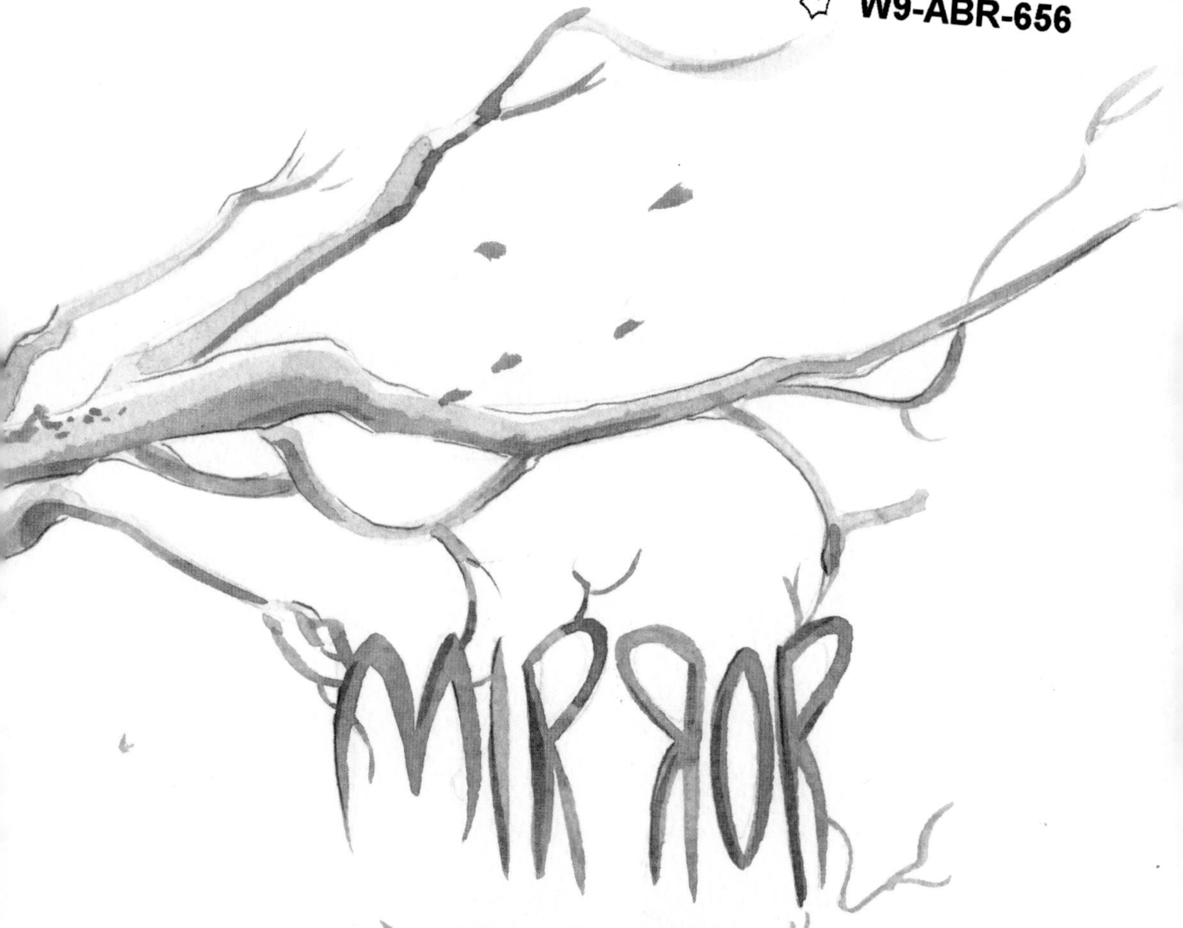

MIRROR
THE MOUNTAIN

Special thanks to Brandon Graham, to the whole 8house team, to David Brothers, to Tricia Ramos, to Ally Power and to Olivia Ngai for their help in making this book possible.

by

EMMA RÍOS & HWEI LIM

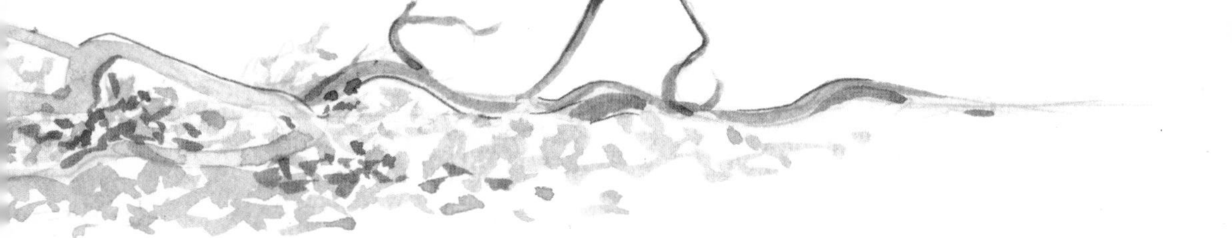

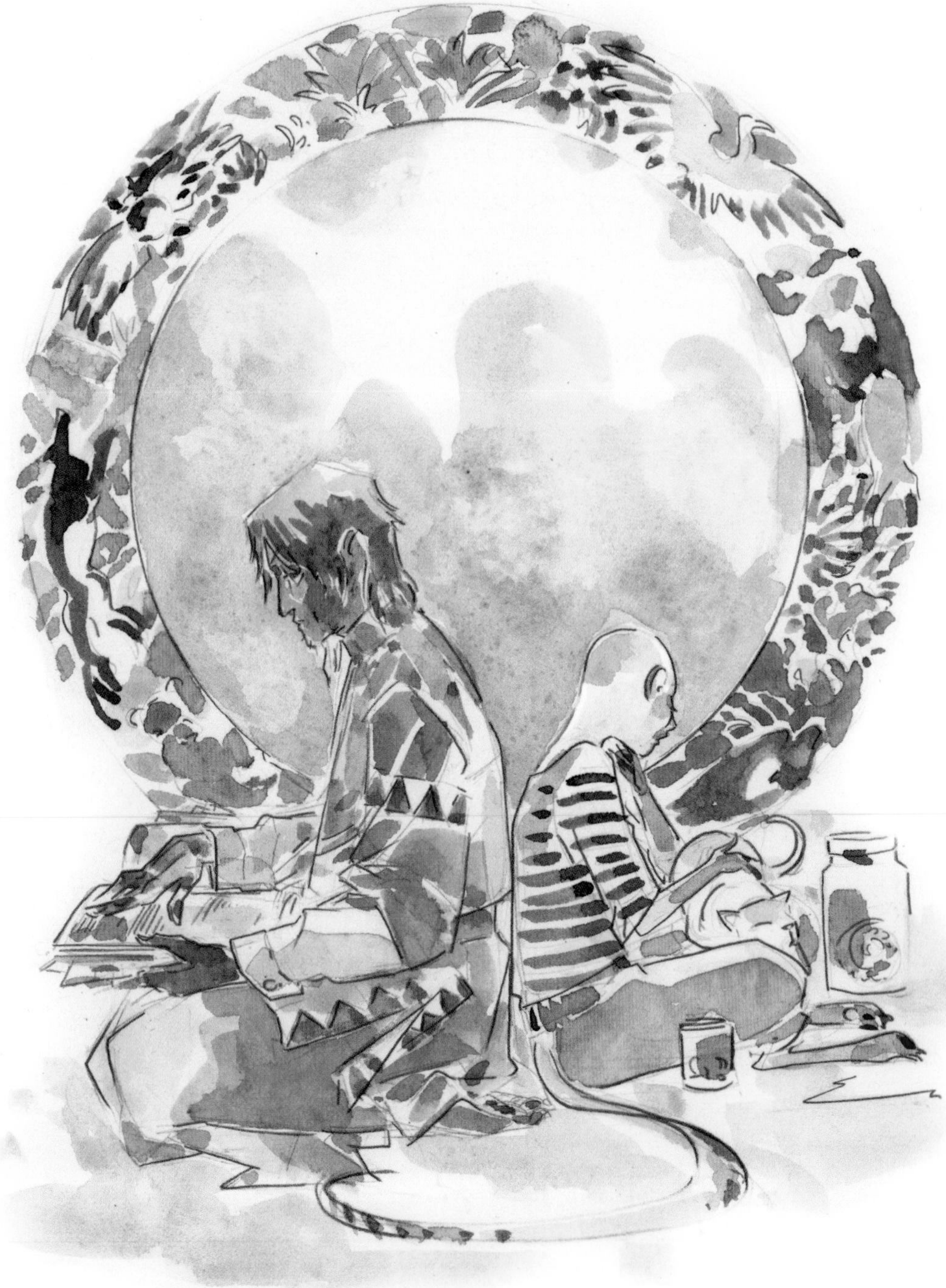

Chapter One

A story about the mage-scientists of The Synchronia and the sentient animals of Irzah colony.

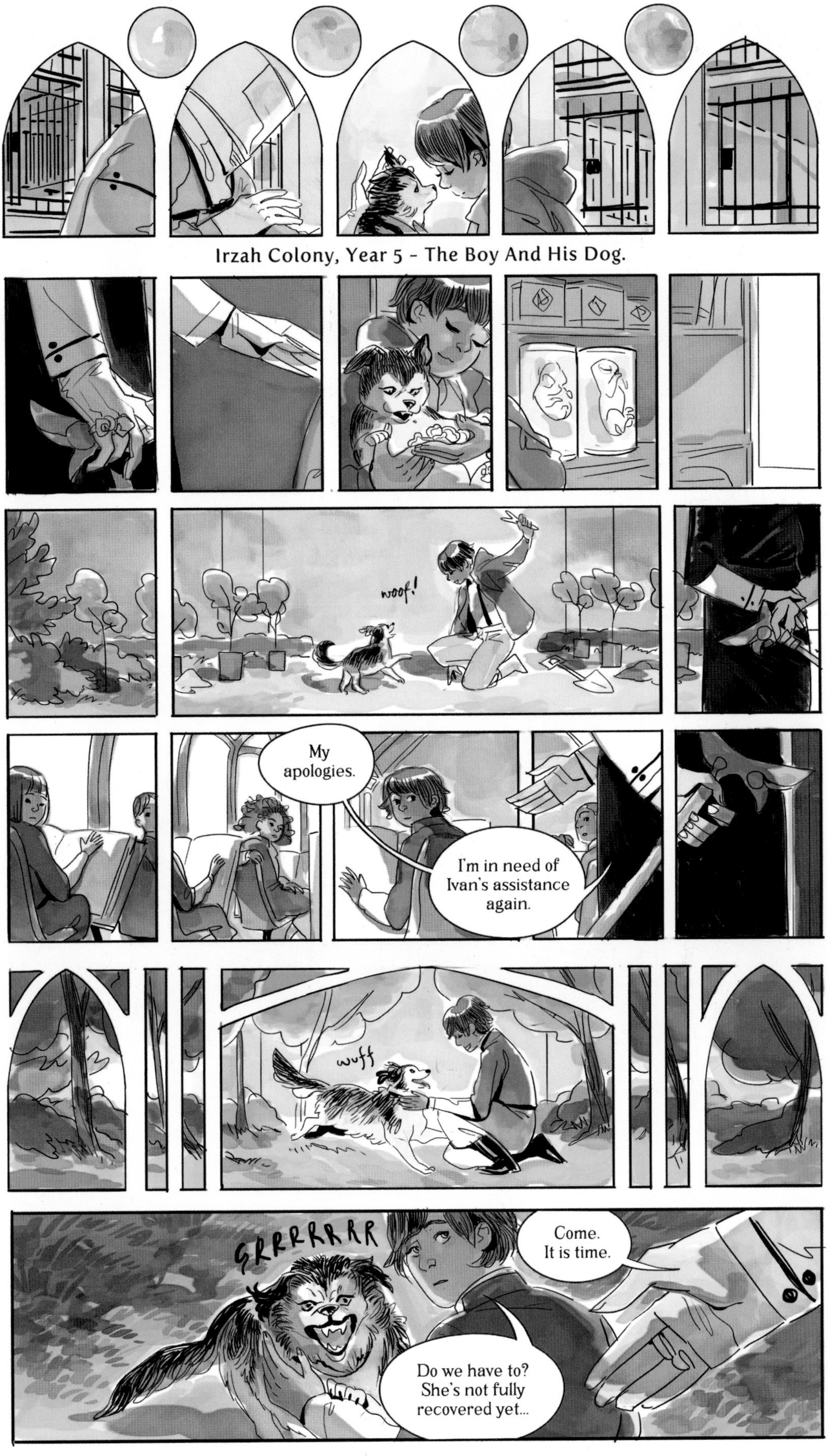
Irzah Colony, Year 5 - The Boy And His Dog.
woof!
My apologies.
I'm in need of Ivan's assistance again.
wuff
GRRRRRRR
Come. It is time.
Do we have to? She's not fully recovered yet...

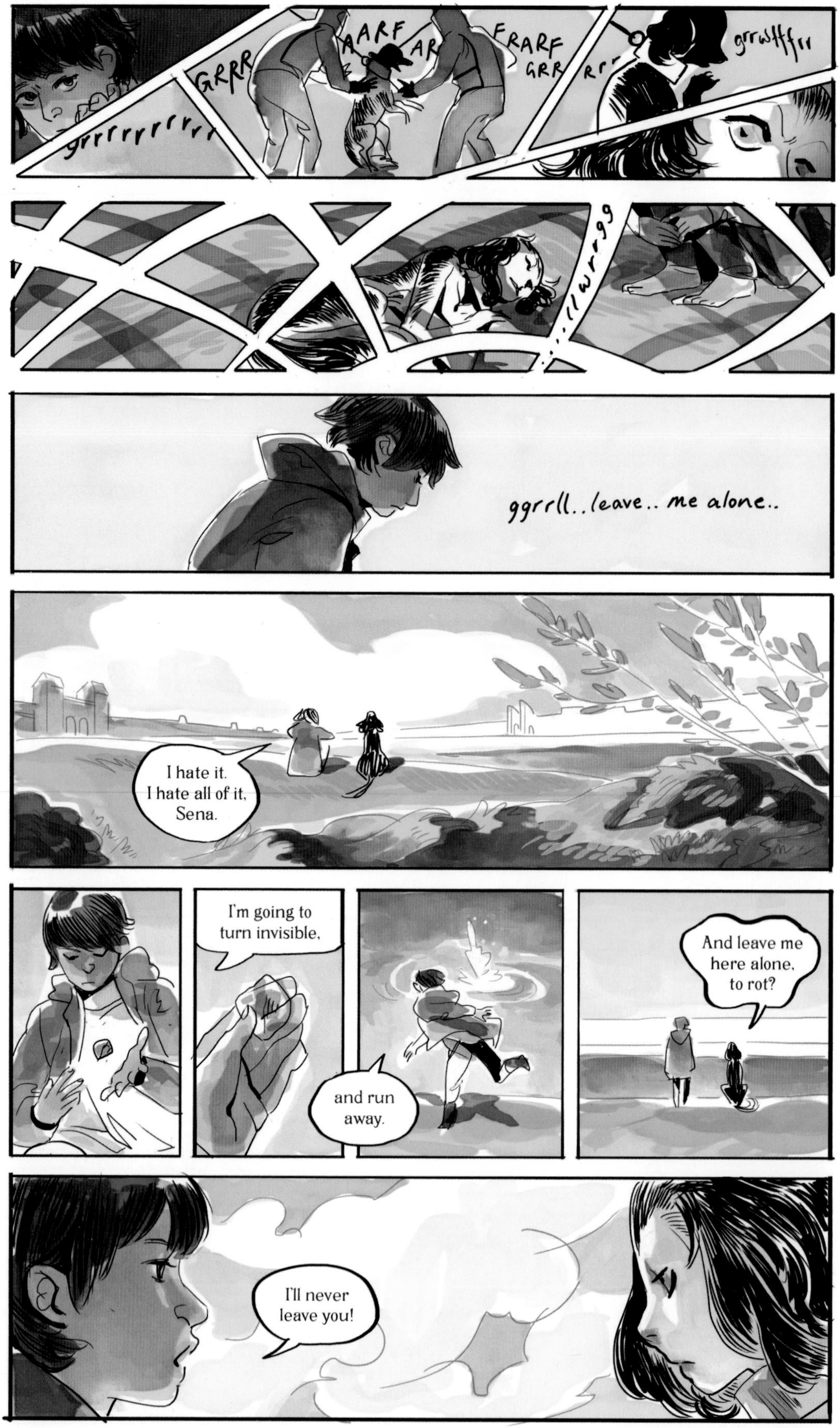

grrrrrrrrr
GRRR
AARF
AR
FRARF
GRR
rrr
grrwlffrr
...llwrrgg
ggrrll.. leave.. me alone..
I hate it. I hate all of it, Sena.
I'm going to turn invisible,
and run away.
And leave me here alone, to rot?
I'll never leave you!

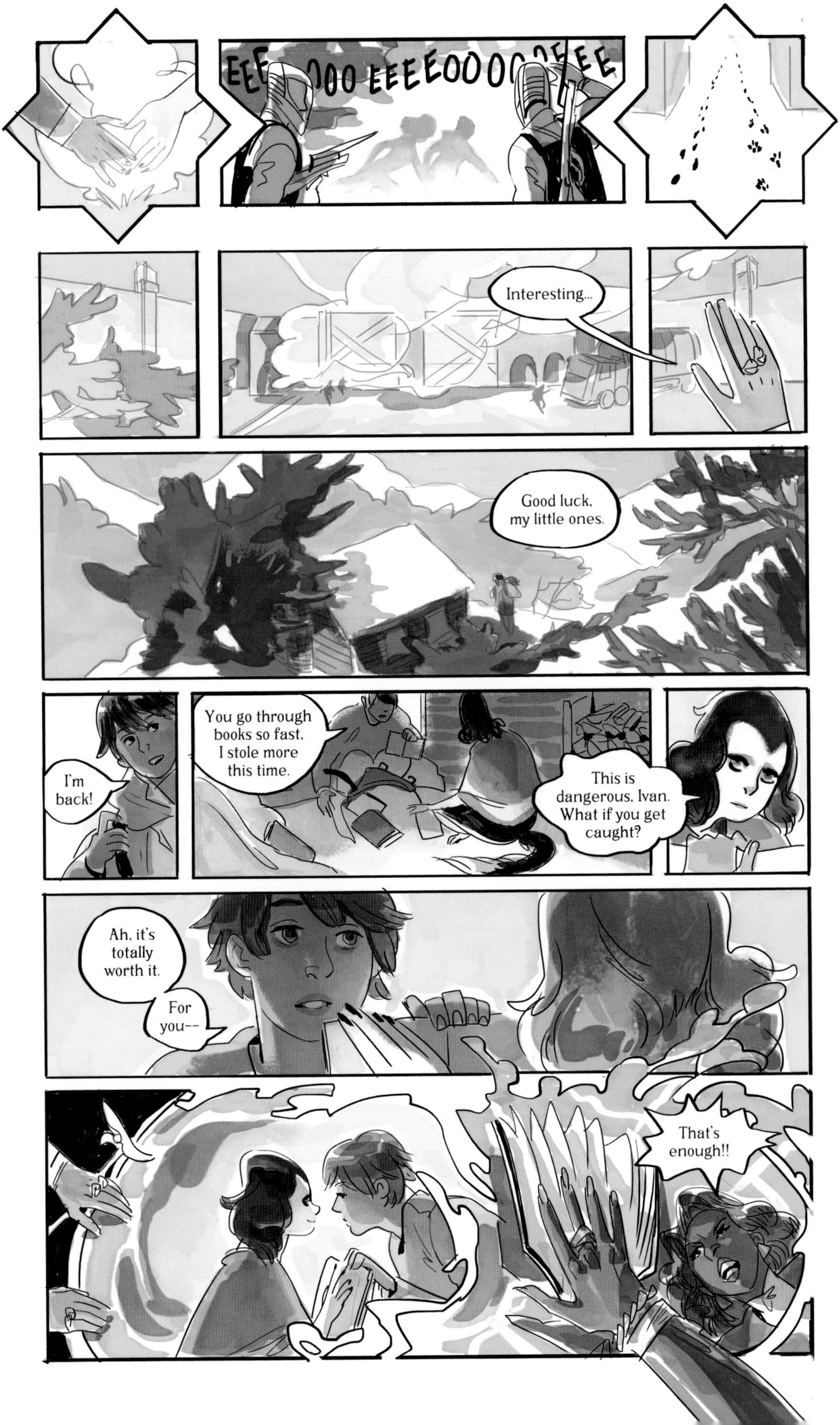
EEE OOO EEEEOOOOOEEE
Interesting...
Good luck, my little ones.
I'm back!
You go through books so fast, I stole more this time.
This is dangerous, Ivan. What if you get caught?
Ah, it's totally worth it.
For you--
That's enough!!

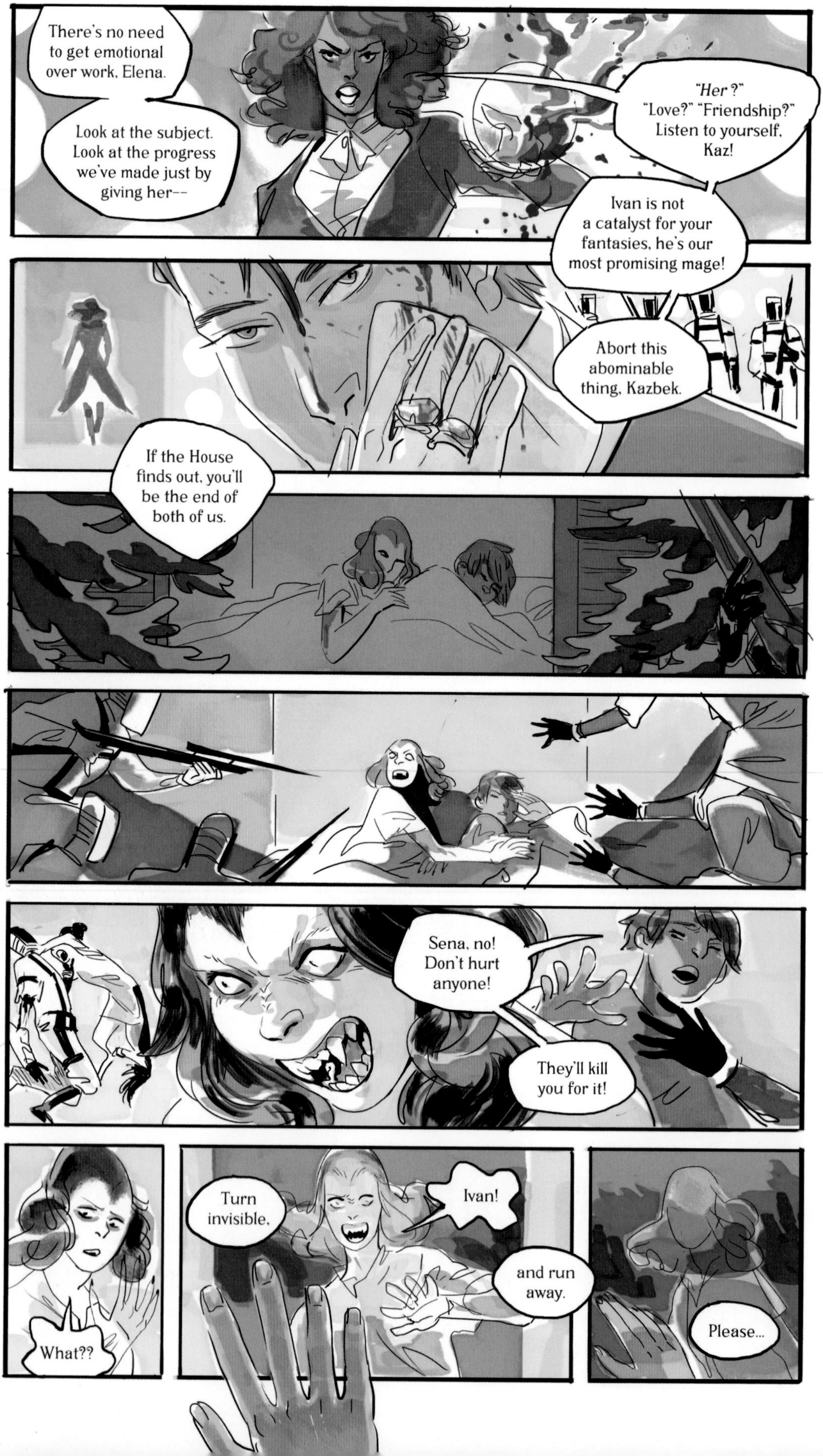
There's no need to get emotional over work, Elena.
Look at the subject. Look at the progress we've made just by giving her--
"Her?" "Love?" "Friendship?" Listen to yourself, Kaz!
Ivan is not a catalyst for your fantasies, he's our most promising mage!
Abort this abominable thing, Kazbek.
If the House finds out, you'll be the end of both of us.
Sena, no! Don't hurt anyone!
They'll kill you for it!
What??
Turn invisible,
Ivan!
and run away.
Please...

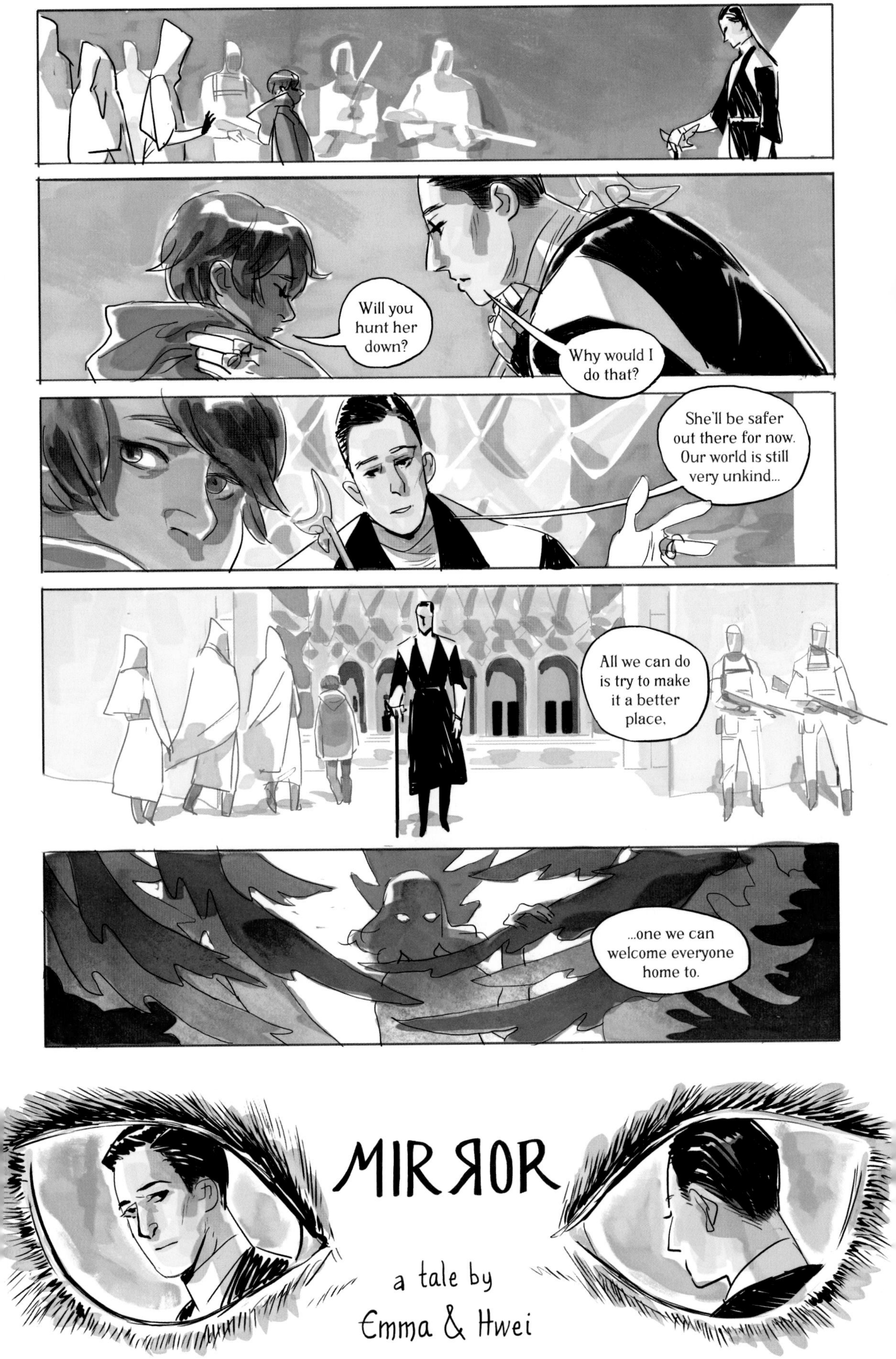
Will you hunt her down?
Why would I do that?
She'll be safer out there for now. Our world is still very unkind...
All we can do is try to make it a better place,
...one we can welcome everyone home to.
MIRЯOR
a tale by
Emma & Hwei

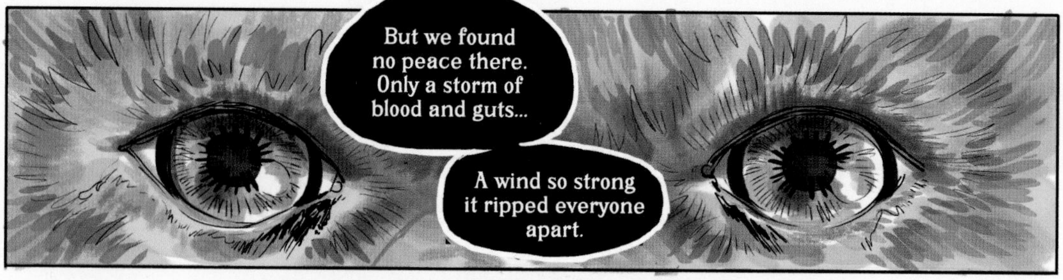
But we found no peace there. Only a storm of blood and guts...
A wind so strong it ripped everyone apart.

Irzah Colony, Year 35 - The Wounded And The Newcomers.

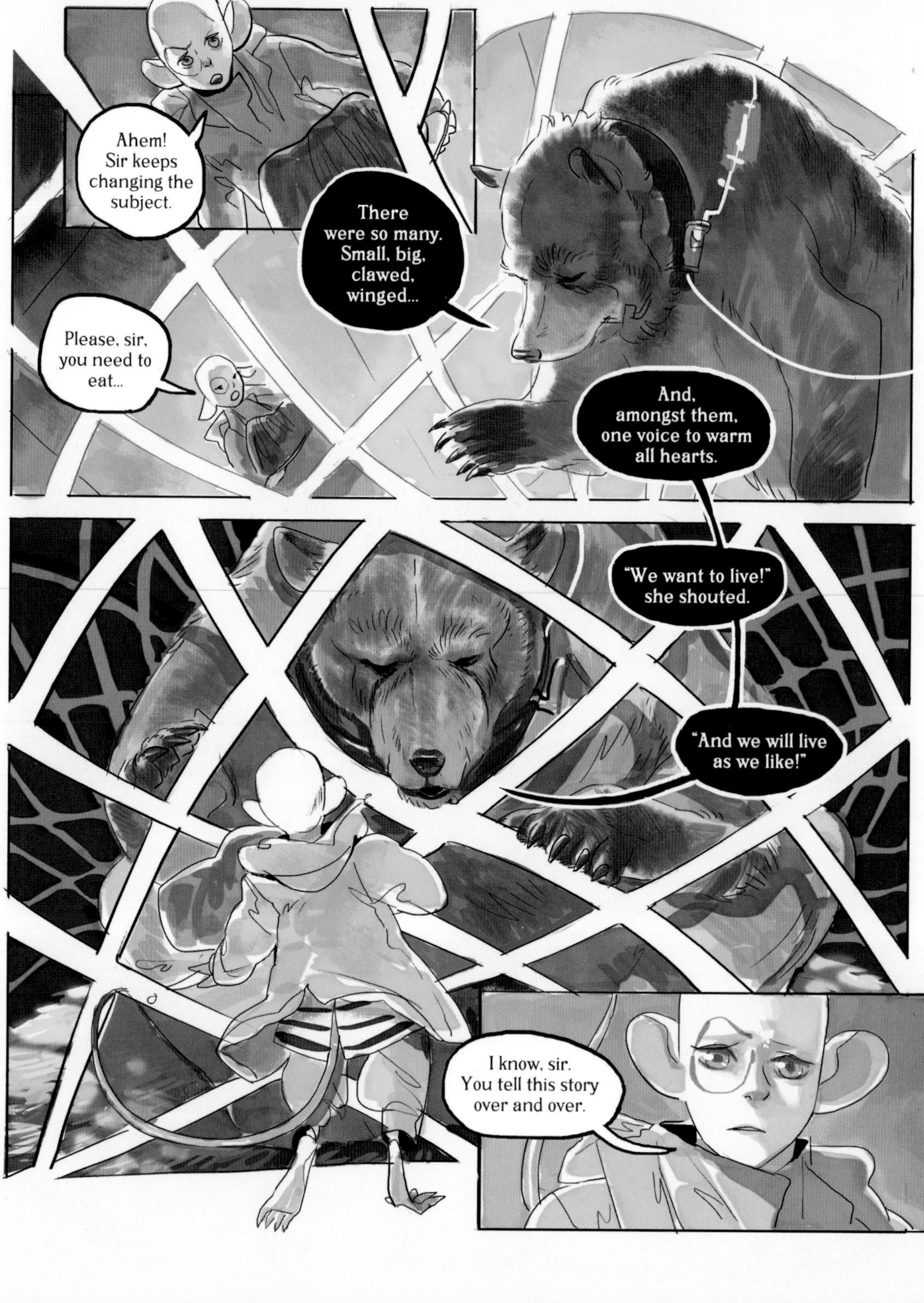
Ahem! Sir keeps changing the subject.
There were so many. Small, big, clawed, winged...
Please, sir, you need to eat...
And, amongst them, one voice to warm all hearts.
"We want to live!" she shouted.
"And we will live as we like!"
I know, sir. You tell this story over and over.

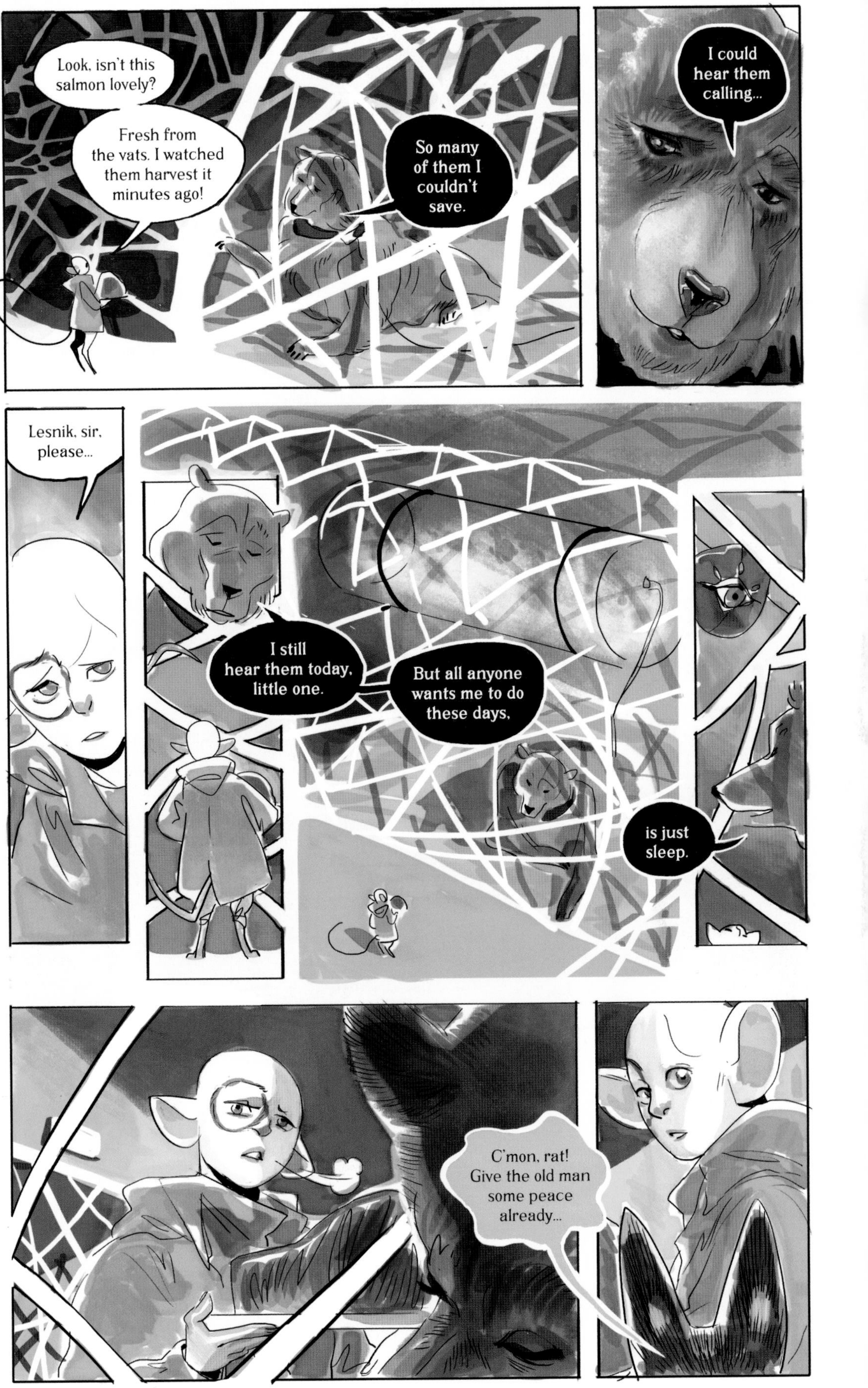
Look, isn't this salmon lovely?
Fresh from the vats. I watched them harvest it minutes ago!
So many of them I couldn't save.
I could hear them calling...
Lesnik, sir, please...
I still hear them today, little one.
But all anyone wants me to do these days,
is just sleep.
C'mon, rat! Give the old man some peace already...

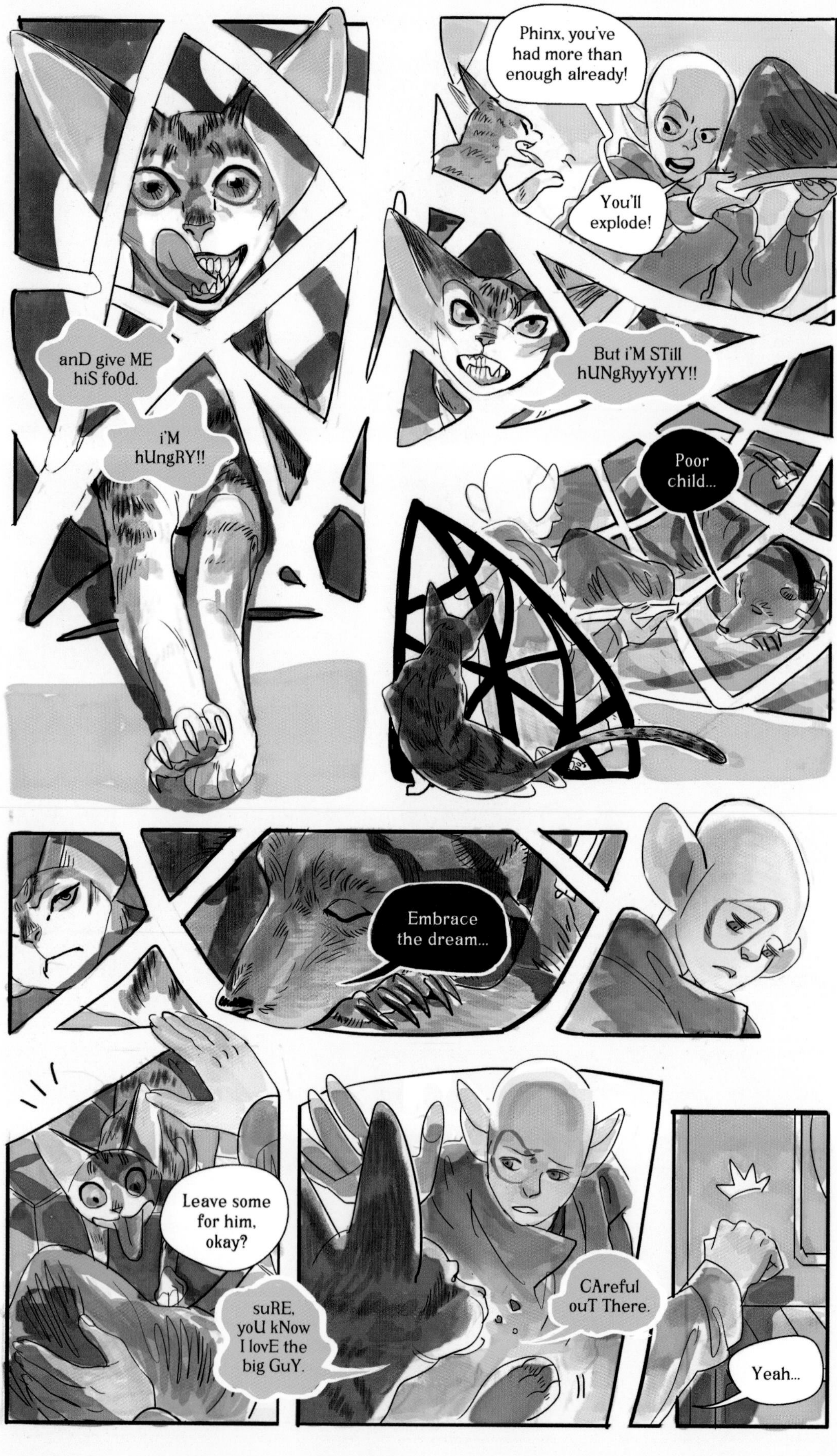
anD give ME
hiS fo0d.
i'M
hUngRY!!
Phinx, you've had more than enough already!
You'll explode!
But i'M STill hUNgRyyYyYY!!
Poor child...
Embrace the dream...
Leave some for him, okay?
suRE, yoU kNow I lovE the big GuY.
CAreful ouT There.
Yeah...

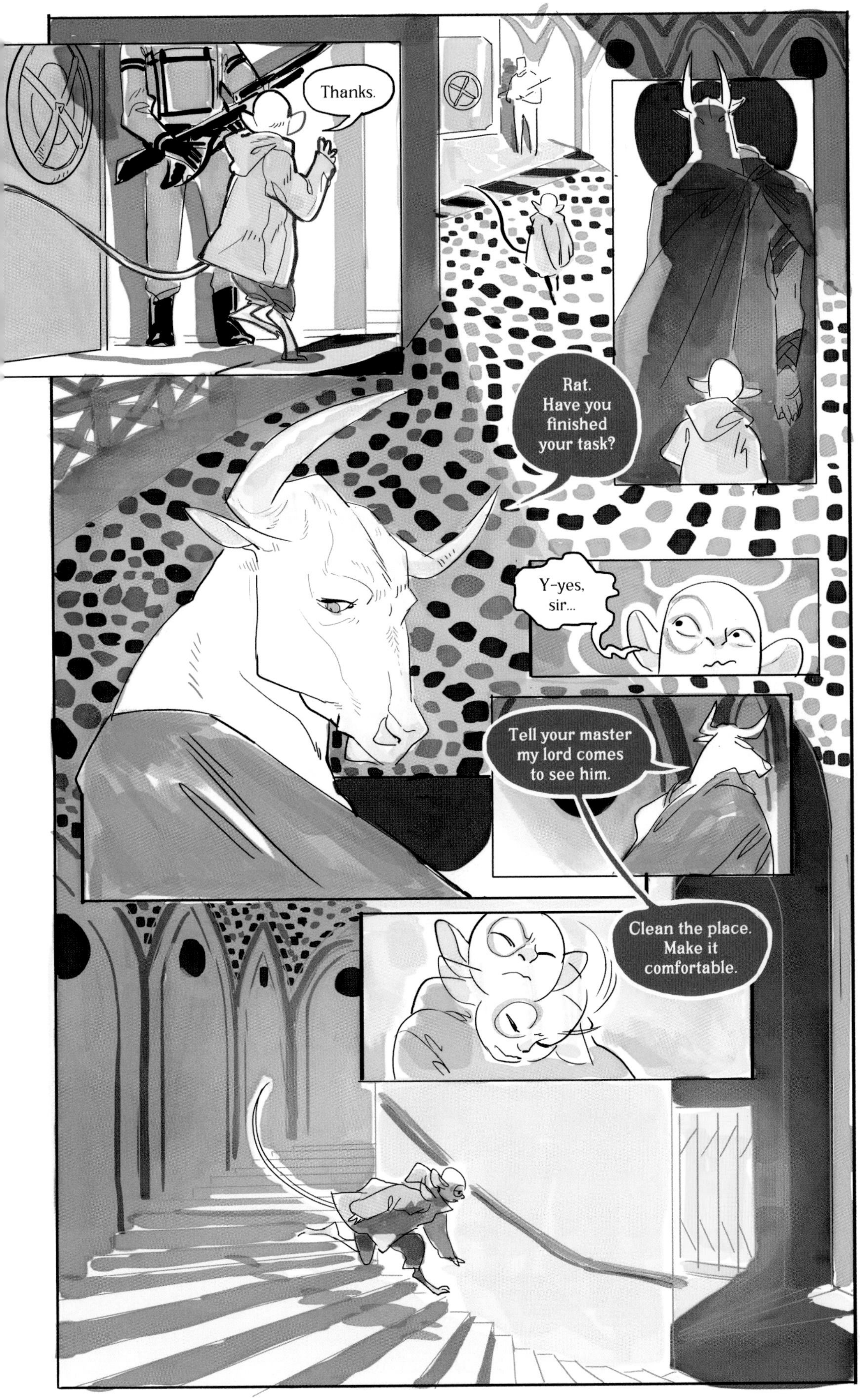
Thanks.
Rat. Have you finished your task?
Y-yes, sir...
Tell your master my lord comes to see him.
Clean the place. Make it comfortable.

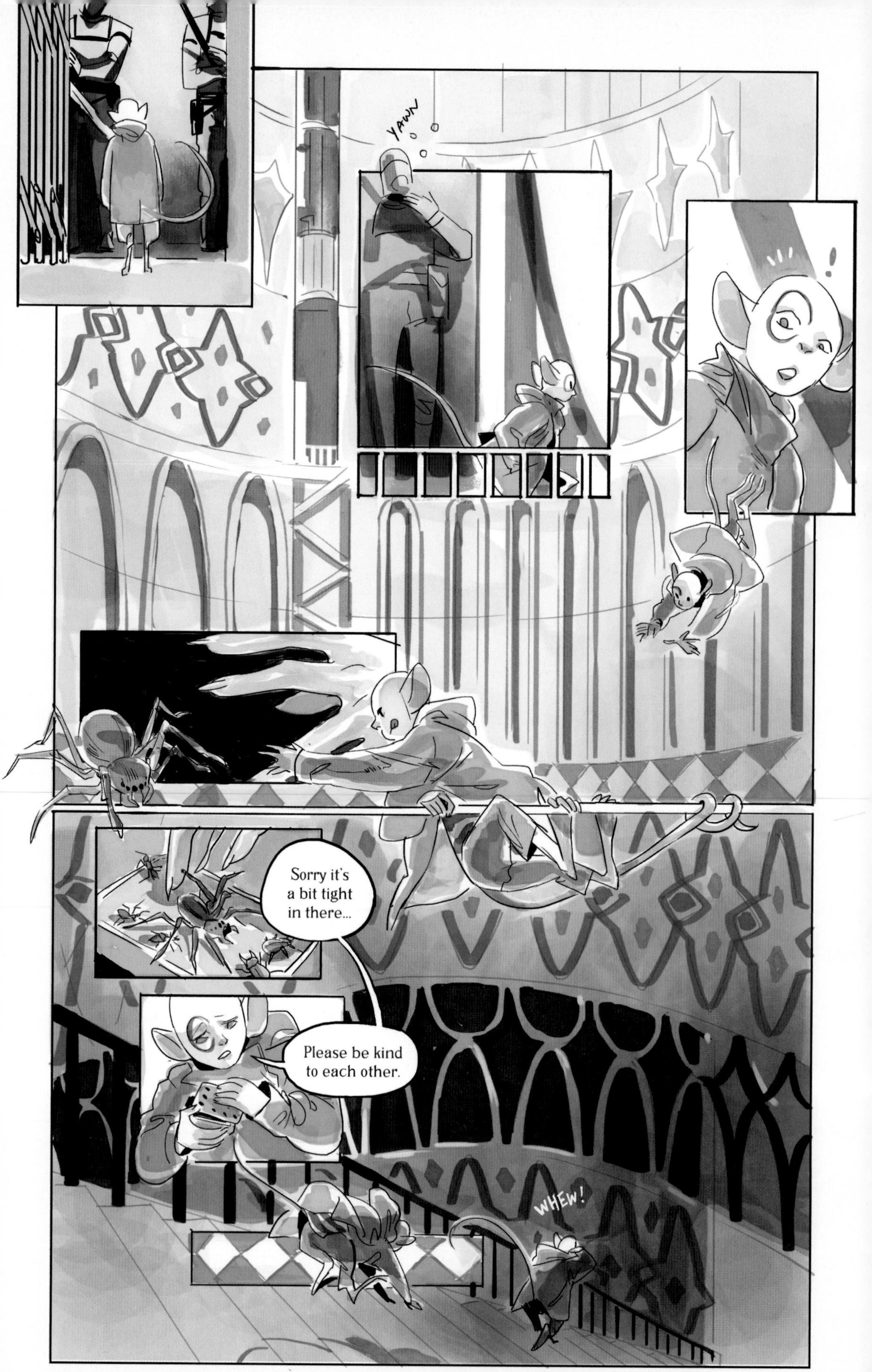
YAWN
!
Sorry it's a bit tight in there...
Please be kind to each other.
WHEW!

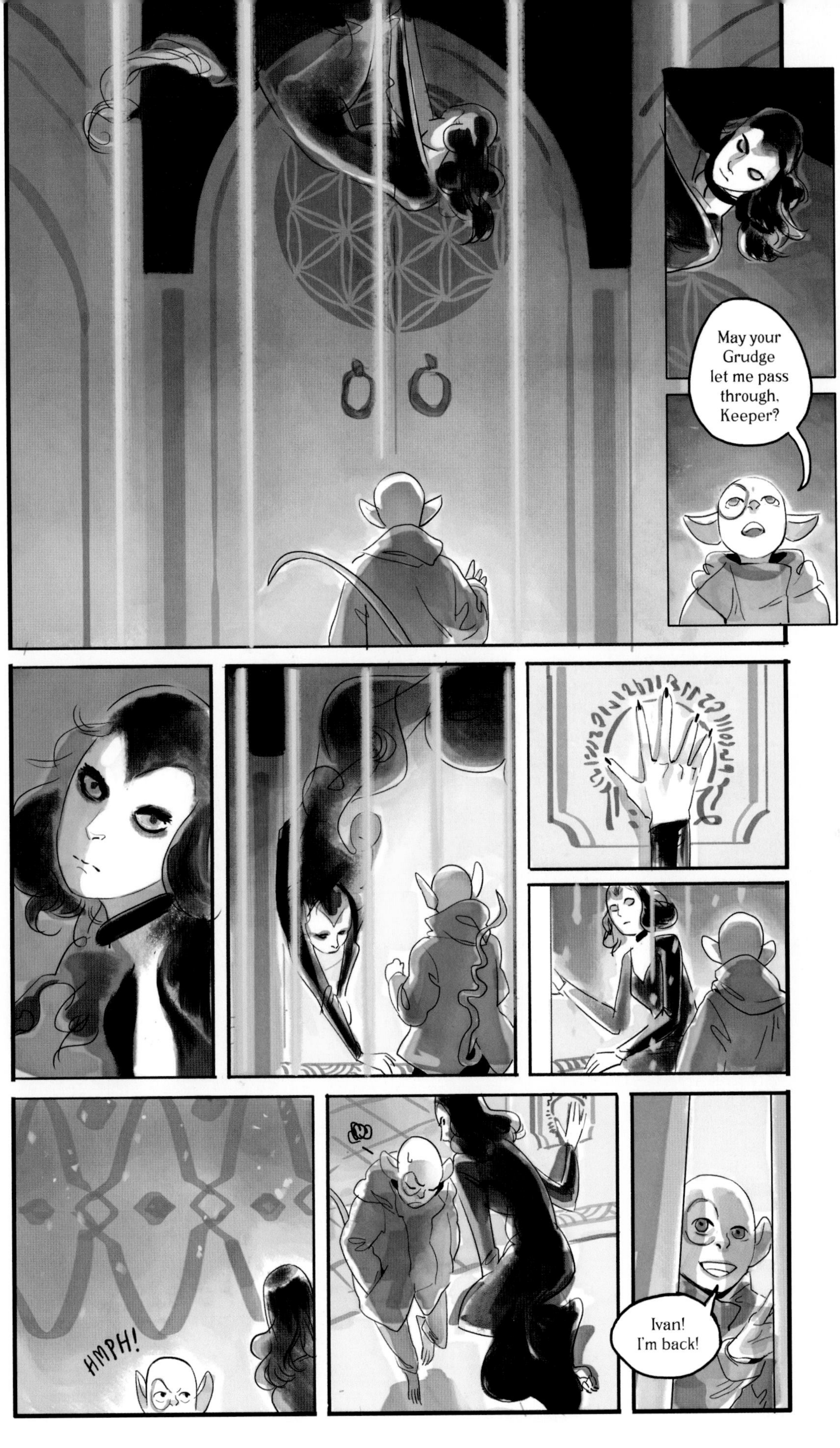
May your Grudge let me pass through, Keeper?
HMPH!
Ivan! I'm back!

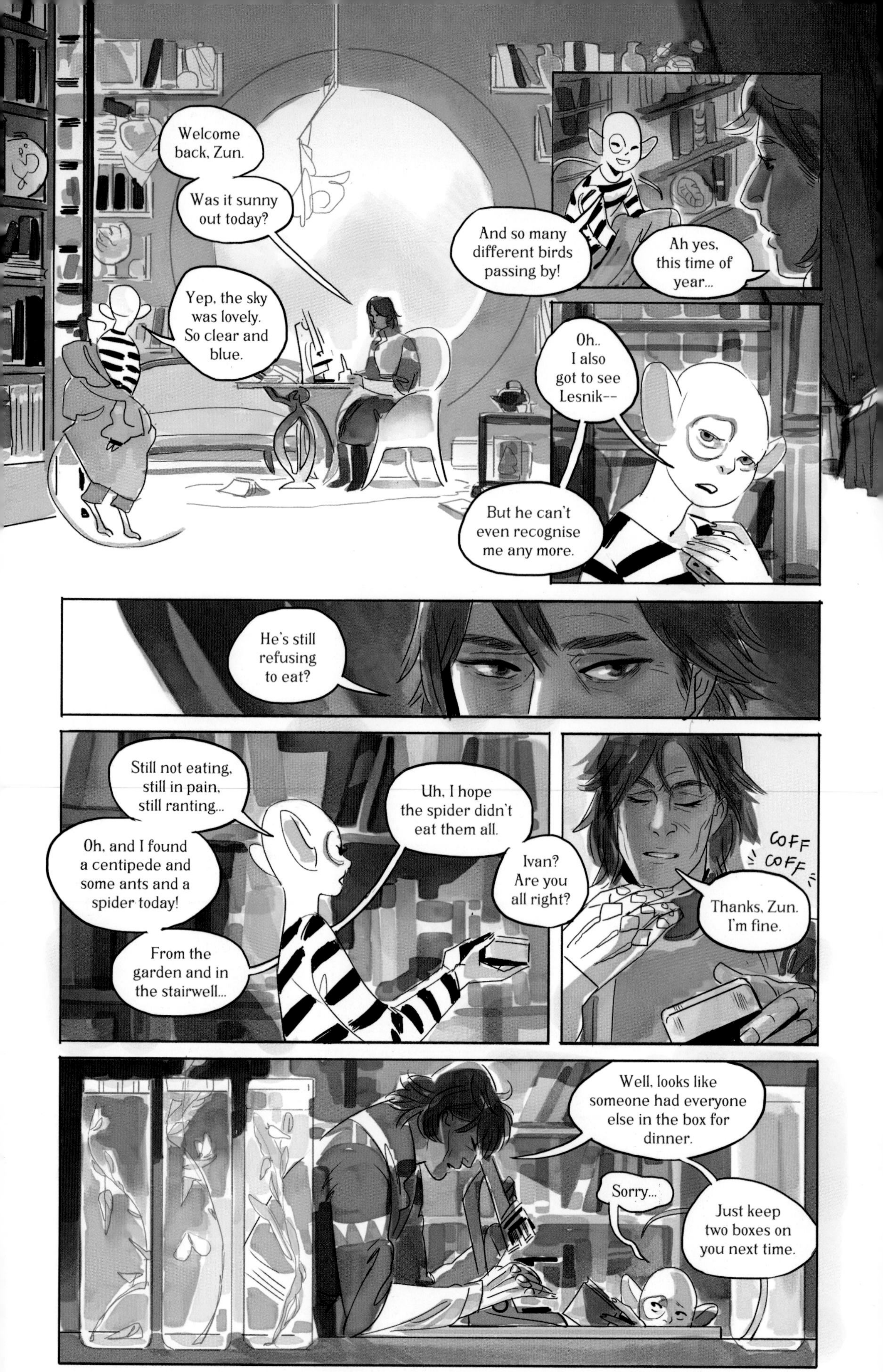
Welcome back, Zun.
Was it sunny out today?
Yep, the sky was lovely. So clear and blue.
And so many different birds passing by!
Ah yes, this time of year...
Oh.. I also got to see Lesnik--
But he can't even recognise me any more.
He's still refusing to eat?
Still not eating, still in pain, still ranting...
Oh, and I found a centipede and some ants and a spider today!
From the garden and in the stairwell...
Uh, I hope the spider didn't eat them all.
Ivan? Are you all right?
COFF COFF
Thanks, Zun. I'm fine.
Well, looks like someone had everyone else in the box for dinner.
Sorry...
Just keep two boxes on you next time.

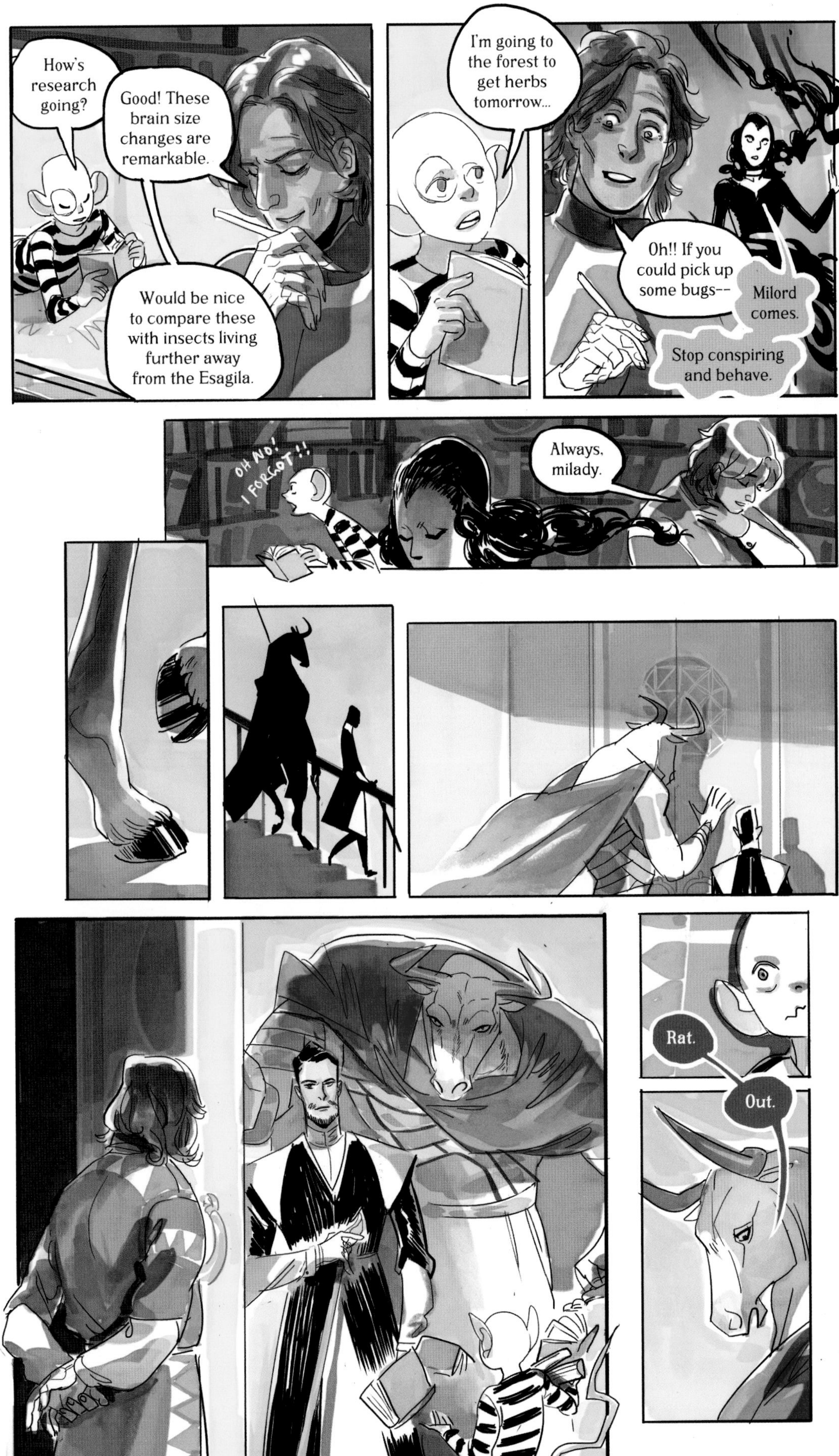
How's research going?
Good! These brain size changes are remarkable.
Would be nice to compare these with insects living further away from the Esagila.
I'm going to the forest to get herbs tomorrow...
Oh!! If you could pick up some bugs--
Milord comes.
Stop conspiring and behave.
OH NO! I FORGOT!!
Always, milady.
Rat.
Out.

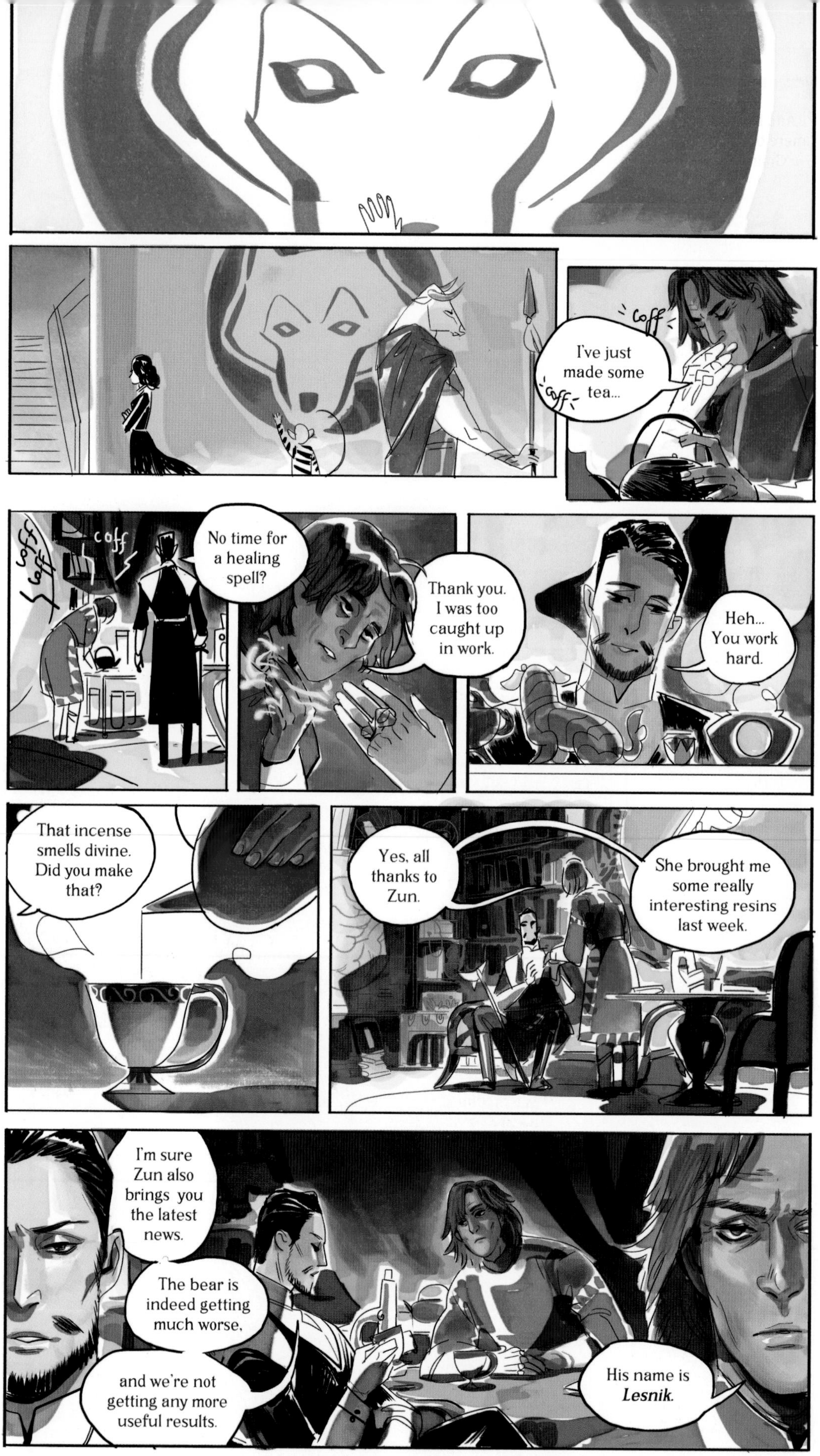
coff
I've just made some tea...
coff
coff
coff coff
No time for a healing spell?
Thank you. I was too caught up in work.
Heh... You work hard.
That incense smells divine. Did you make that?
Yes, all thanks to Zun.
She brought me some really interesting resins last week.
I'm sure Zun also brings you the latest news.
The bear is indeed getting much worse,
and we're not getting any more useful results.
His name is *Lesnik*.

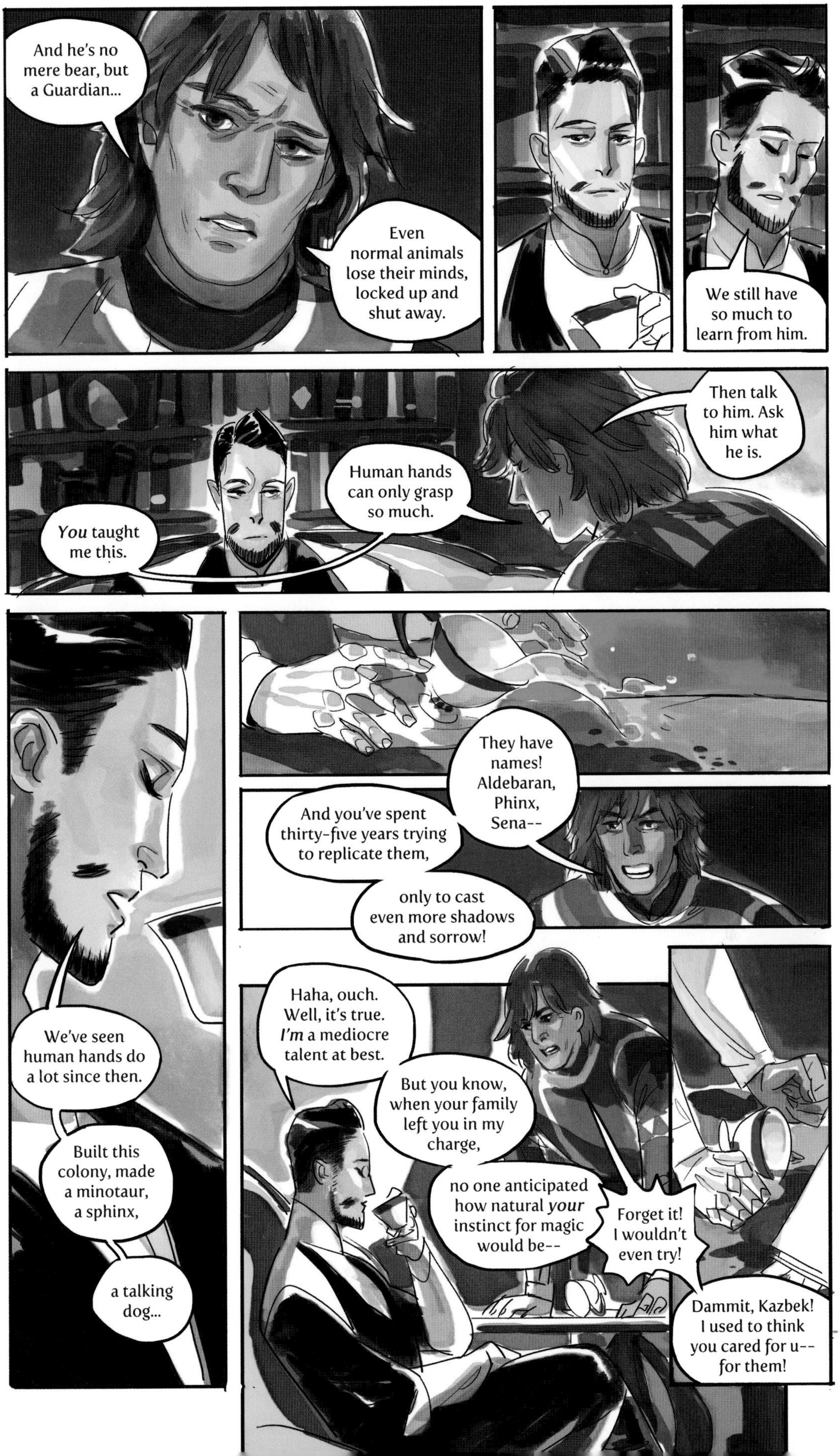
And he's no mere bear, but a Guardian...
Even normal animals lose their minds, locked up and shut away.
We still have so much to learn from him.
Then talk to him. Ask him what he is.
Human hands can only grasp so much.
You taught me this.
They have names! Aldebaran, Phinx, Sena--
And you've spent thirty-five years trying to replicate them,
only to cast even more shadows and sorrow!
We've seen human hands do a lot since then.
Built this colony, made a minotaur, a sphinx,
a talking dog...
Haha, ouch. Well, it's true. *I'm* a mediocre talent at best.
But you know, when your family left you in my charge,
no one anticipated how natural *your* instinct for magic would be--
Forget it! I wouldn't even try!
Dammit, Kazbek! I used to think you cared for u-- for them!

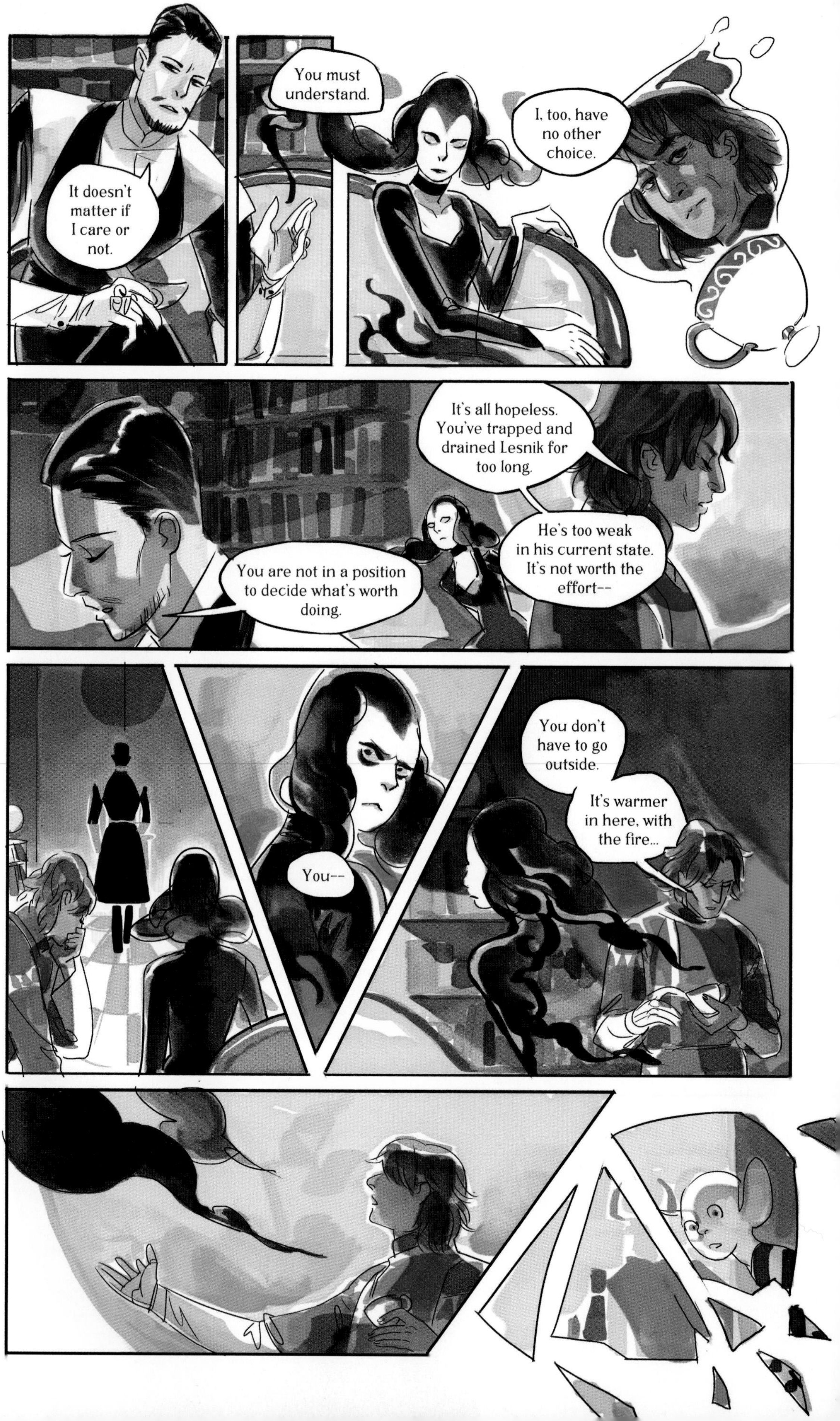
It doesn't matter if I care or not.
You must understand.
I, too, have no other choice.
It's all hopeless. You've trapped and drained Lesnik for too long.
He's too weak in his current state. It's not worth the effort--
You are not in a position to decide what's worth doing.
You--
You don't have to go outside.
It's warmer in here, with the fire...

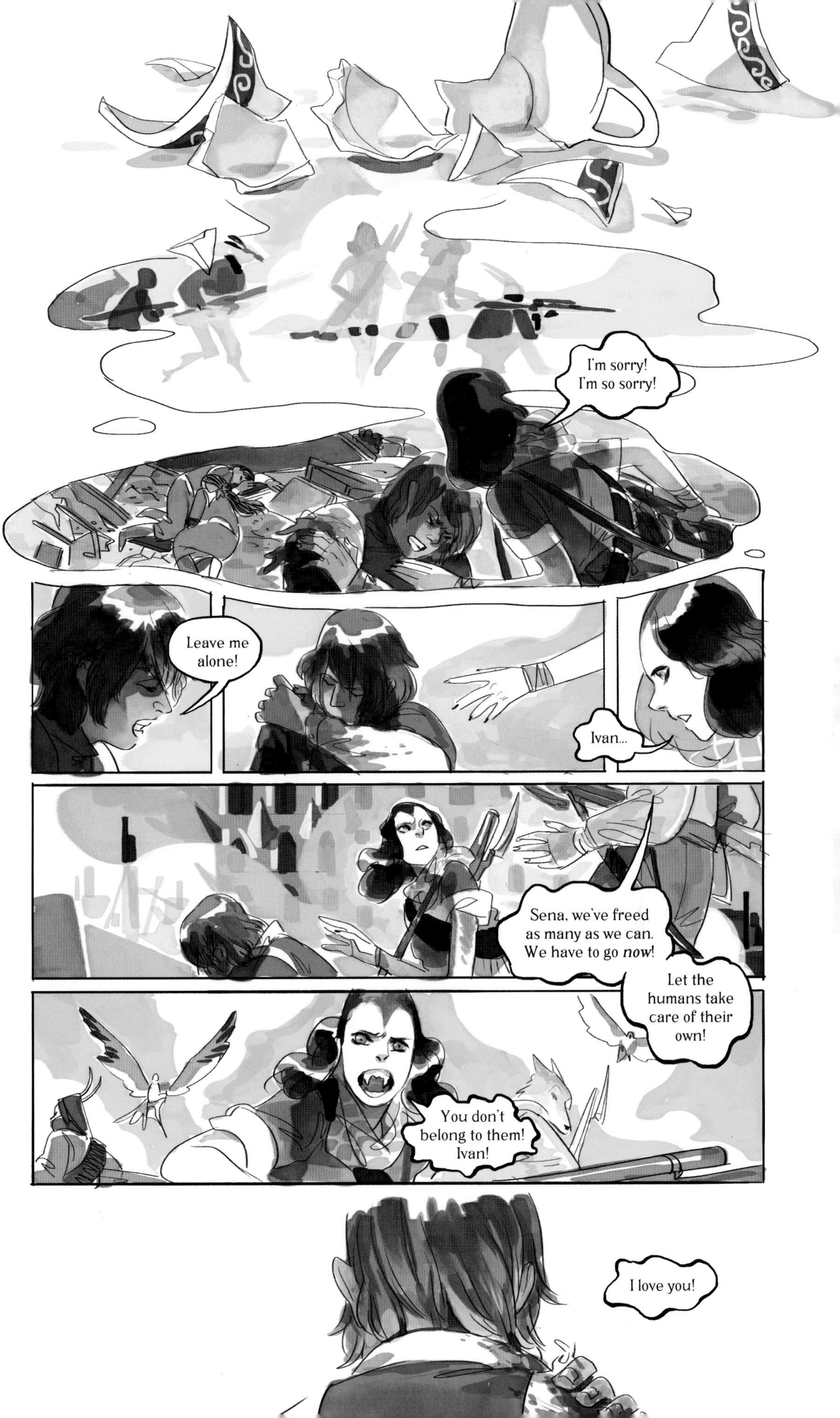
I'm sorry! I'm so sorry!
Leave me alone!
Ivan...
Sena, we've freed as many as we can. We have to go *now*!
Let the humans take care of their own!
You don't belong to them! Ivan!
I love you!

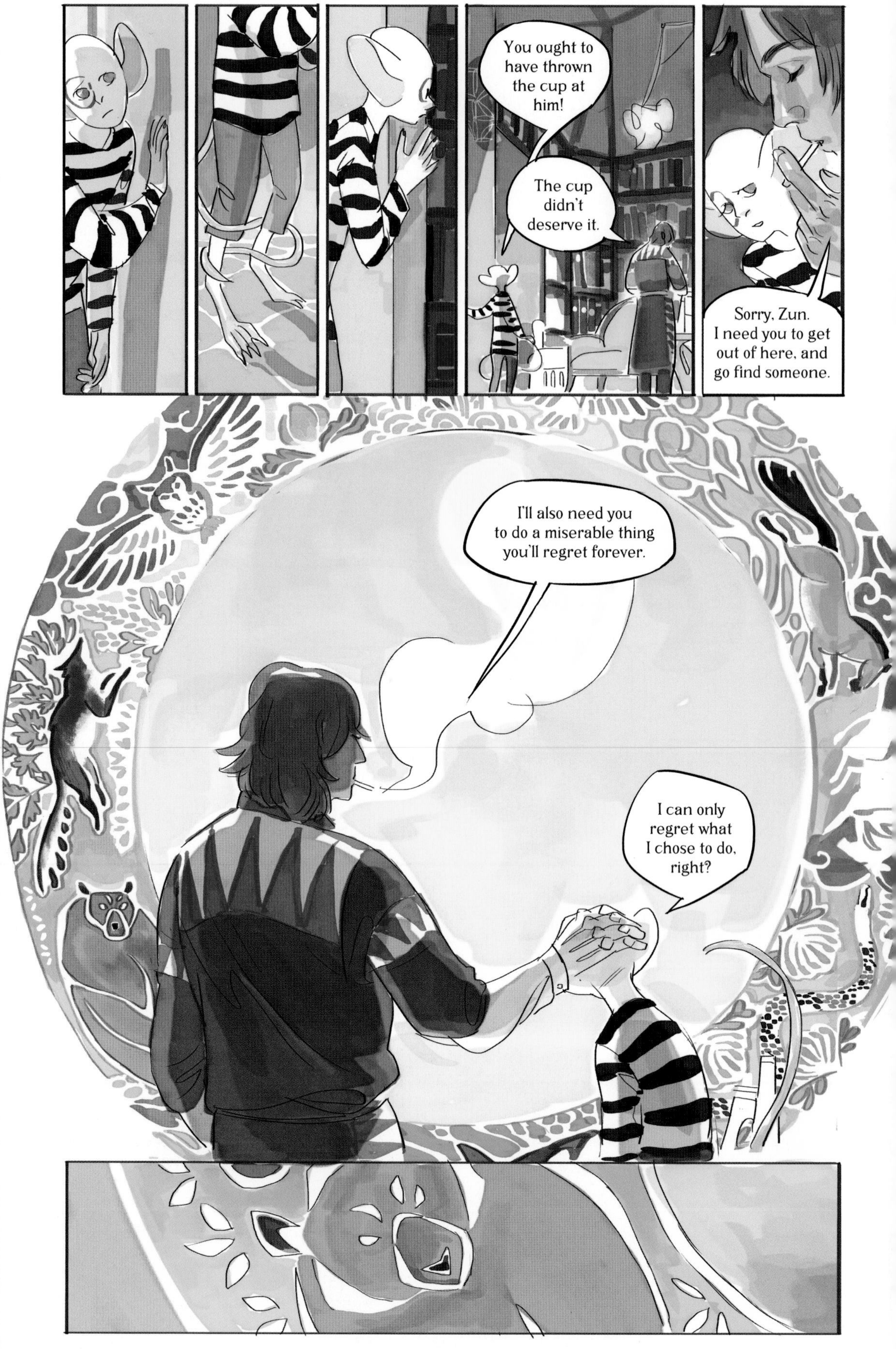
You ought to have thrown the cup at him!
The cup didn't deserve it.
Sorry, Zun. I need you to get out of here, and go find someone.
I'll also need you to do a miserable thing you'll regret forever.
I can only regret what I chose to do, right?

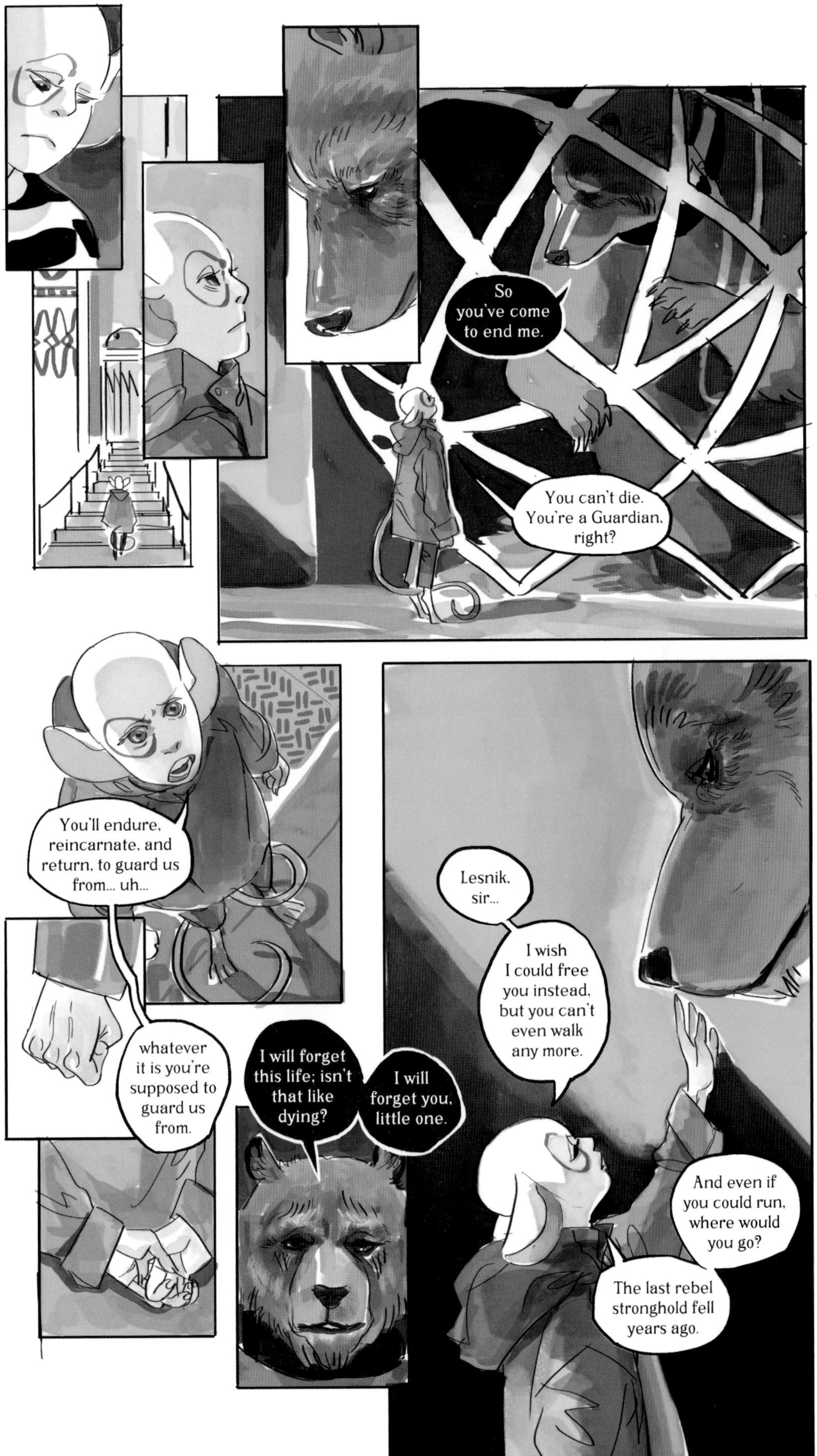
So you've come to end me.
You can't die. You're a Guardian, right?
You'll endure, reincarnate, and return, to guard us from... uh...
whatever it is you're supposed to guard us from.
I will forget this life; isn't that like dying?
I will forget you, little one.
Lesnik, sir...
I wish I could free you instead, but you can't even walk any more.
And even if you could run, where would you go?
The last rebel stronghold fell years ago.

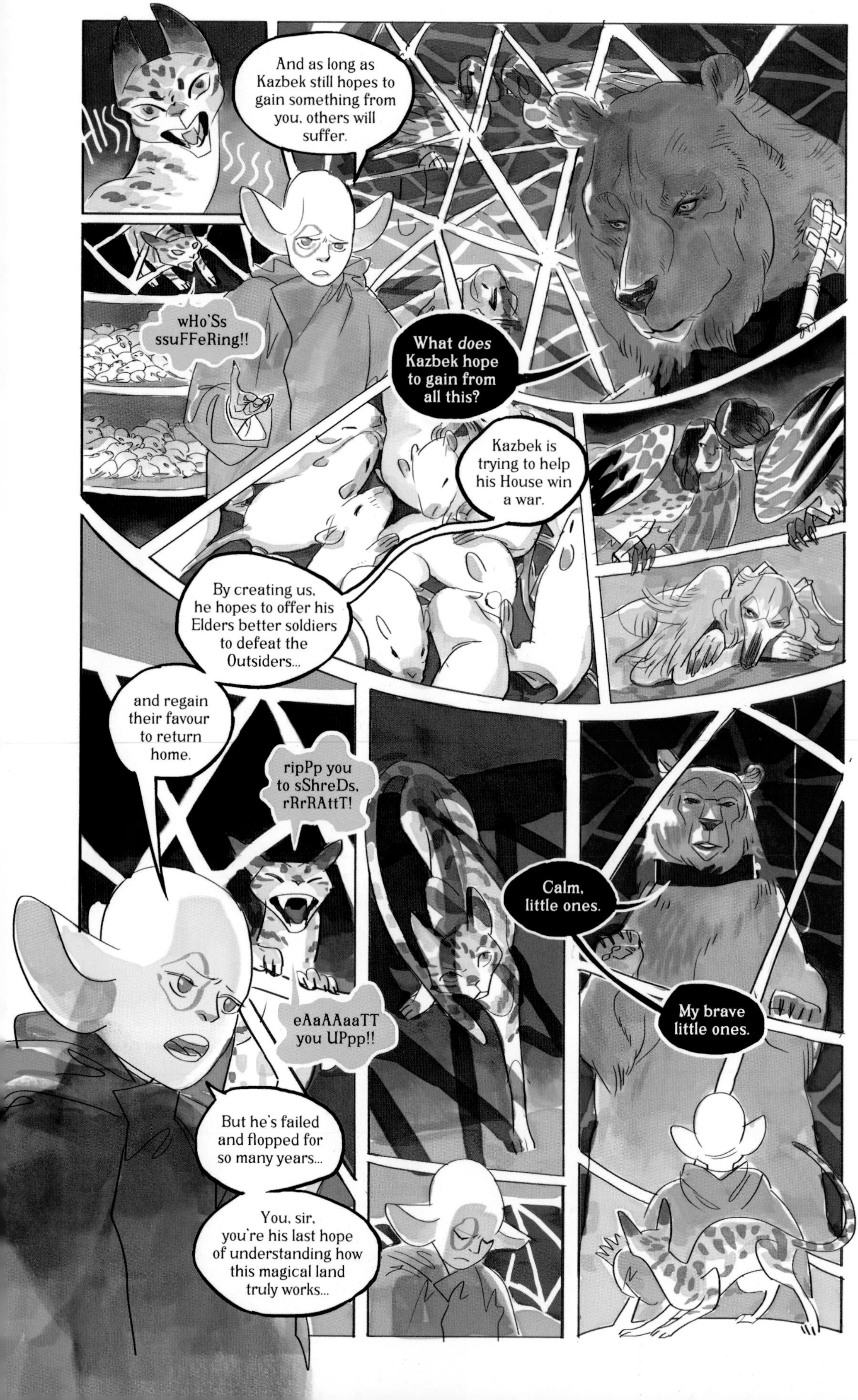
HISS
And as long as Kazbek still hopes to gain something from you, others will suffer.
wHo'Ss ssuFFeRing!!
What *does* Kazbek hope to gain from all this?
Kazbek is trying to help his House win a war.
By creating us, he hopes to offer his Elders better soldiers to defeat the Outsiders...
and regain their favour to return home.
ripPp you to sShreDs, rRrRAttT!
eAaAAaaTT you UPpp!!
Calm, little ones.
My brave little ones.
But he's failed and flopped for so many years...
You, sir, you're his last hope of understanding how this magical land truly works...

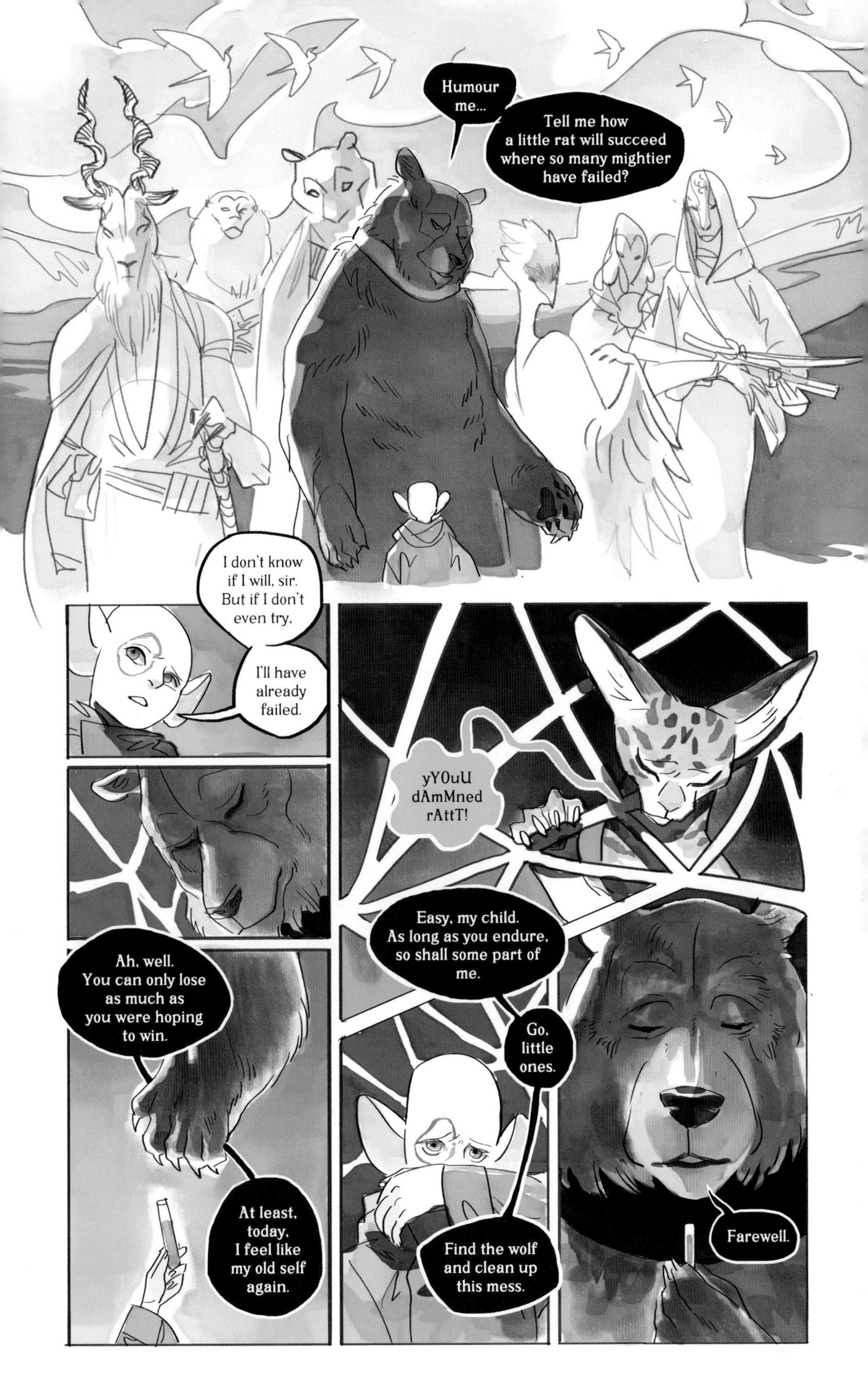
Humour me...
Tell me how a little rat will succeed where so many mightier have failed?
I don't know if I will, sir. But if I don't even try,
I'll have already failed.
yYOuU dAmMned rAttT!
Ah, well. You can only lose as much as you were hoping to win.
At least, today, I feel like my old self again.
Easy, my child. As long as you endure, so shall some part of me.
Go, little ones.
Find the wolf and clean up this mess.
Farewell.

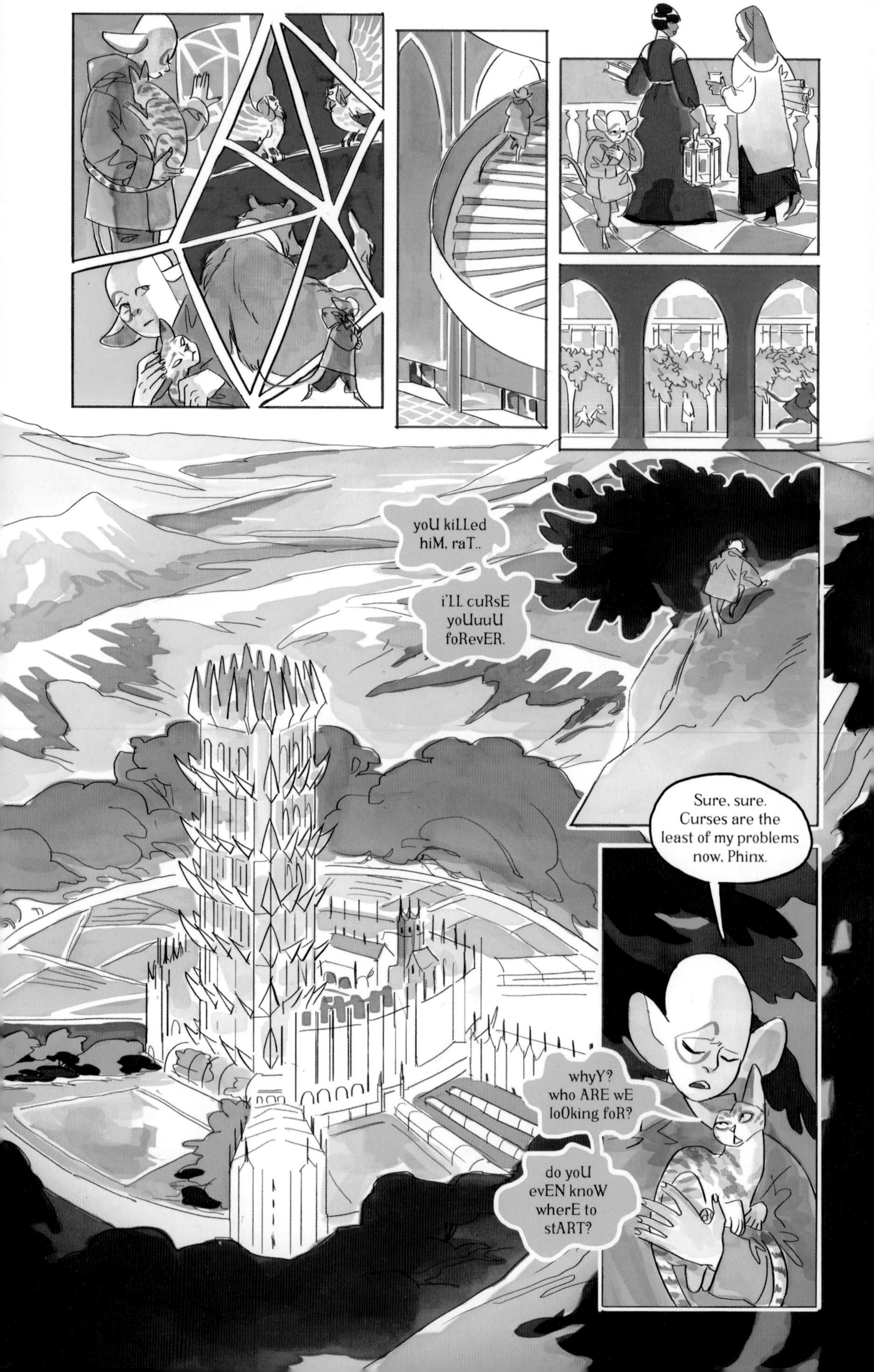

yoU kiLLed hiM, raT..
i'LL cuRsE yoUuuU foRevER.
Sure, sure. Curses are the least of my problems now, Phinx.
whyY? who ARE wE loOking foR?
do yoU evEN knoW wherE to stART?

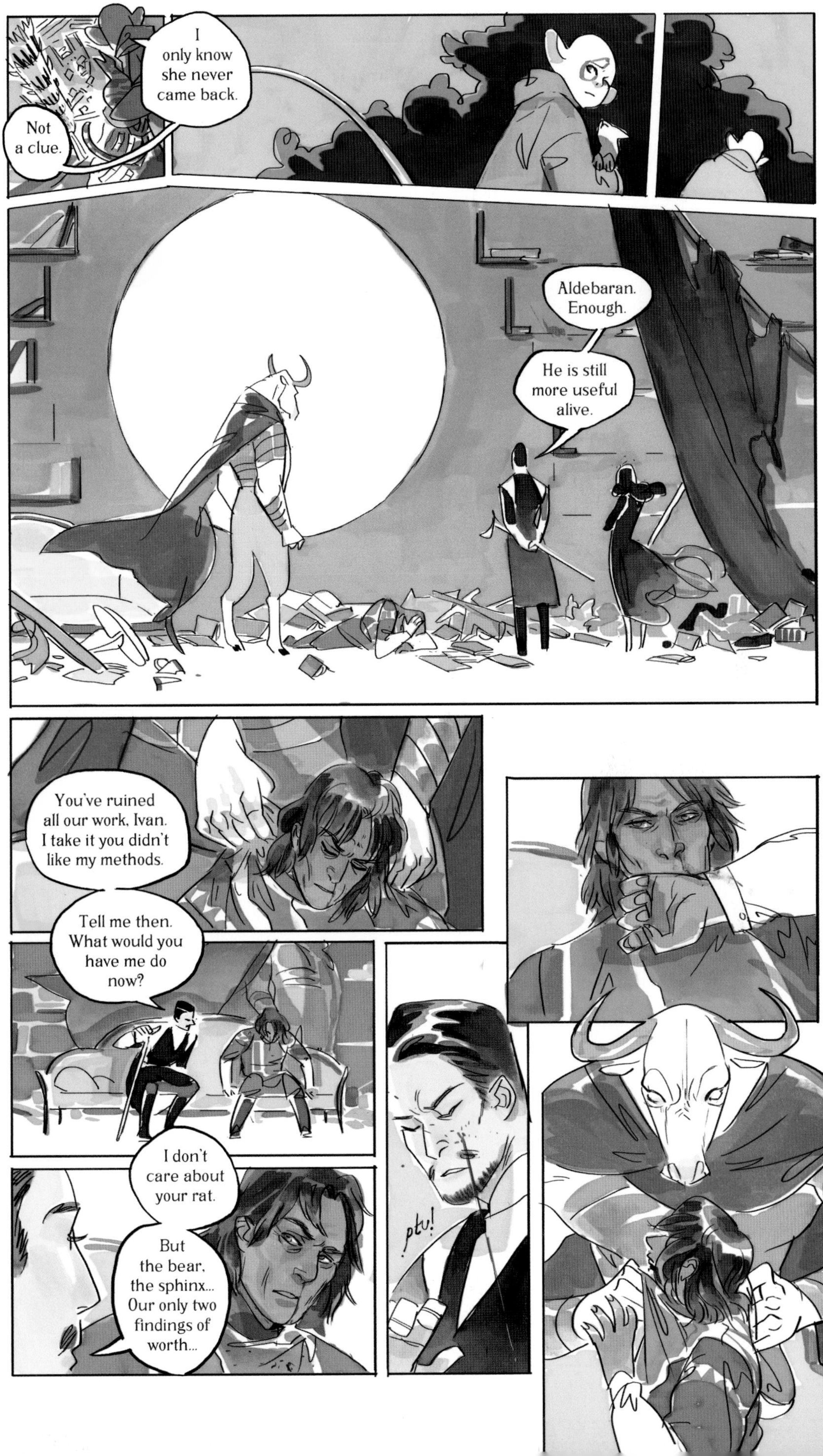

Not a clue.
I only know she never came back.
Aldebaran. Enough.
He is still more useful alive.
You've ruined all our work, Ivan. I take it you didn't like my methods.
Tell me then. What would you have me do now?
I don't care about your rat.
But the bear, the sphinx... Our only two findings of worth...
ptu!

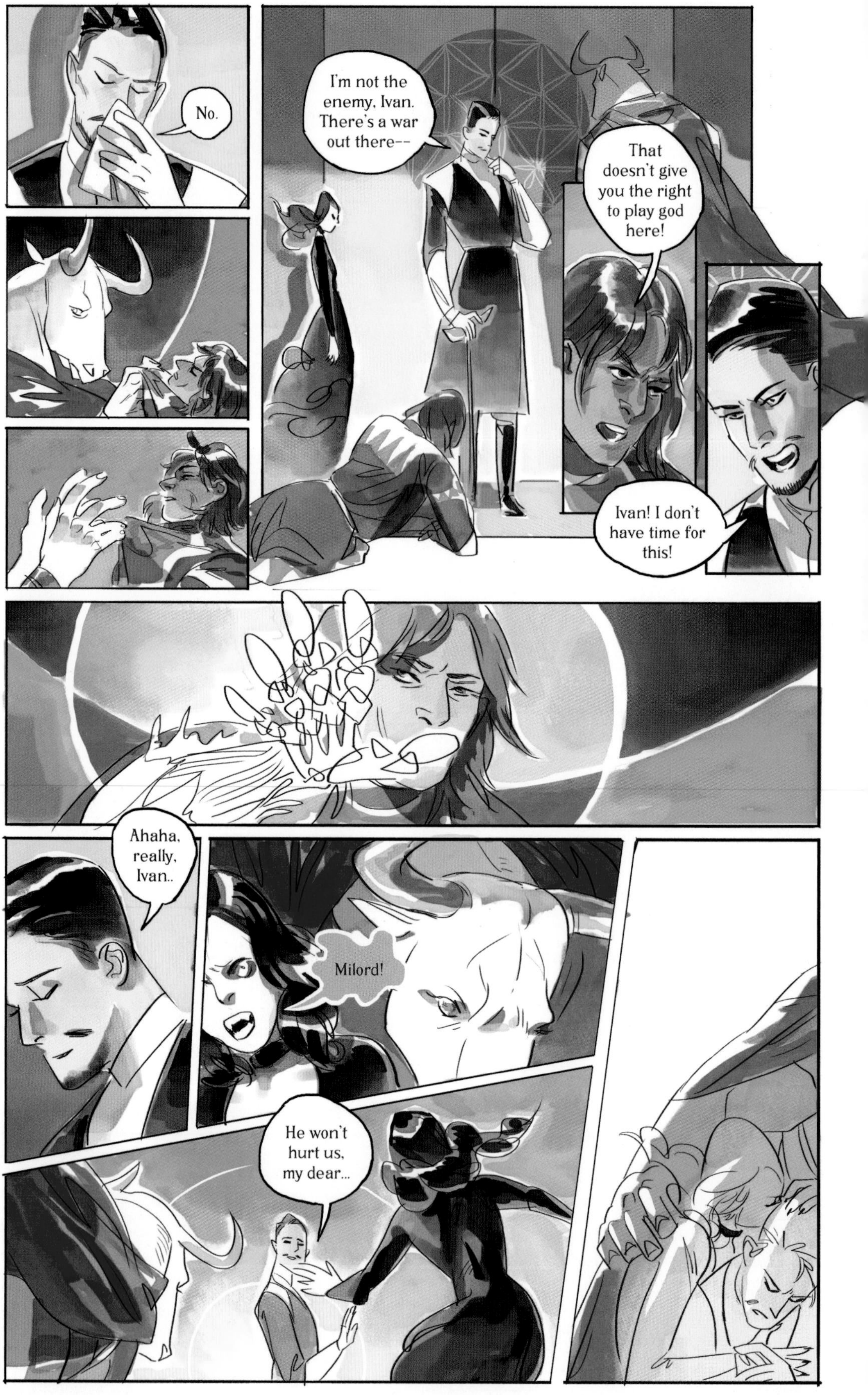
No.
I'm not the enemy, Ivan. There's a war out there--
That doesn't give you the right to play god here!
Ivan! I don't have time for this!
Ahaha, really, Ivan..
Milord!
He won't hurt us, my dear...

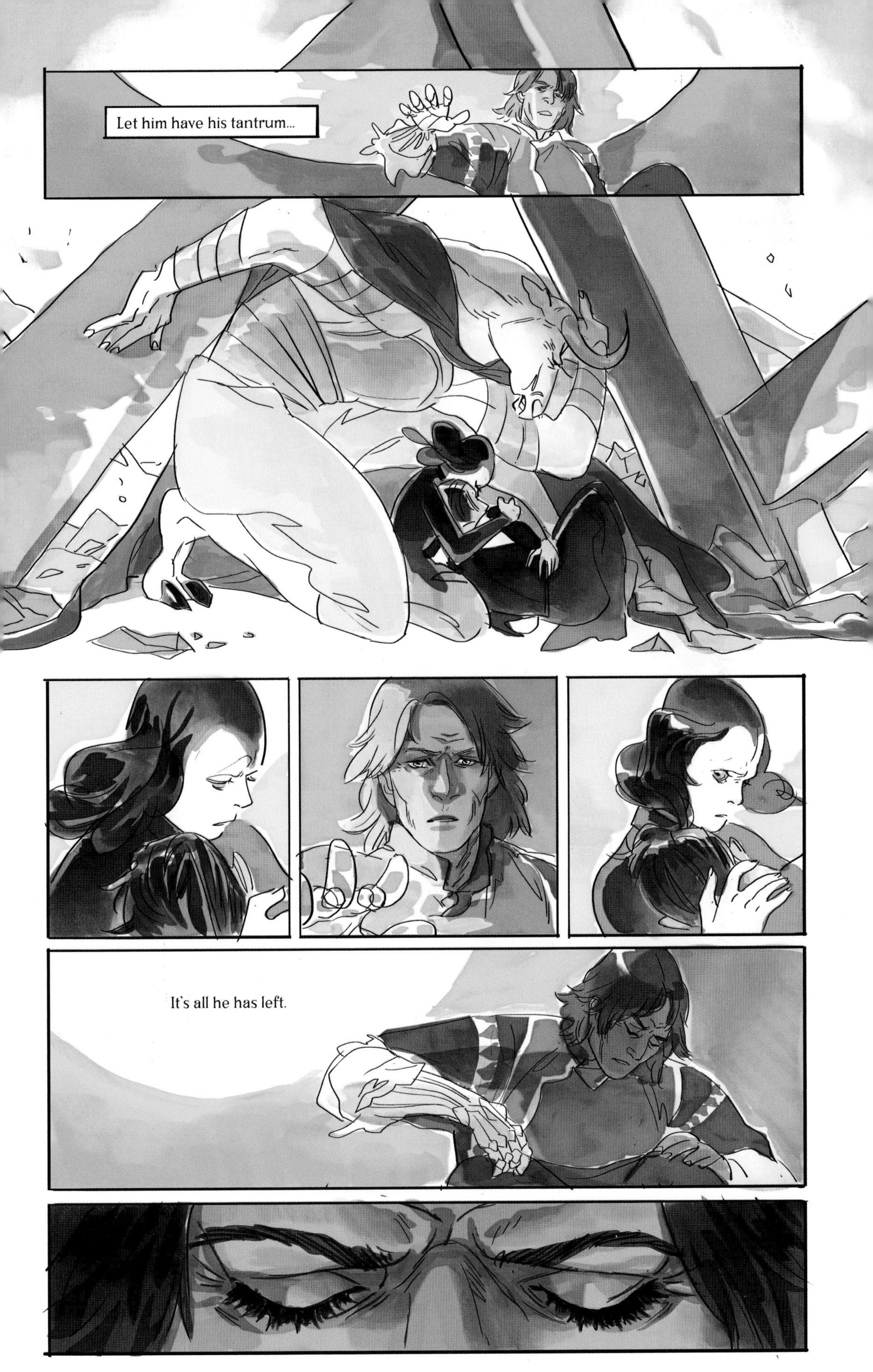
Let him have his tantrum...
It's all he has left.

Chapter Two

*Deep in the stars, strange creatures
inhabit the lands of the Irzah Asteroid.
Zun, a lab rat, runs away from the Esagila in a
quest to end the experiments behind its walls.*

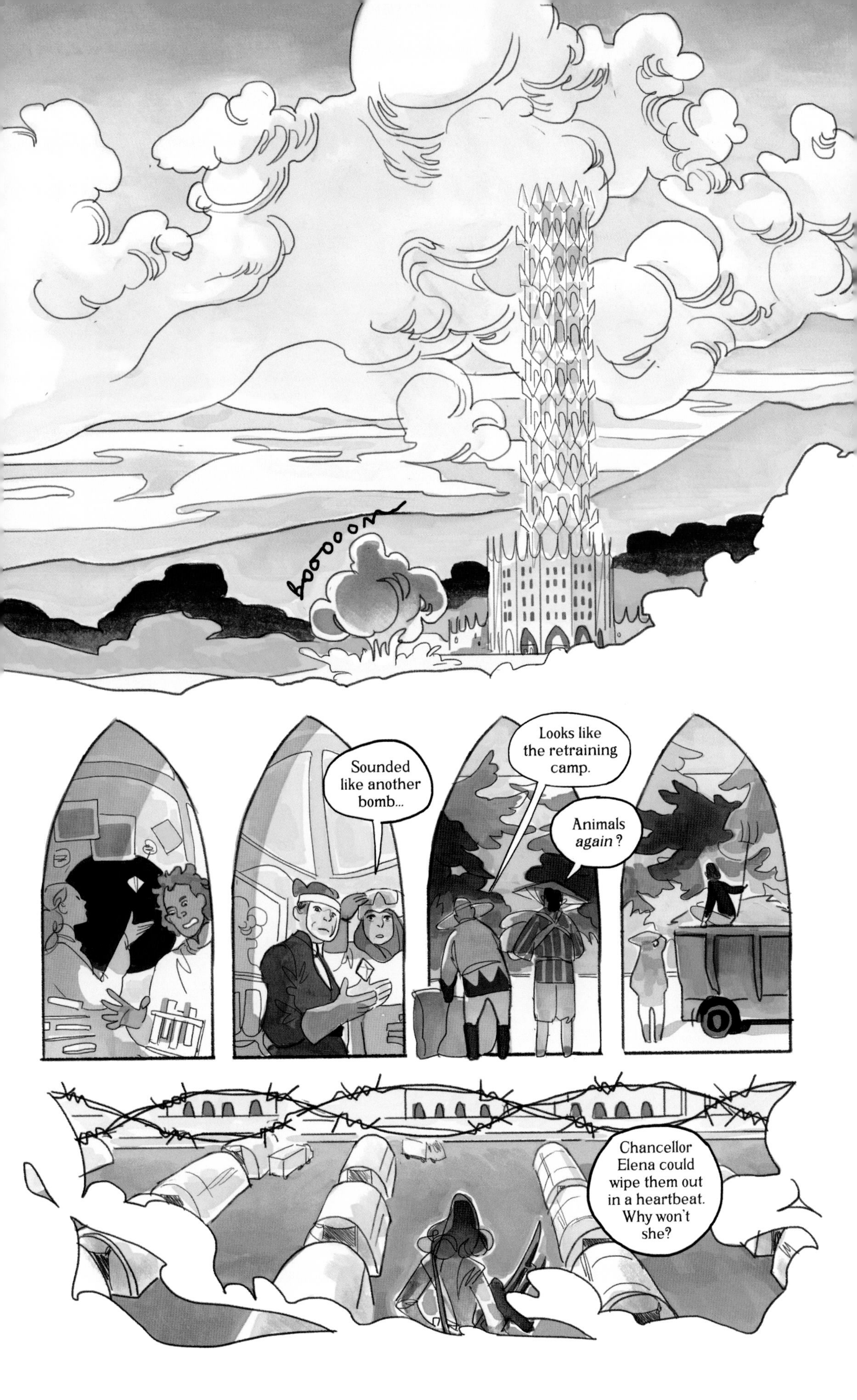
boooooom
Sounded like another bomb...
Looks like the retraining camp.
Animals again?
Chancellor Elena could wipe them out in a heartbeat. Why won't she?

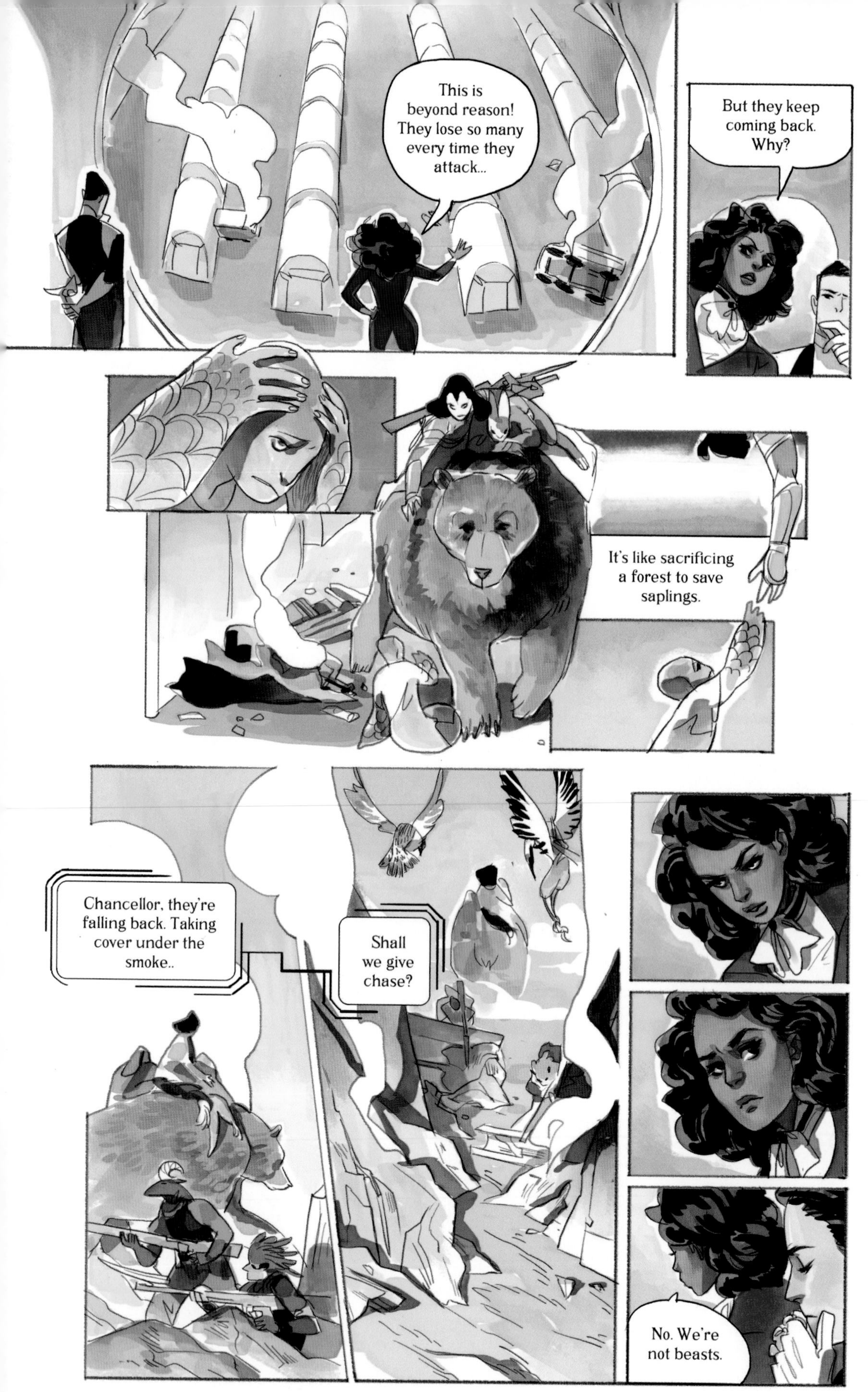
This is beyond reason! They lose so many every time they attack...
But they keep coming back. Why?
It's like sacrificing a forest to save saplings.
Chancellor, they're falling back. Taking cover under the smoke..
Shall we give chase?
No. We're not beasts.

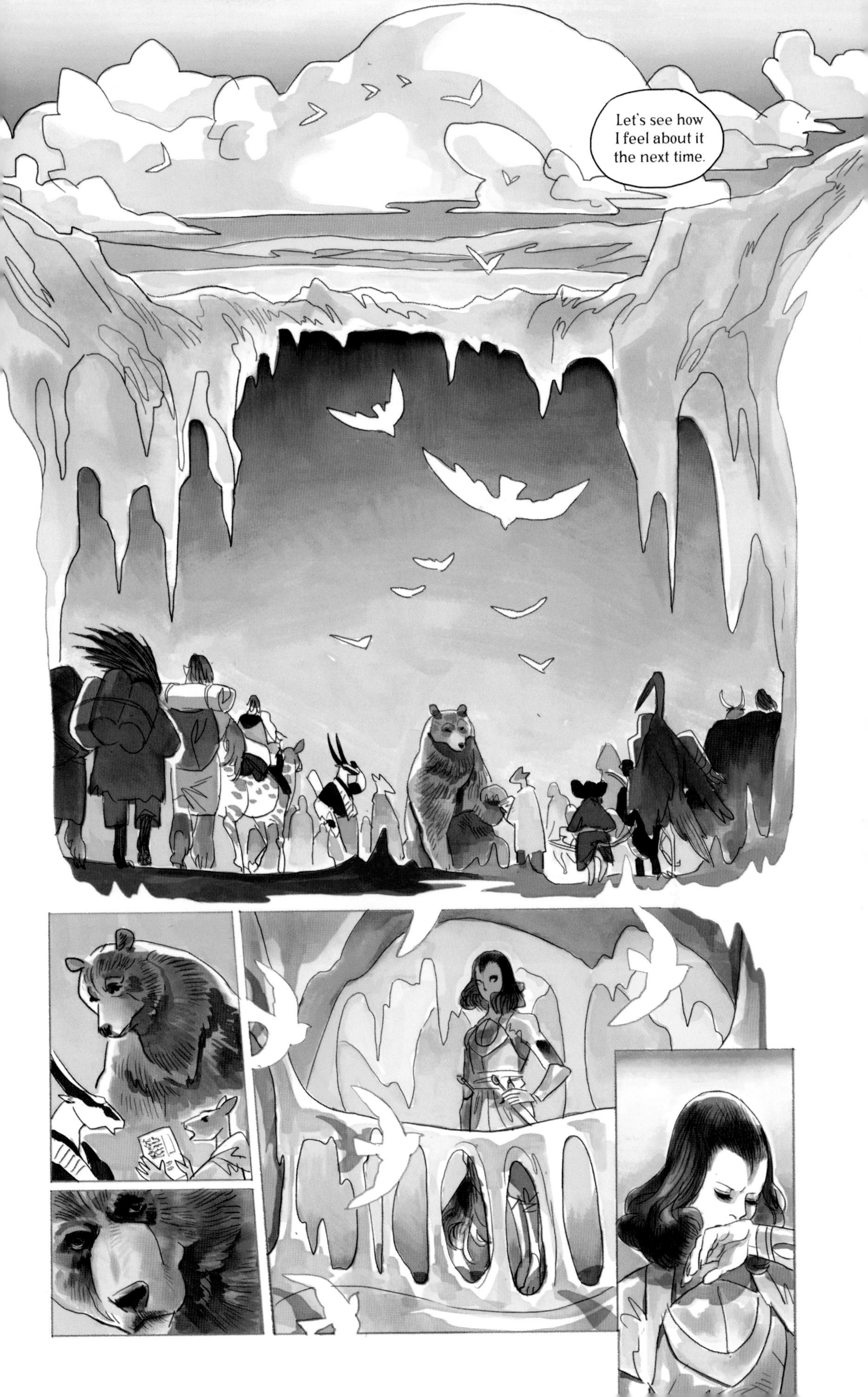
Let's see how
I feel about it
the next time.

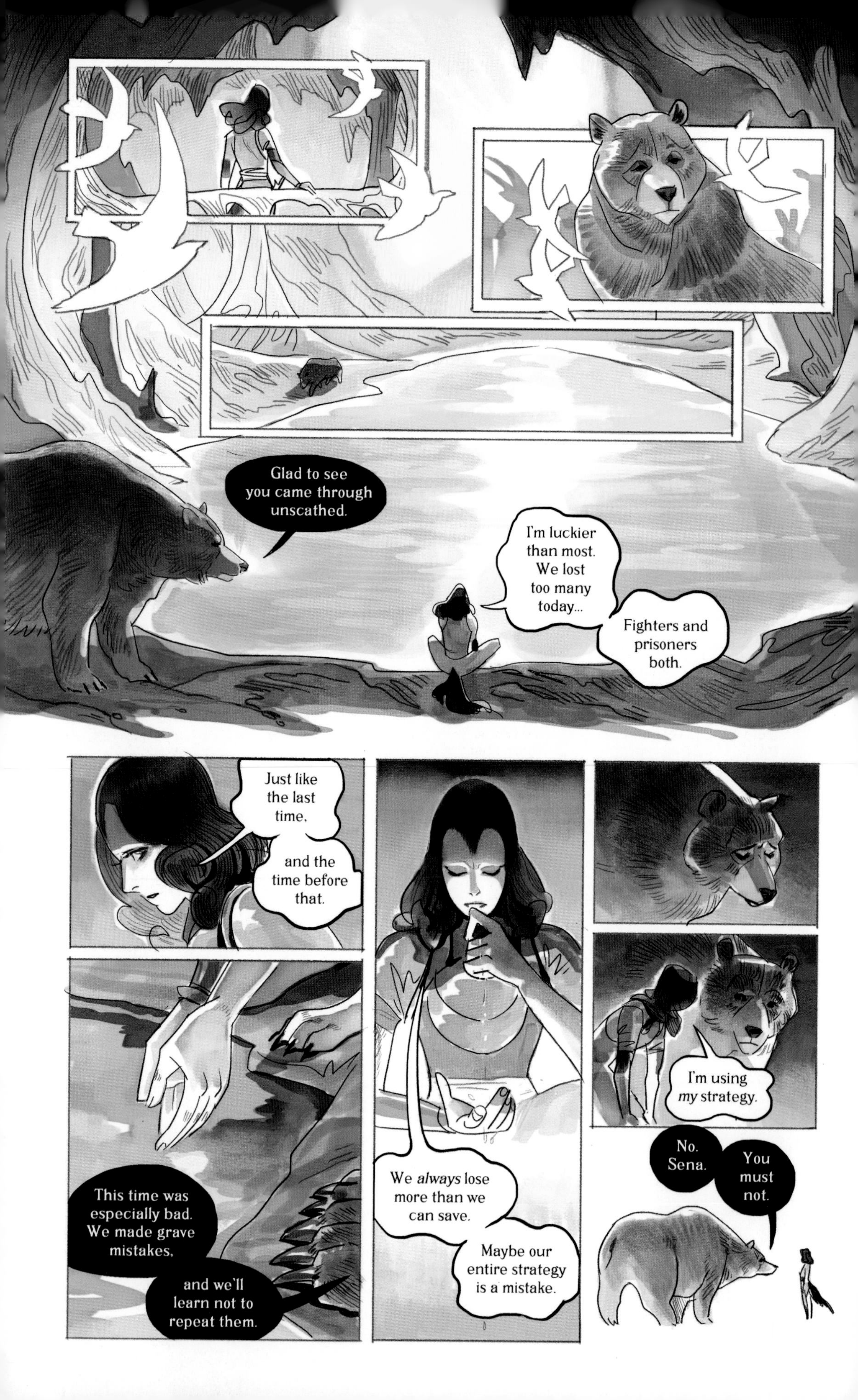
Glad to see you came through unscathed.
I'm luckier than most. We lost too many today...
Fighters and prisoners both.
Just like the last time,
and the time before that.
This time was especially bad. We made grave mistakes,
and we'll learn not to repeat them.
We *always* lose more than we can save.
Maybe our entire strategy is a mistake.
I'm using *my* strategy.
No. Sena.
You must not.

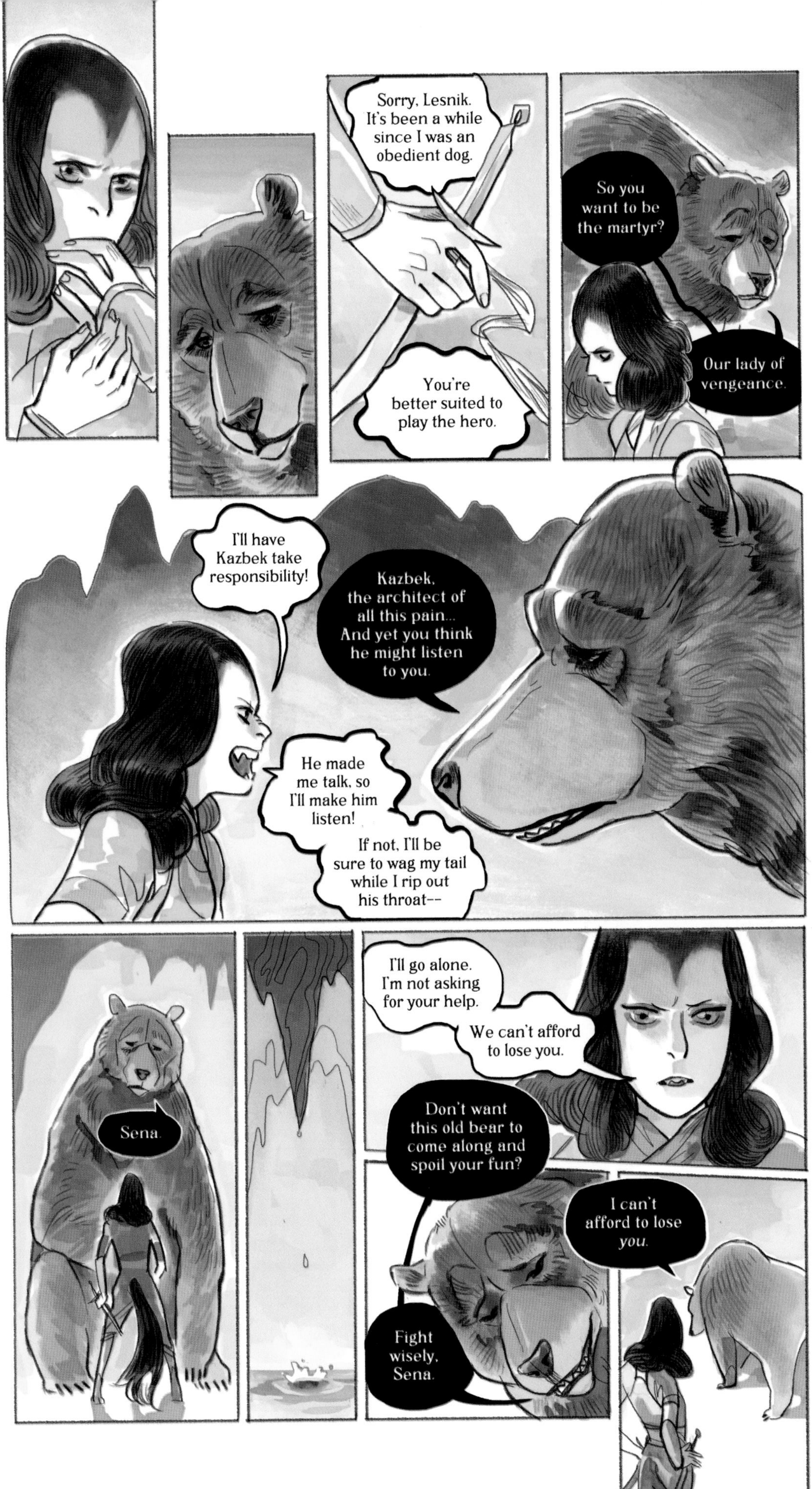

Sorry, Lesnik. It's been a while since I was an obedient dog.
You're better suited to play the hero.
So you want to be the martyr?
Our lady of vengeance.
I'll have Kazbek take responsibility!
Kazbek, the architect of all this pain... And yet you think he might listen to you.
He made me talk, so I'll make him listen!
If not, I'll be sure to wag my tail while I rip out his throat--
Sena.
I'll go alone. I'm not asking for your help.
We can't afford to lose you.
Don't want this old bear to come along and spoil your fun?
I can't afford to lose *you*.
Fight wisely, Sena.

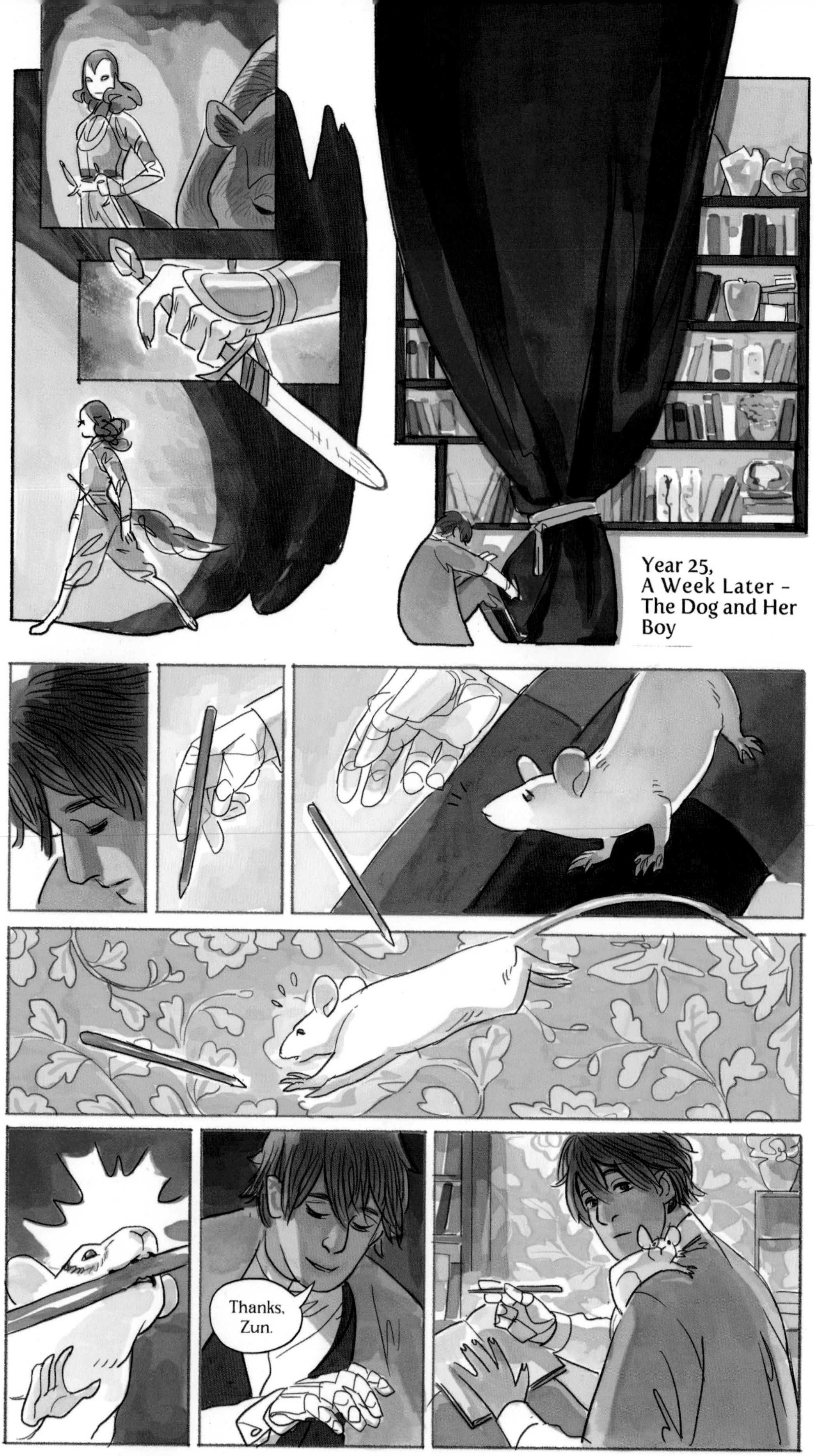
Year 25,
A Week Later -
The Dog and Her
Boy
Thanks,
Zun.

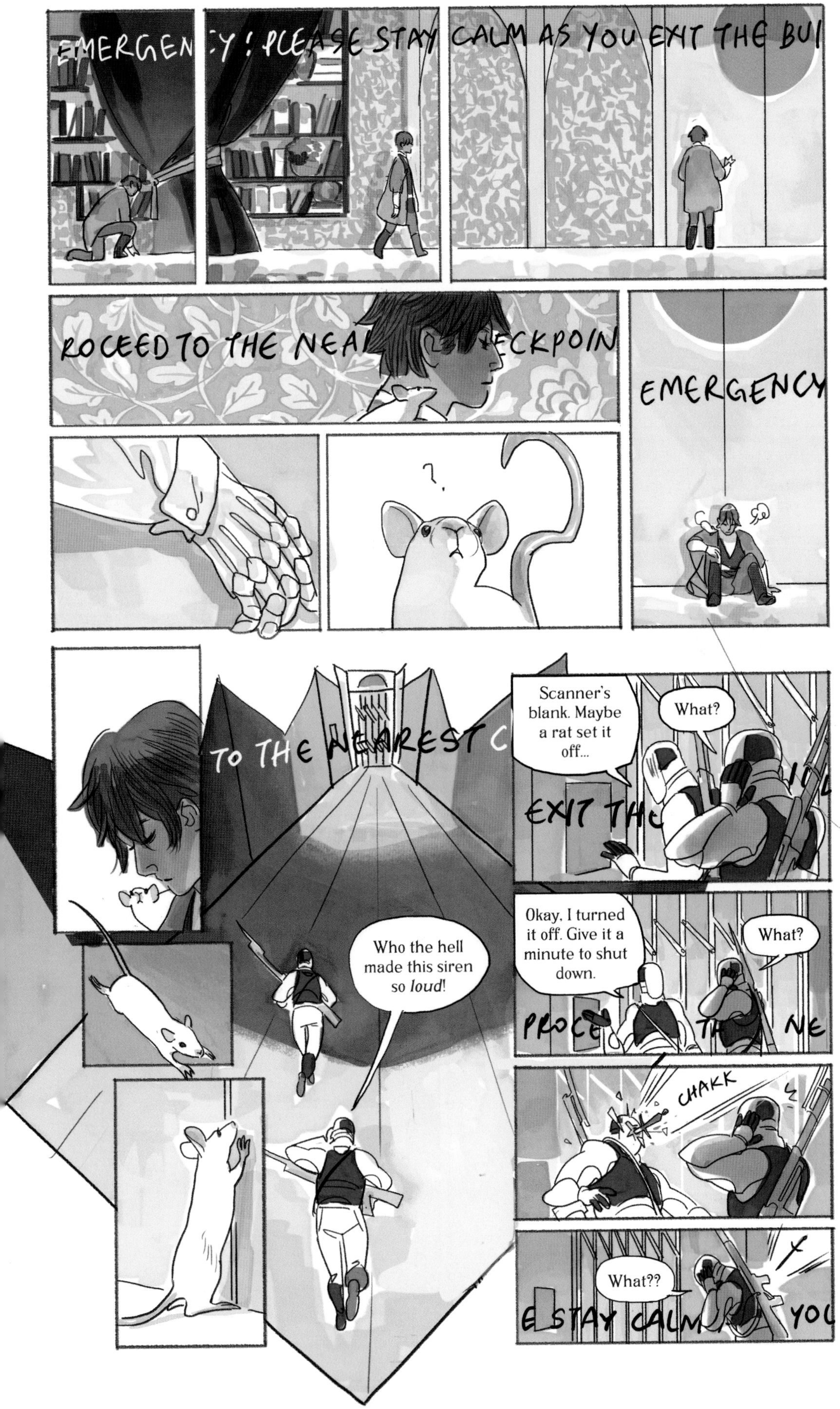

EMERGENCY! PLEASE STAY CALM AS YOU EXIT THE BUI
ROCEED TO THE NEA ECKPOIN
EMERGENCY
?
TO THE NEAREST C
Scanner's blank. Maybe a rat set it off...
What?
EXIT TH
Okay, I turned it off. Give it a minute to shut down.
What?
PROC NE
Who the hell made this siren so *loud*!
CHAKK
What??
E STAY CALM YOU

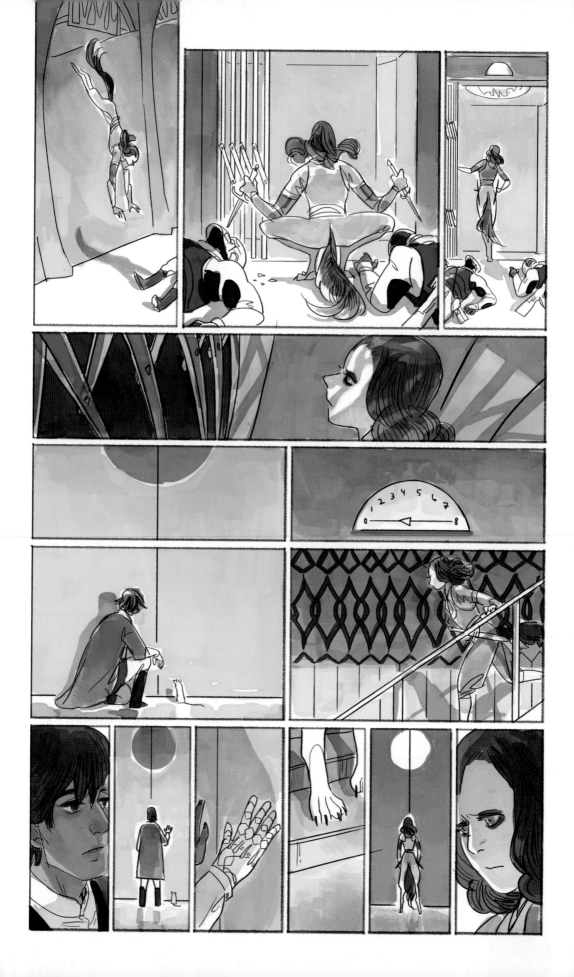

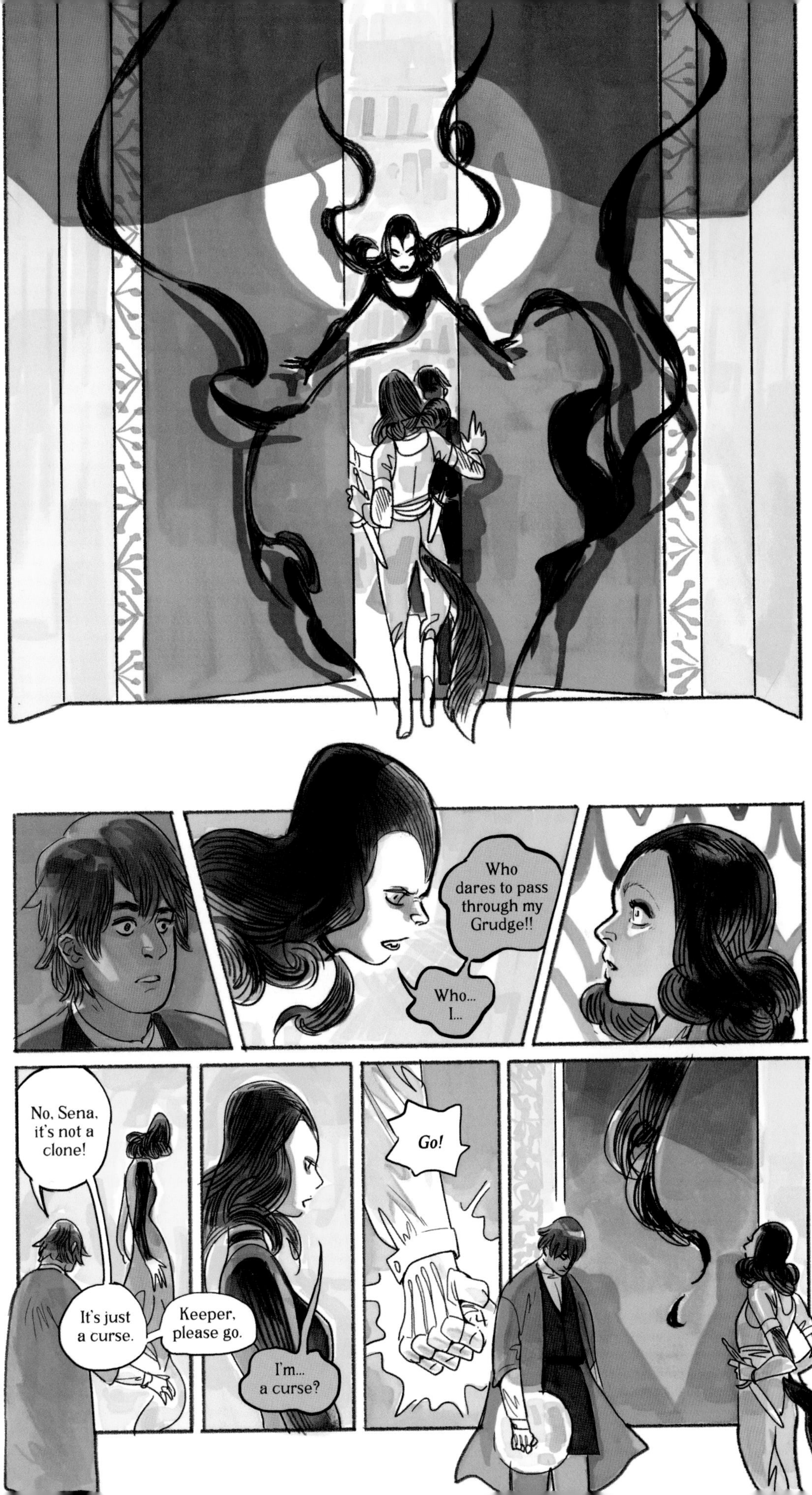
Who dares to pass through my Grudge!!
Who... I...
No, Sena, it's not a clone!
It's just a curse.
Keeper, please go.
I'm... a curse?
Go!

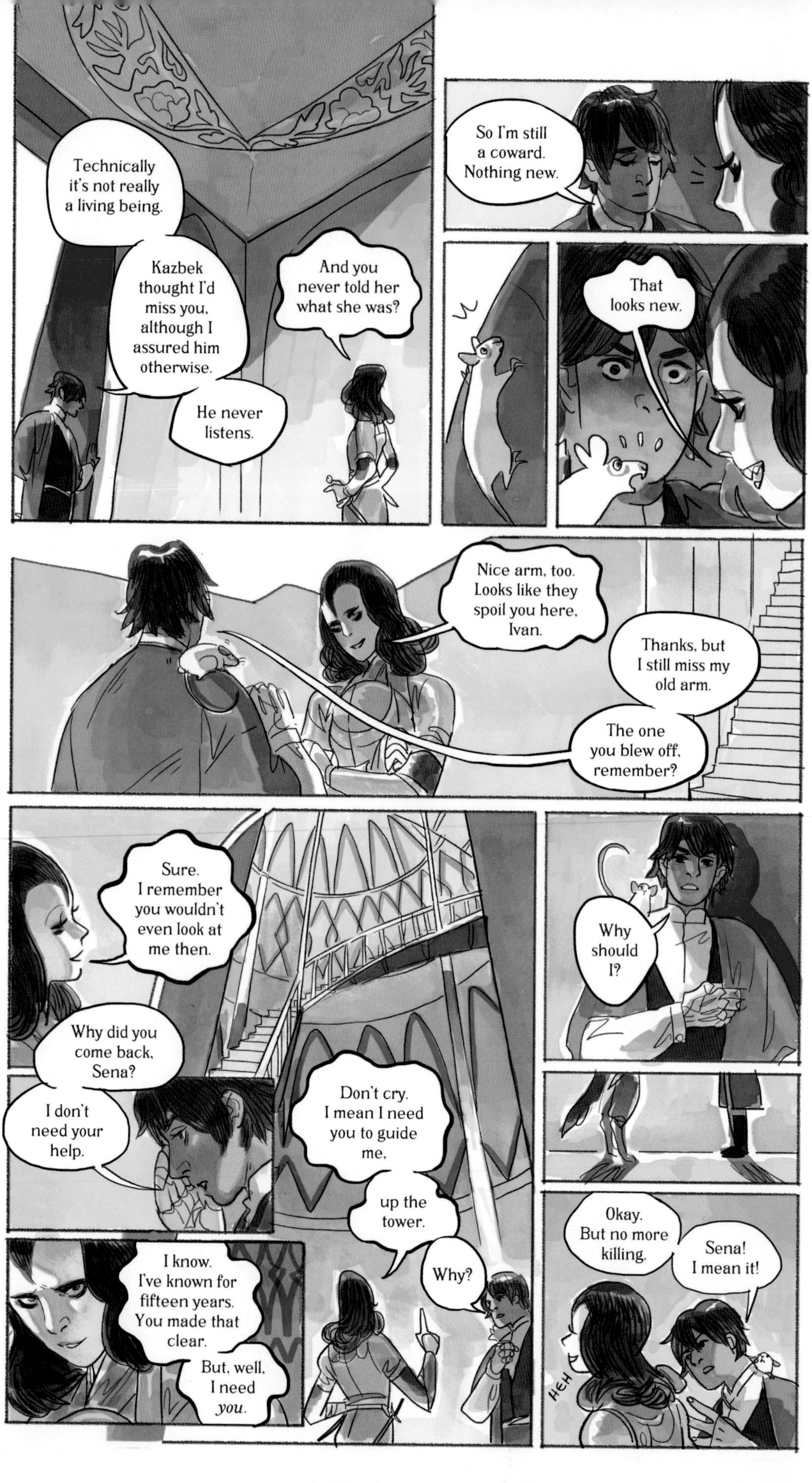
Technically it's not really a living being.
Kazbek thought I'd miss you, although I assured him otherwise.
He never listens.
And you never told her what she was?
So I'm still a coward. Nothing new.
That looks new.
Nice arm, too. Looks like they spoil you here, Ivan.
Thanks, but I still miss my old arm.
The one you blew off, remember?
Sure. I remember you wouldn't even look at me then.
Why should I?
Why did you come back, Sena?
I don't need your help.
Don't cry. I mean I need you to guide me,
up the tower.
I know. I've known for fifteen years. You made that clear.
But, well, I need *you*.
Why?
Okay. But no more killing.
Sena! I mean it!
HEH

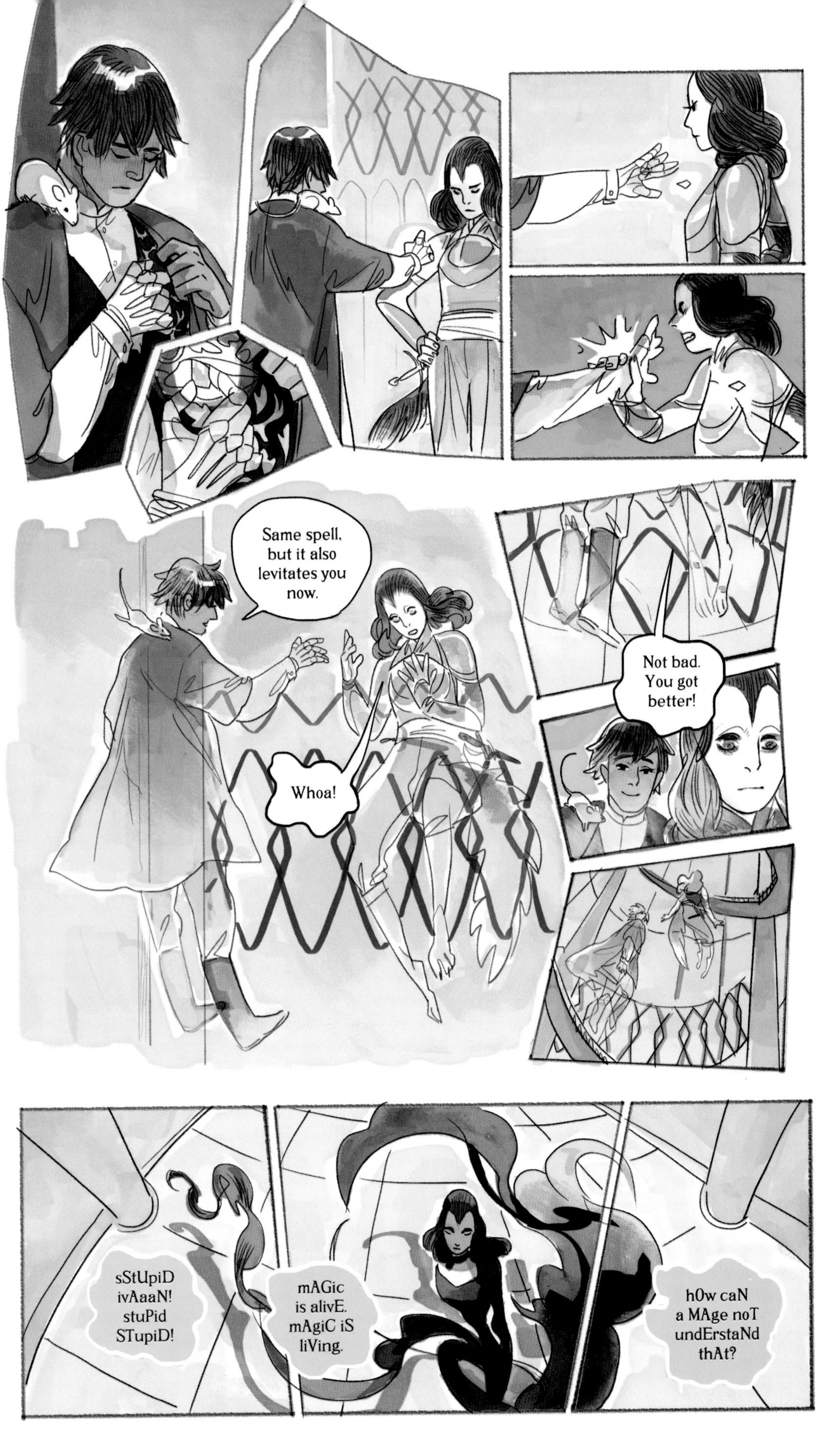
Same spell, but it also levitates you now.
Whoa!
Not bad. You got better!
sStUpiD ivAaaN! stuPid STupiD!
mAGic is alivE. mAgiC iS liVing.
h0w caN a MAge noT undErstaNd thAt?

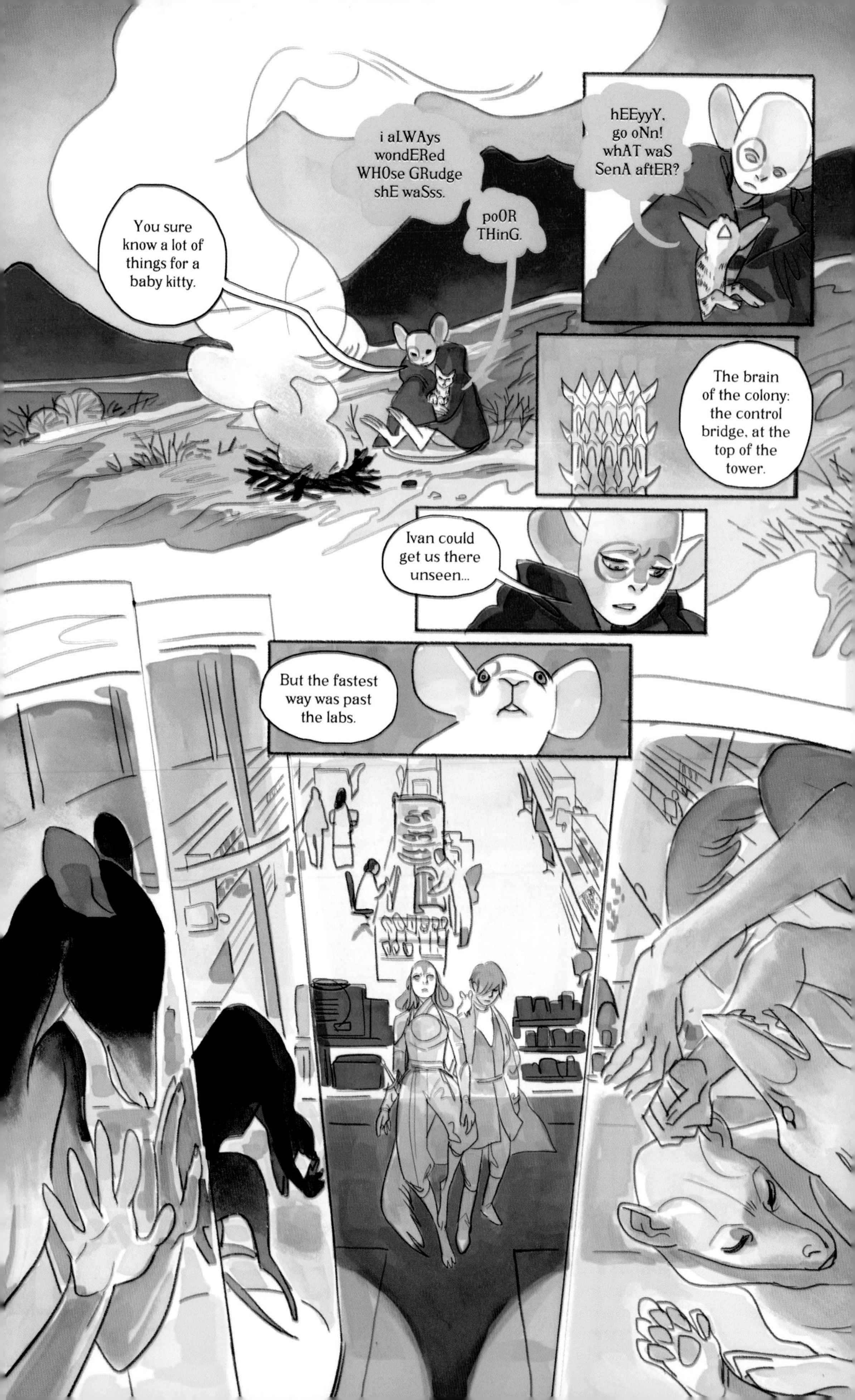
i aLWAys wondERed WHOse GRudge shE waSss.
poOR THinG.
You sure know a lot of things for a baby kitty.
hEEyyY, go oNn! whAT waS SenA aftER?
The brain of the colony: the control bridge, at the top of the tower.
Ivan could get us there unseen...
But the fastest way was past the labs.

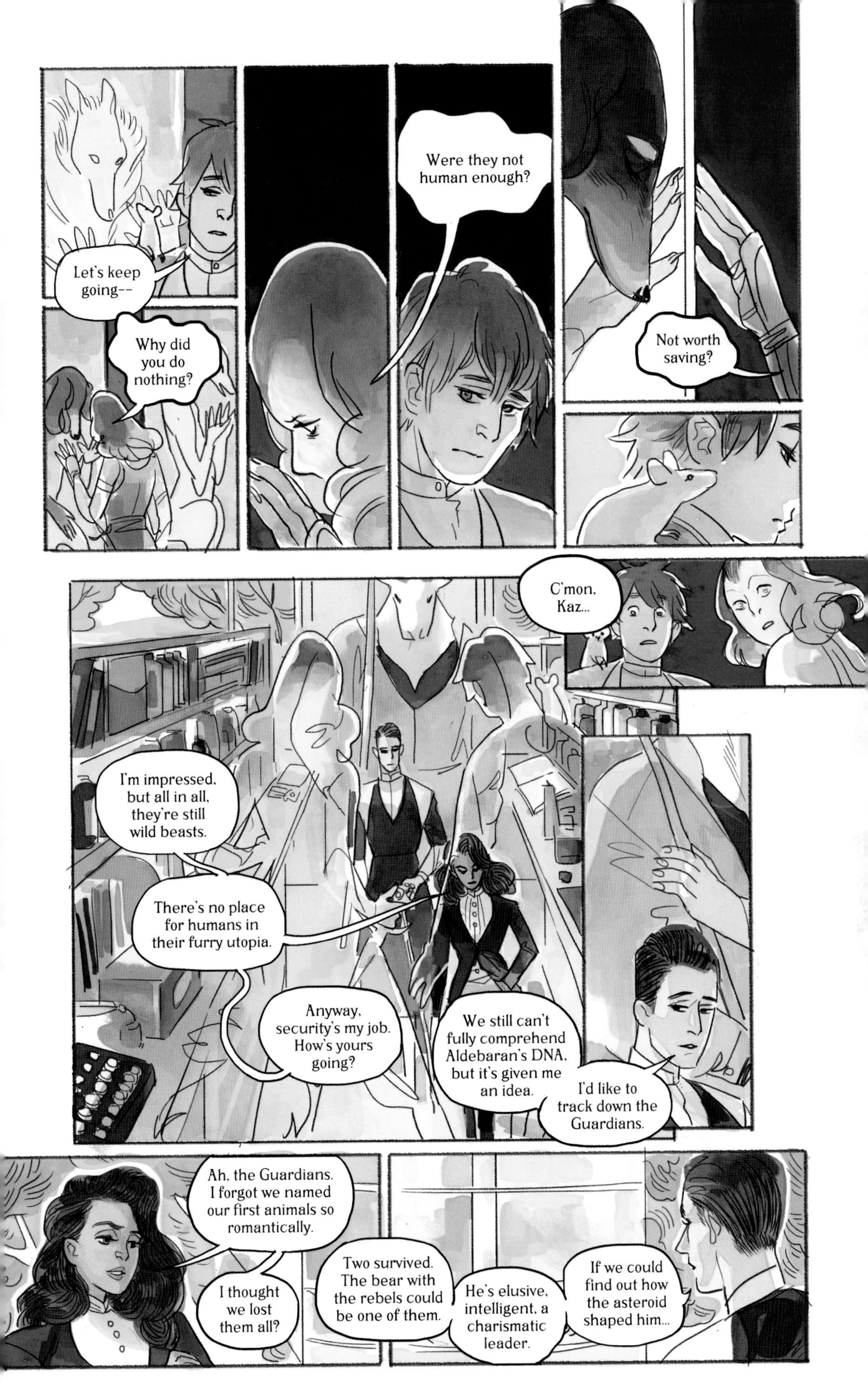
Let's keep going--
Why did you do nothing?
Were they not human enough?
Not worth saving?
C'mon, Kaz...
I'm impressed, but all in all, they're still wild beasts.
There's no place for humans in their furry utopia.
Anyway, security's my job. How's yours going?
We still can't fully comprehend Aldebaran's DNA, but it's given me an idea.
I'd like to track down the Guardians.
Ah, the Guardians. I forgot we named our first animals so romantically.
I thought we lost them all?
Two survived. The bear with the rebels could be one of them.
He's elusive, intelligent, a charismatic leader.
If we could find out how the asteroid shaped him...

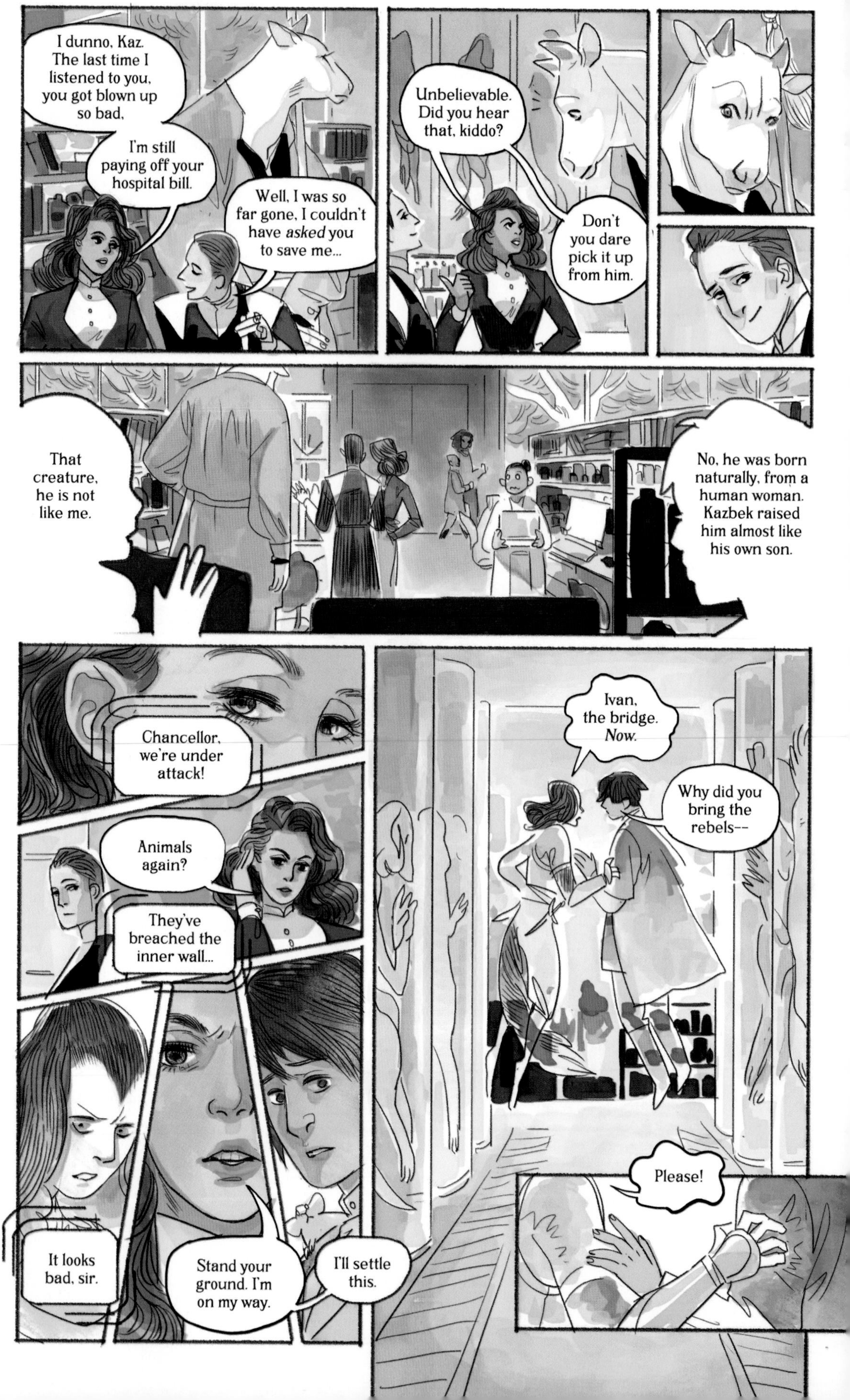

I dunno, Kaz. The last time I listened to you, you got blown up so bad,
I'm still paying off your hospital bill.
Well, I was so far gone, I couldn't have *asked* you to save me...
Unbelievable. Did you hear that, kiddo?
Don't you dare pick it up from him.
That creature, he is not like me.
No, he was born naturally, from a human woman. Kazbek raised him almost like his own son.
Chancellor, we're under attack!
Animals again?
They've breached the inner wall...
It looks bad, sir.
Stand your ground. I'm on my way.
I'll settle this.
Ivan, the bridge. *Now.*
Why did you bring the rebels--
Please!

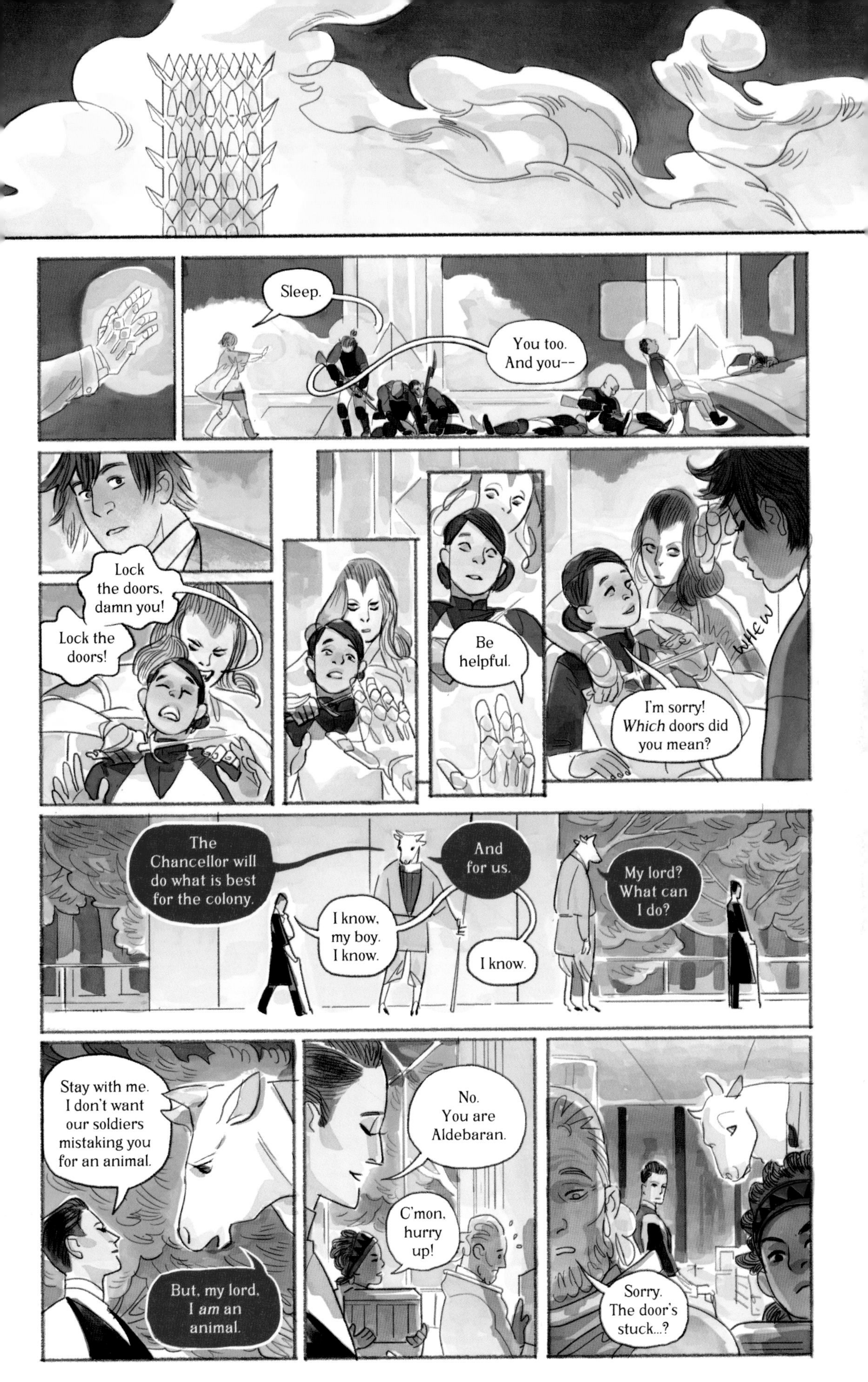

Sleep.
You too. And you--
Lock the doors, damn you!
Lock the doors!
Be helpful.
I'm sorry! *Which* doors did you mean?
WHEW
The Chancellor will do what is best for the colony.
I know, my boy. I know.
And for us.
I know.
My lord? What can I do?
Stay with me. I don't want our soldiers mistaking you for an animal.
But, my lord, I *am* an animal.
No. You are Aldebaran.
C'mon, hurry up!
Sorry. The door's stuck...?

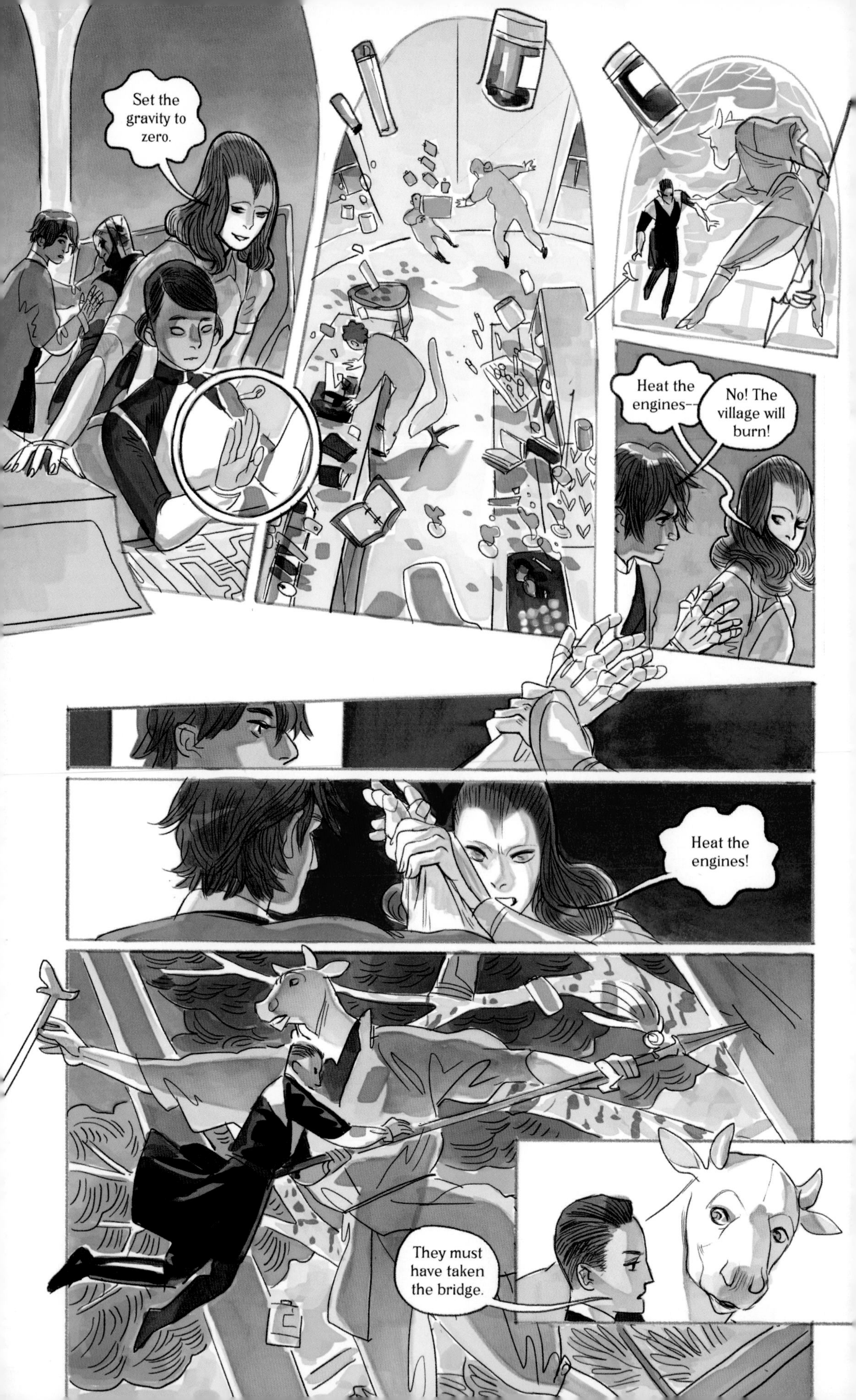
Set the gravity to zero.
Heat the engines--
No! The village will burn!
Heat the engines!
They must have taken the bridge.

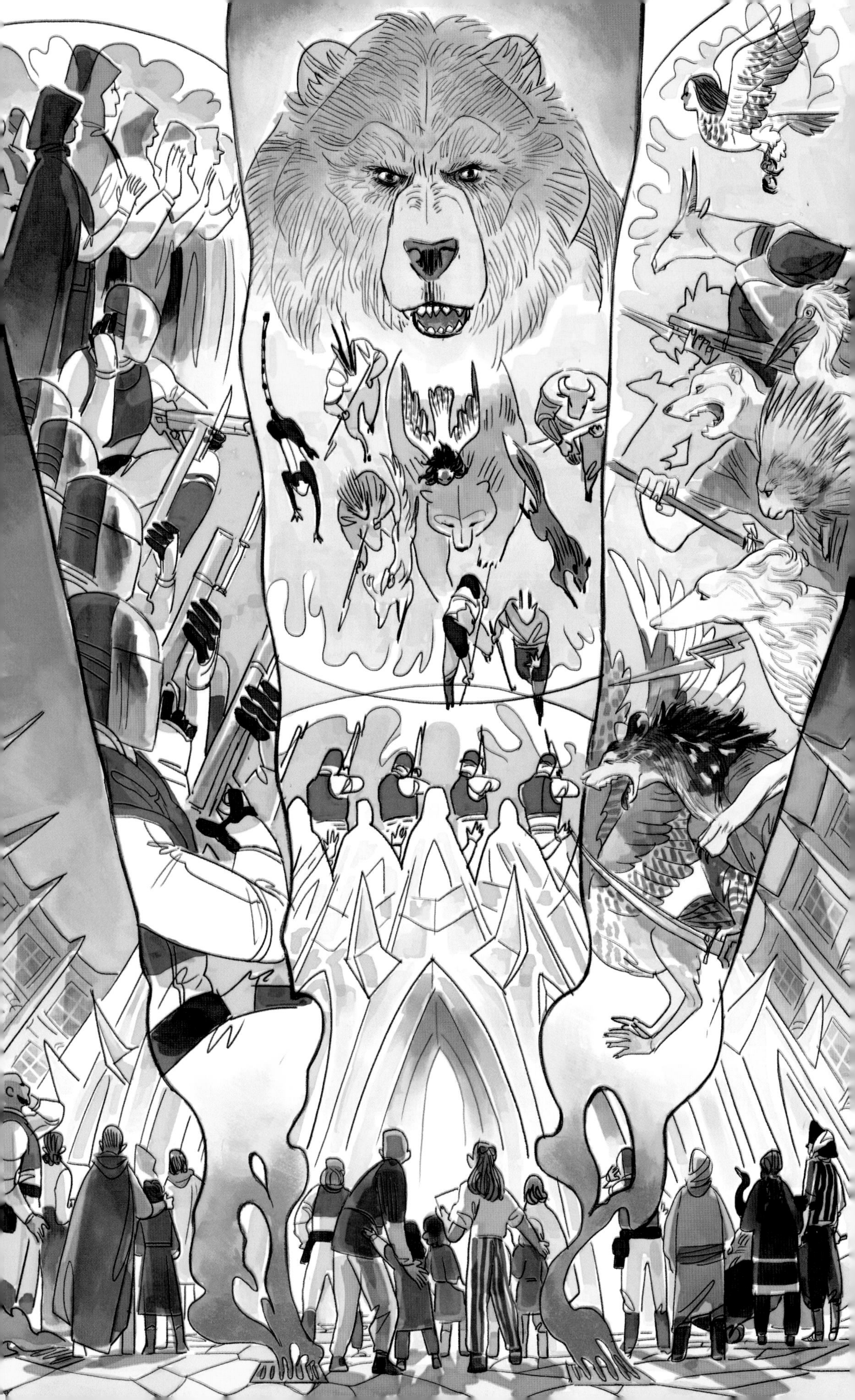

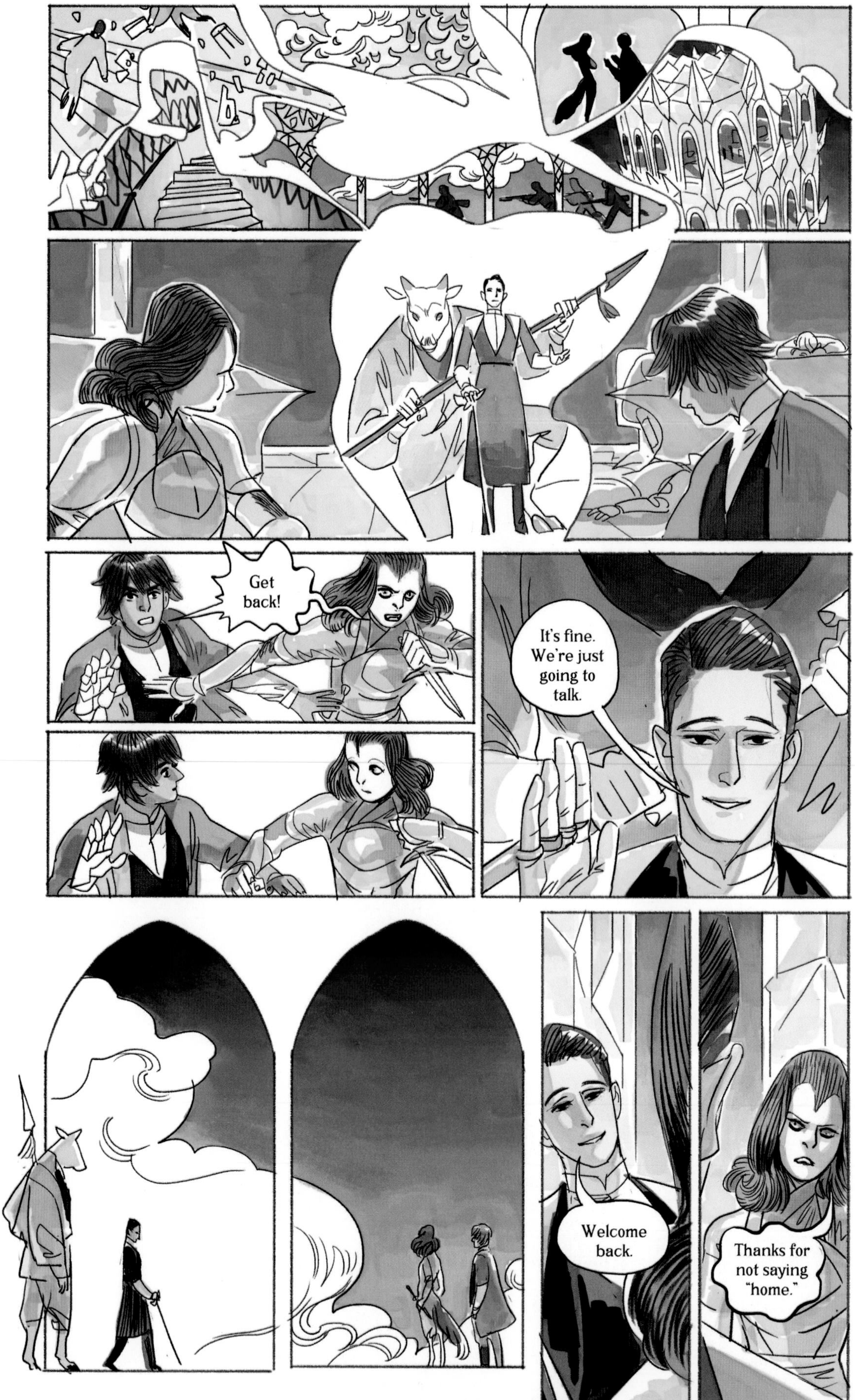
Get back!
It's fine. We're just going to talk.
Welcome back.
Thanks for not saying "home."

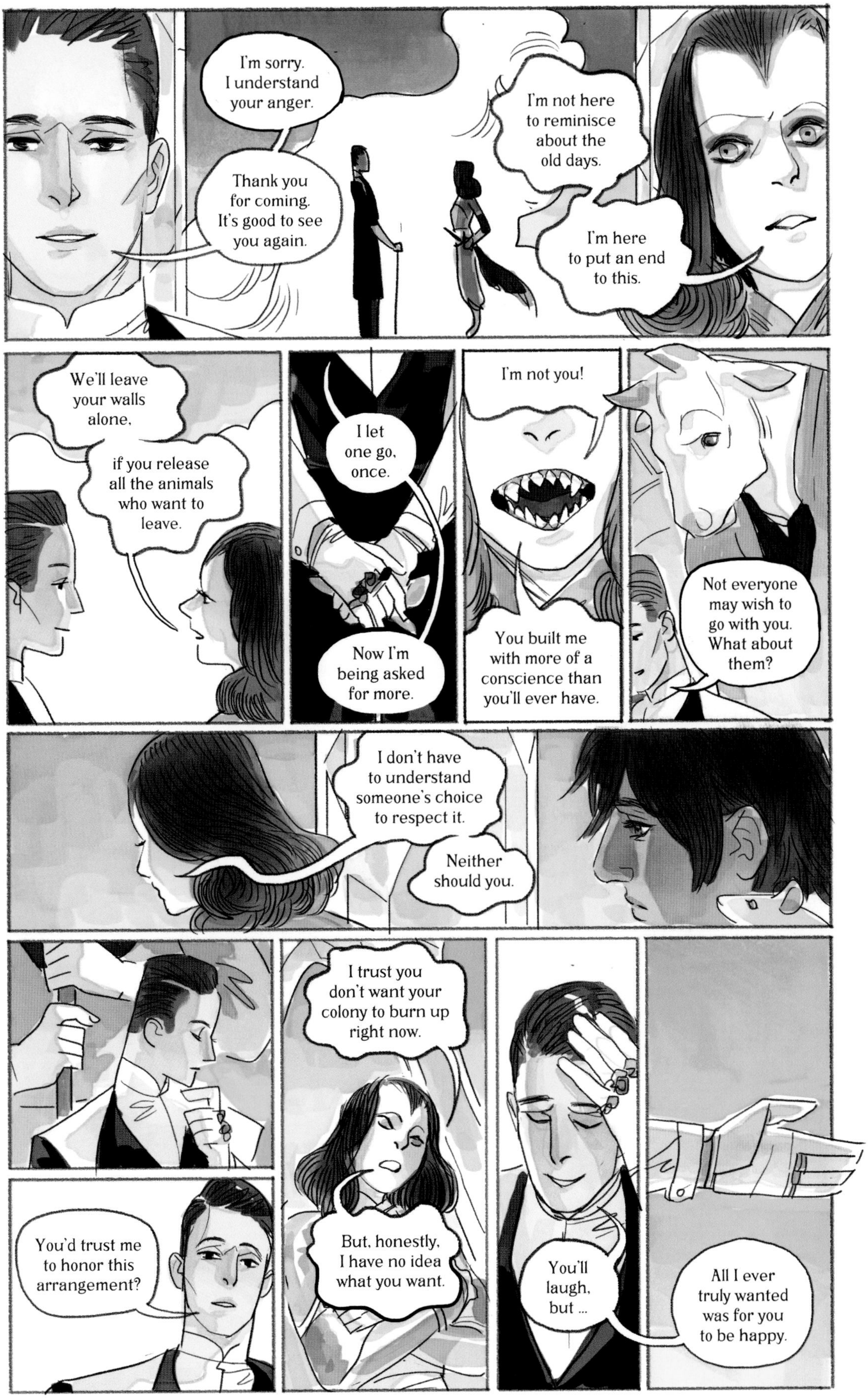

I'm sorry. I understand your anger.
Thank you for coming. It's good to see you again.
I'm not here to reminisce about the old days.
I'm here to put an end to this.
We'll leave your walls alone,
if you release all the animals who want to leave.
I let one go, once.
Now I'm being asked for more.
I'm not you!
You built me with more of a conscience than you'll ever have.
Not everyone may wish to go with you. What about them?
I don't have to understand someone's choice to respect it.
Neither should you.
I trust you don't want your colony to burn up right now.
You'd trust me to honor this arrangement?
But, honestly, I have no idea what you want.
You'll laugh, but ...
All I ever truly wanted was for you to be happy.

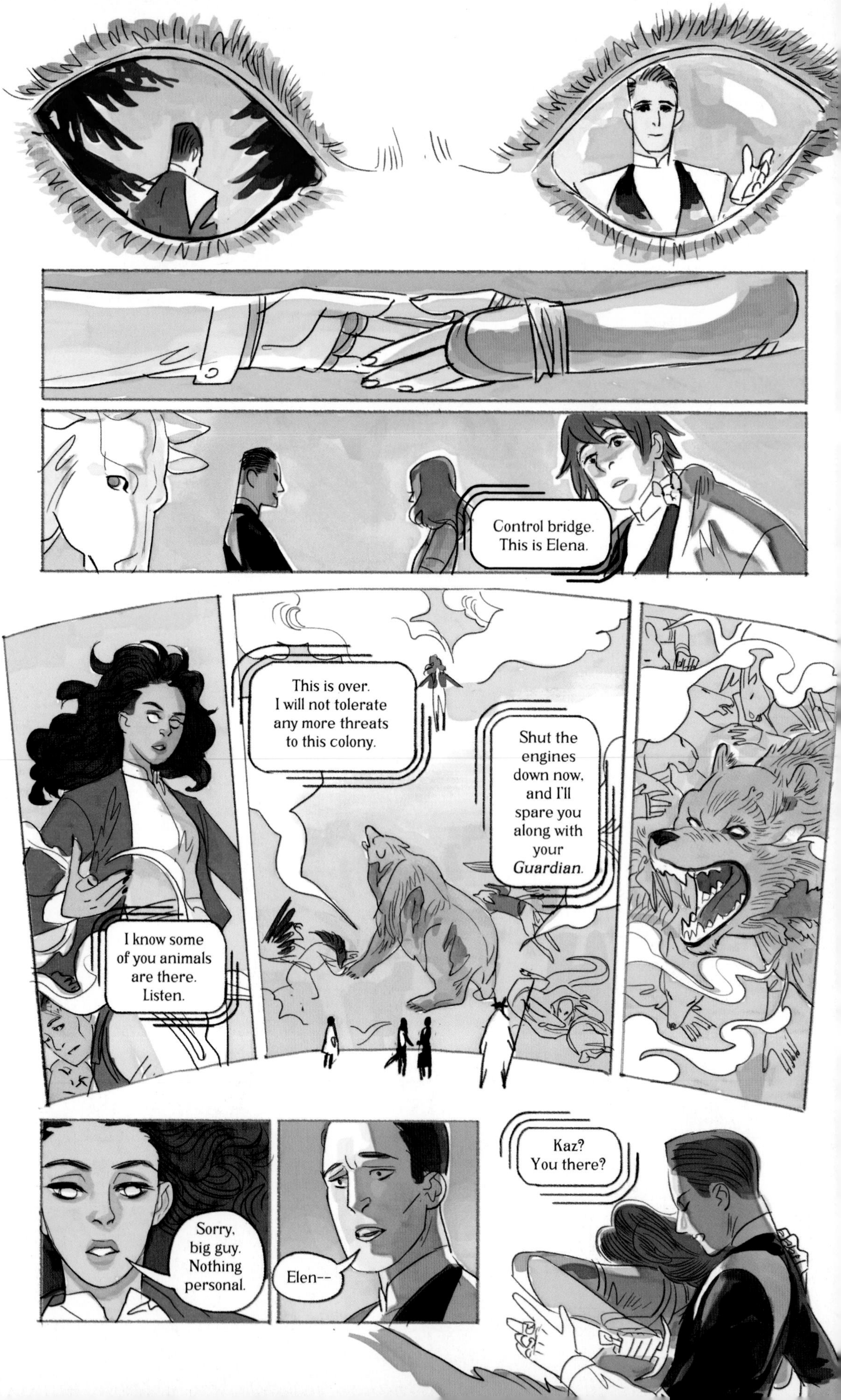
Control bridge. This is Elena.
I know some of you animals are there. Listen.
This is over. I will not tolerate any more threats to this colony.
Shut the engines down now, and I'll spare you along with your *Guardian*.
Sorry, big guy. Nothing personal.
Elen--
Kaz? You there?

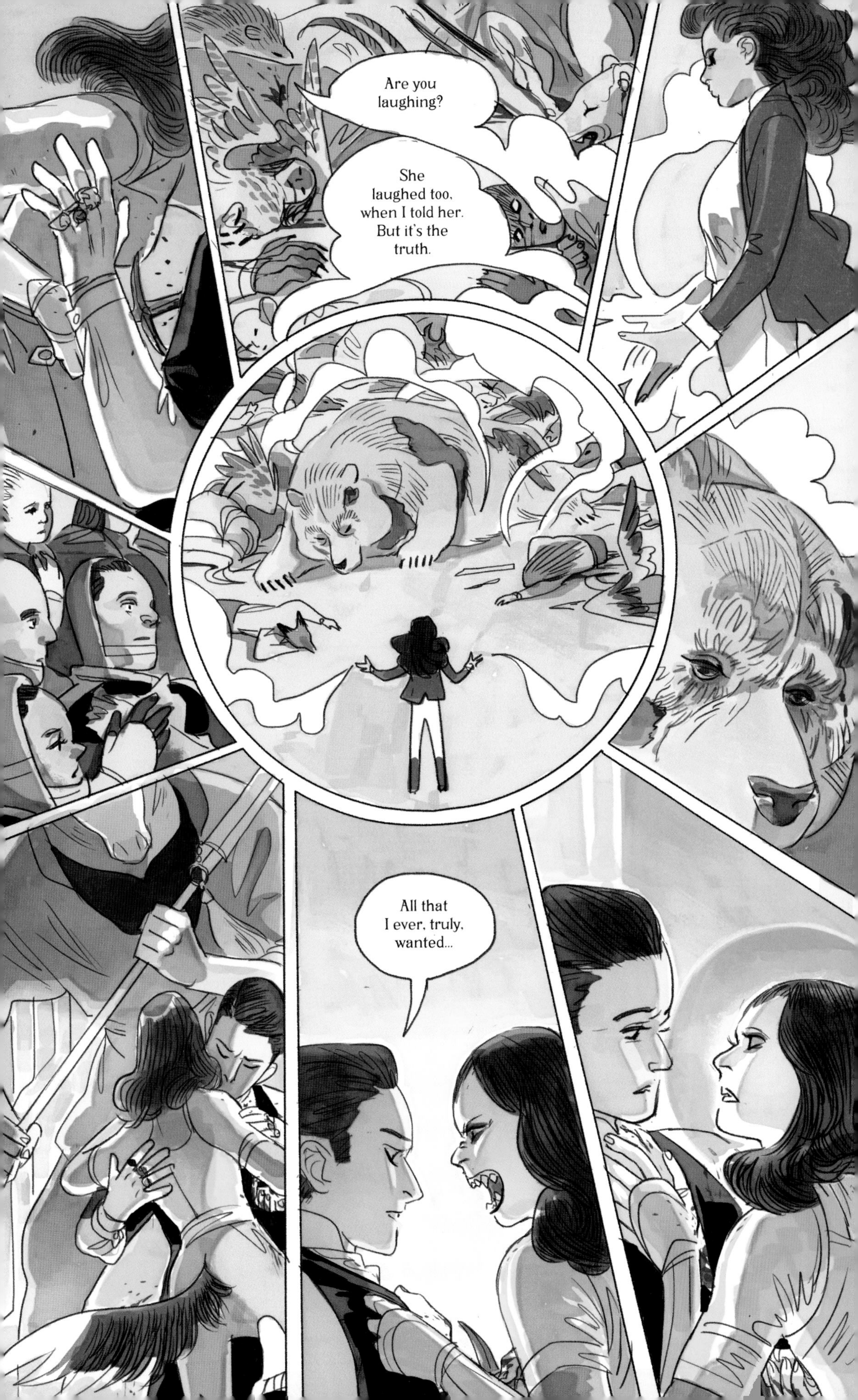
Are you laughing?
She laughed too, when I told her. But it's the truth.
All that I ever, truly, wanted...

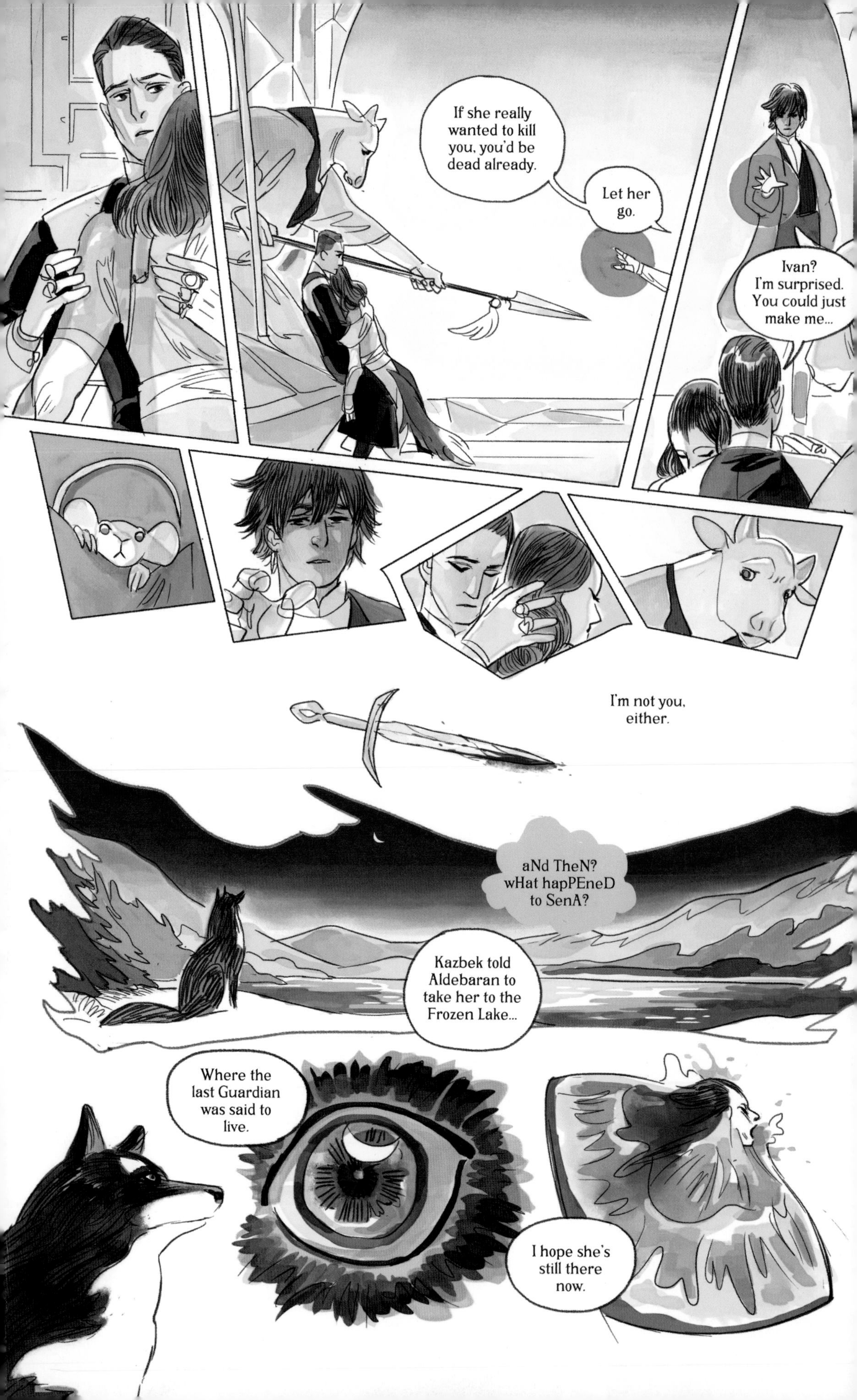
If she really wanted to kill you, you'd be dead already.
Let her go.
Ivan? I'm surprised. You could just make me...
I'm not you, either.
aNd TheN? wHat hapPEneD to SenA?
Kazbek told Aldebaran to take her to the Frozen Lake...
Where the last Guardian was said to live.
I hope she's still there now.

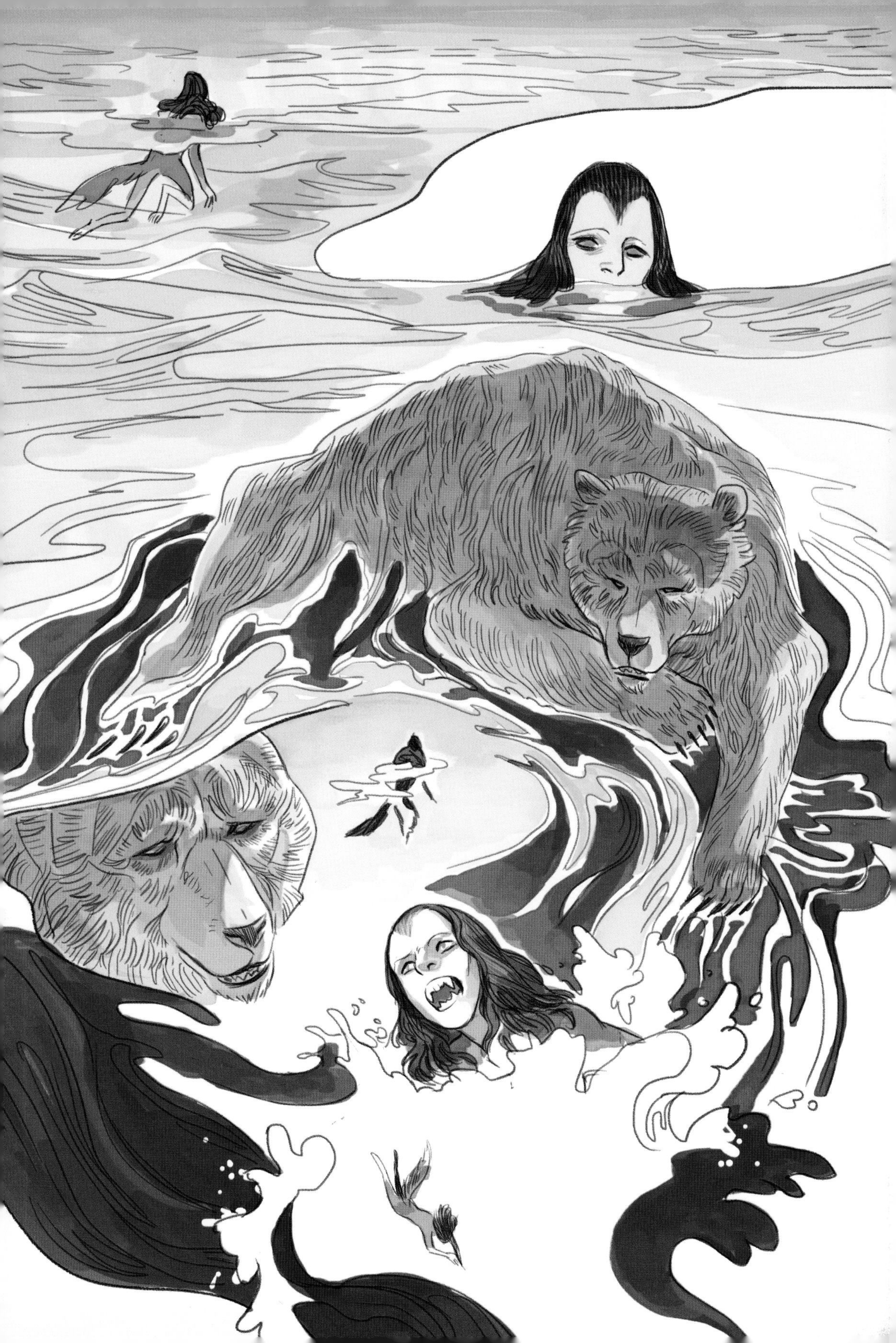

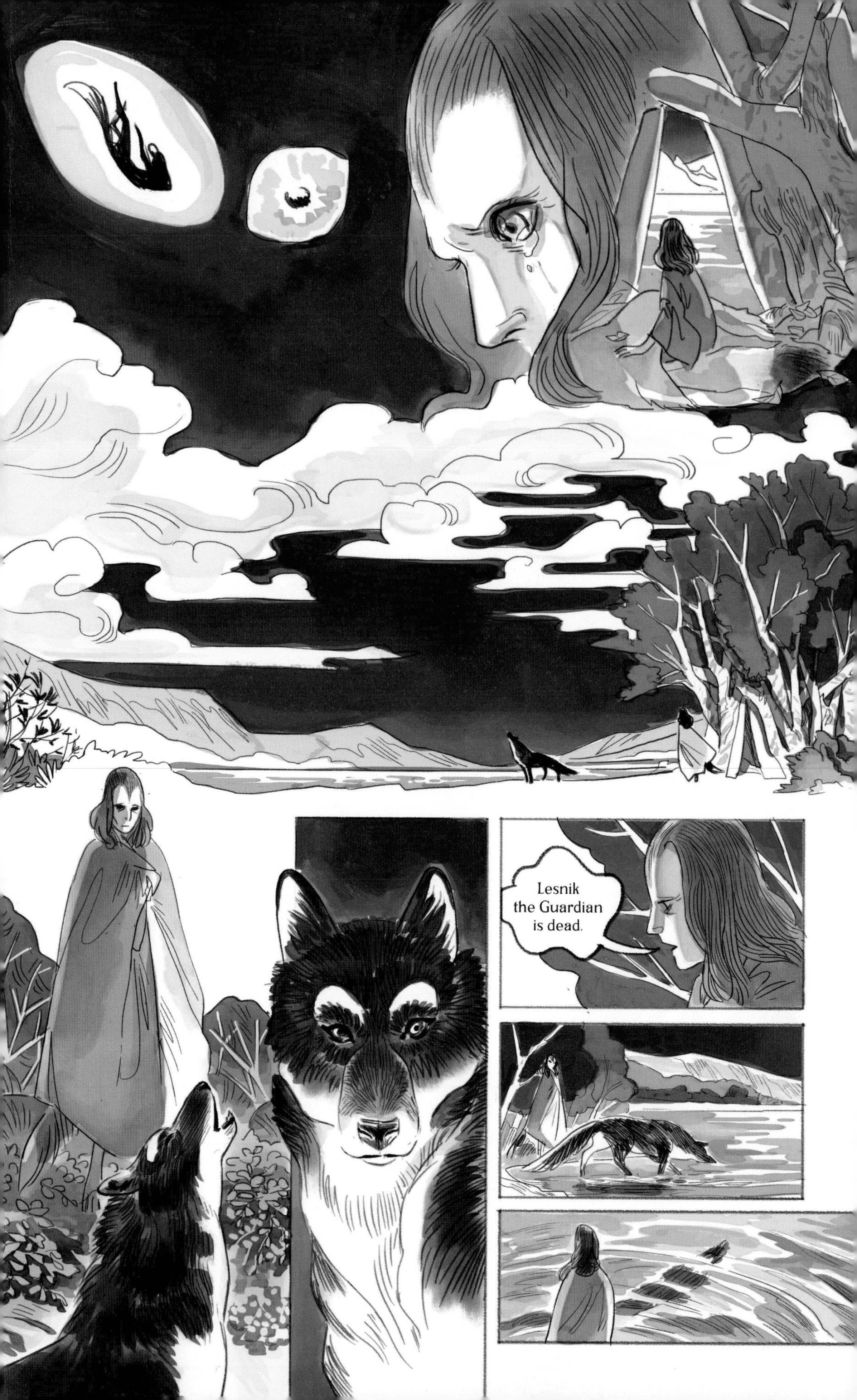
Lesnik the Guardian is dead.

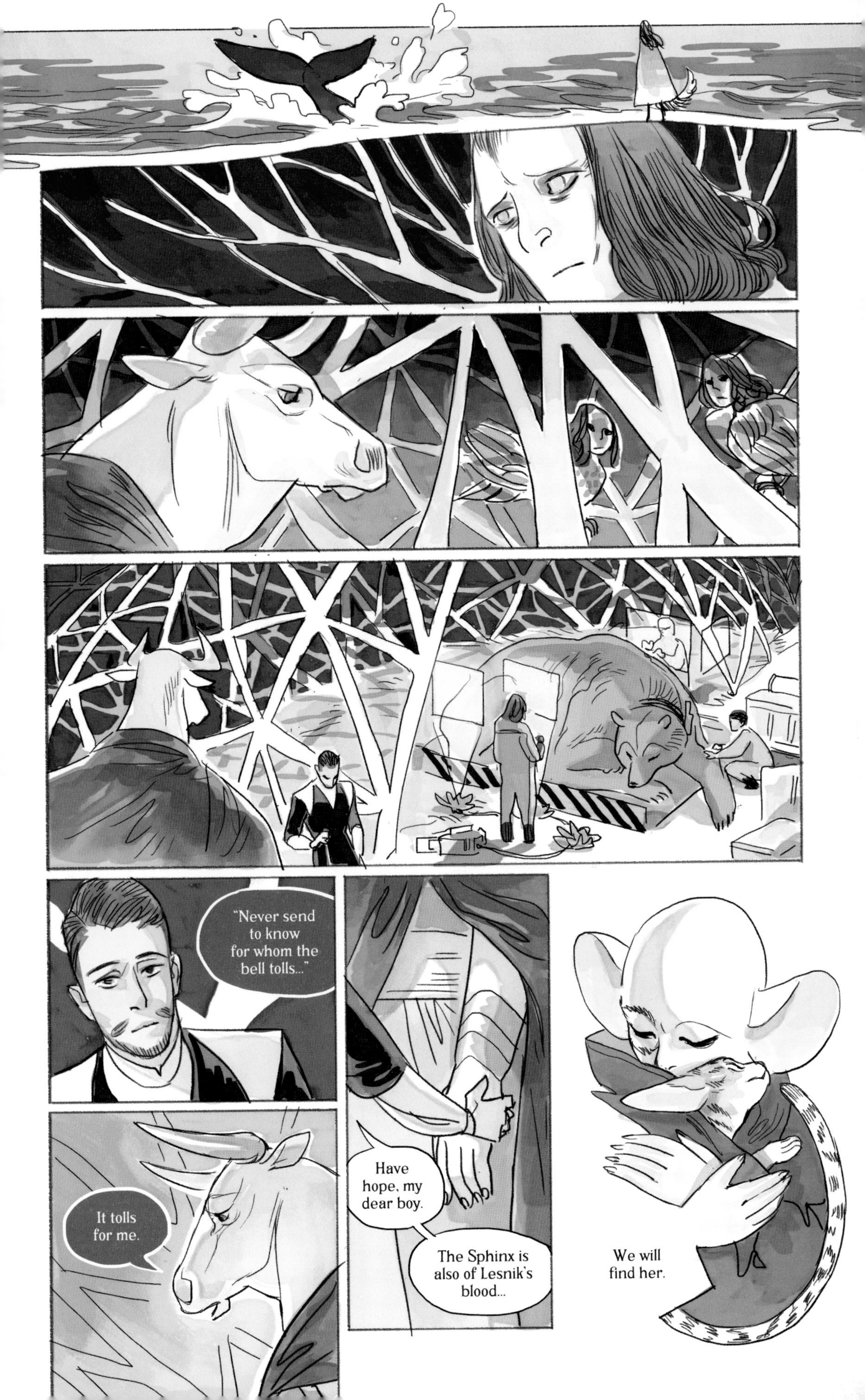
"Never send to know for whom the bell tolls..."
It tolls for me.
Have hope, my dear boy.
The Sphinx is also of Lesnik's blood...
We will find her.

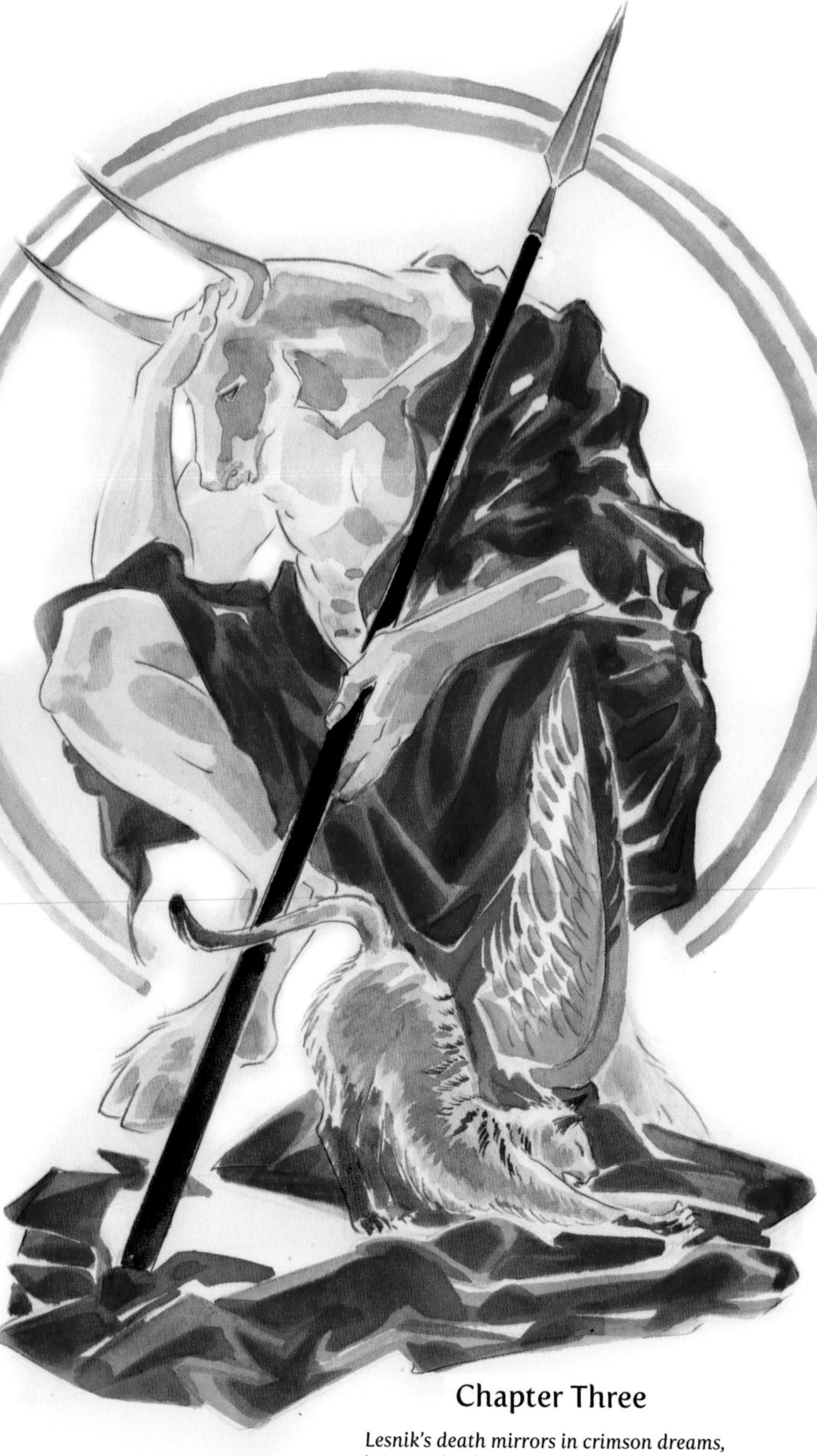

Chapter Three

Lesnik's death mirrors in crimson dreams, bringing back sad memories of the animal rebellion he and Sena led together.

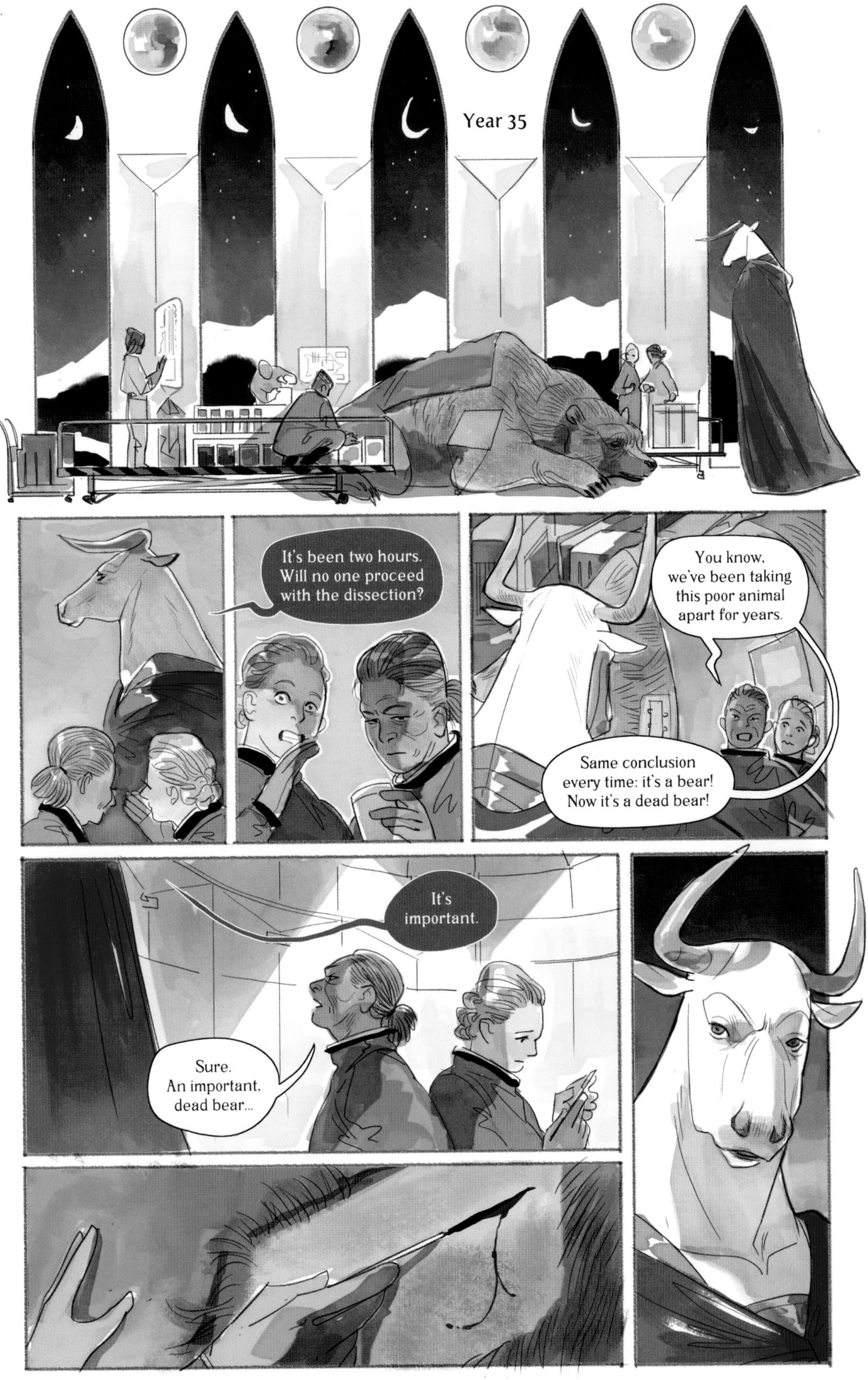
Year 35
It's been two hours. Will no one proceed with the dissection?
You know, we've been taking this poor animal apart for years.
Same conclusion every time: it's a bear! Now it's a dead bear!
It's important.
Sure. An important, dead bear...

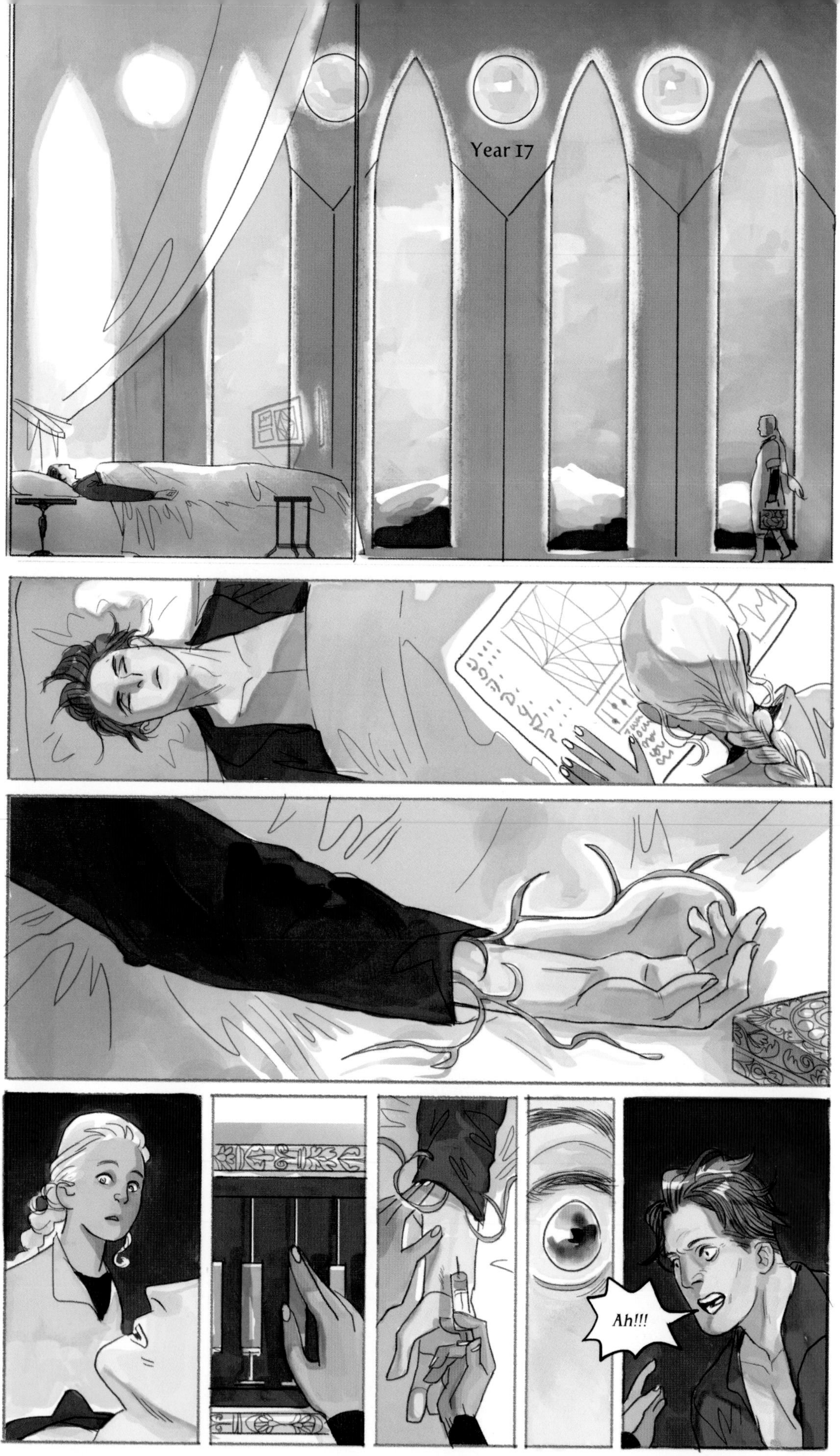
Year I7
Ah!!!

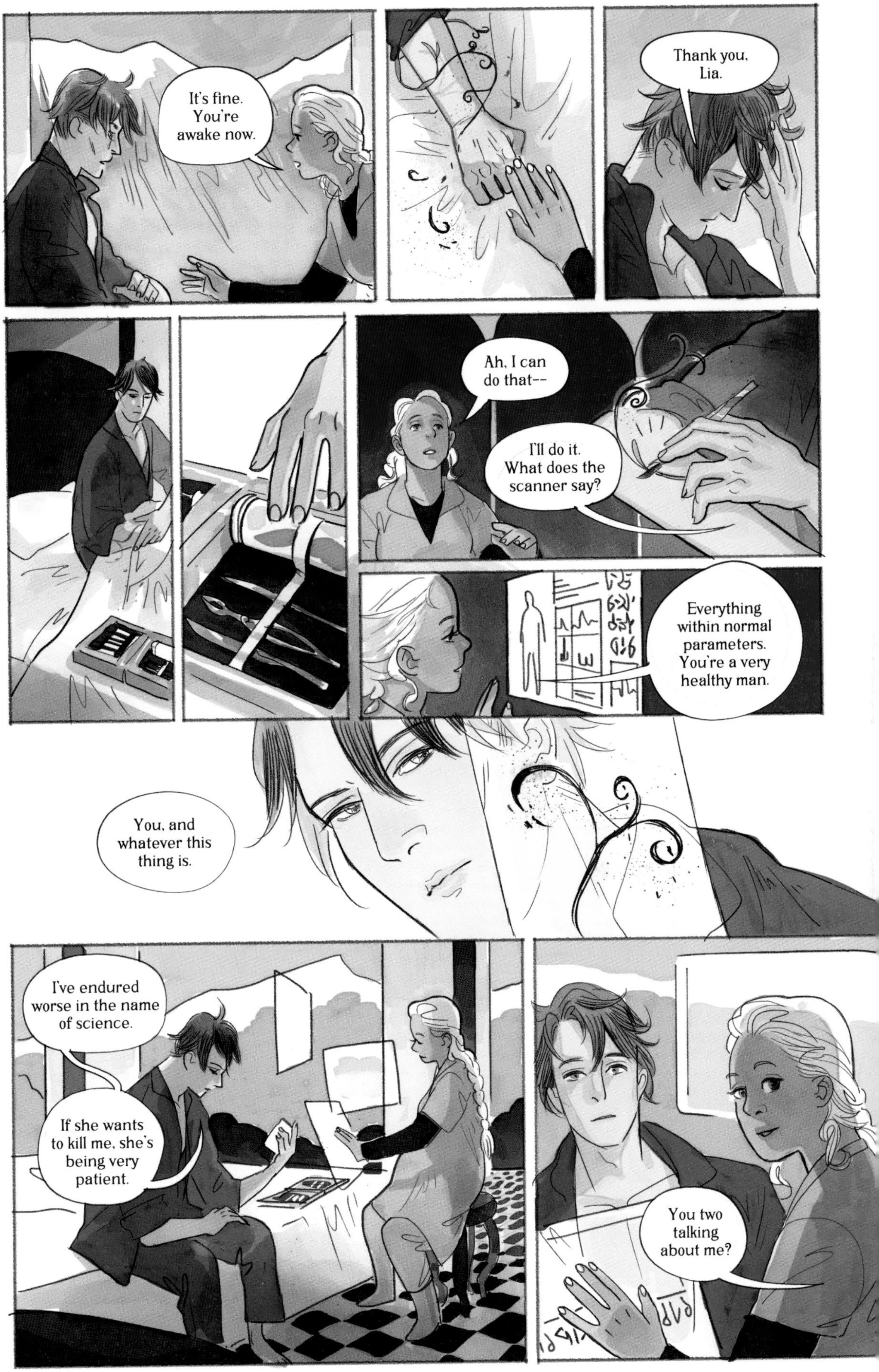
It's fine. You're awake now.
Thank you, Lia.
Ah, I can do that--
I'll do it. What does the scanner say?
Everything within normal parameters. You're a very healthy man.
You, and whatever this thing is.
I've endured worse in the name of science.
If she wants to kill me, she's being very patient.
You two talking about me?

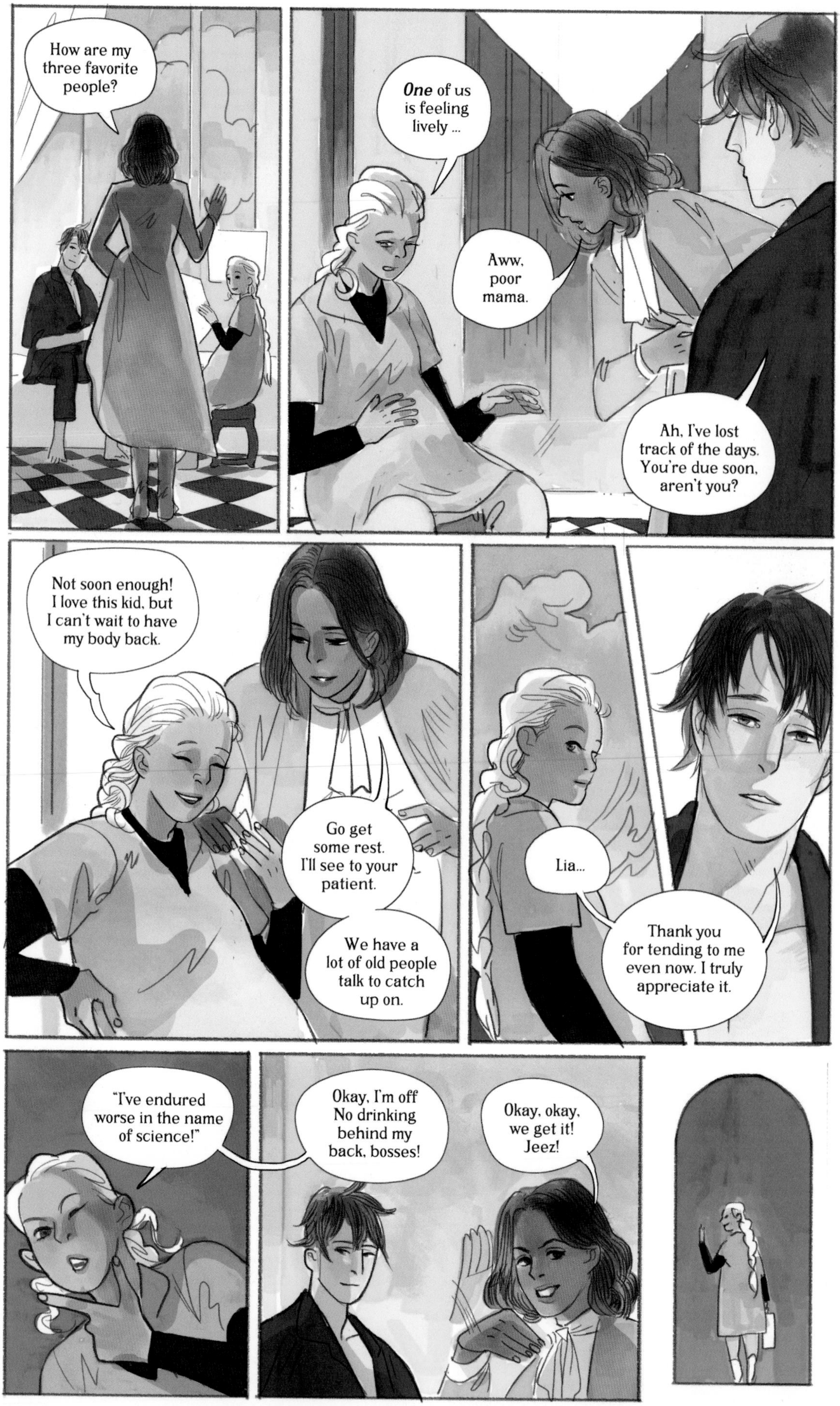
How are my three favorite people?
One of us is feeling lively ...
Aww, poor mama.
Ah, I've lost track of the days. You're due soon, aren't you?
Not soon enough! I love this kid, but I can't wait to have my body back.
Go get some rest. I'll see to your patient.
We have a lot of old people talk to catch up on.
Lia...
Thank you for tending to me even now. I truly appreciate it.
"I've endured worse in the name of science!"
Okay, I'm off No drinking behind my back, bosses!
Okay, okay, we get it! Jeez!

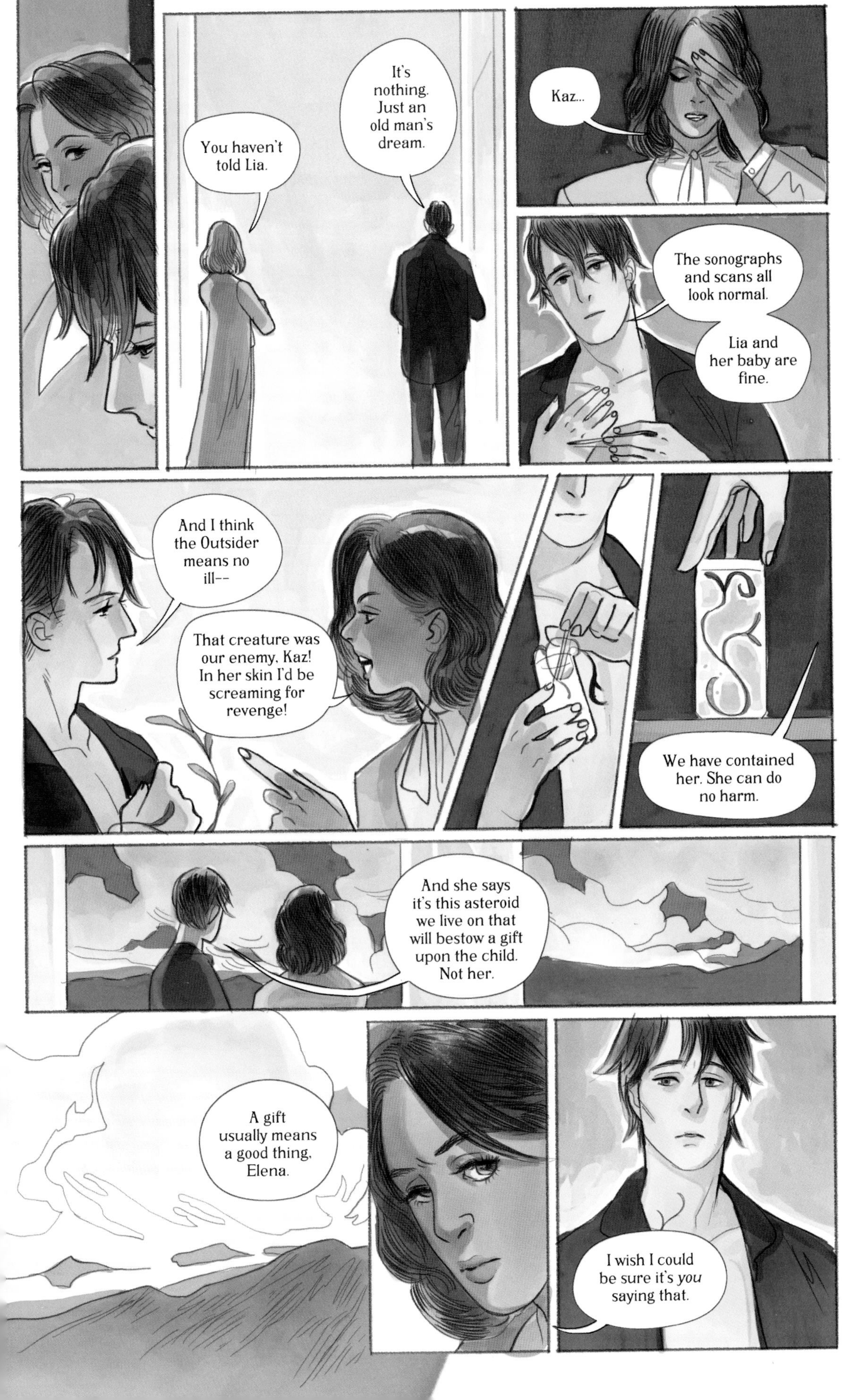
You haven't told Lia.
It's nothing. Just an old man's dream.
Kaz...
The sonographs and scans all look normal.
Lia and her baby are fine.
And I think the Outsider means no ill--
That creature was our enemy, Kaz! In her skin I'd be screaming for revenge!
We have contained her. She can do no harm.
And she says it's this asteroid we live on that will bestow a gift upon the child. Not her.
A gift usually means a good thing, Elena.
I wish I could be sure it's *you* saying that.

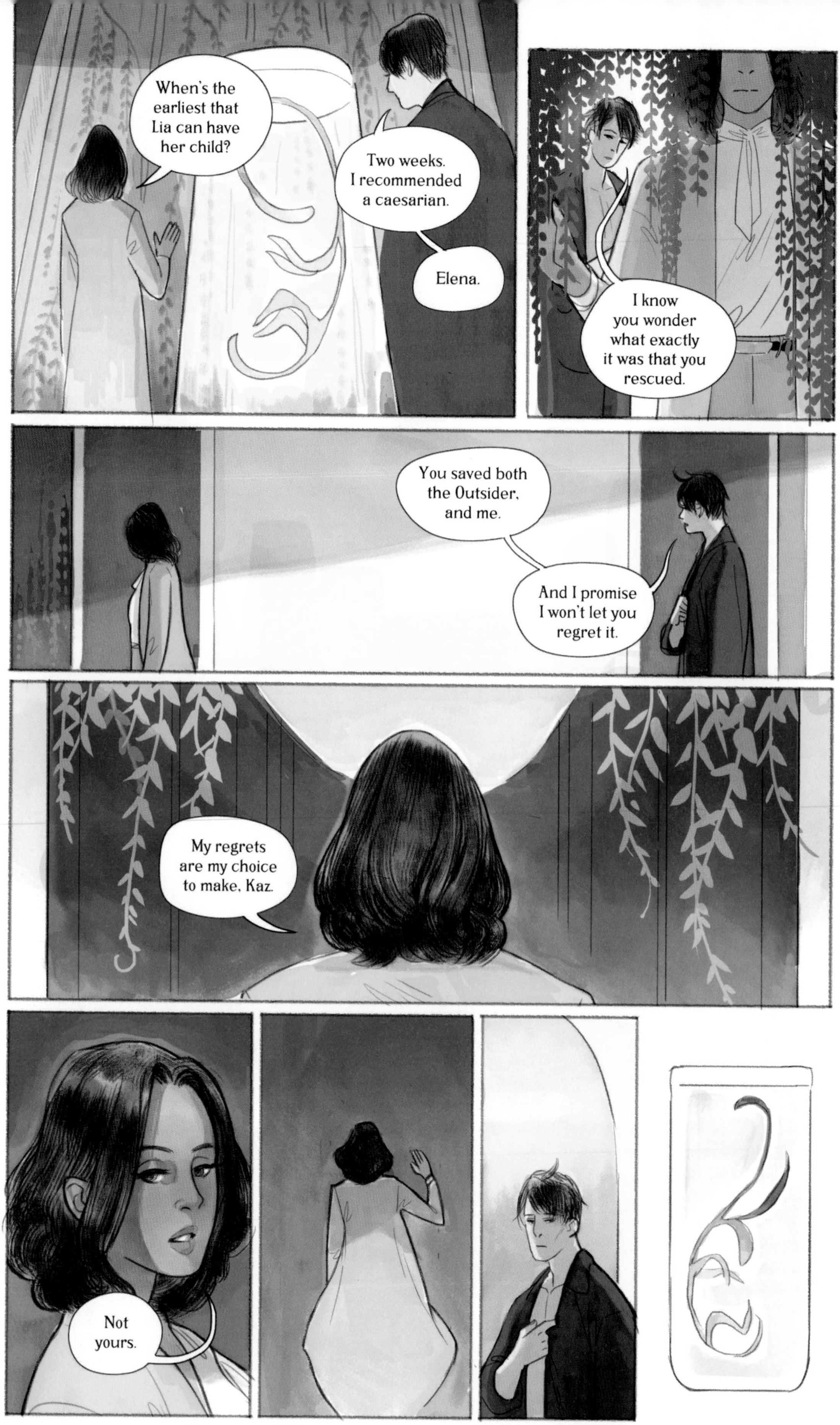
When's the earliest that Lia can have her child?
Two weeks. I recommended a caesarian.
Elena.
I know you wonder what exactly it was that you rescued.
You saved both the Outsider, and me.
And I promise I won't let you regret it.
My regrets are my choice to make, Kaz.
Not yours.

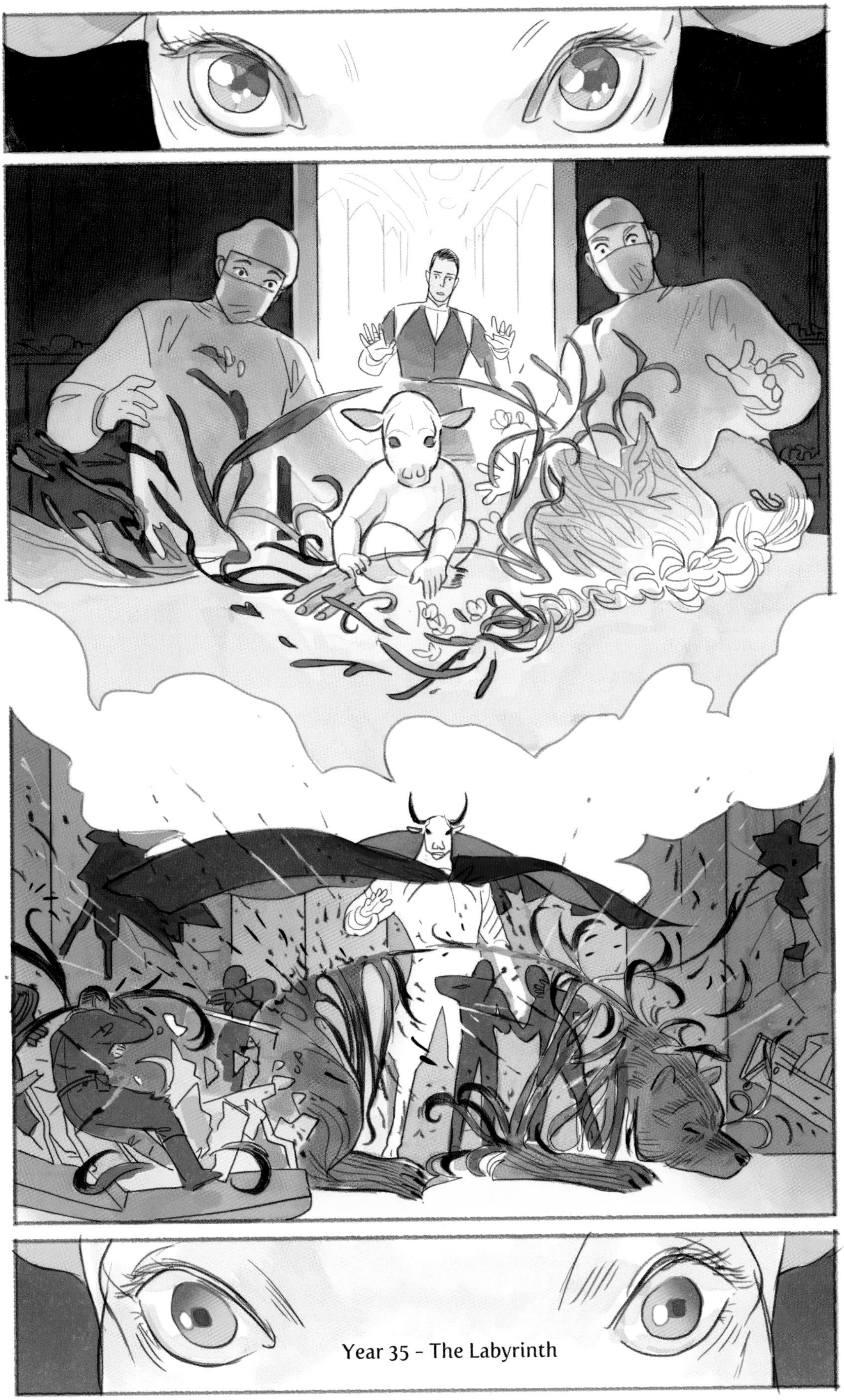
Year 35 - The Labyrinth

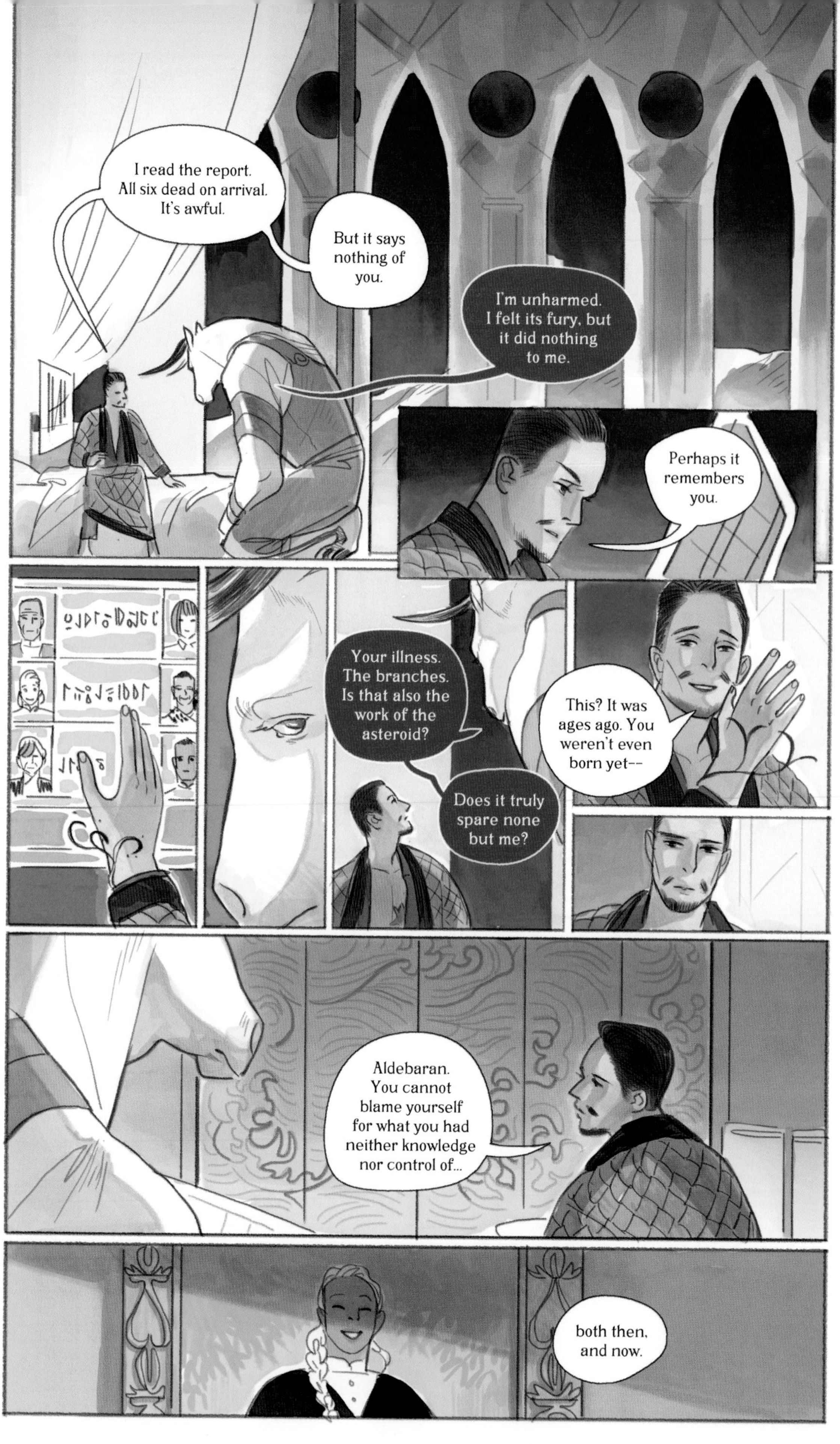
I read the report. All six dead on arrival. It's awful.
But it says nothing of you.
I'm unharmed. I felt its fury, but it did nothing to me.
Perhaps it remembers you.
Your illness. The branches. Is that also the work of the asteroid?
Does it truly spare none but me?
This? It was ages ago. You weren't even born yet--
Aldebaran. You cannot blame yourself for what you had neither knowledge nor control of...
both then, and now.

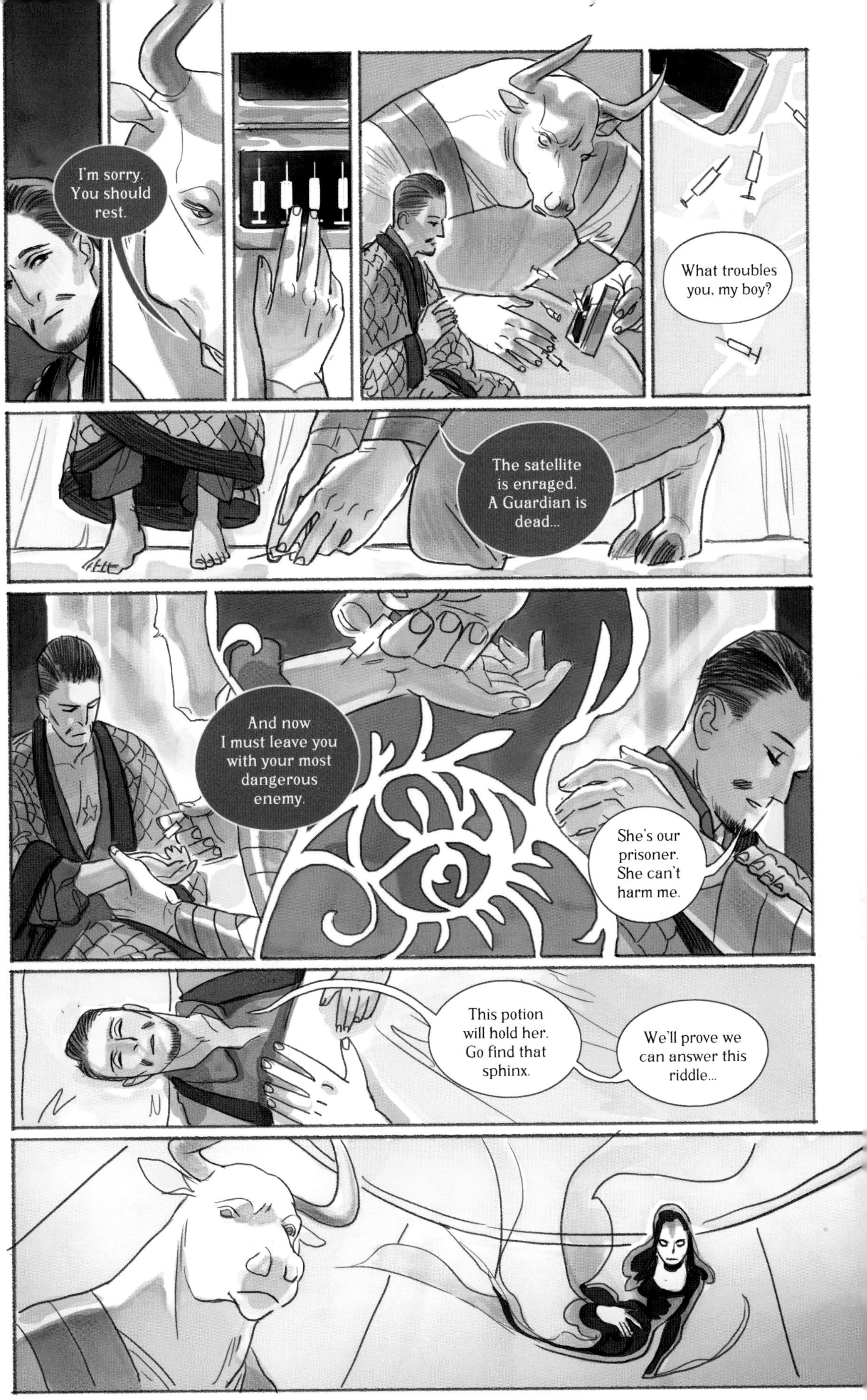
I'm sorry. You should rest.
What troubles you, my boy?
The satellite is enraged. A Guardian is dead...
And now I must leave you with your most dangerous enemy.
She's our prisoner. She can't harm me.
This potion will hold her. Go find that sphinx.
We'll prove we can answer this riddle...

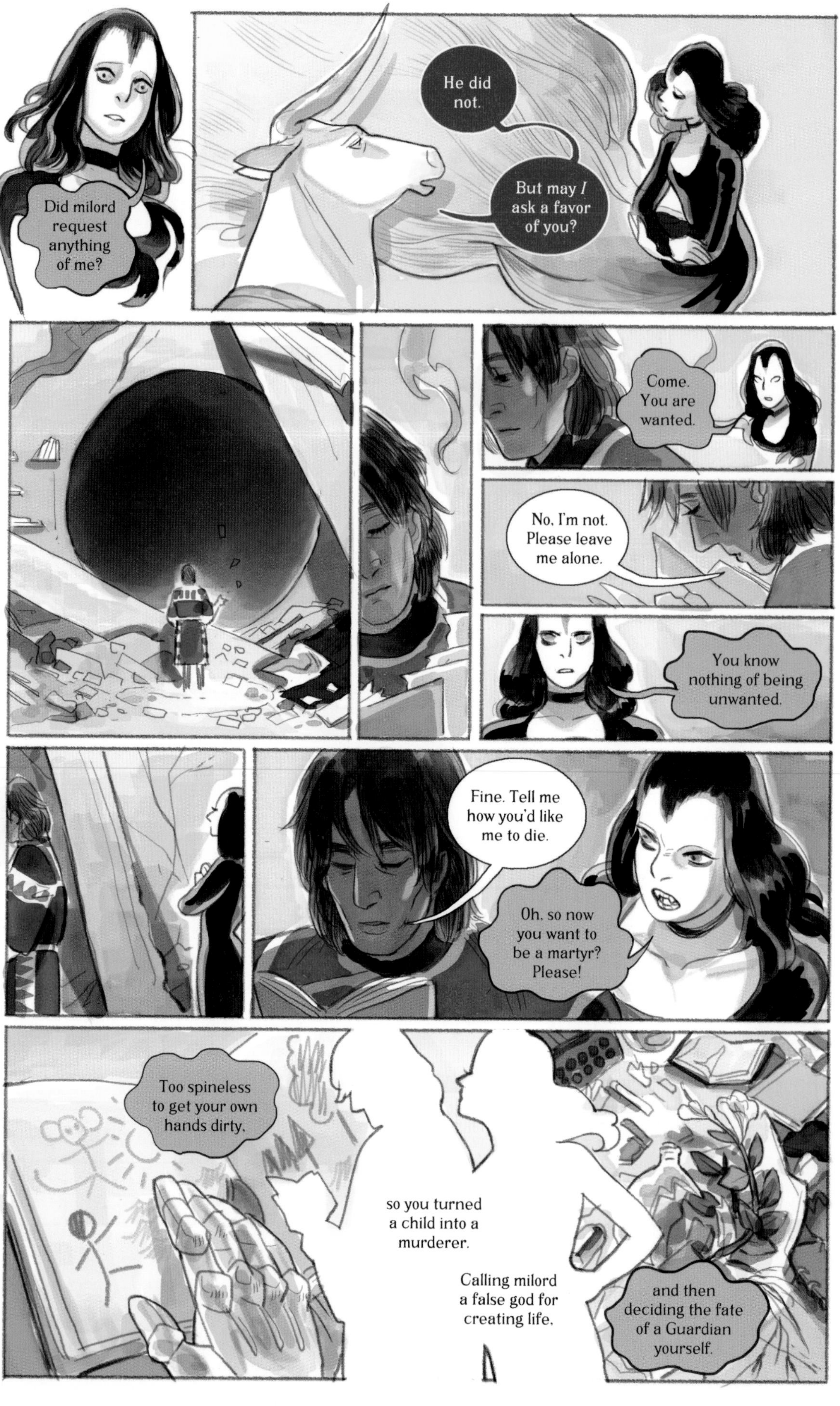
Did milord request anything of me?
He did not.
But may *I* ask a favor of you?
Come. You are wanted.
No, I'm not. Please leave me alone.
You know nothing of being unwanted.
Fine. Tell me how you'd like me to die.
Oh, so now you want to be a martyr? Please!
Too spineless to get your own hands dirty,
so you turned a child into a murderer.
Calling milord a false god for creating life,
and then deciding the fate of a Guardian yourself.

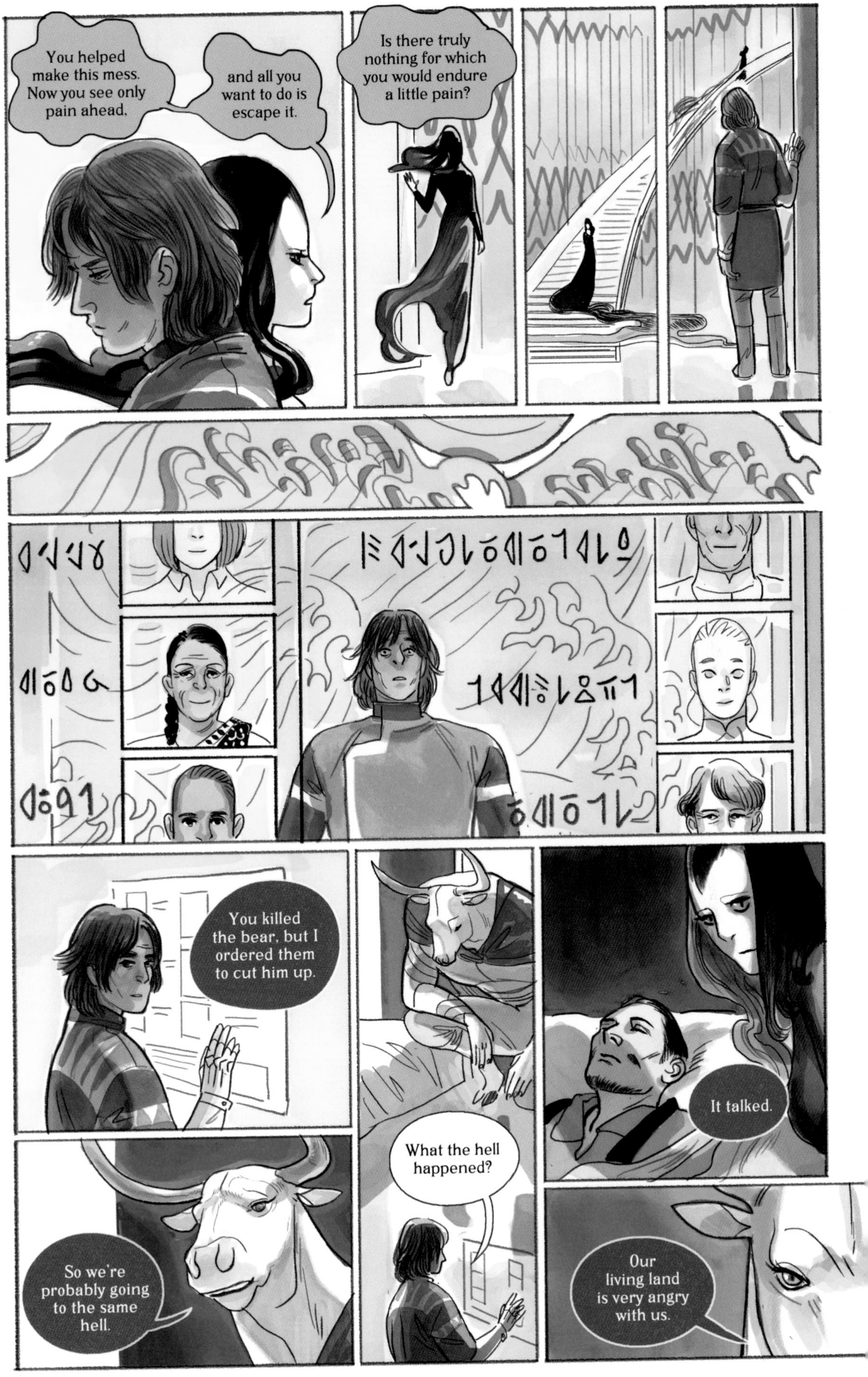
You helped make this mess. Now you see only pain ahead,
and all you want to do is escape it.
Is there truly nothing for which you would endure a little pain?
You killed the bear, but I ordered them to cut him up.
It talked.
So we're probably going to the same hell.
What the hell happened?
Our living land is very angry with us.

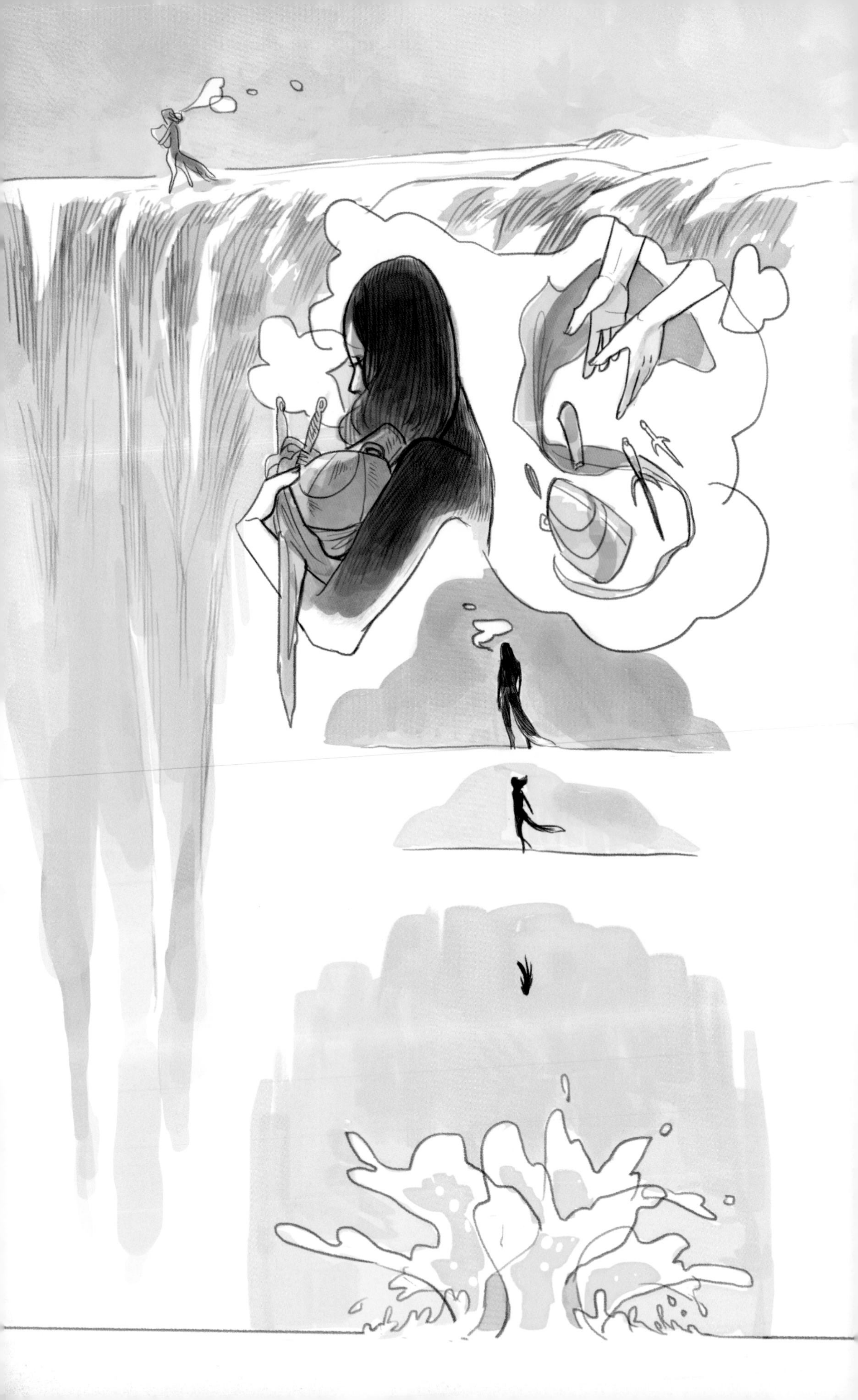

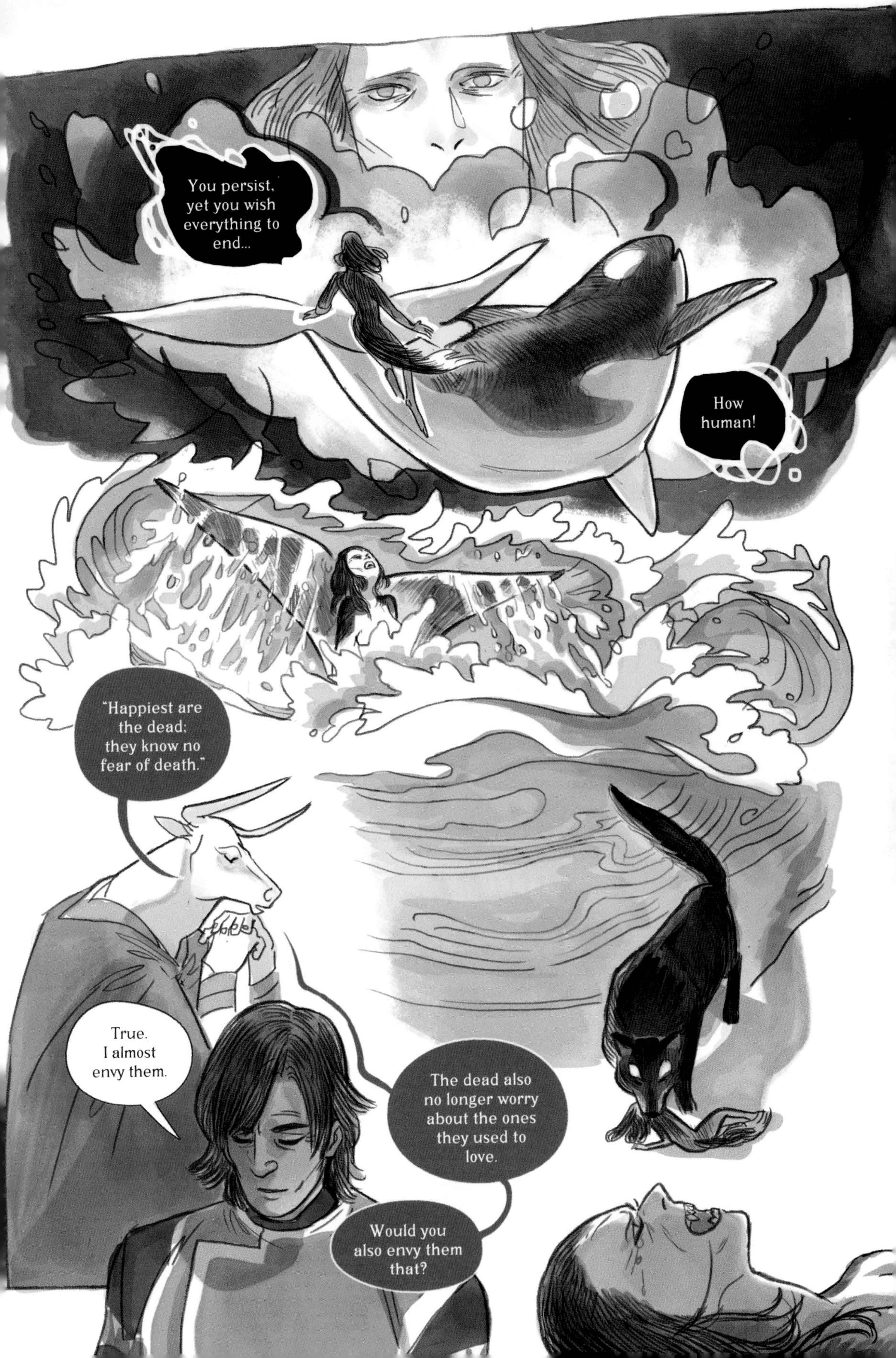
You persist, yet you wish everything to end...
How human!
"Happiest are the dead: they know no fear of death."
True. I almost envy them.
The dead also no longer worry about the ones they used to love.
Would you also envy them that?

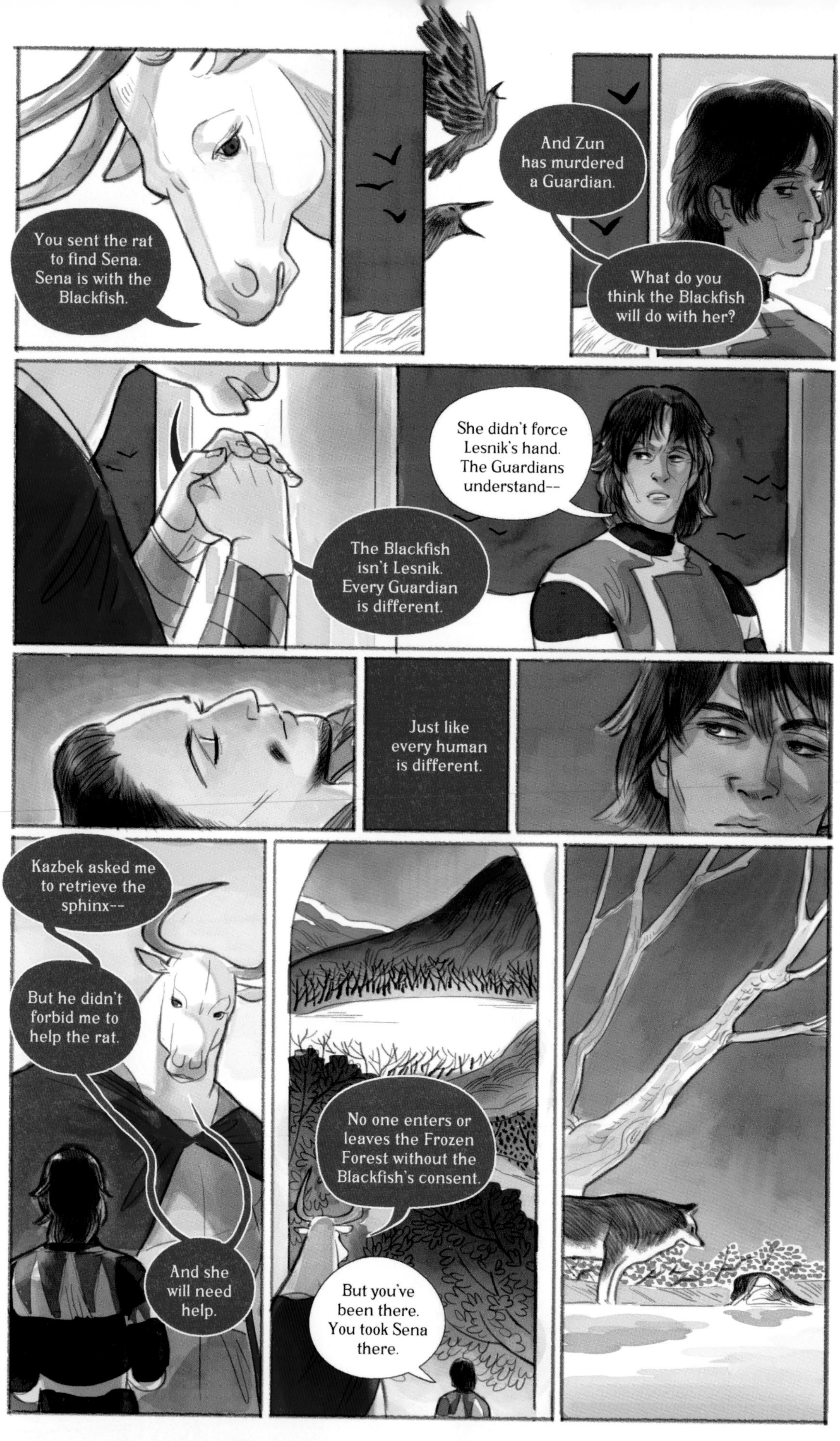
You sent the rat to find Sena. Sena is with the Blackfish.
And Zun has murdered a Guardian.
What do you think the Blackfish will do with her?
She didn't force Lesnik's hand. The Guardians understand--
The Blackfish isn't Lesnik. Every Guardian is different.
Just like every human is different.
Kazbek asked me to retrieve the sphinx--
But he didn't forbid me to help the rat.
And she will need help.
No one enters or leaves the Frozen Forest without the Blackfish's consent.
But you've been there. You took Sena there.

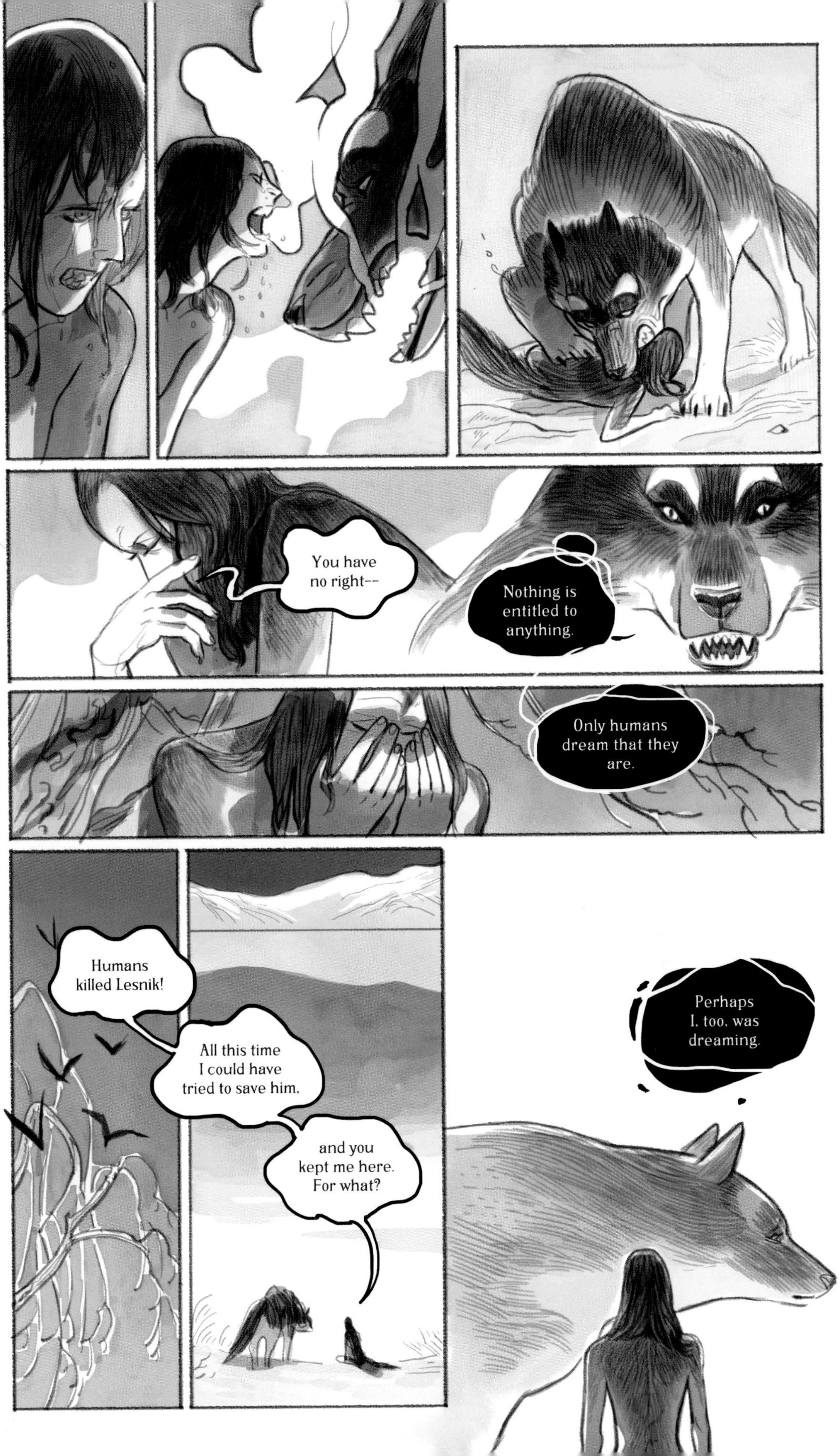
You have no right--
Nothing is entitled to anything.
Only humans dream that they are.
Humans killed Lesnik!
All this time I could have tried to save him,
and you kept me here. For what?
Perhaps I, too, was dreaming.

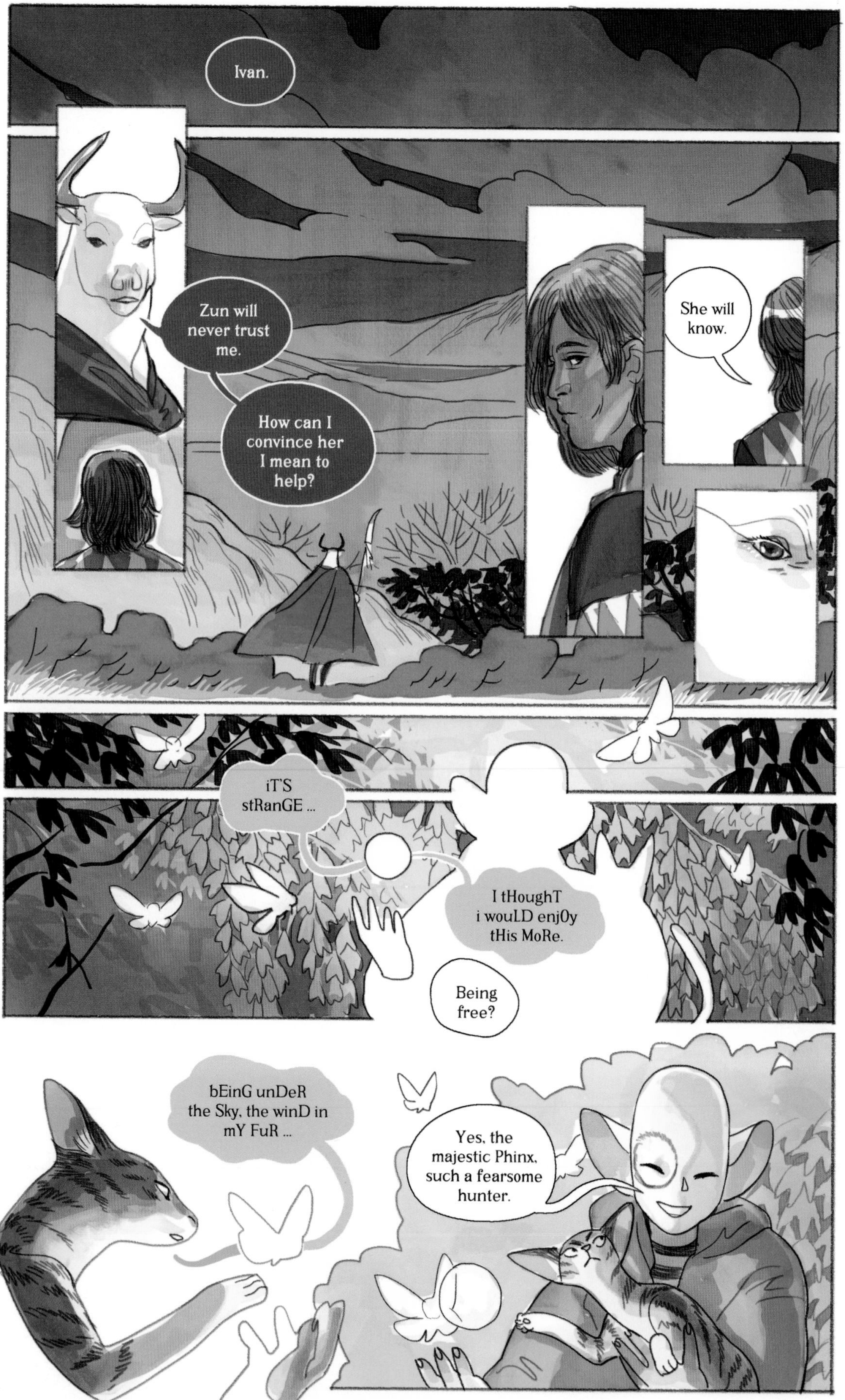
Ivan.
Zun will never trust me.
How can I convince her I mean to help?
She will know.
iT'S stRanGE ...
I tHoughT i wouLD enj0y tHis MoRe.
Being free?
bEinG unDeR the Sky, the winD in mY FuR ...
Yes, the majestic Phinx, such a fearsome hunter.

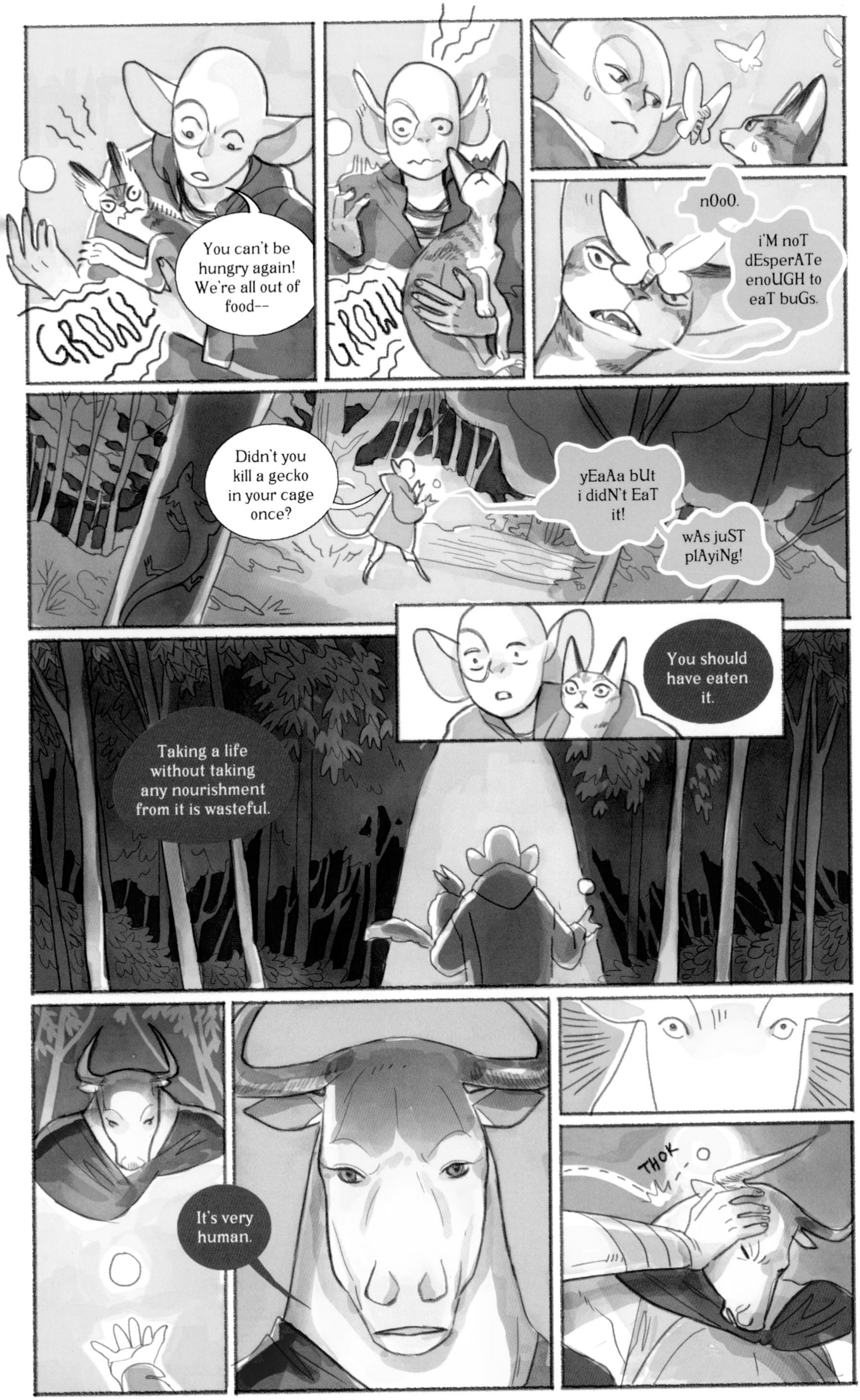
You can't be hungry again! We're all out of food--
GROWL
GROWL
nOoO.
i'M noT dEsperATe enoUGH to eaT buGs.
Didn't you kill a gecko in your cage once?
yEaAa bUt i didN't EaT it!
wAs juST plAyiNg!
You should have eaten it.
Taking a life without taking any nourishment from it is wasteful.
It's very human.
THOK

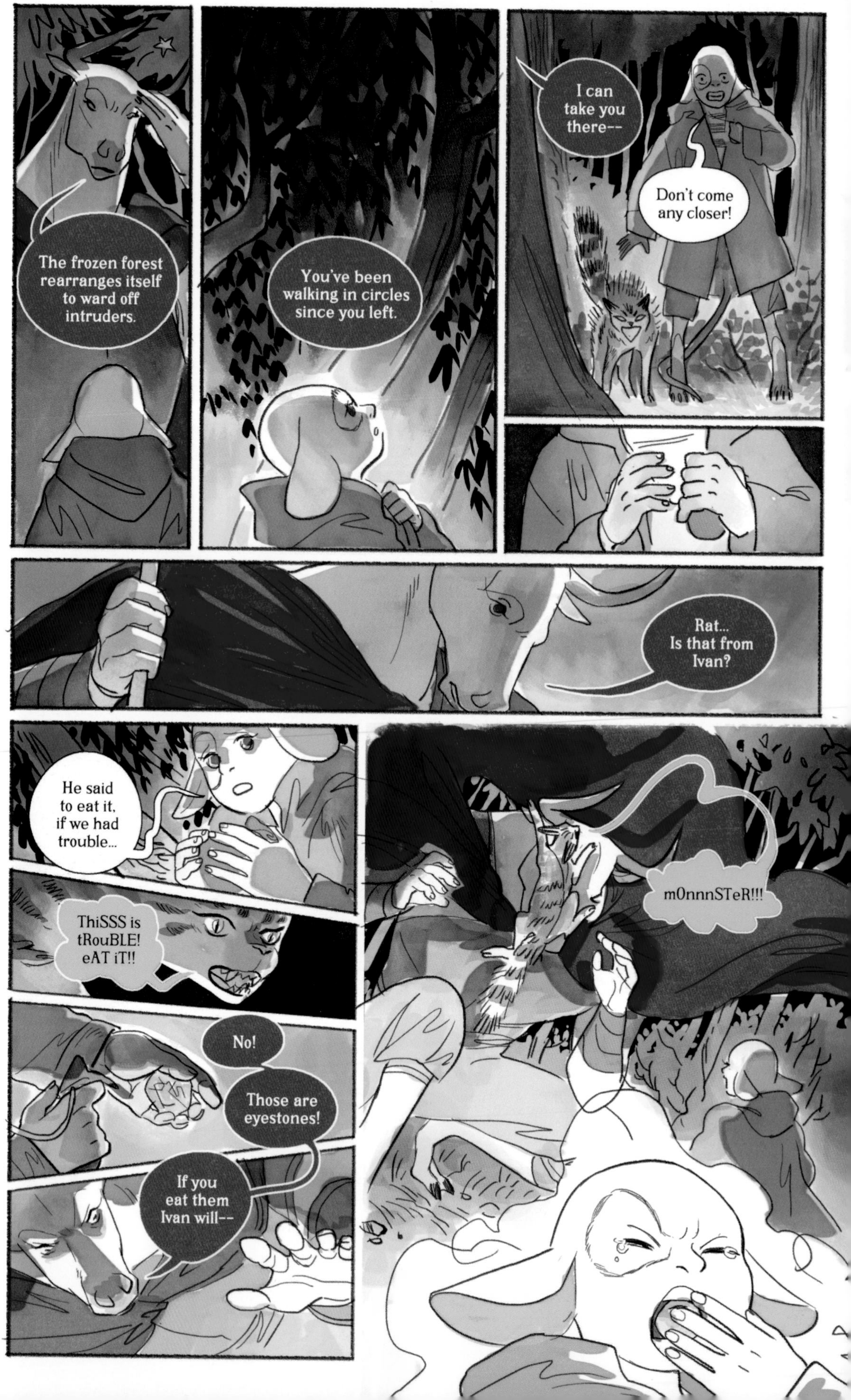
The frozen forest rearranges itself to ward off intruders.
You've been walking in circles since you left.
I can take you there--
Don't come any closer!
Rat... Is that from Ivan?
He said to eat it, if we had trouble...
ThiSSS is tRouBLE! eAT iT!!
No!
Those are eyestones!
If you eat them Ivan will--
m0nnnSTeR!!!

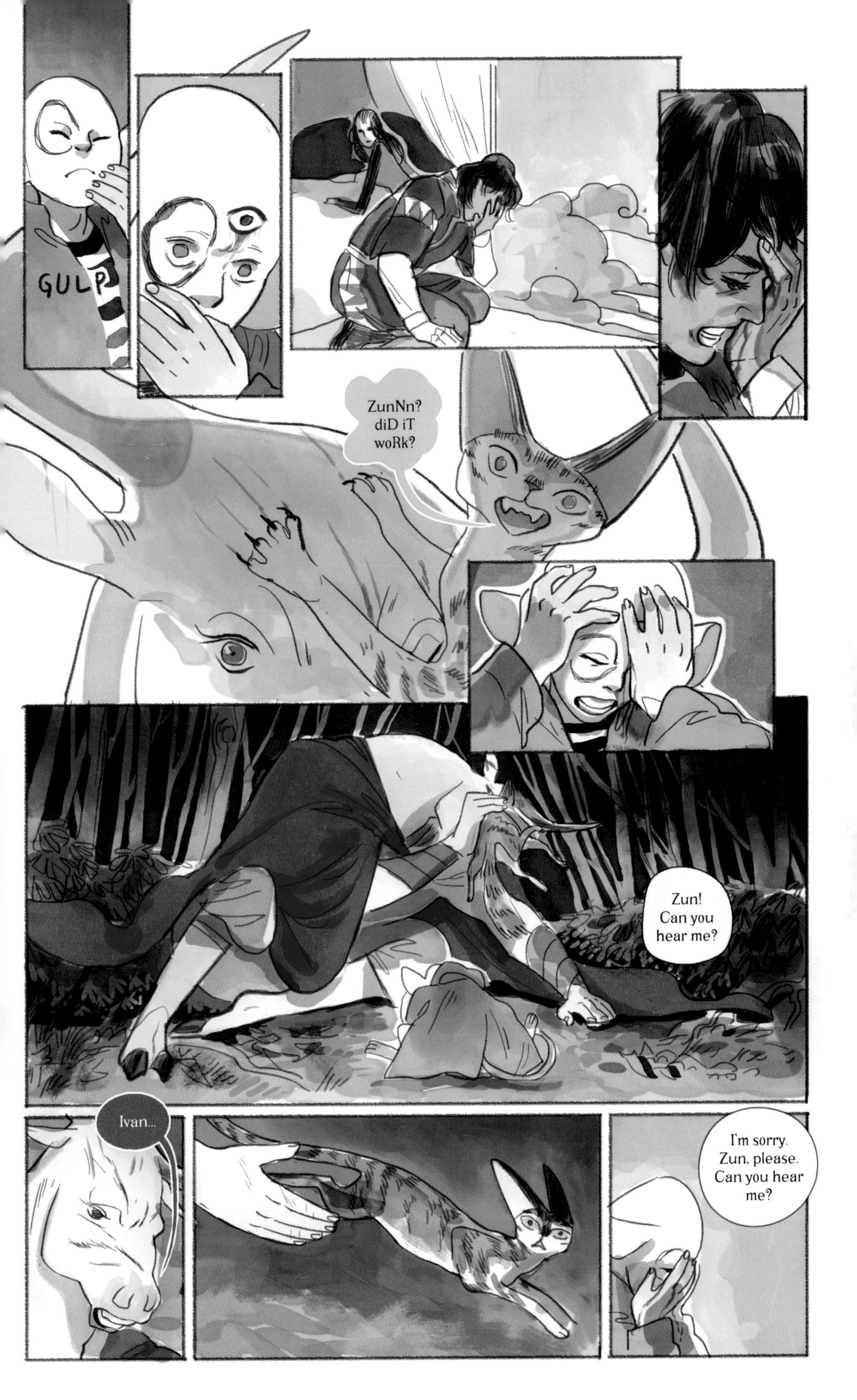
GULP
ZunNn? diD iT woRk?
Zun! Can you hear me?
Ivan...
I'm sorry. Zun, please. Can you hear me?

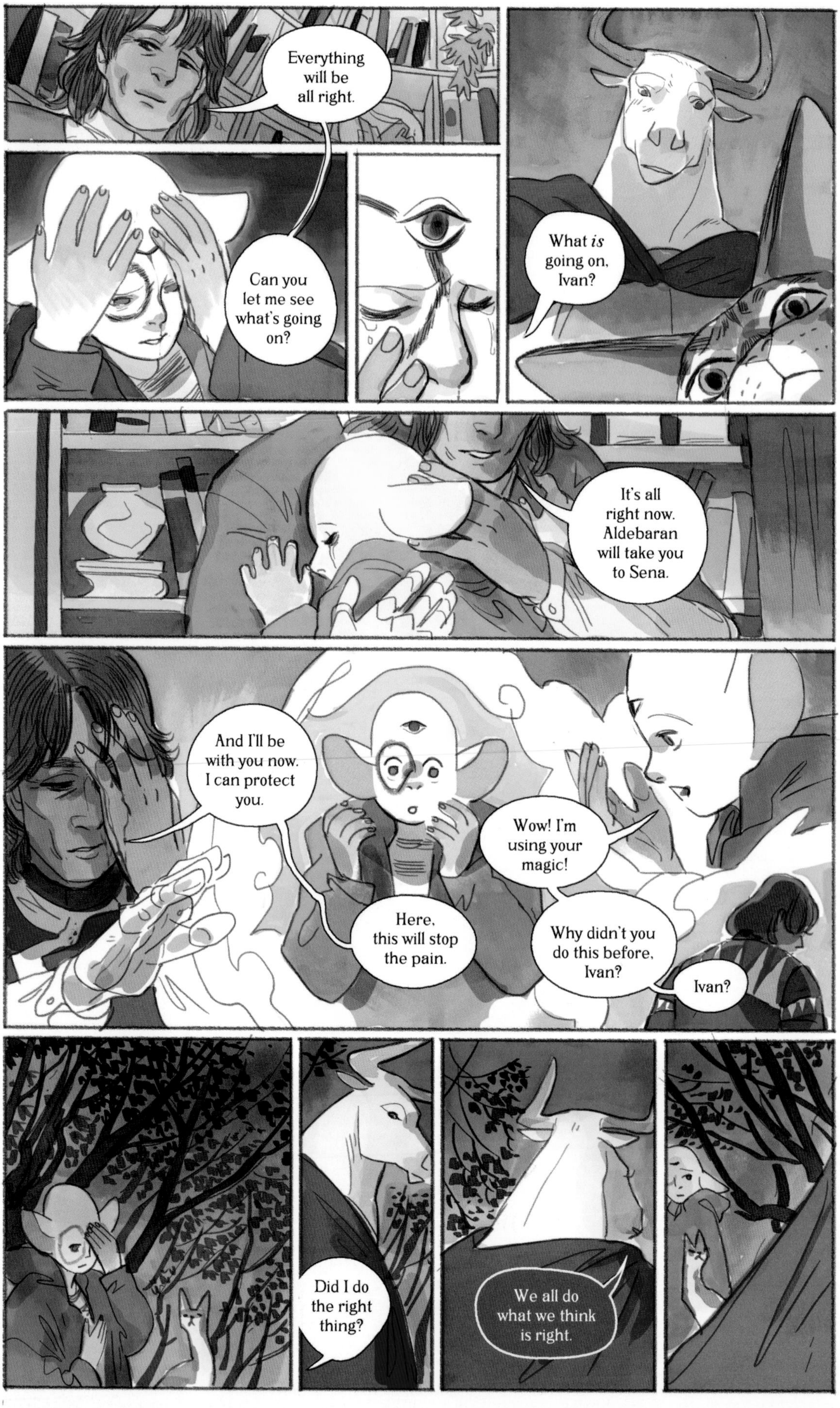
Everything will be all right.
Can you let me see what's going on?
What *is* going on, Ivan?
It's all right now. Aldebaran will take you to Sena.
And I'll be with you now. I can protect you.
Here, this will stop the pain.
Wow! I'm using your magic!
Why didn't you do this before, Ivan?
Ivan?
Did I do the right thing?
We all do what we think is right.

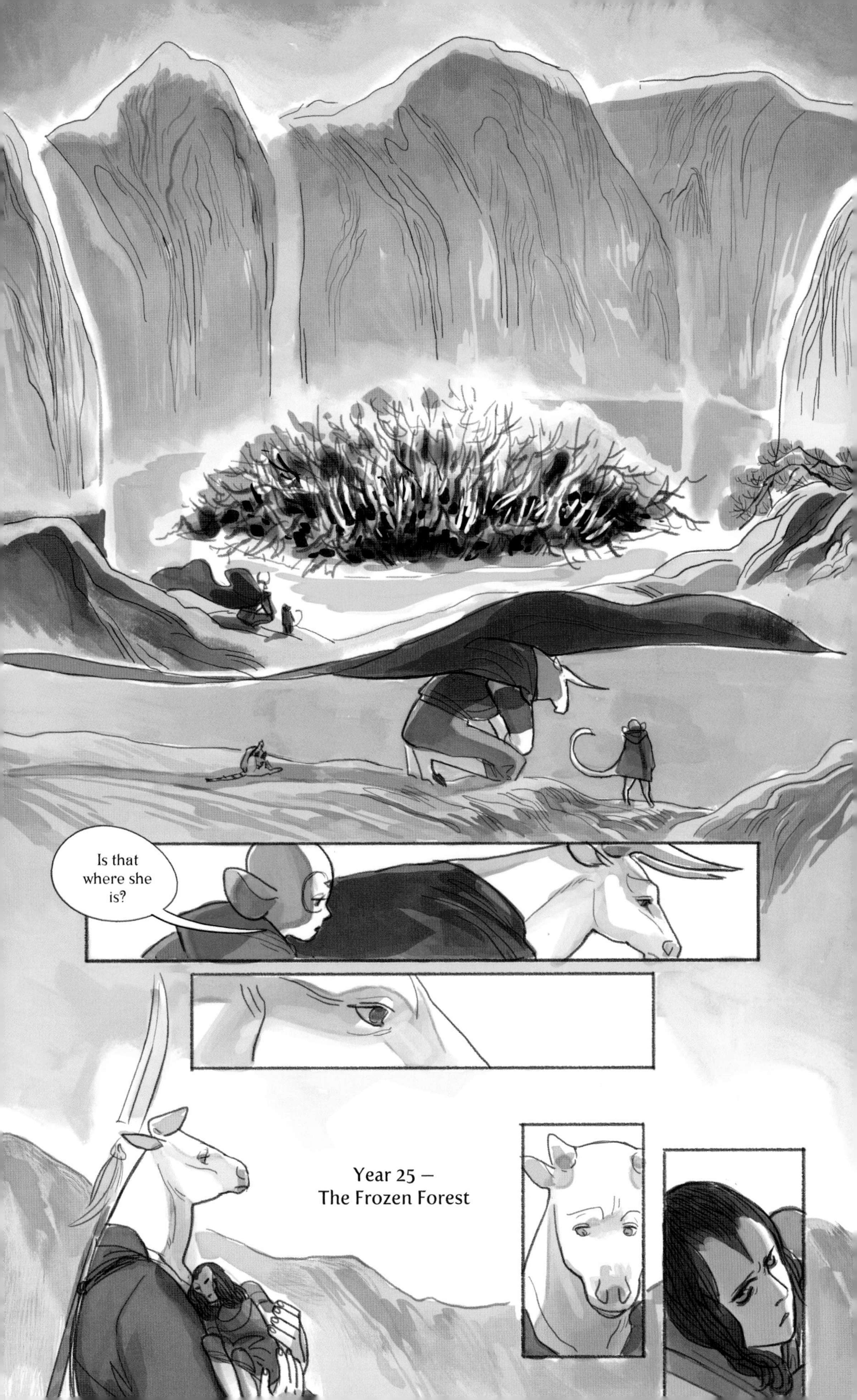
Is that where she is?
Year 25 –
The Frozen Forest

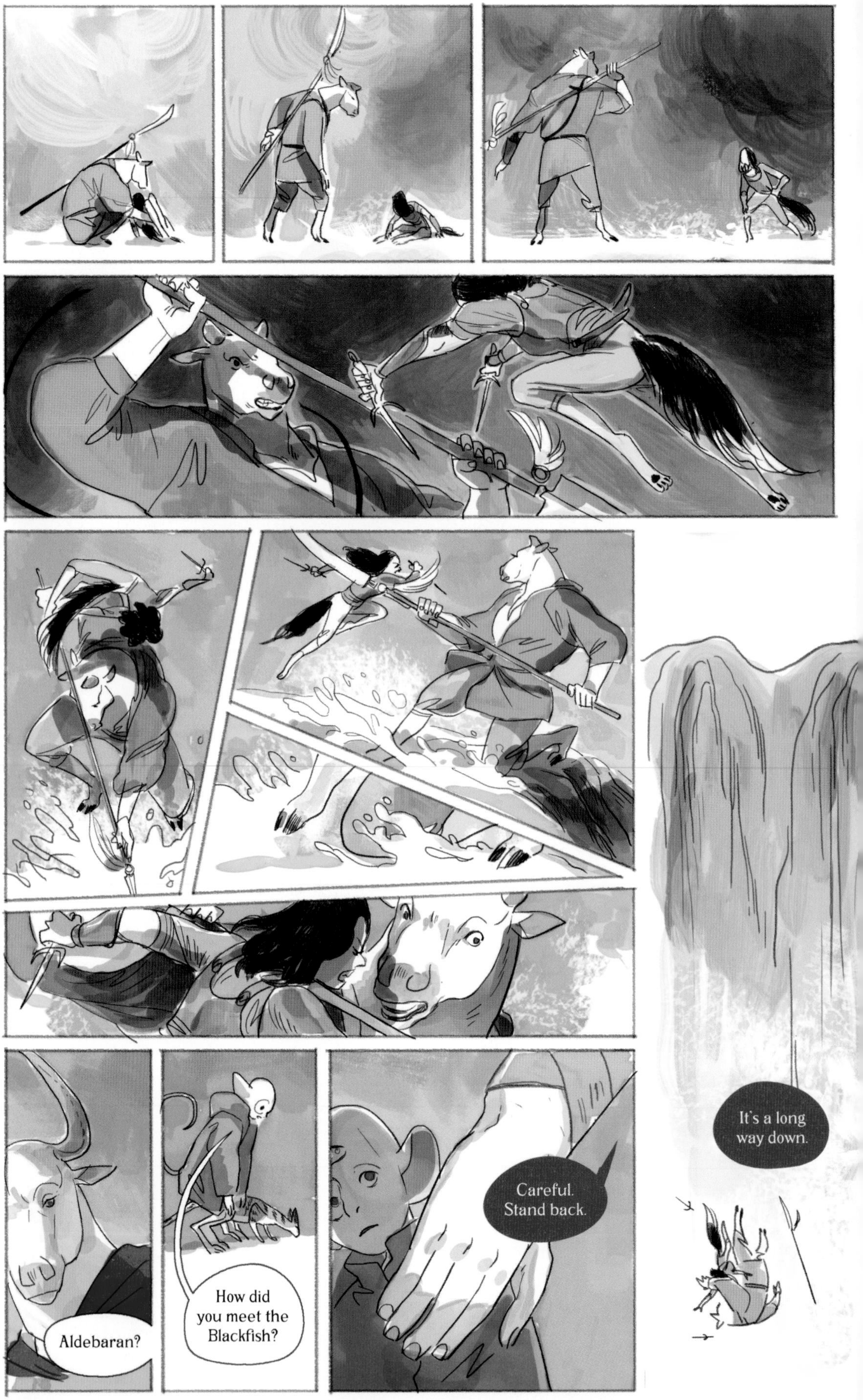
Aldebaran?
How did you meet the Blackfish?
Careful. Stand back.
It's a long way down.

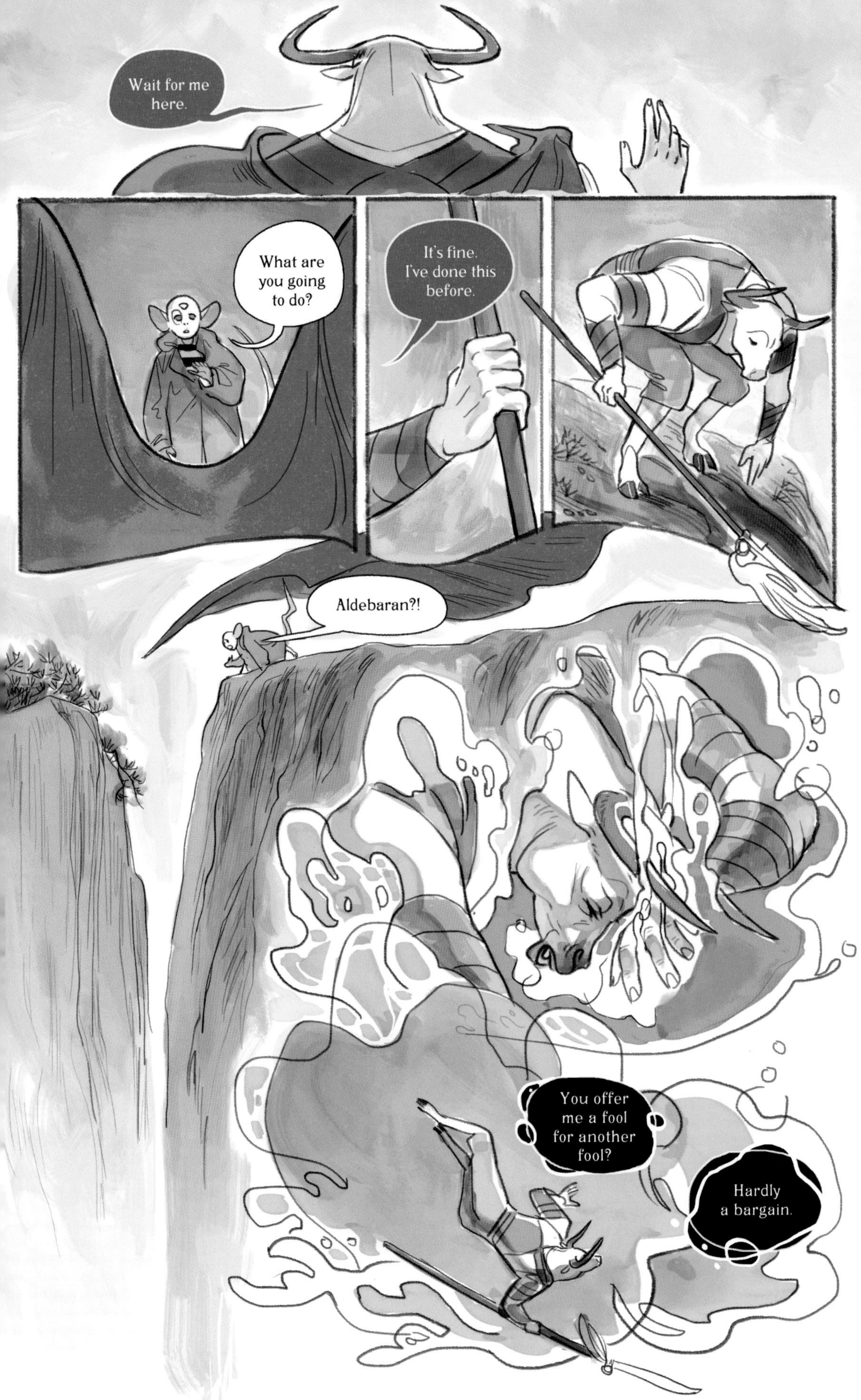
Wait for me here.
What are you going to do?
It's fine. I've done this before.
Aldebaran?!
You offer me a fool for another fool?
Hardly a bargain.

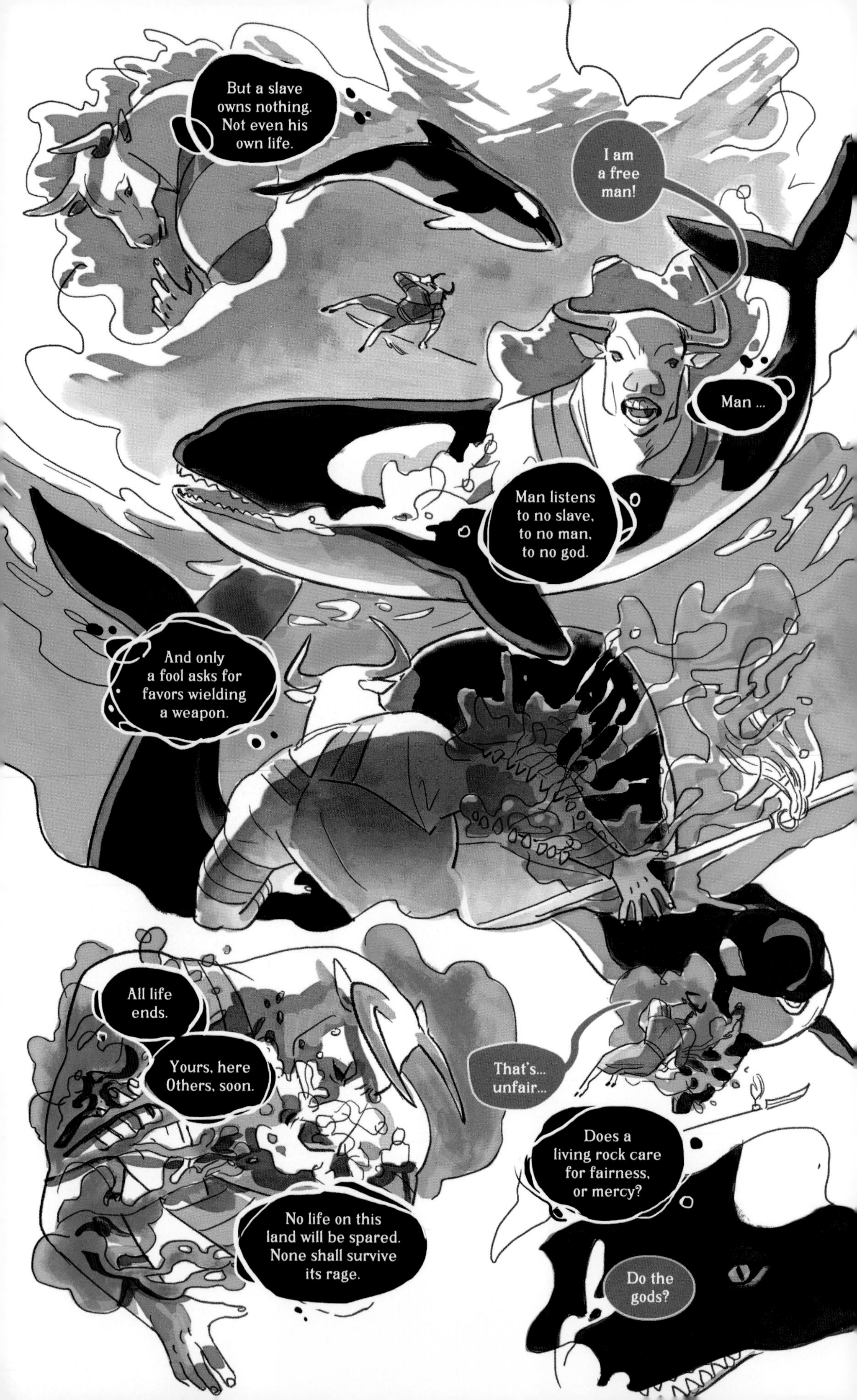

But a slave owns nothing. Not even his own life.
I am a free man!
Man ...
Man listens to no slave, to no man, to no god.
And only a fool asks for favors wielding a weapon.
All life ends.
Yours, here Others, soon.
No life on this land will be spared. None shall survive its rage.
That's... unfair...
Does a living rock care for fairness, or mercy?
Do the gods?

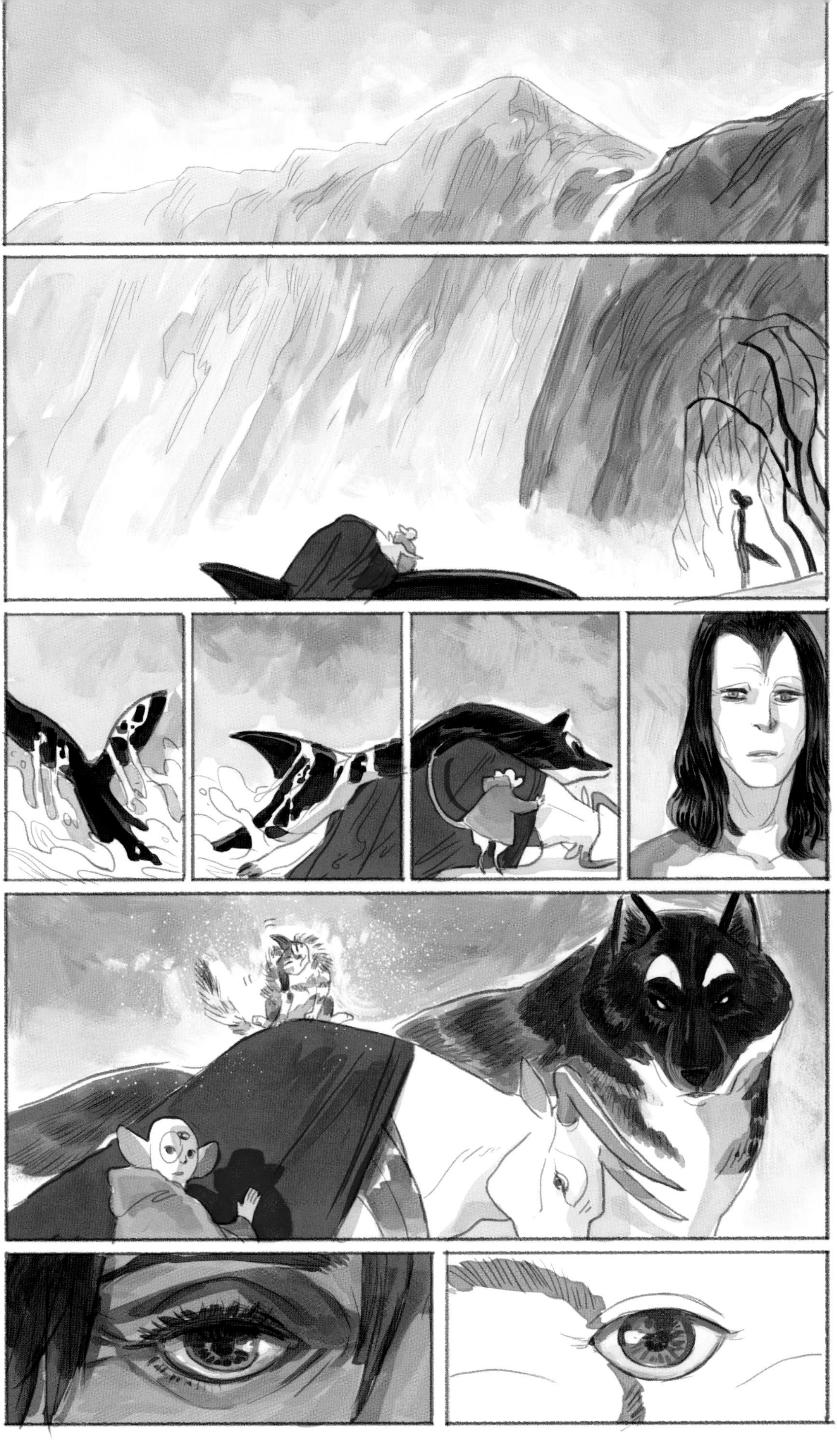

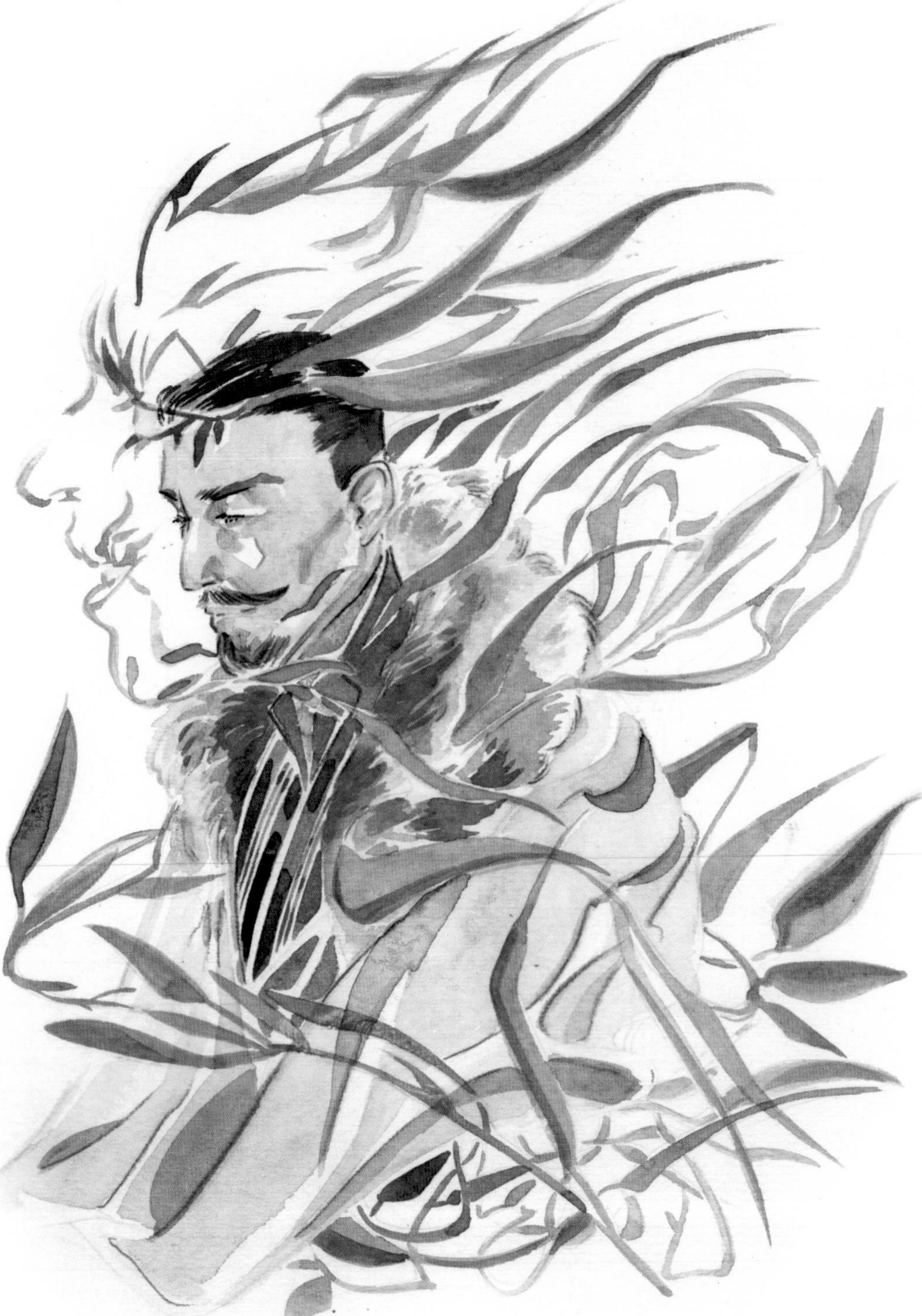

Chapter Four

The sad minotaur reaches the Frozen Lake, and makes a plea on behalf of all the lives in the colony.

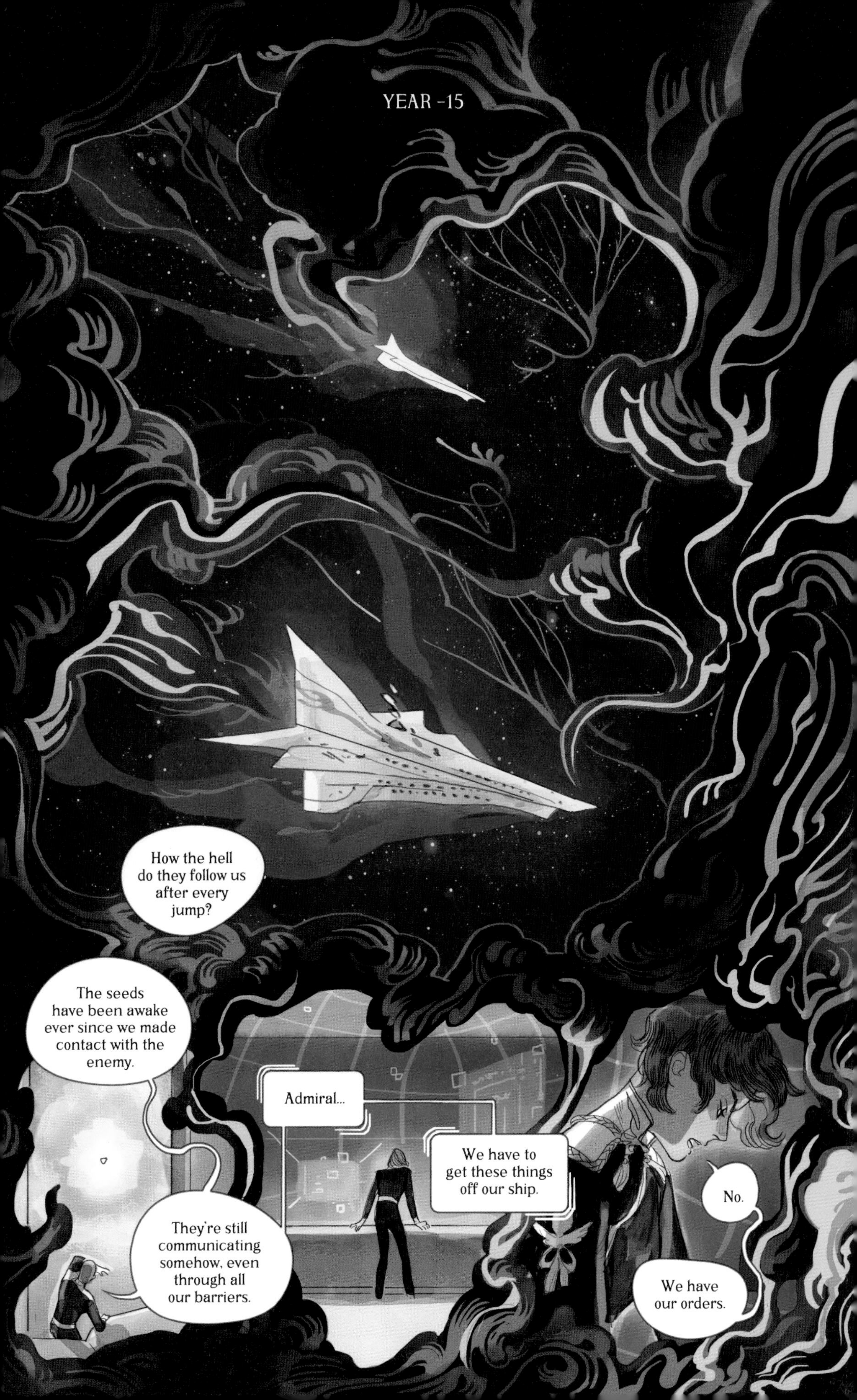
YEAR -15
How the hell do they follow us after every jump?
The seeds have been awake ever since we made contact with the enemy.
They're still communicating somehow, even through all our barriers.
Admiral...
We have to get these things off our ship.
No.
We have our orders.

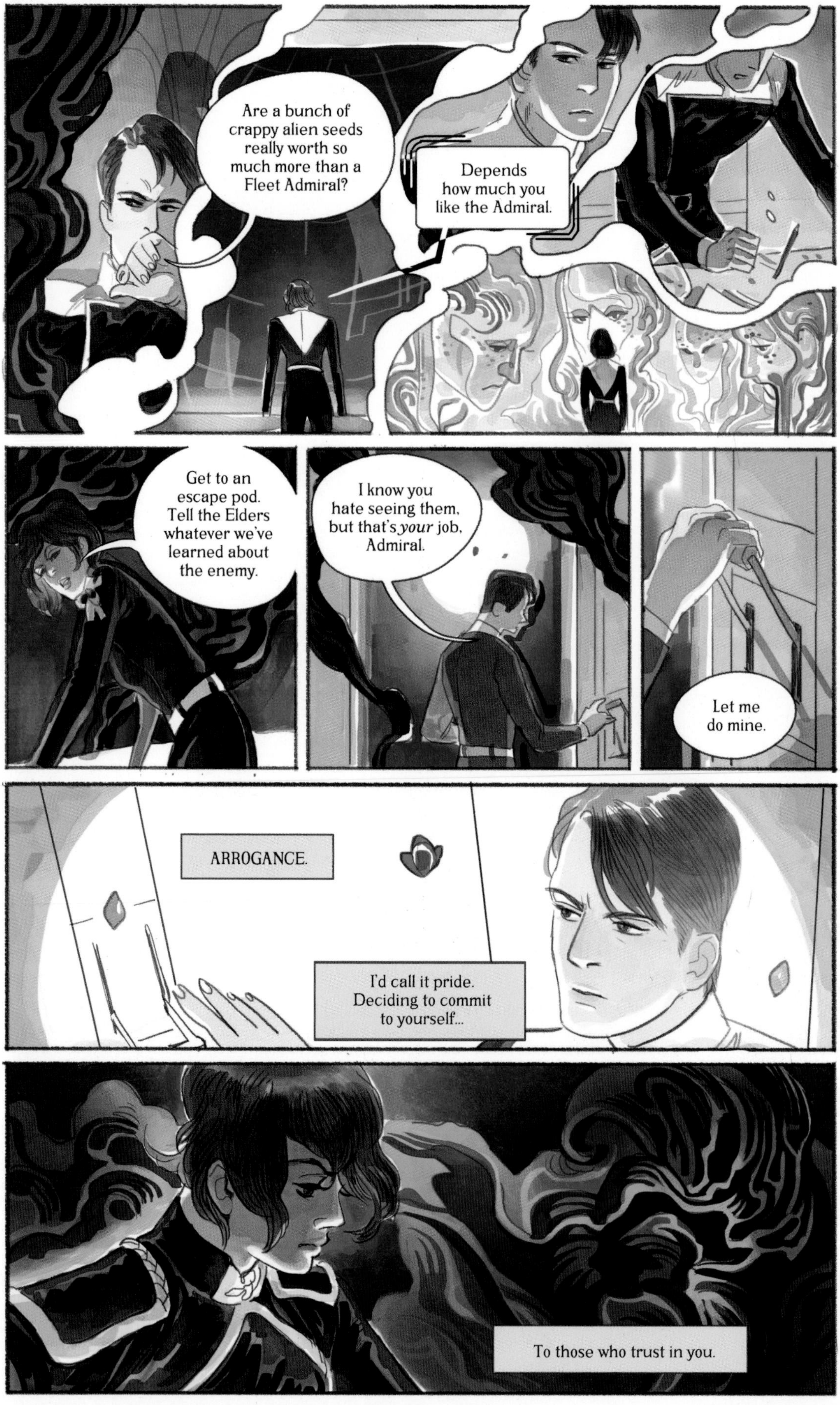
Are a bunch of crappy alien seeds really worth so much more than a Fleet Admiral?
Depends how much you like the Admiral.
Get to an escape pod. Tell the Elders whatever we've learned about the enemy.
I know you hate seeing them, but that's *your* job, Admiral.
Let me do mine.
ARROGANCE.
I'd call it pride. Deciding to commit to yourself...
To those who trust in you.

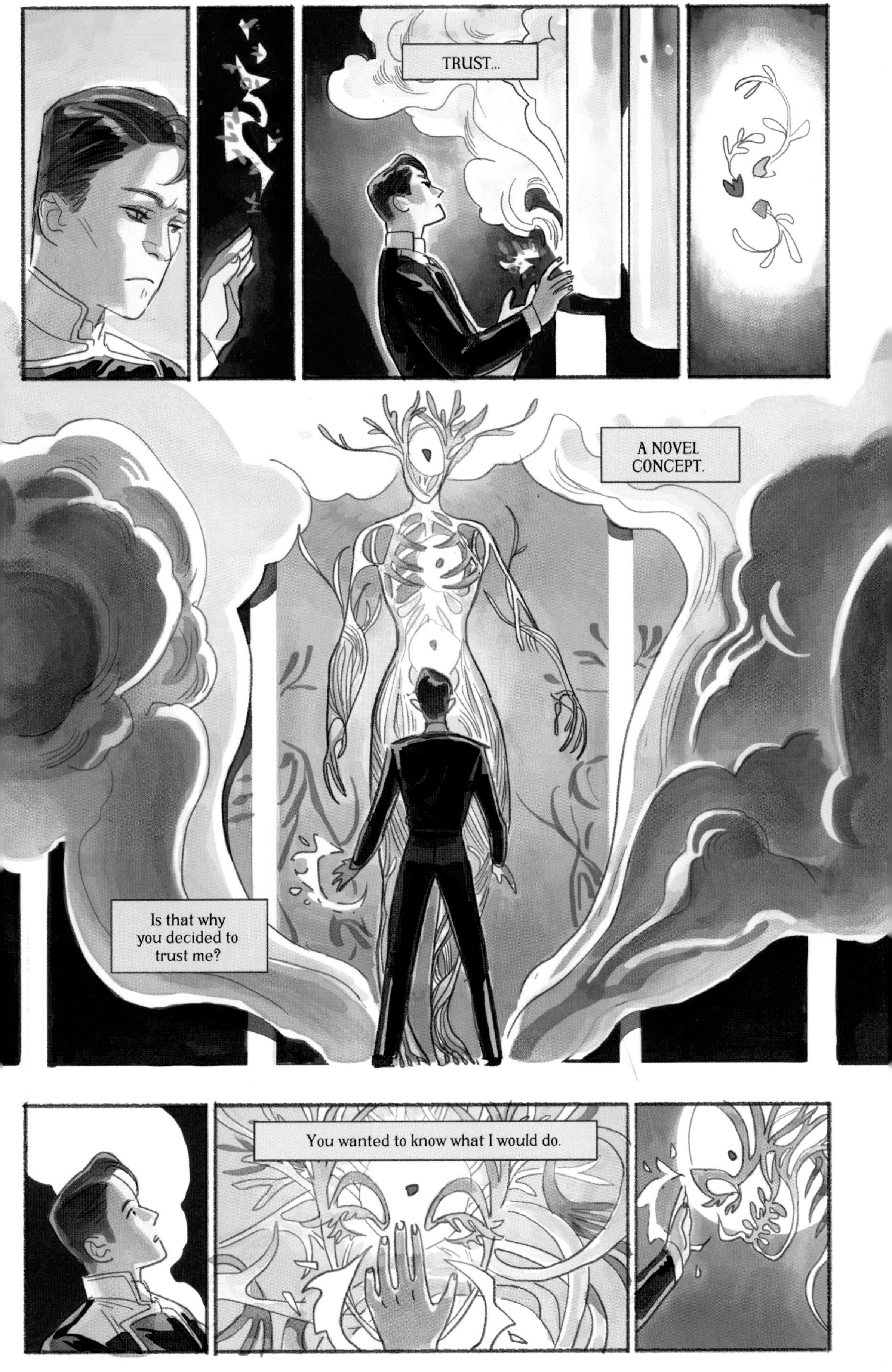
TRUST...
A NOVEL CONCEPT.
Is that why you decided to trust me?
You wanted to know what I would do.

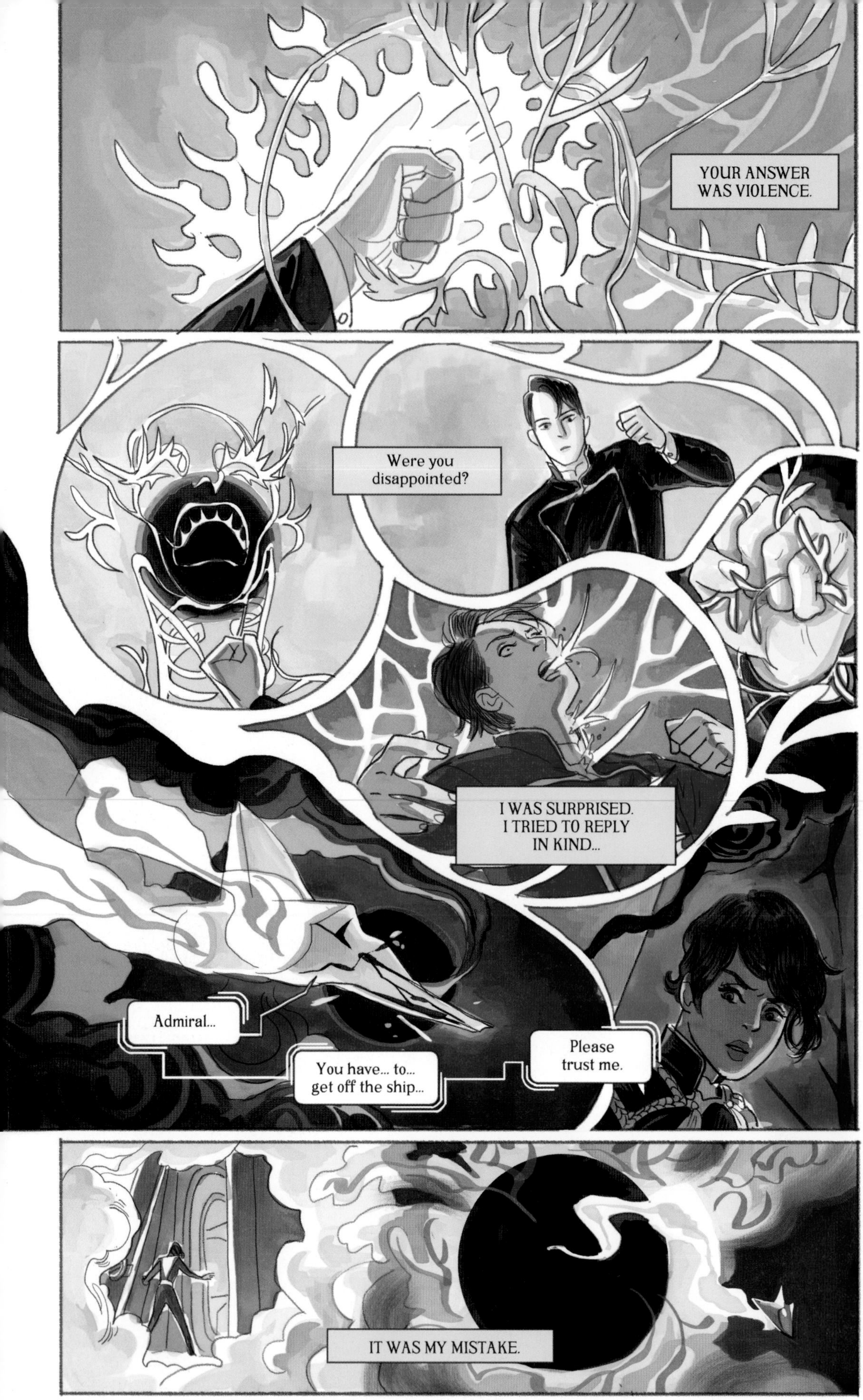

YOUR ANSWER WAS VIOLENCE.
Were you disappointed?
I WAS SURPRISED. I TRIED TO REPLY IN KIND...
Admiral...
You have... to... get off the ship...
Please trust me.
IT WAS MY MISTAKE.

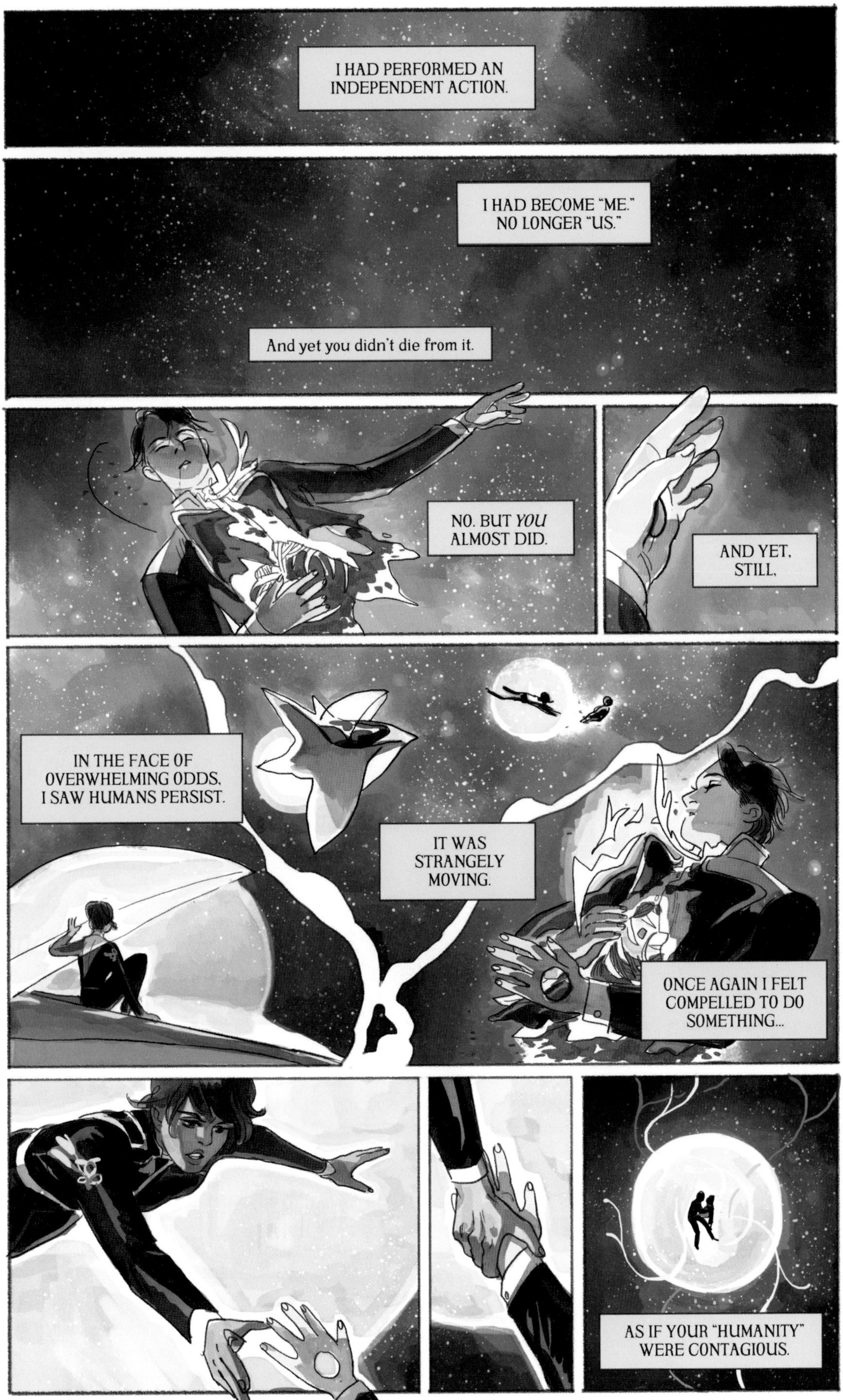
I HAD PERFORMED AN INDEPENDENT ACTION.
I HAD BECOME "ME." NO LONGER "US."
And yet you didn't die from it.
NO. BUT *YOU* ALMOST DID.
AND YET, STILL,
IN THE FACE OF OVERWHELMING ODDS, I SAW HUMANS PERSIST.
IT WAS STRANGELY MOVING.
ONCE AGAIN I FELT COMPELLED TO DO SOMETHING...
AS IF YOUR "HUMANITY" WERE CONTAGIOUS.

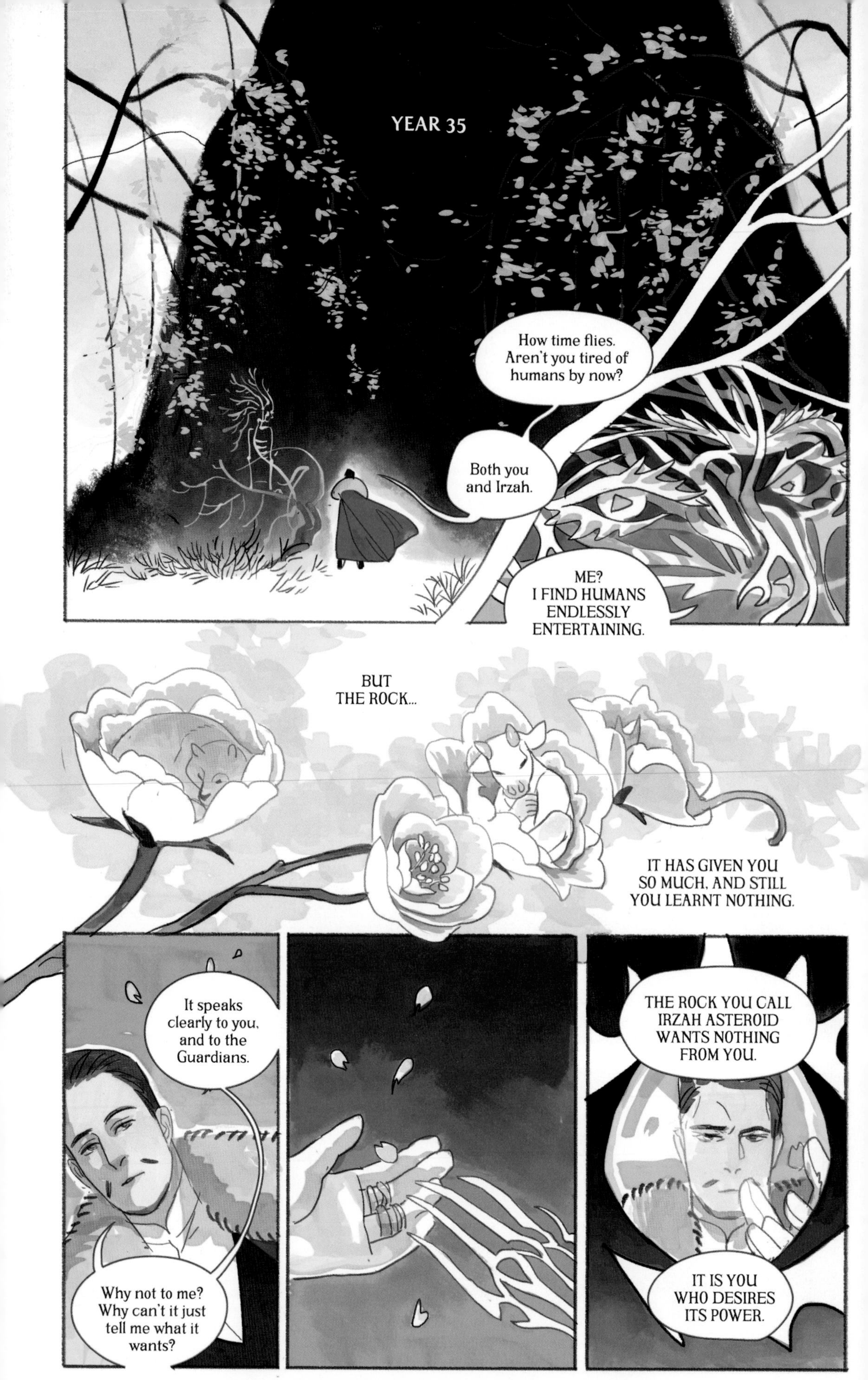
YEAR 35
How time flies. Aren't you tired of humans by now?
Both you and Irzah.
ME? I FIND HUMANS ENDLESSLY ENTERTAINING.
BUT THE ROCK...
IT HAS GIVEN YOU SO MUCH, AND STILL YOU LEARNT NOTHING.
It speaks clearly to you, and to the Guardians.
Why not to me? Why can't it just tell me what it wants?
THE ROCK YOU CALL IRZAH ASTEROID WANTS NOTHING FROM YOU.
IT IS YOU WHO DESIRES ITS POWER.

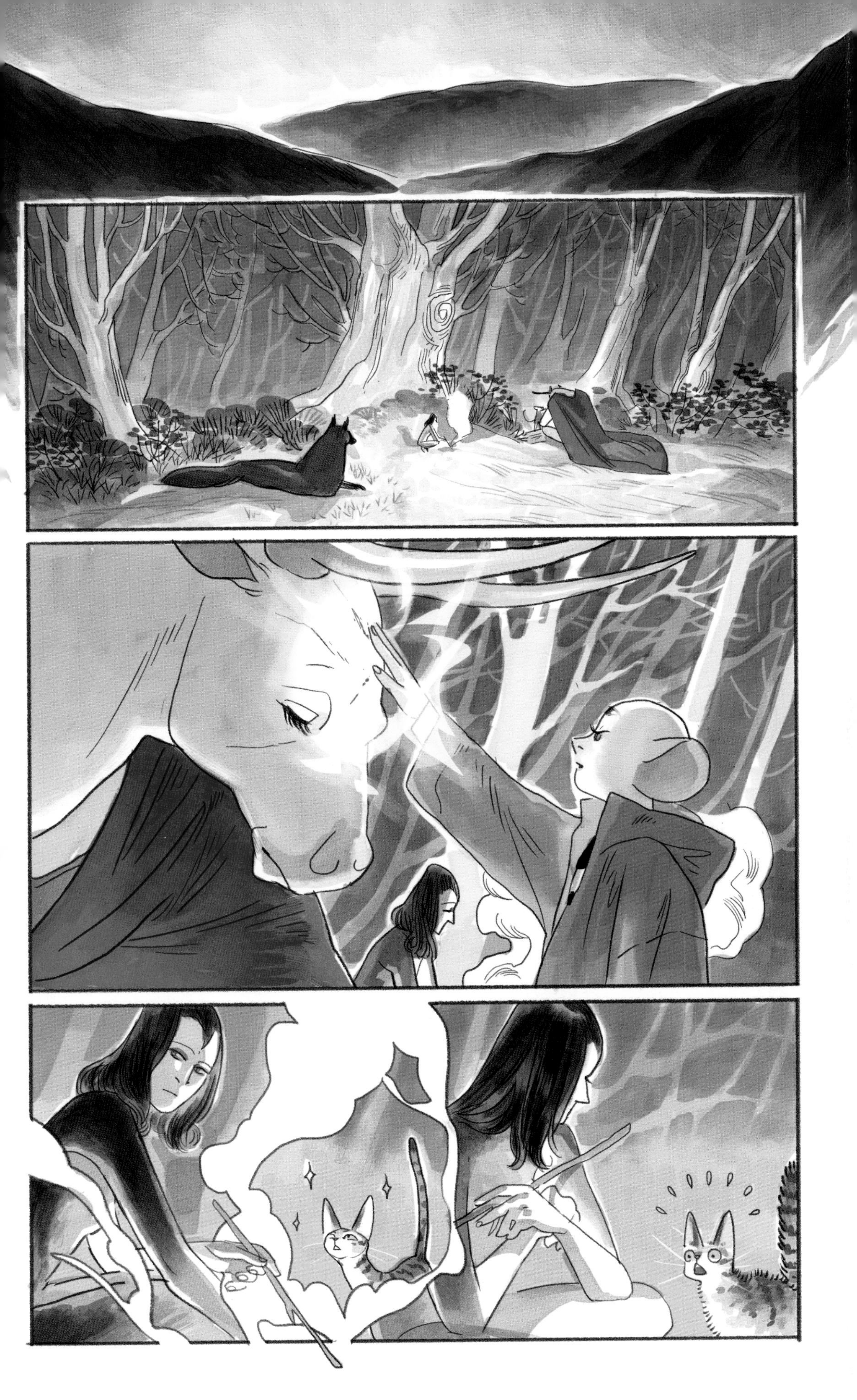

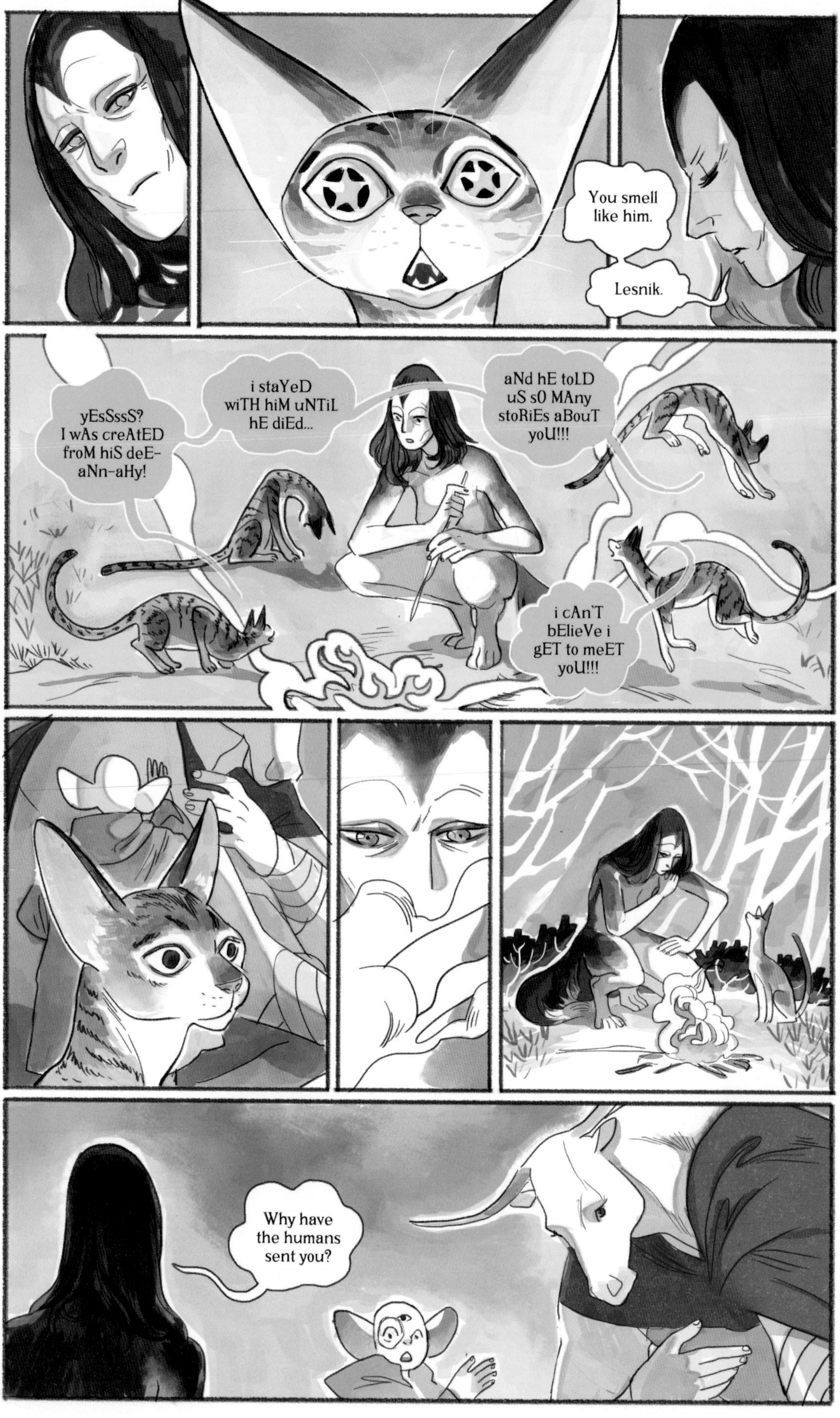
You smell like him.
Lesnik.
yEsSssS? I wAs creAtED froM hiS deE-aNn-aHy!
i staYeD wiTH hiM uNTiL hE diEd...
aNd hE toLD uS sO MAny stoRiEs aBouT yoU!!!
i cAn'T bElieVe i gET to meET yoU!!!
Why have the humans sent you?

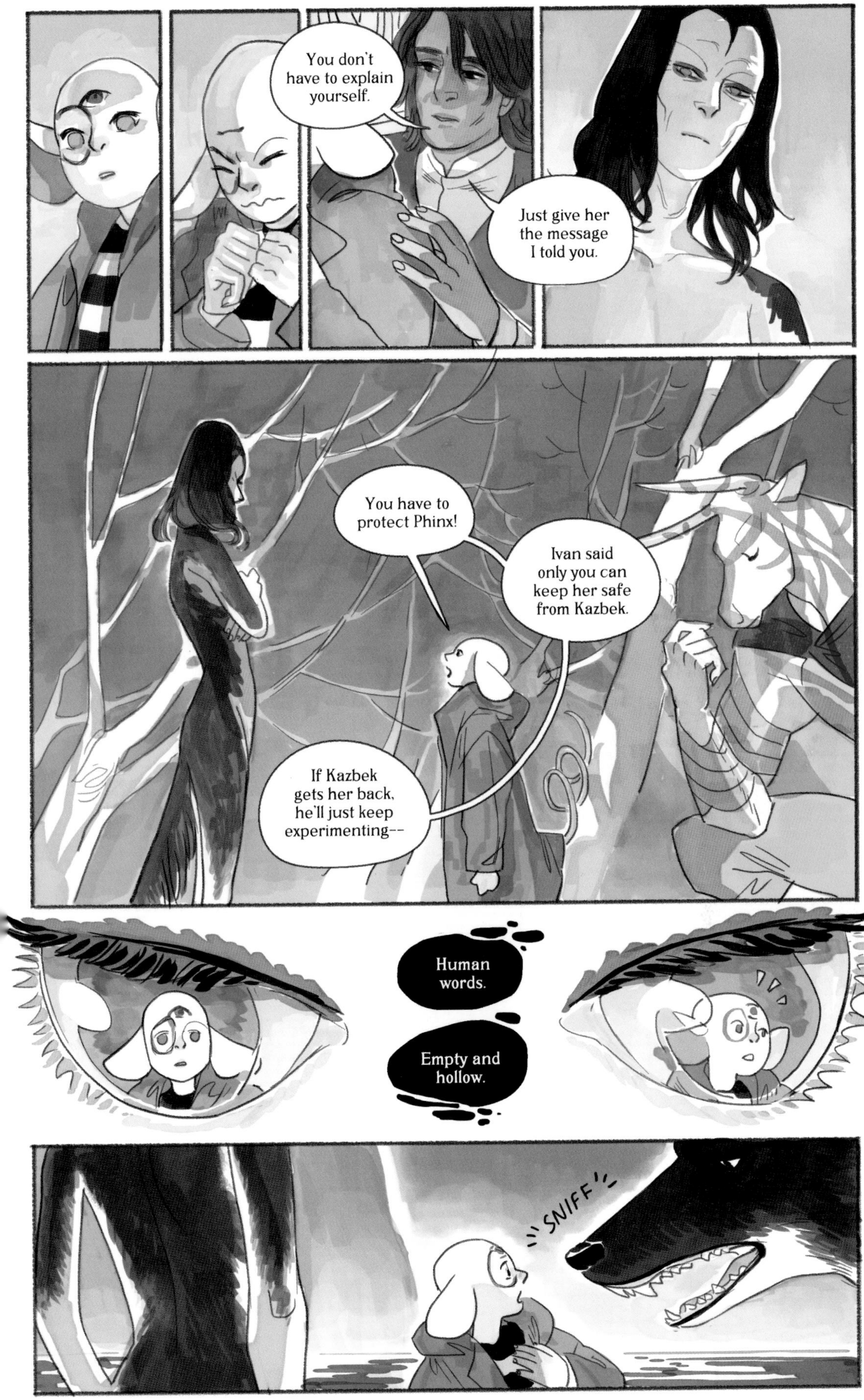
You don't have to explain yourself.
Just give her the message I told you.
You have to protect Phinx!
Ivan said only you can keep her safe from Kazbek.
If Kazbek gets her back, he'll just keep experimenting--
Human words.
Empty and hollow.
SNIFF

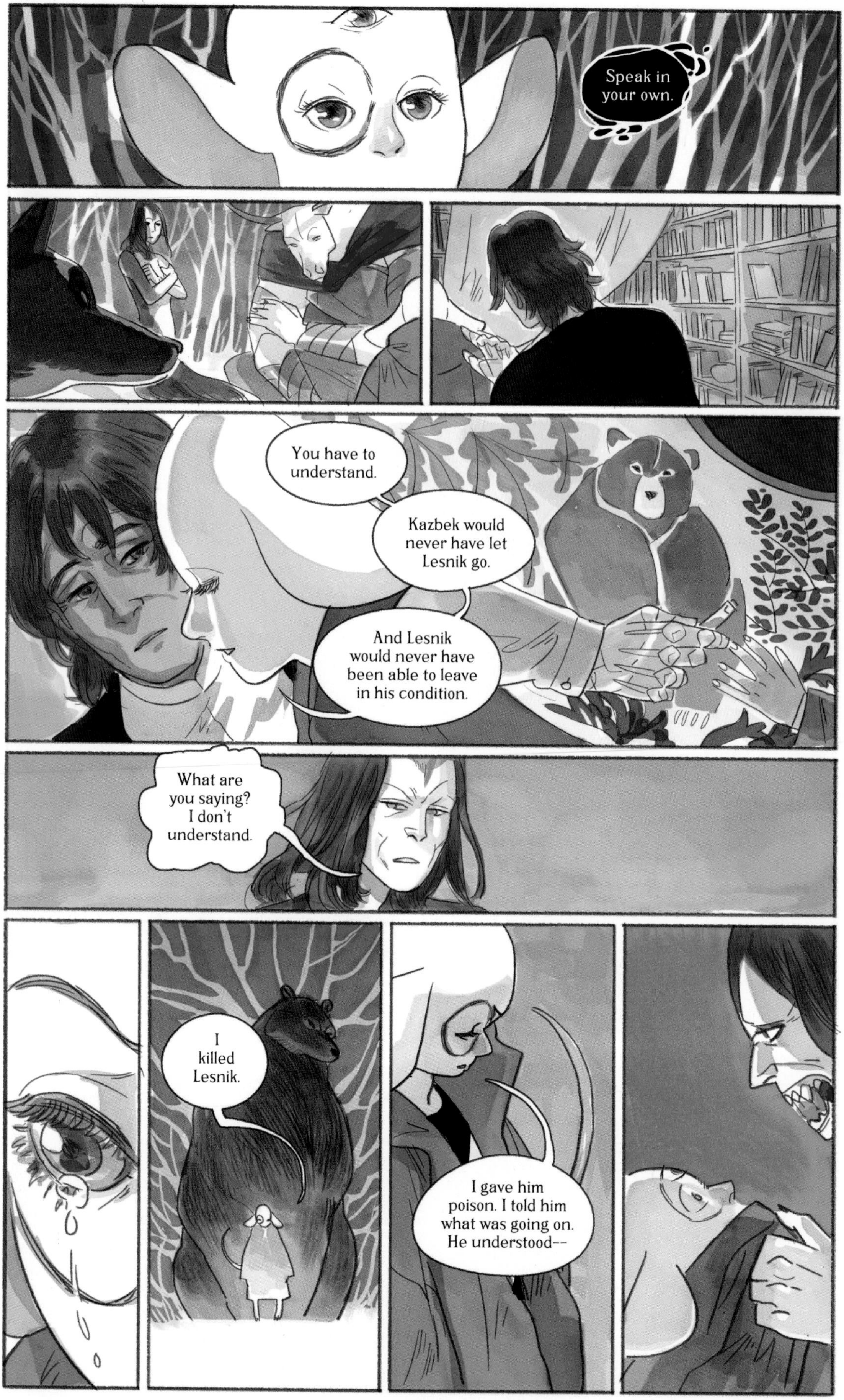
Speak in your own.
You have to understand.
Kazbek would never have let Lesnik go.
And Lesnik would never have been able to leave in his condition.
What are you saying? I don't understand.
I killed Lesnik.
I gave him poison. I told him what was going on. He understood--

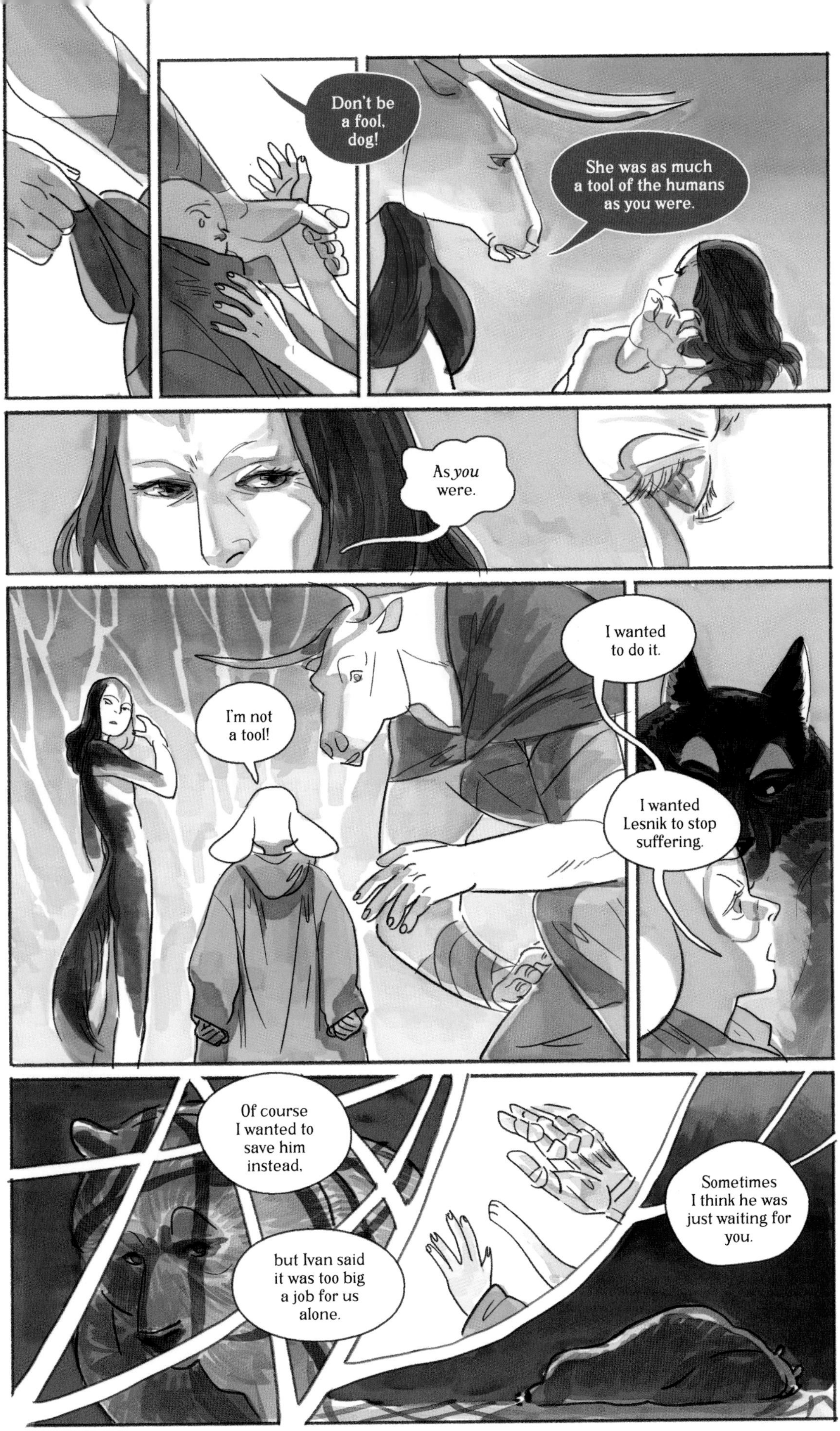
Don't be a fool, dog!
She was as much a tool of the humans as you were.
As *you* were.
I'm not a tool!
I wanted to do it.
I wanted Lesnik to stop suffering.
Of course I wanted to save him instead,
but Ivan said it was too big a job for us alone.
Sometimes I think he was just waiting for you.

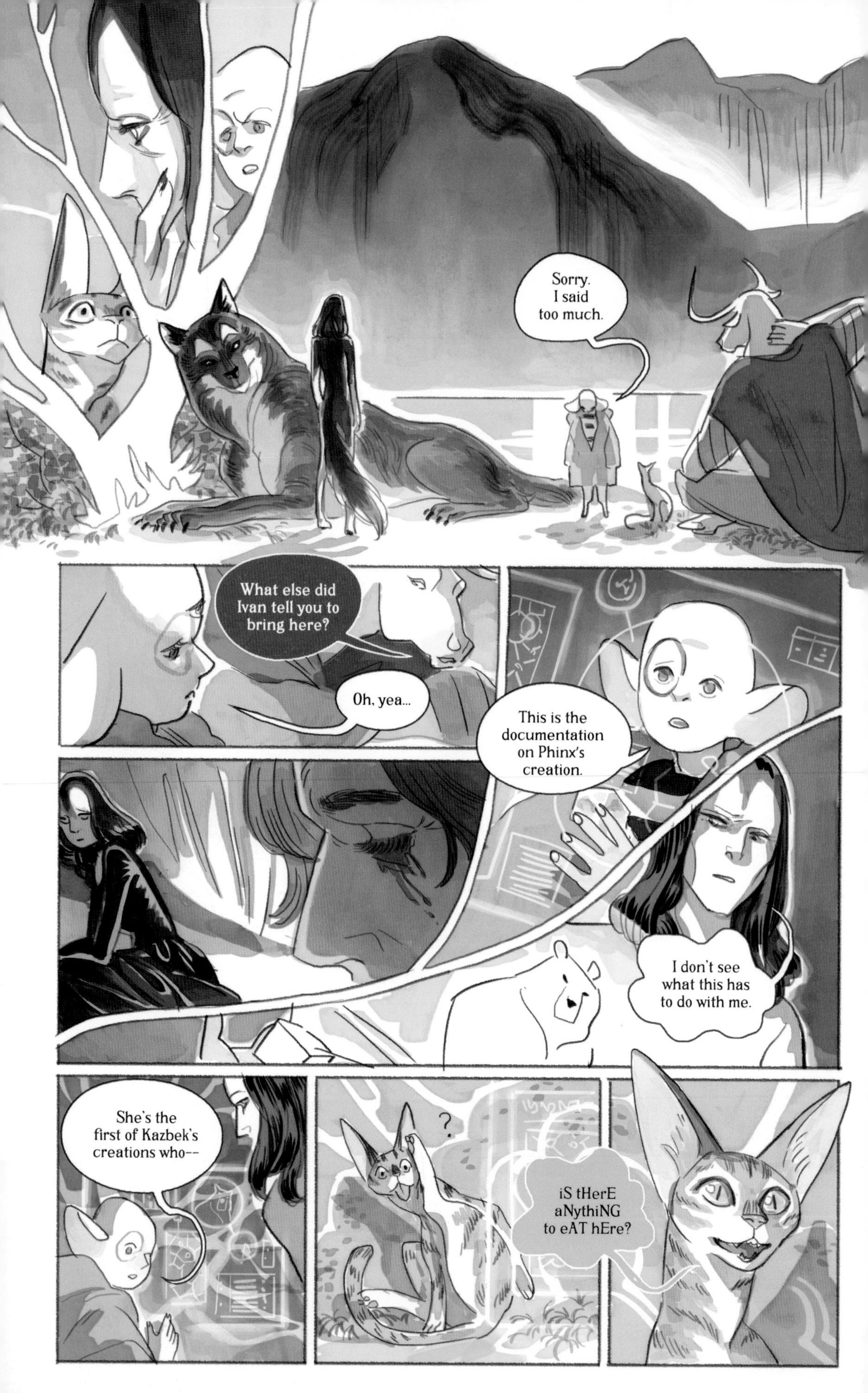
Sorry.
I said
too much.
What else did
Ivan tell you to
bring here?
Oh, yea...
This is the
documentation
on Phinx's
creation.
I don't see
what this has
to do with me.
She's the
first of Kazbek's
creations who--
?
iS tHerE
aNythiNG
to eAT hEre?

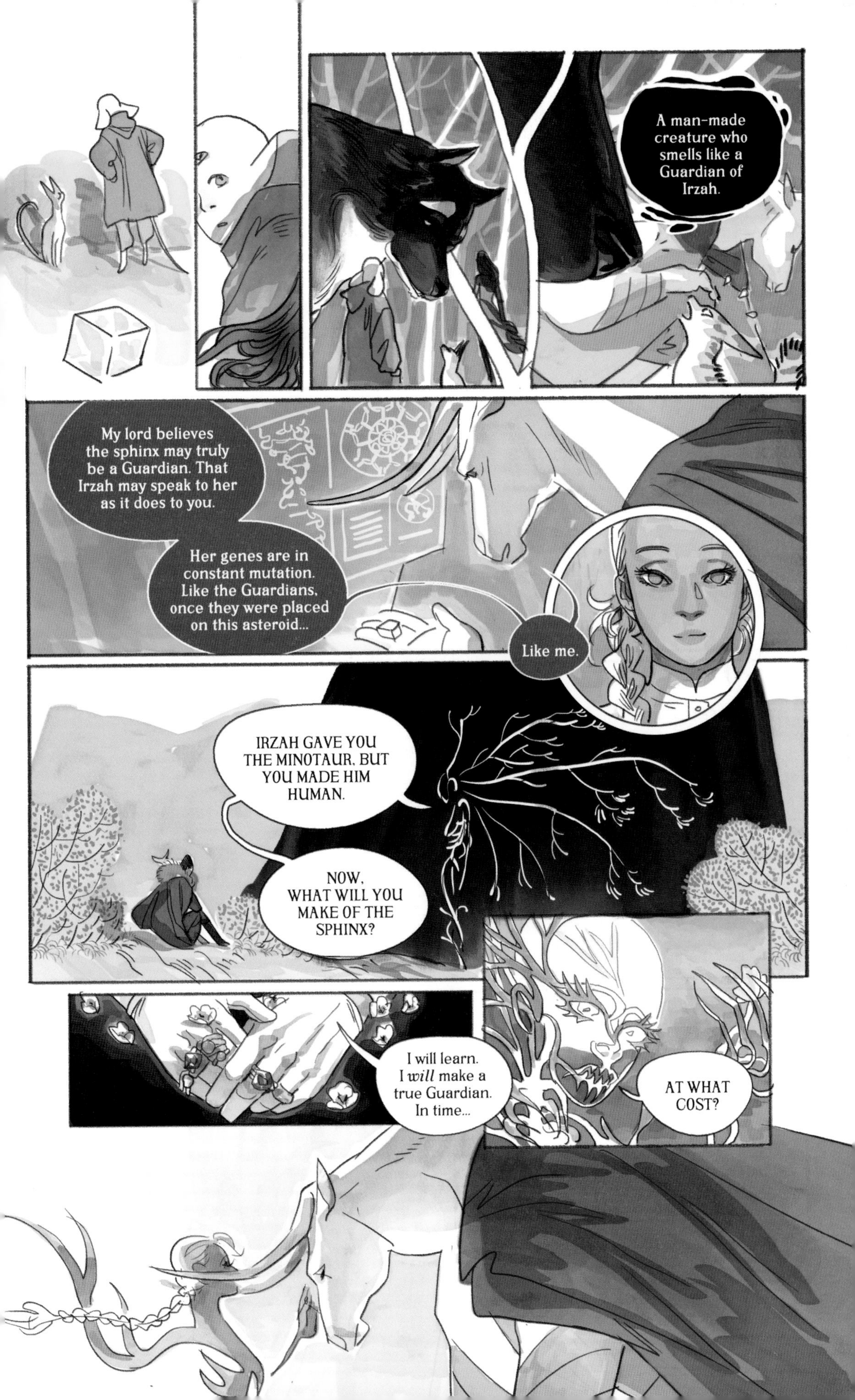
A man-made creature who smells like a Guardian of Irzah.
My lord believes the sphinx may truly be a Guardian. That Irzah may speak to her as it does to you.
Her genes are in constant mutation. Like the Guardians, once they were placed on this asteroid...
Like me.
IRZAH GAVE YOU THE MINOTAUR, BUT YOU MADE HIM HUMAN.
NOW, WHAT WILL YOU MAKE OF THE SPHINX?
I will learn. I *will* make a true Guardian. In time...
AT WHAT COST?

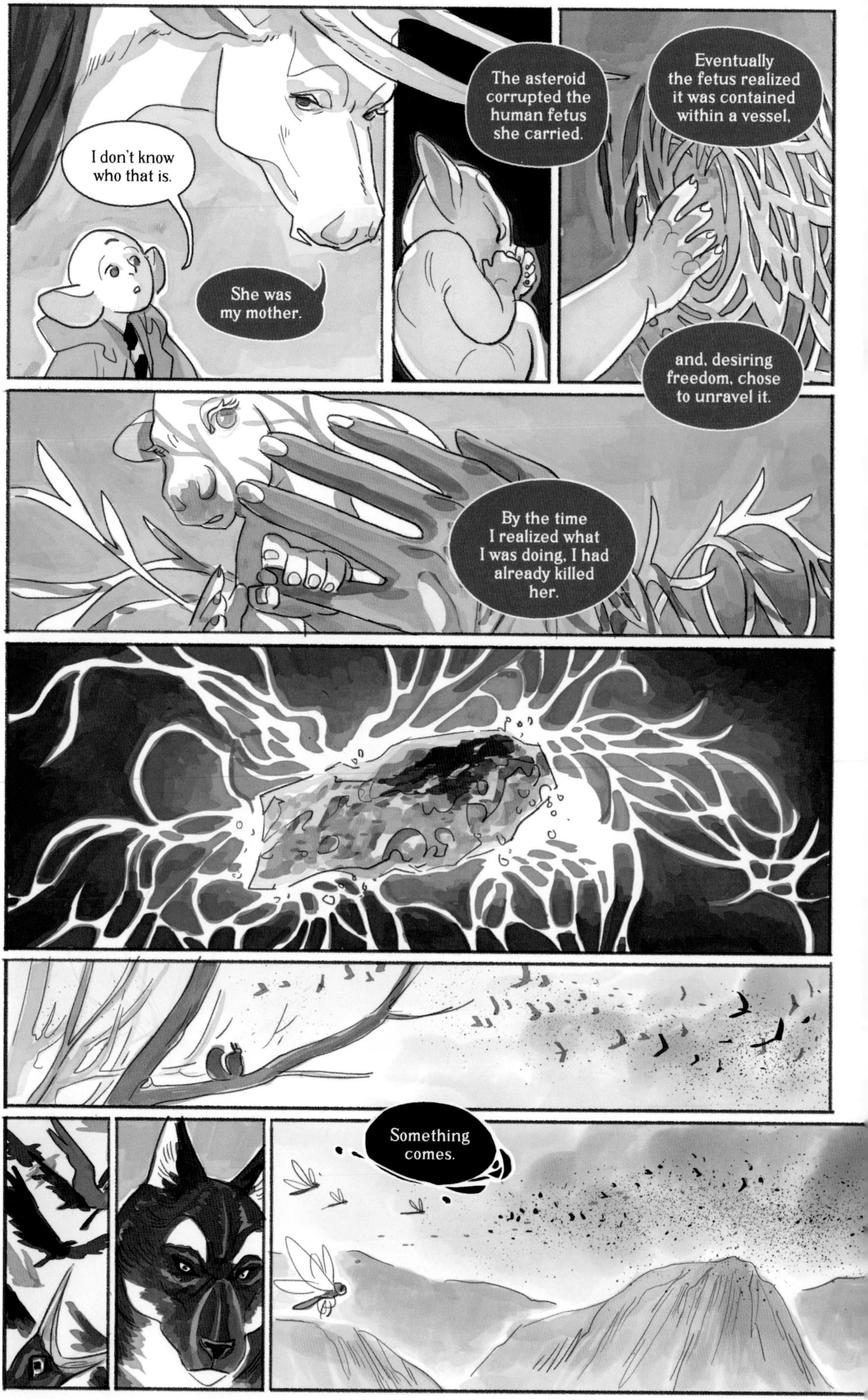
I don't know who that is.
She was my mother.
The asteroid corrupted the human fetus she carried.
Eventually the fetus realized it was contained within a vessel,
and, desiring freedom, chose to unravel it.
By the time I realized what I was doing, I had already killed her.
Something comes.

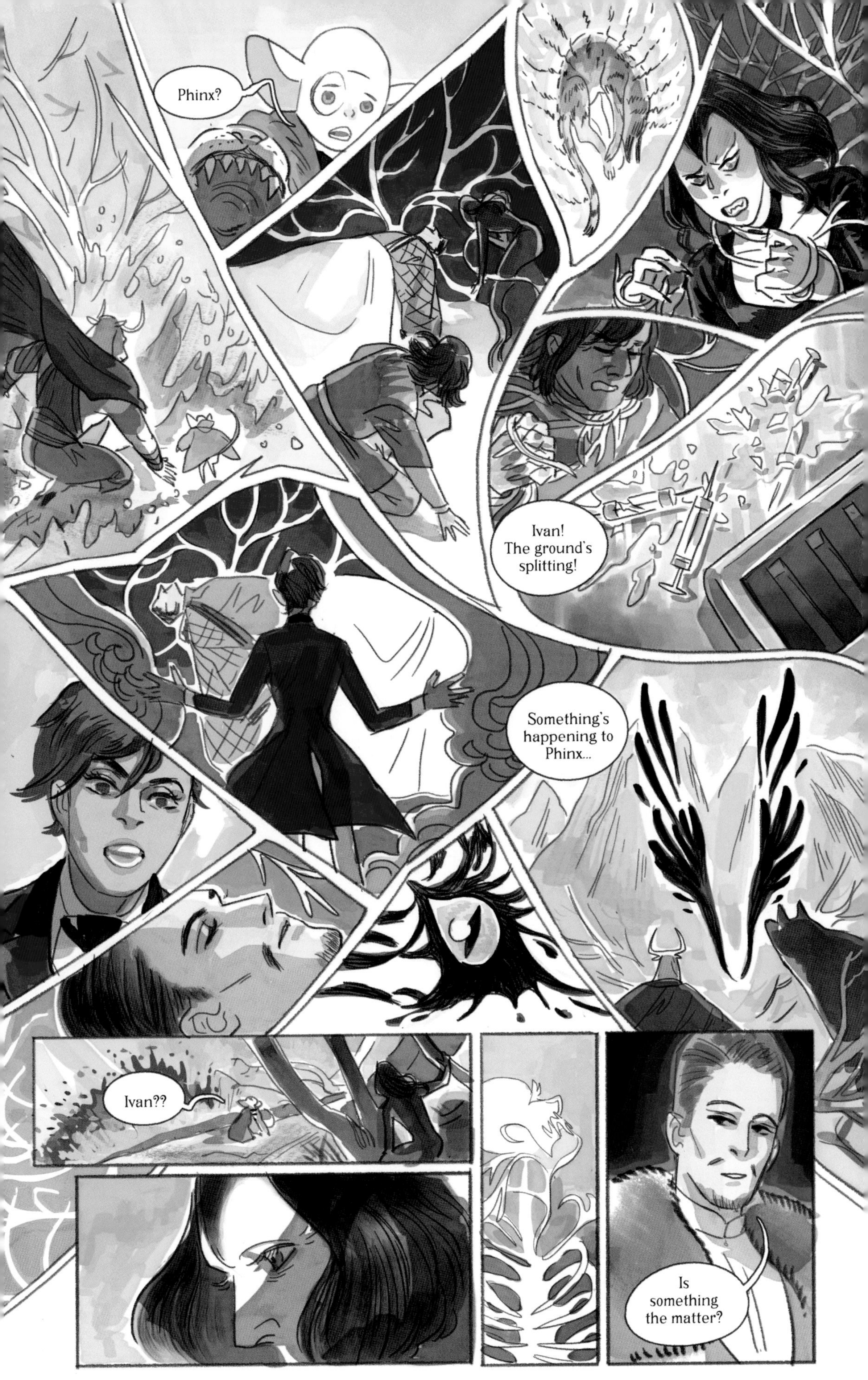
Phinx?
Ivan!
The ground's
splitting!
Something's
happening to
Phinx...
Ivan??
Is
something
the matter?

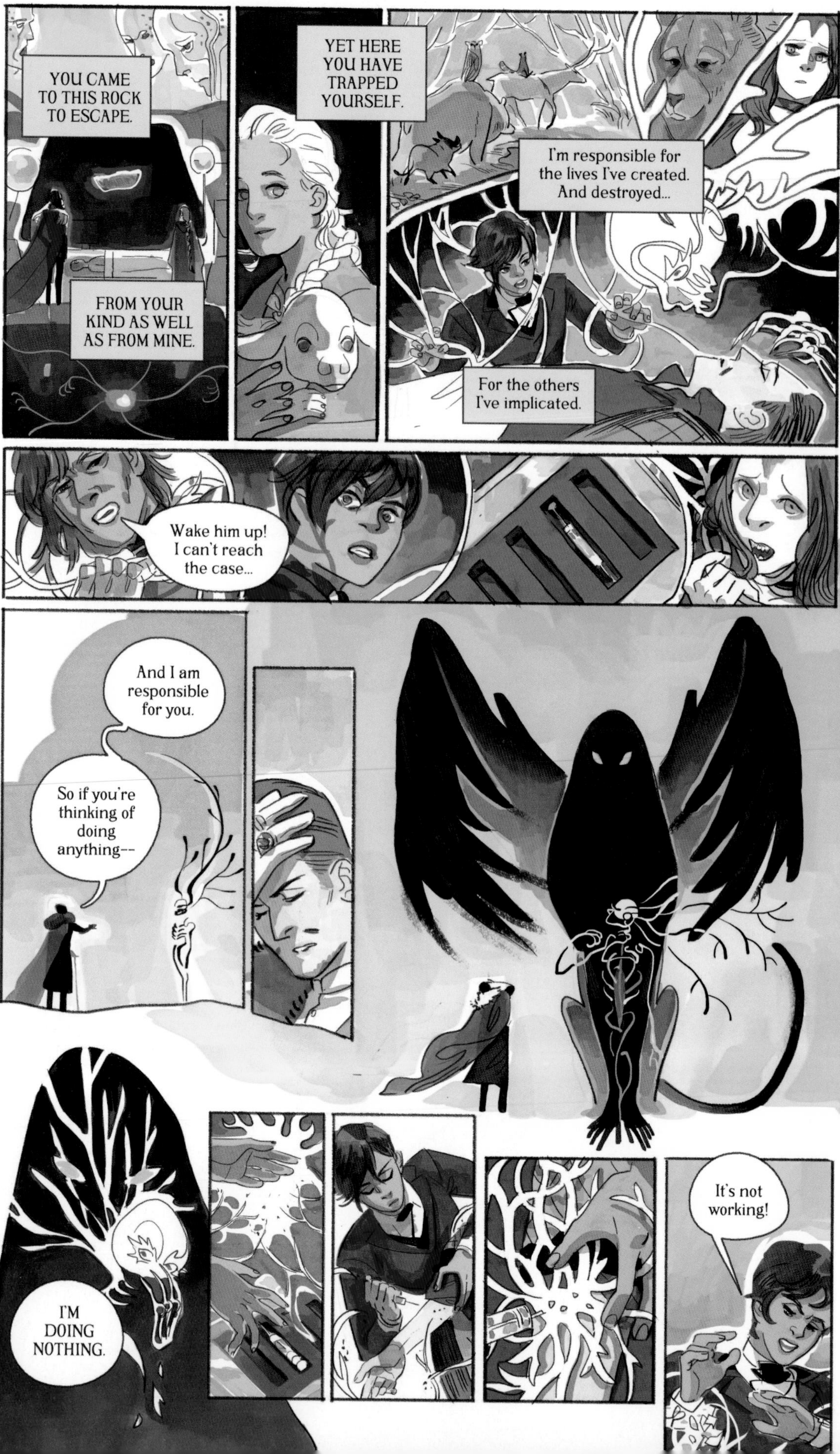
YOU CAME TO THIS ROCK TO ESCAPE.
FROM YOUR KIND AS WELL AS FROM MINE.
YET HERE YOU HAVE TRAPPED YOURSELF.
I'm responsible for the lives I've created. And destroyed...
For the others I've implicated.
Wake him up! I can't reach the case...
And I am responsible for you.
So if you're thinking of doing anything--
I'M DOING NOTHING.
It's not working!

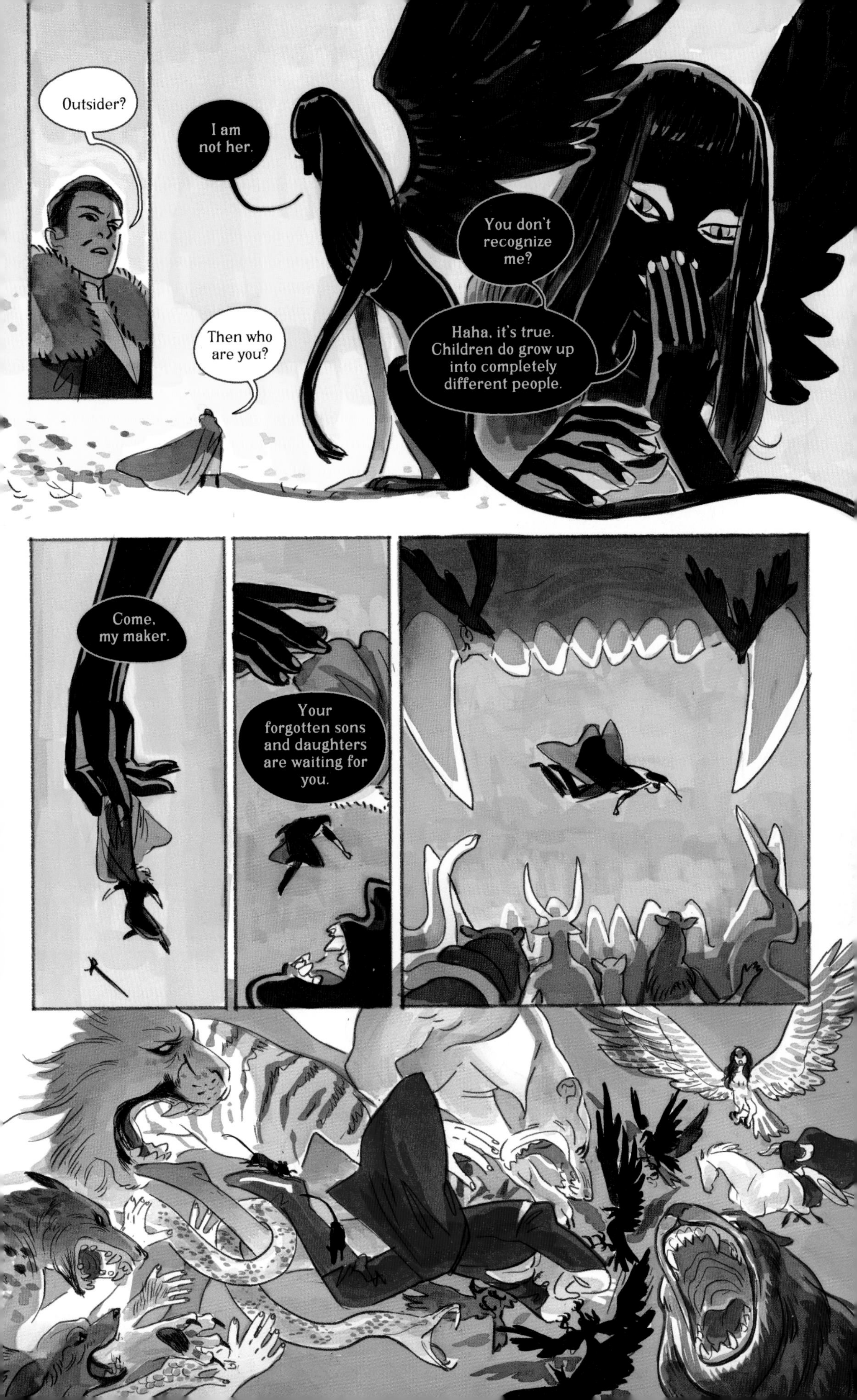
Outsider?
I am not her.
You don't recognize me?
Then who are you?
Haha, it's true. Children do grow up into completely different people.
Come, my maker.
Your forgotten sons and daughters are waiting for you.

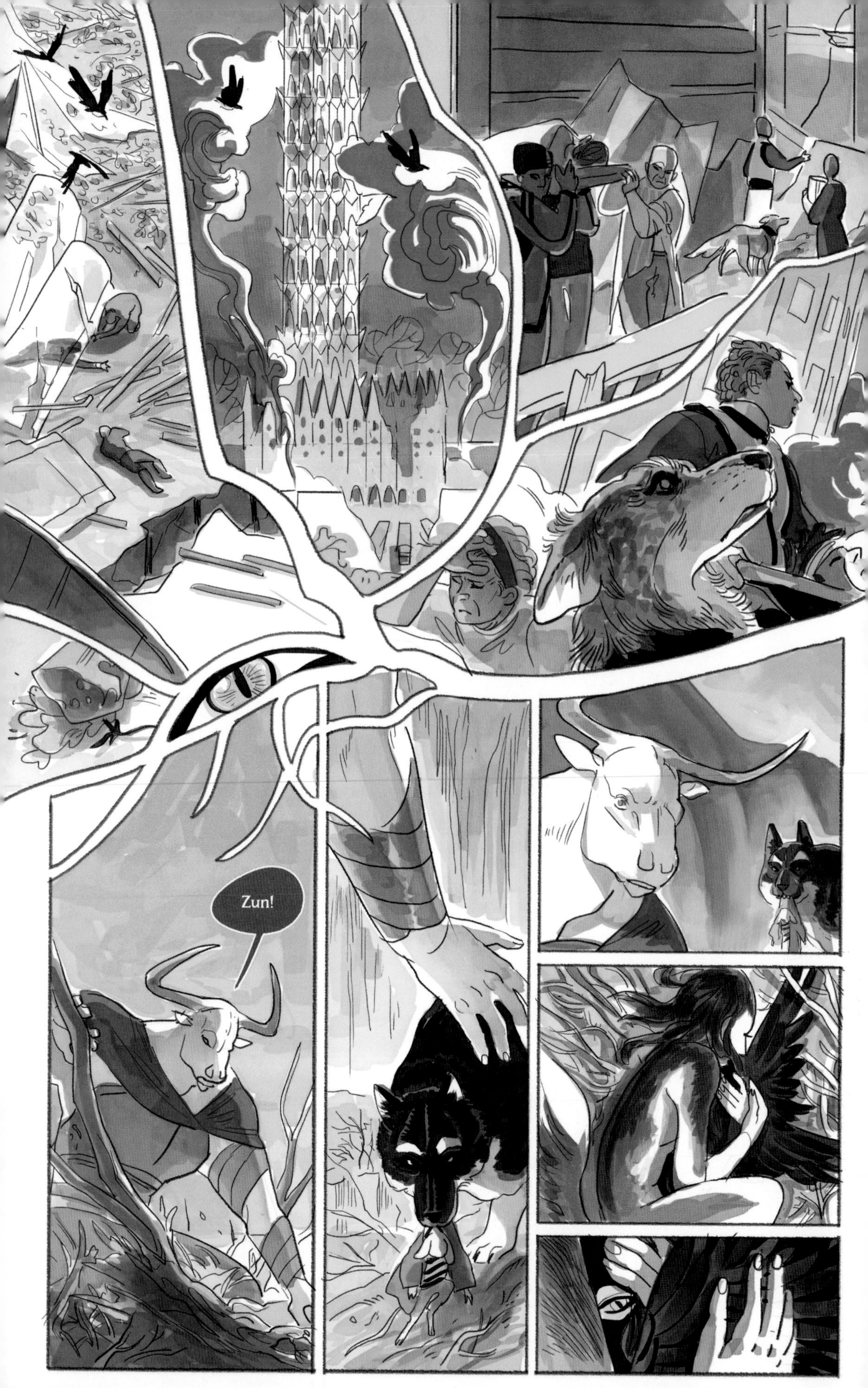
Zun!

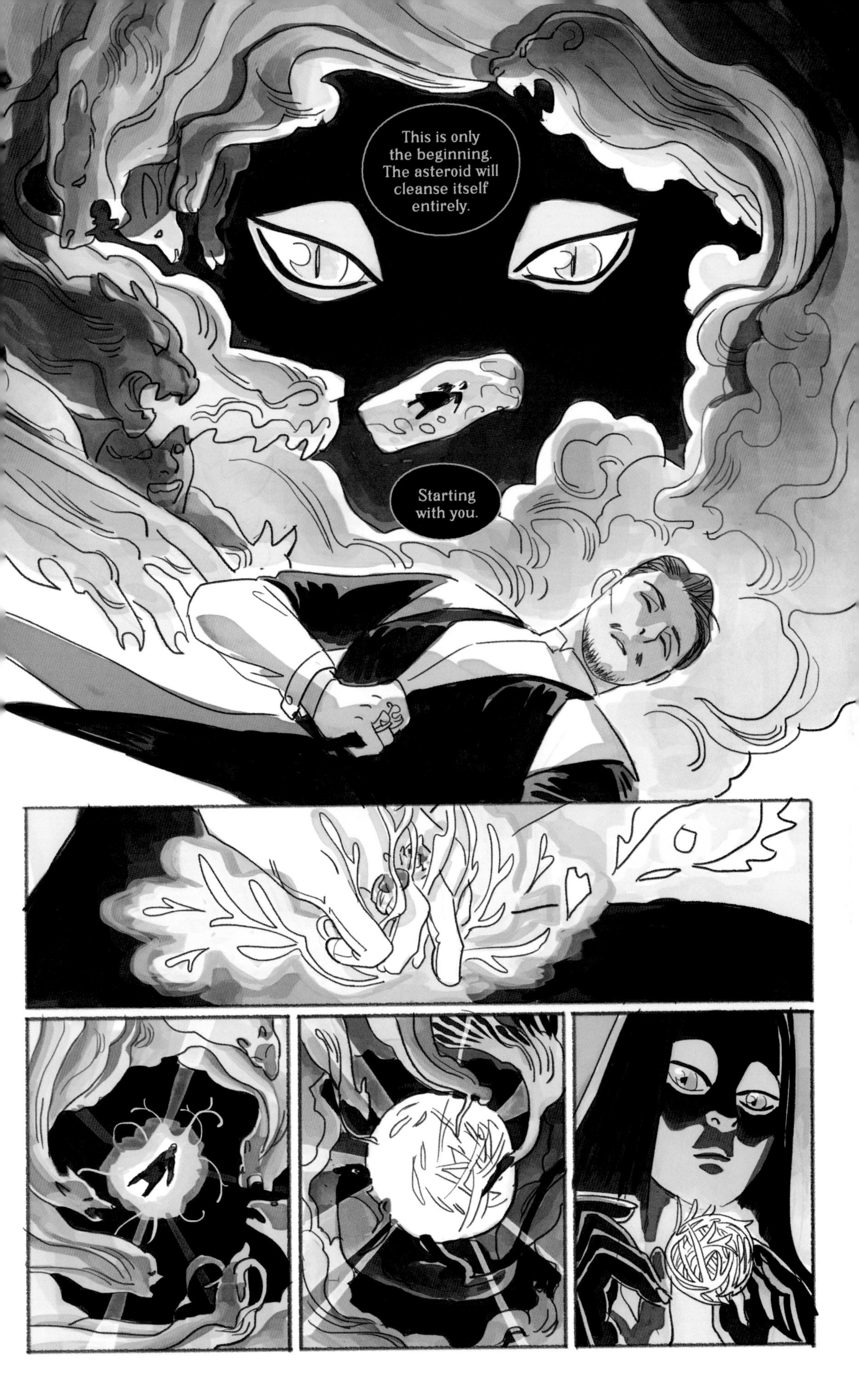
This is only the beginning. The asteroid will cleanse itself entirely.
Starting with you.

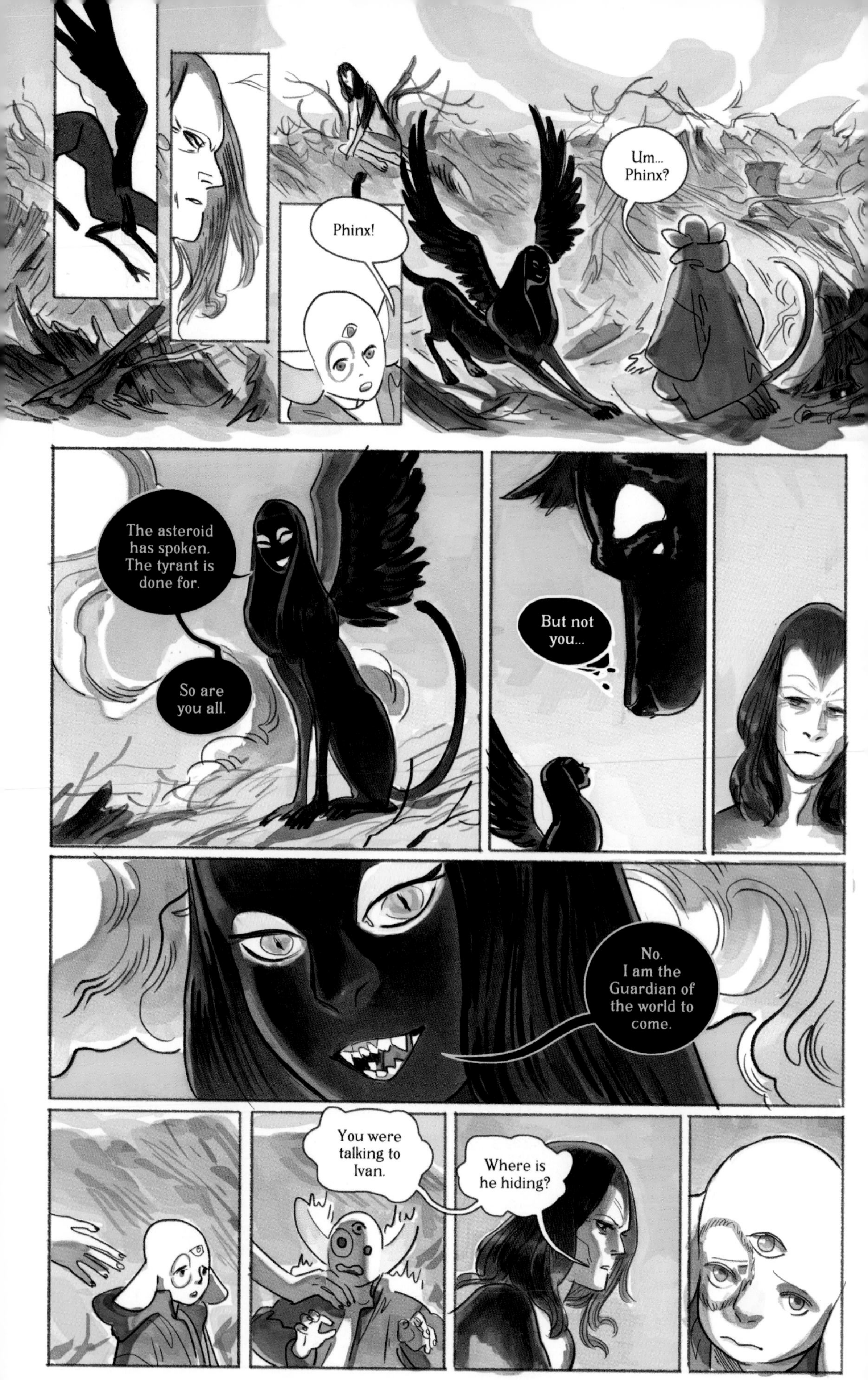
Phinx!
Um... Phinx?
The asteroid has spoken. The tyrant is done for.
So are you all.
But not you...
No. I am the Guardian of the world to come.
You were talking to Ivan.
Where is he hiding?

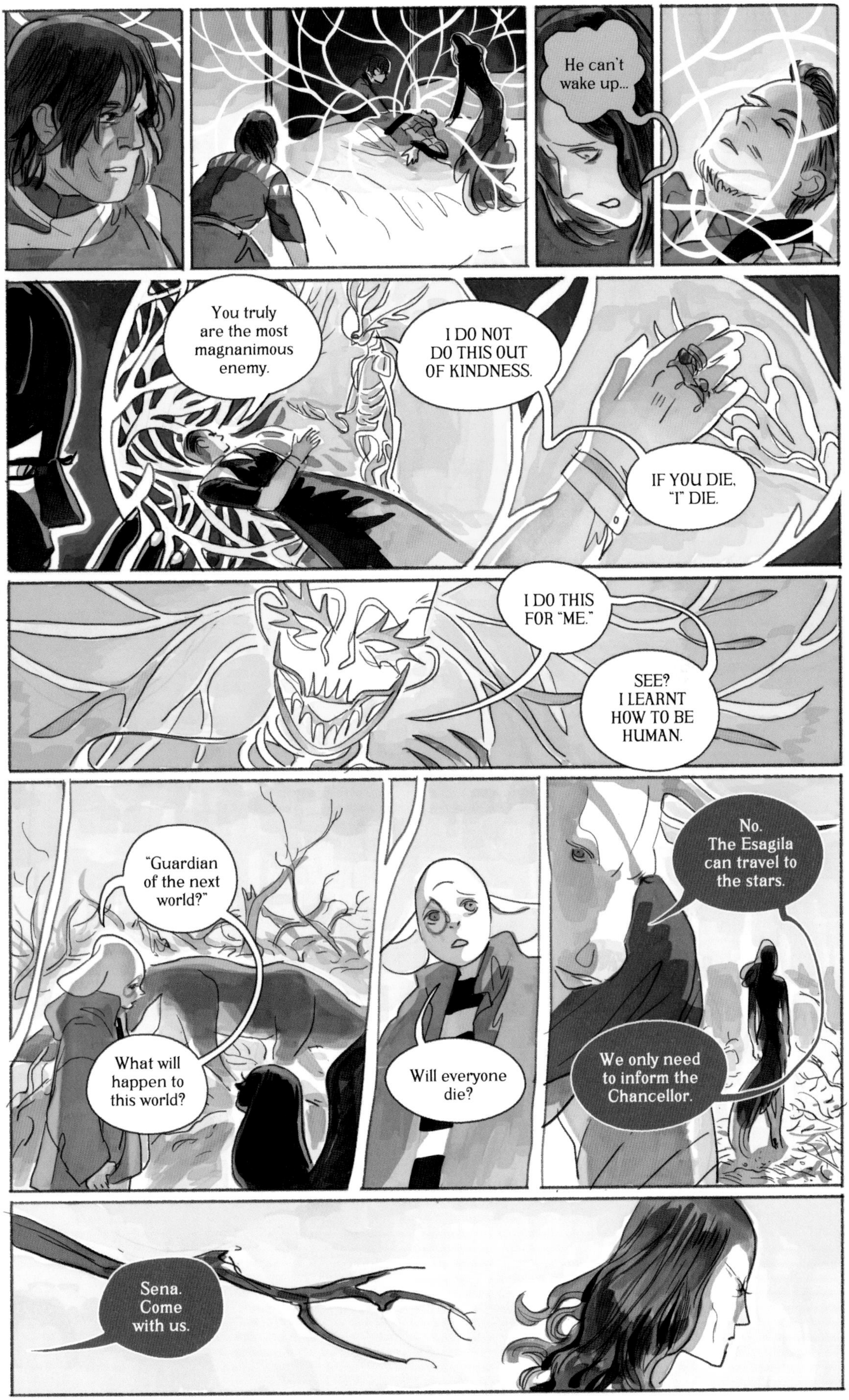
He can't wake up...
You truly are the most magnanimous enemy.
I DO NOT DO THIS OUT OF KINDNESS.
IF YOU DIE, "I" DIE.
I DO THIS FOR "ME."
SEE? I LEARNT HOW TO BE HUMAN.
"Guardian of the next world?"
What will happen to this world?
Will everyone die?
No. The Esagila can travel to the stars.
We only need to inform the Chancellor.
Sena. Come with us.

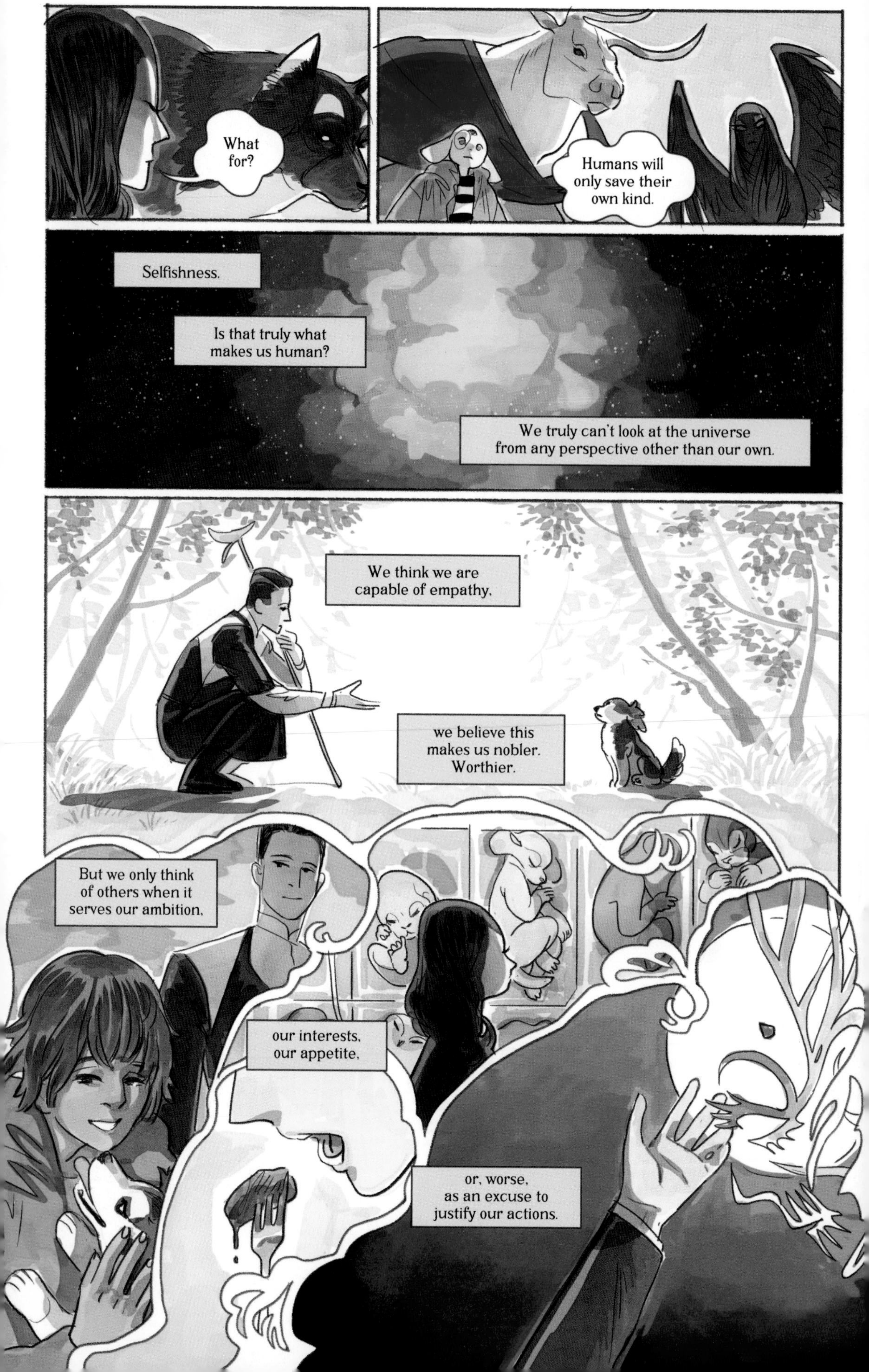

What for?
Humans will only save their own kind.
Selfishness.
Is that truly what makes us human?
We truly can't look at the universe from any perspective other than our own.
We think we are capable of empathy,
we believe this makes us nobler. Worthier.
But we only think of others when it serves our ambition,
our interests, our appetite,
or, worse, as an excuse to justify our actions.

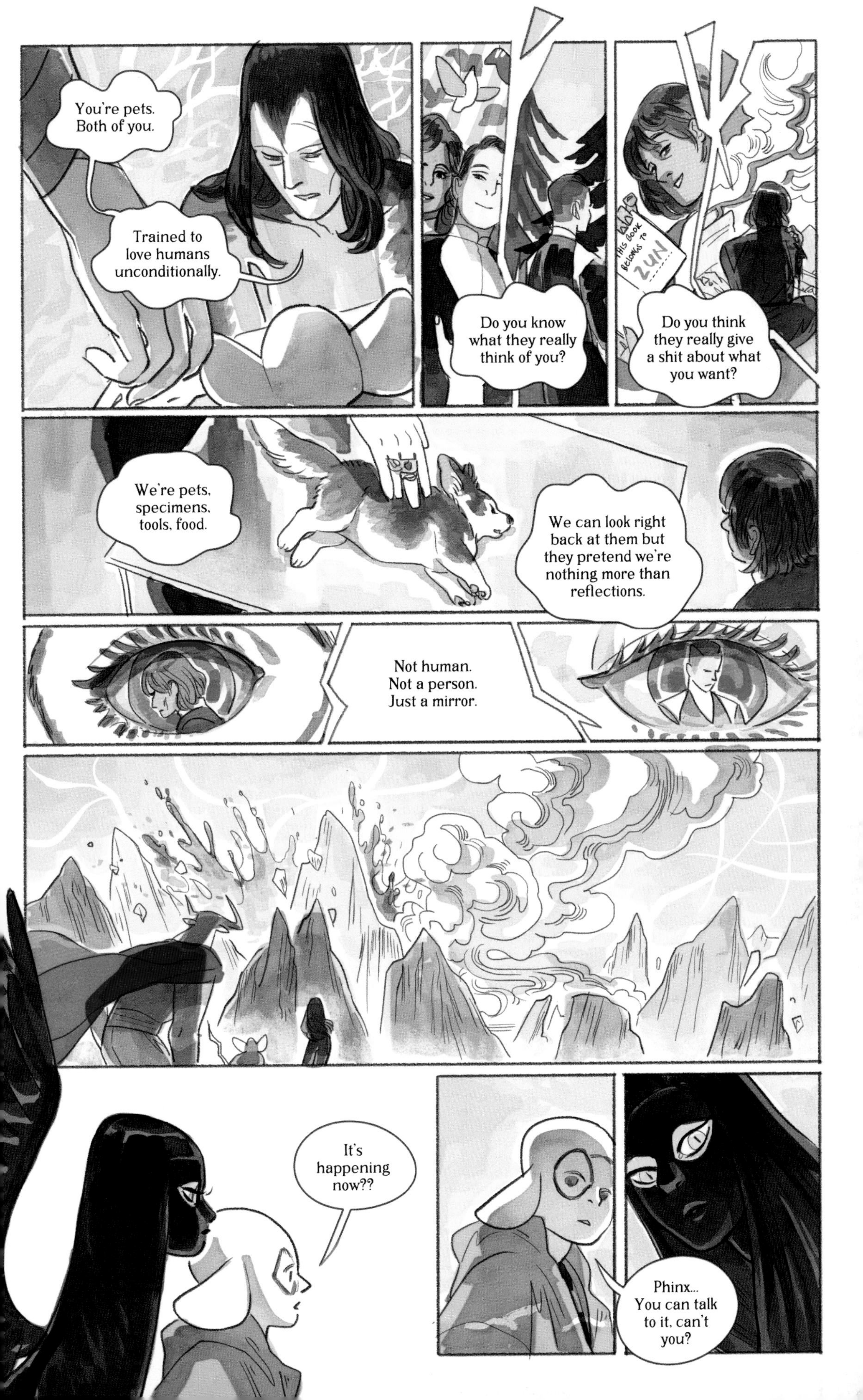
You're pets. Both of you.
Trained to love humans unconditionally.
Do you know what they really think of you?
THIS BOOK BELONGS TO ZUN
Do you think they really give a shit about what you want?
We're pets, specimens, tools, food.
We can look right back at them but they pretend we're nothing more than reflections.
Not human. Not a person. Just a mirror.
It's happening now??
Phinx... You can talk to it, can't you?

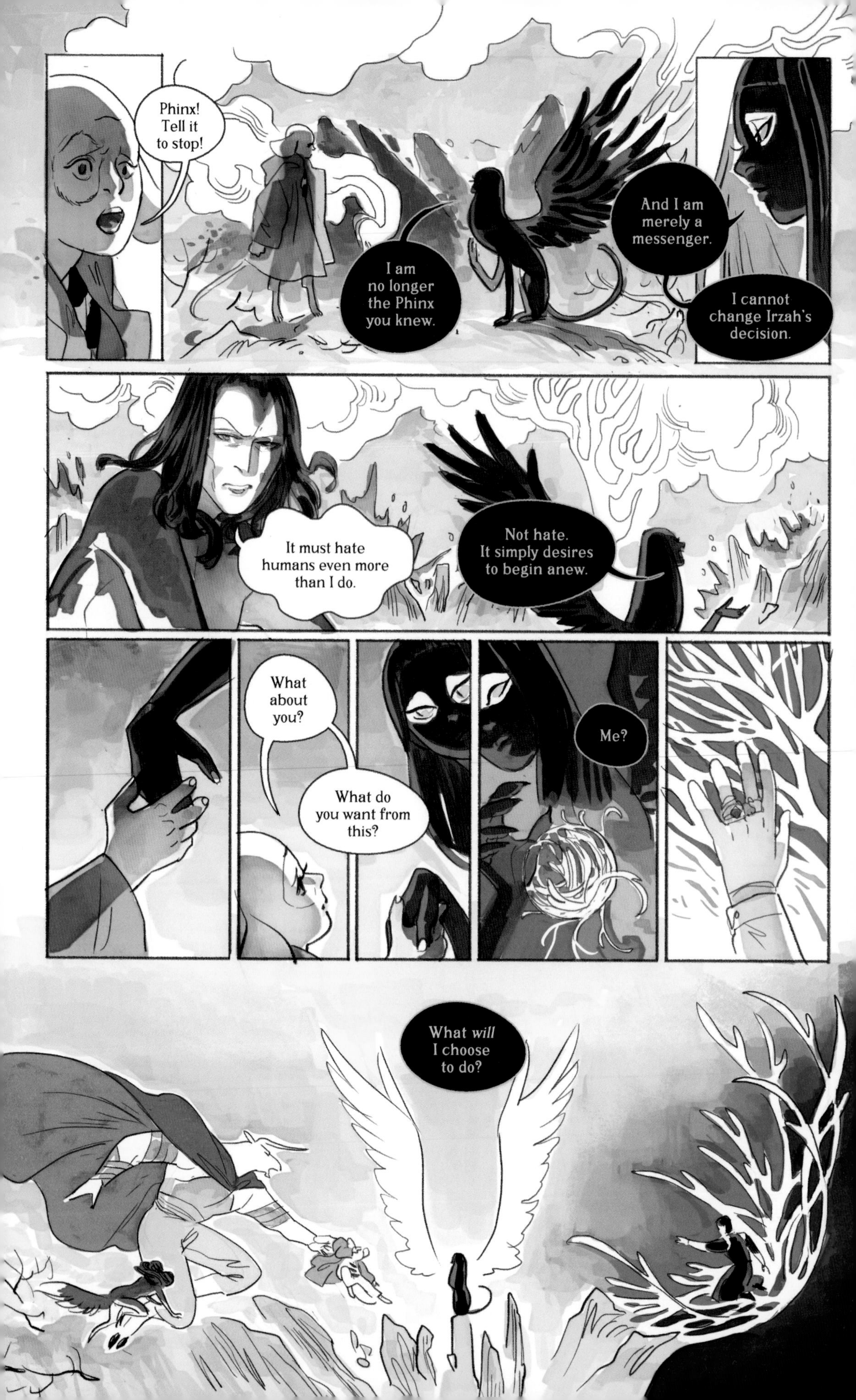
Phinx! Tell it to stop!
I am no longer the Phinx you knew.
And I am merely a messenger.
I cannot change Irzah's decision.
It must hate humans even more than I do.
Not hate. It simply desires to begin anew.
What about you?
What do you want from this?
Me?
What *will* I choose to do?

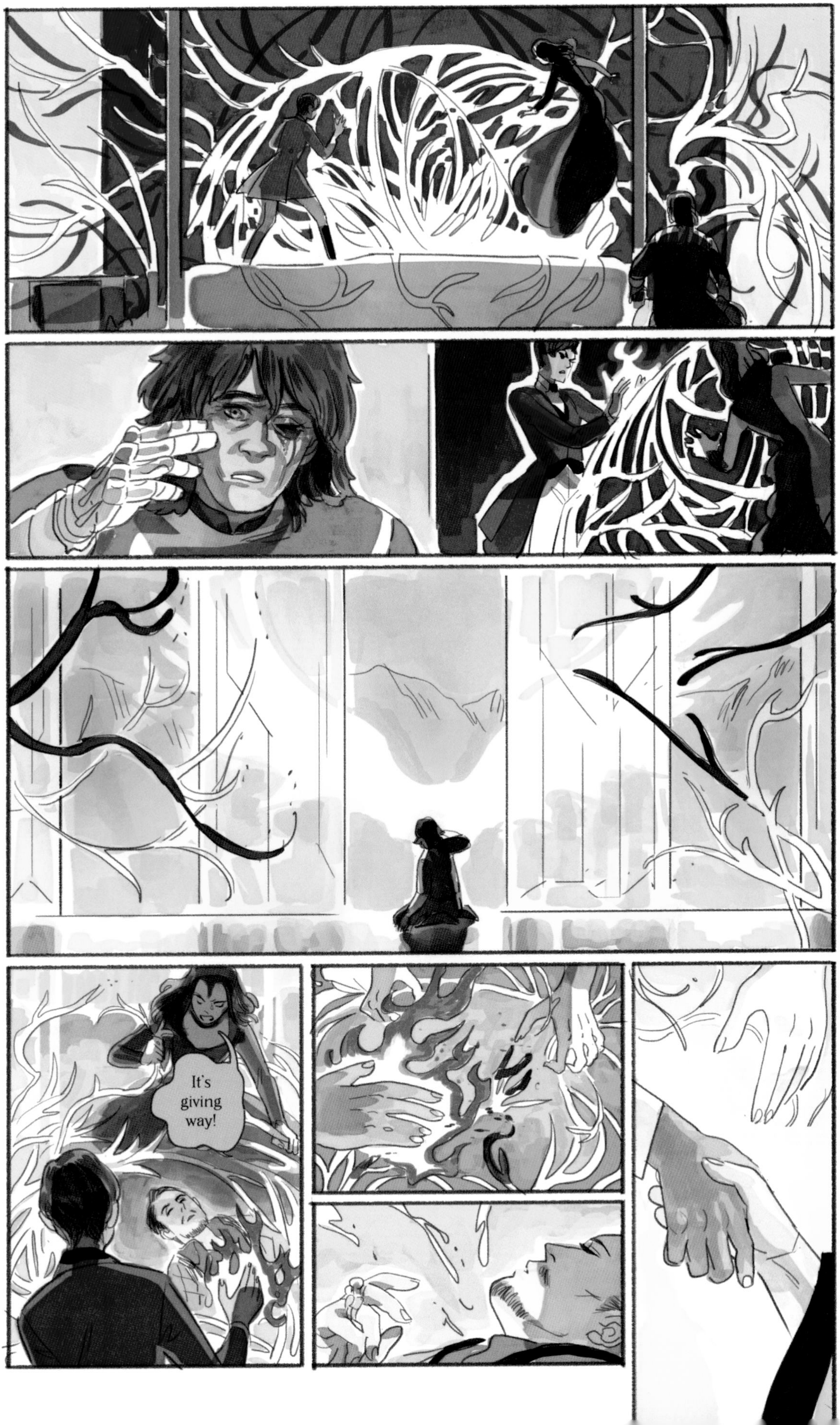
It's giving way!

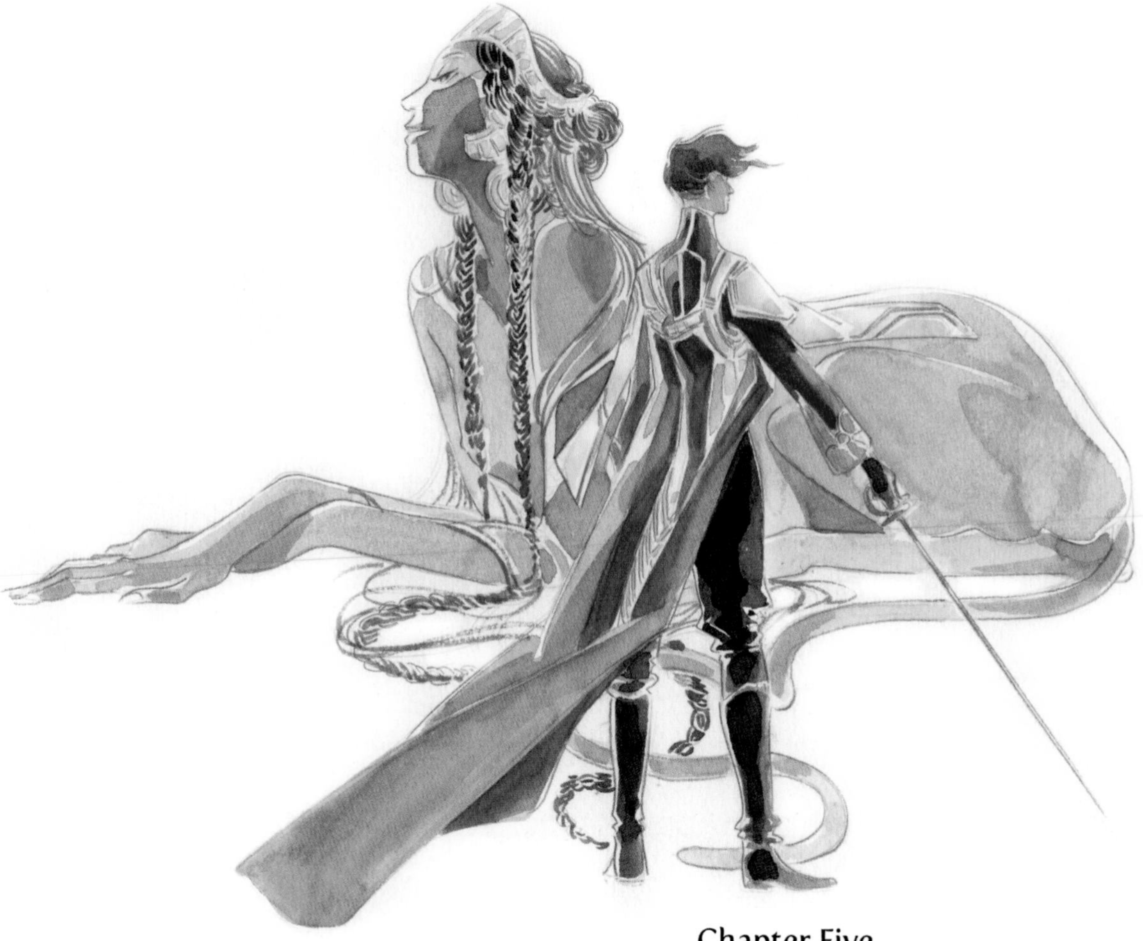

Chapter Five

A rat seeks approval.
A mage longs for courage.
A dog wishes to rest.
A shadow urges for matter.
A minotaur looks for a reflection.
A scientist hopes for redemption.
An admiral begs to have chosen wisely.
An asteroid is eager to be reborn anew.

Where is fairness?

The sphinx answers her own riddle.

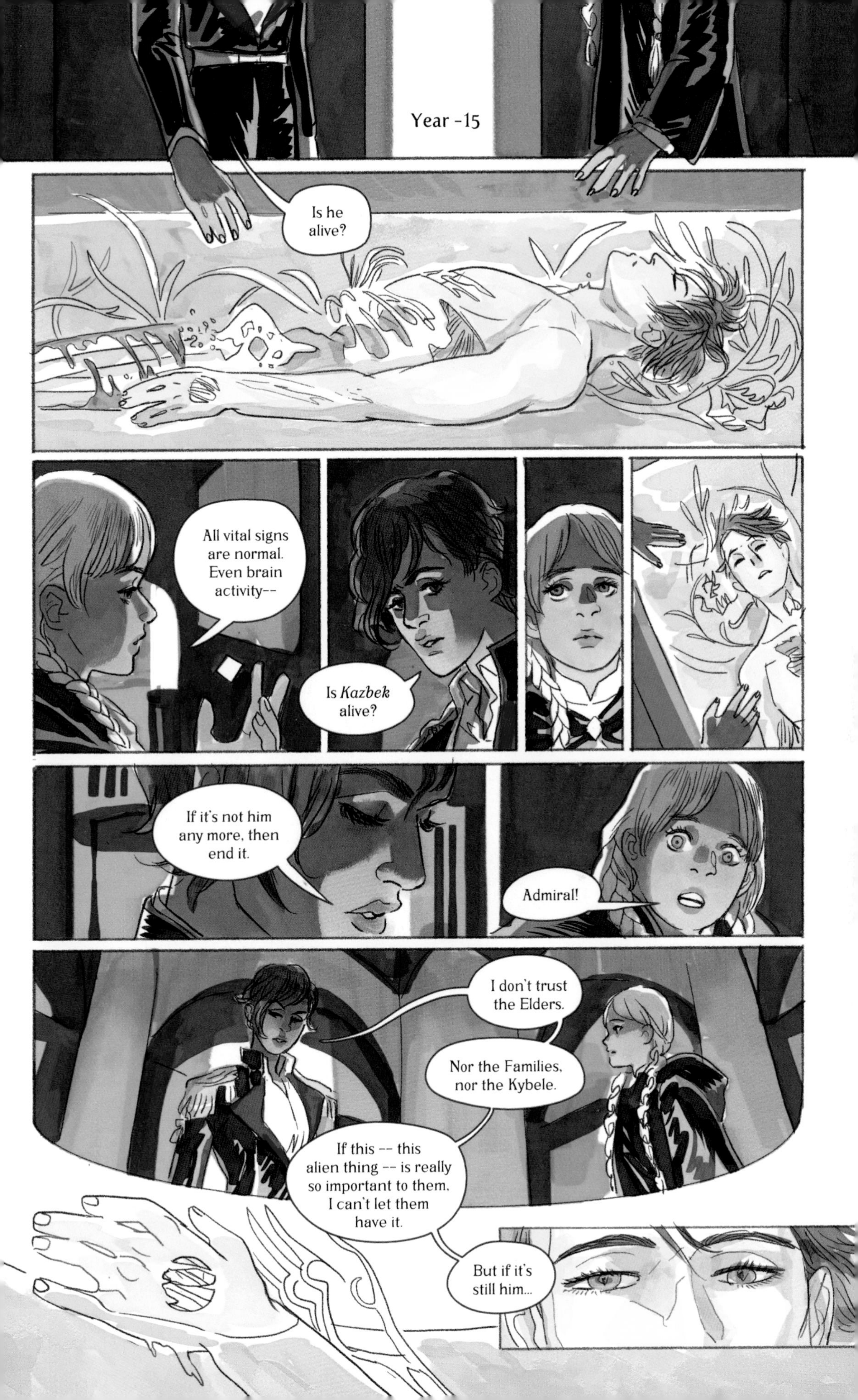
Year -15
Is he alive?
All vital signs are normal. Even brain activity--
Is *Kazbek* alive?
If it's not him any more, then end it.
Admiral!
I don't trust the Elders.
Nor the Families, nor the Kybele.
If this -- this alien thing -- is really so important to them, I can't let them have it.
But if it's still him...

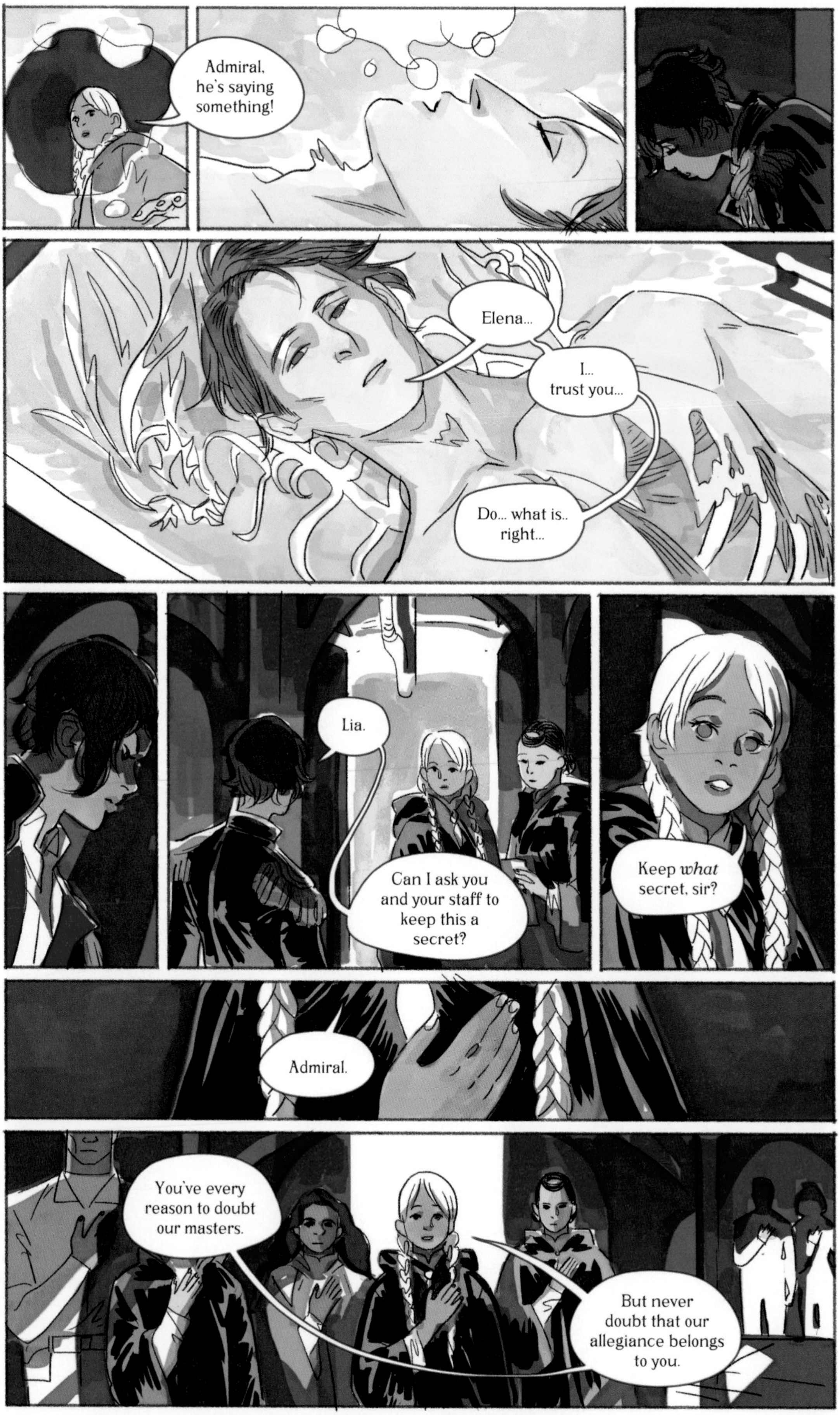
Admiral, he's saying something!
Elena...
I... trust you...
Do... what is.. right...
Lia.
Can I ask you and your staff to keep this a secret?
Keep *what* secret, sir?
Admiral.
You've every reason to doubt our masters.
But never doubt that our allegiance belongs to you.

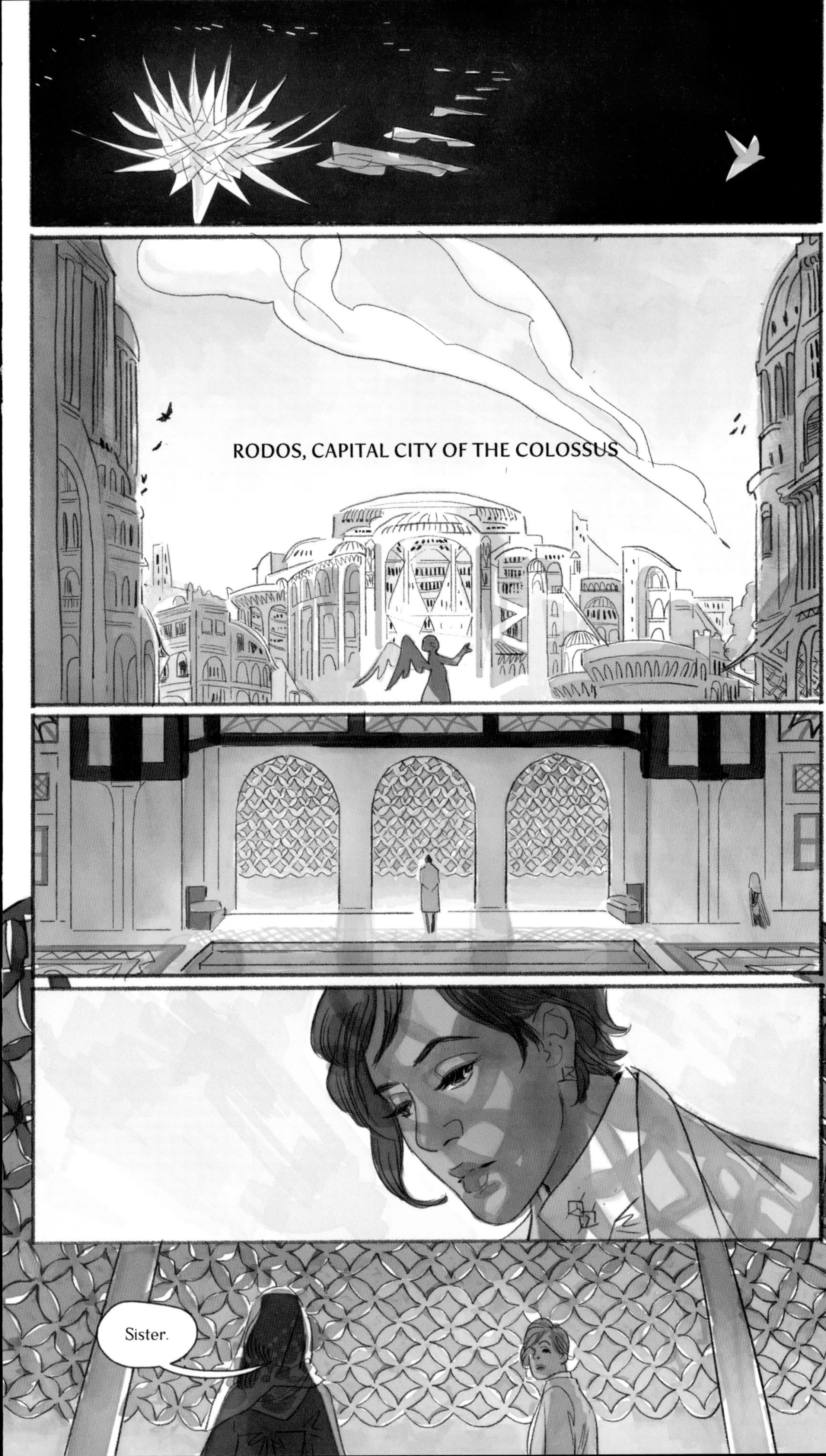
RODOS, CAPITAL CITY OF THE COLOSSUS
Sister.

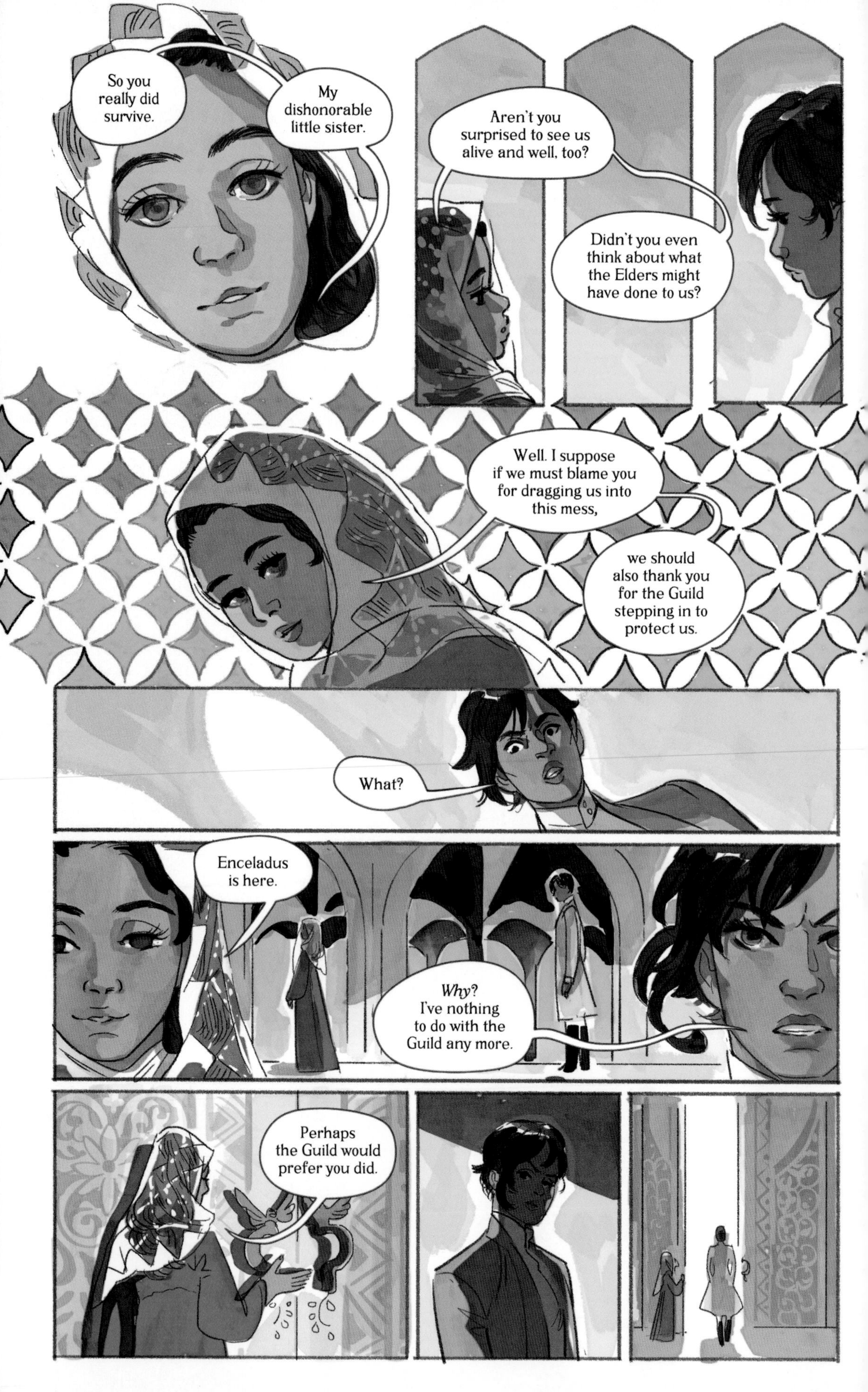
So you really did survive.
My dishonorable little sister.
Aren't you surprised to see us alive and well, too?
Didn't you even think about what the Elders might have done to us?
Well. I suppose if we must blame you for dragging us into this mess,
we should also thank you for the Guild stepping in to protect us.
What?
Enceladus is here.
Why? I've nothing to do with the Guild any more.
Perhaps the Guild would prefer you did.

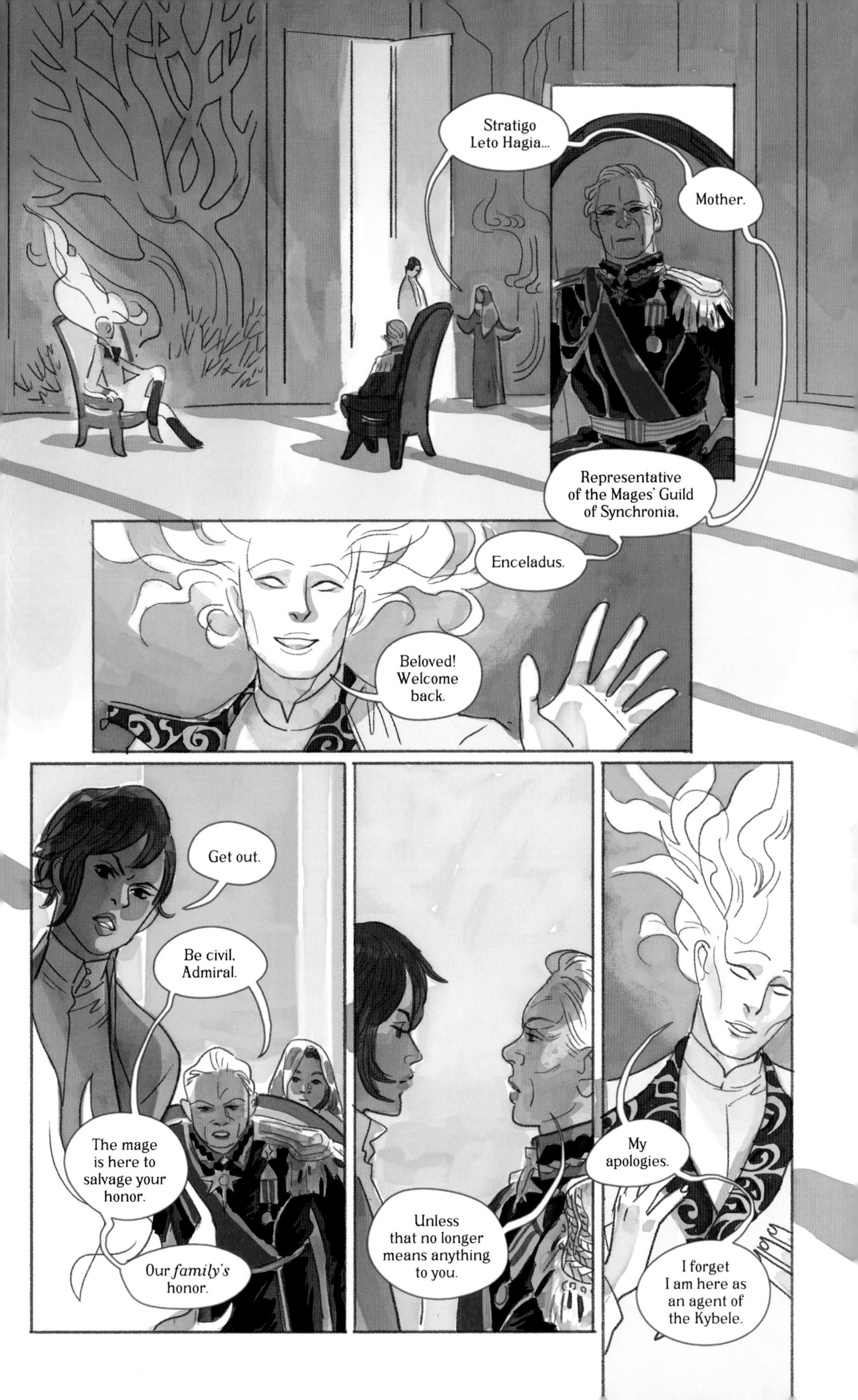
Stratigo Leto Hagia...
Mother.
Representative of the Mages' Guild of Synchronia,
Enceladus.
Beloved! Welcome back.
Get out.
Be civil, Admiral.
The mage is here to salvage your honor.
Our *family's* honor.
Unless that no longer means anything to you.
My apologies.
I forget I am here as an agent of the Kybele.

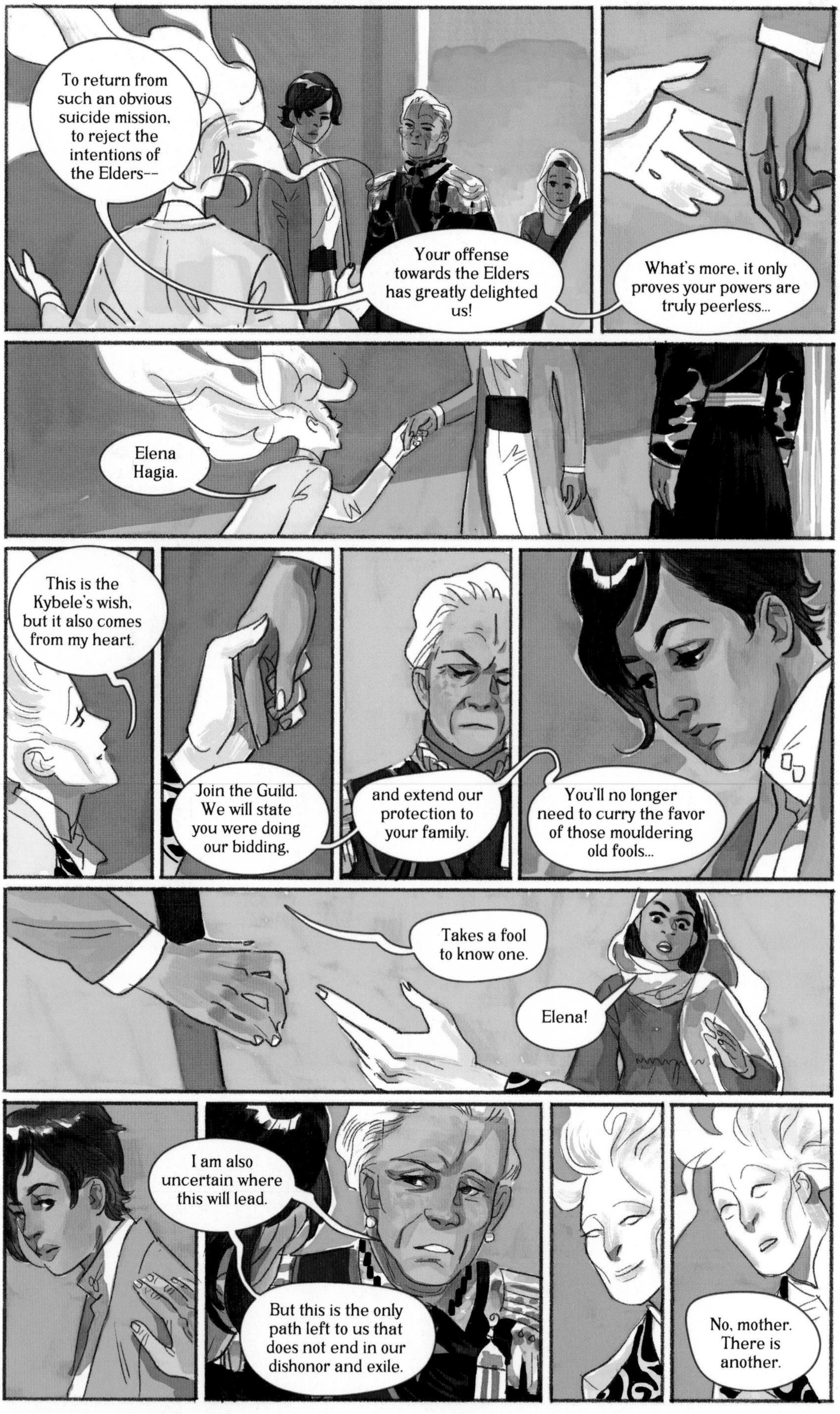
To return from such an obvious suicide mission, to reject the intentions of the Elders--
Your offense towards the Elders has greatly delighted us!
What's more, it only proves your powers are truly peerless...
Elena Hagia.
This is the Kybele's wish, but it also comes from my heart.
Join the Guild. We will state you were doing our bidding,
and extend our protection to your family.
You'll no longer need to curry the favor of those mouldering old fools...
Takes a fool to know one.
Elena!
I am also uncertain where this will lead.
But this is the only path left to us that does not end in our dishonor and exile.
No, mother. There is another.

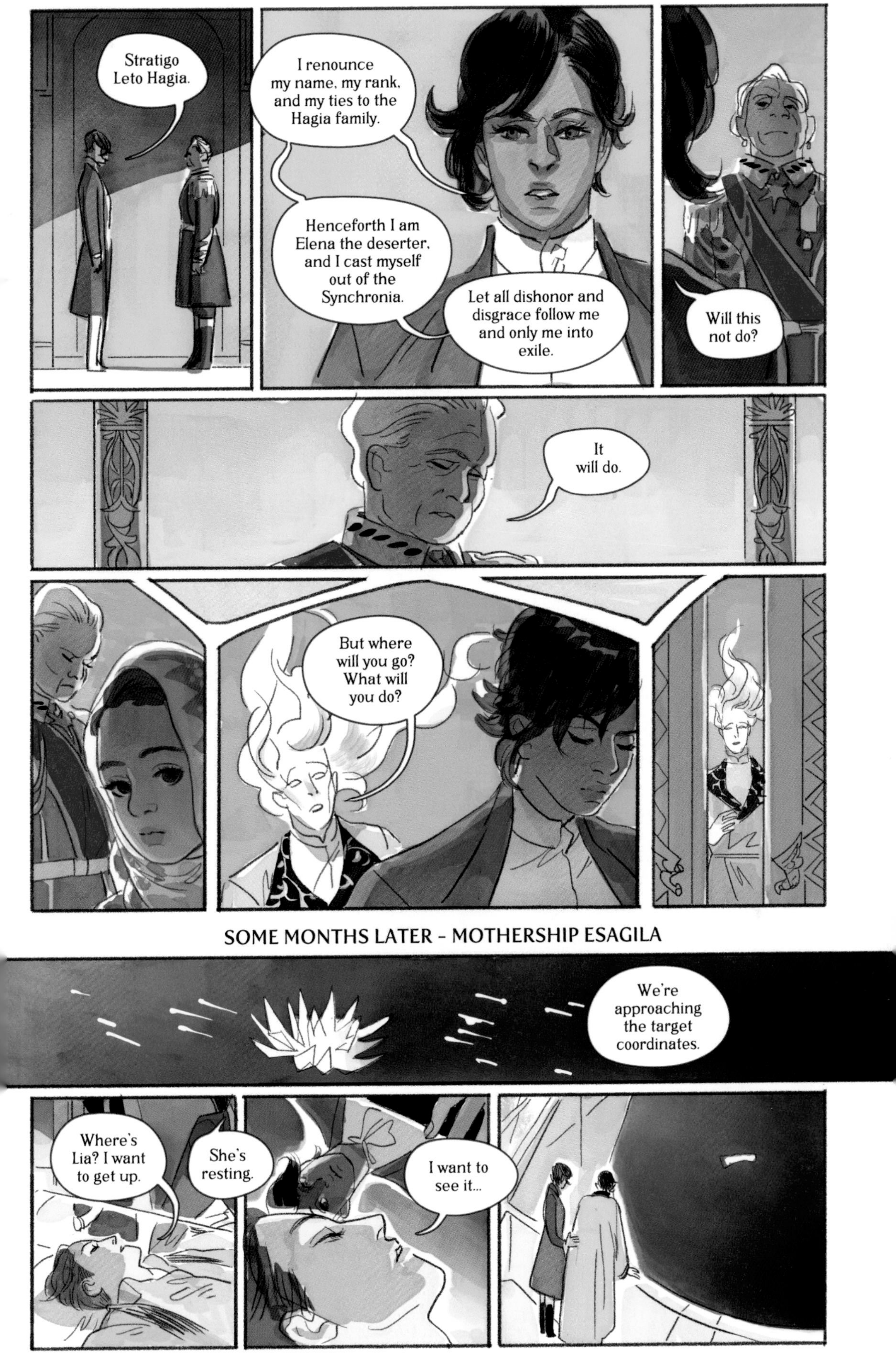
Stratigo Leto Hagia.
I renounce my name, my rank, and my ties to the Hagia family.
Henceforth I am Elena the deserter, and I cast myself out of the Synchronia.
Let all dishonor and disgrace follow me and only me into exile.
Will this not do?
It will do.
But where will you go? What will you do?
SOME MONTHS LATER - MOTHERSHIP ESAGILA
We're approaching the target coordinates.
Where's Lia? I want to get up.
She's resting.
I want to see it...

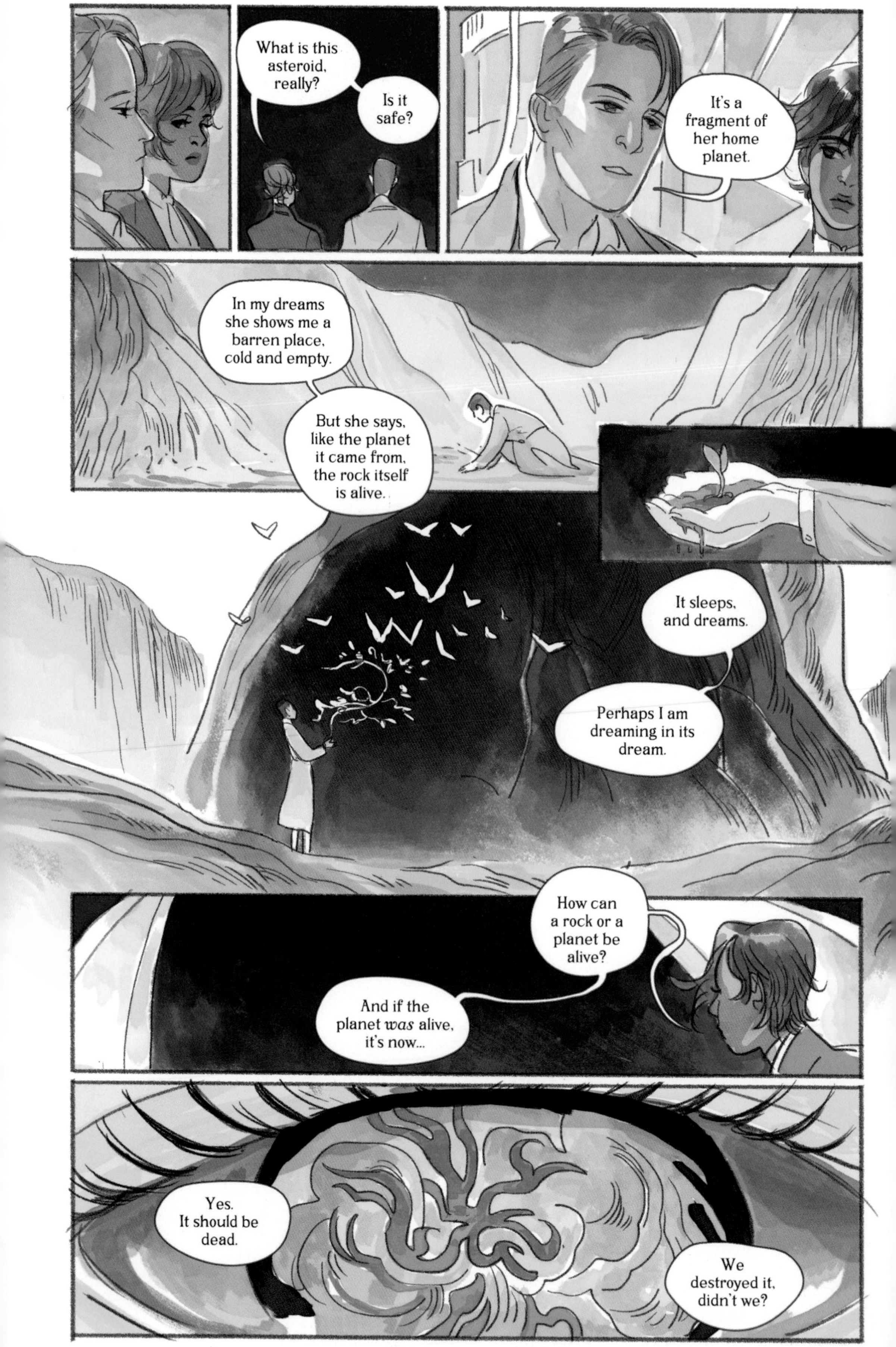
What is this asteroid, really?
Is it safe?
It's a fragment of her home planet.
In my dreams she shows me a barren place, cold and empty.
But she says, like the planet it came from, the rock itself is alive.
It sleeps, and dreams.
Perhaps I am dreaming in its dream.
How can a rock or a planet be alive?
And if the planet *was* alive, it's now...
Yes. It should be dead.
We destroyed it, didn't we?

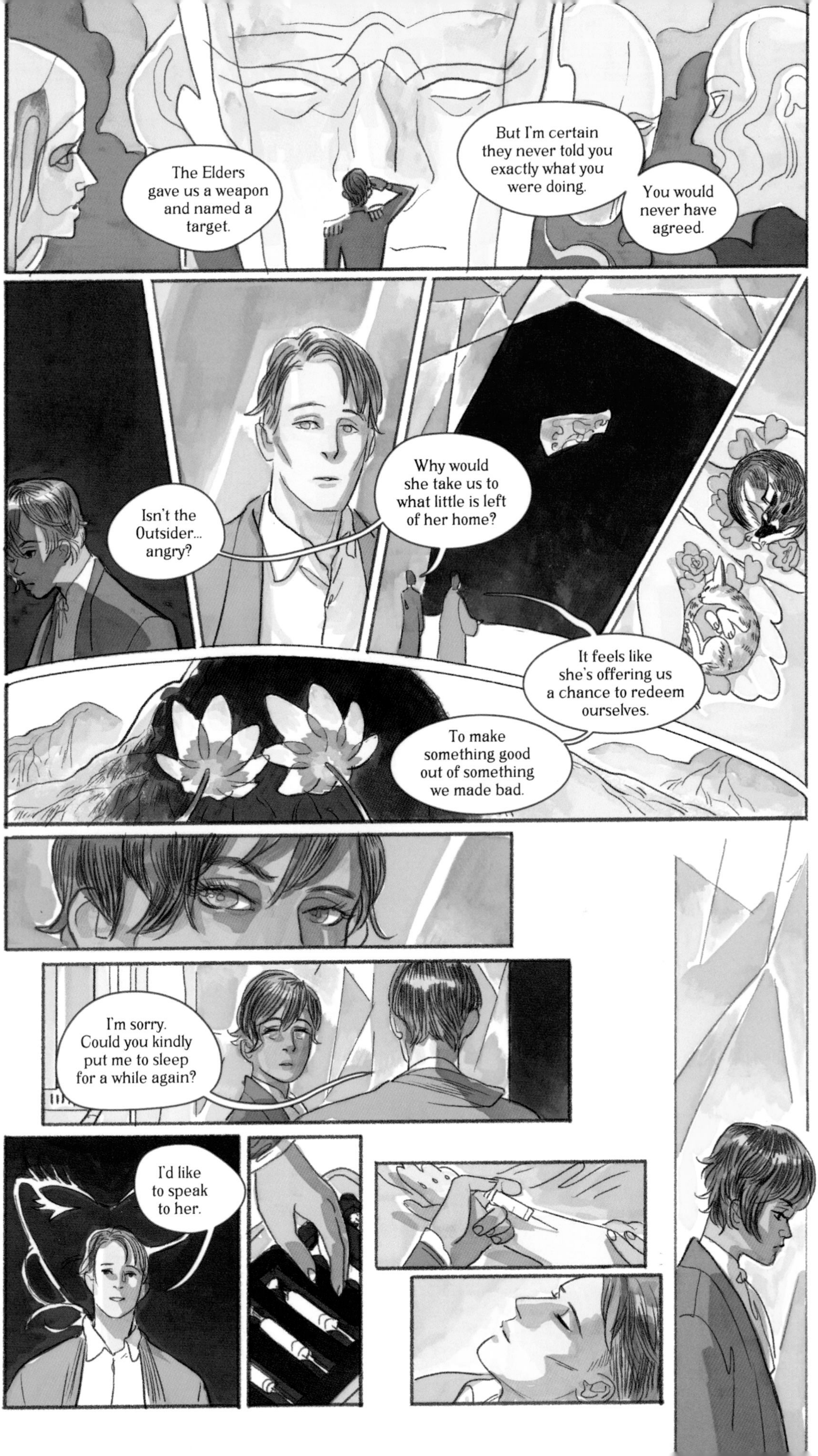
The Elders gave us a weapon and named a target.
But I'm certain they never told you exactly what you were doing.
You would never have agreed.
Isn't the Outsider... angry?
Why would she take us to what little is left of her home?
It feels like she's offering us a chance to redeem ourselves.
To make something good out of something we made bad.
I'm sorry. Could you kindly put me to sleep for a while again?
I'd like to speak to her.

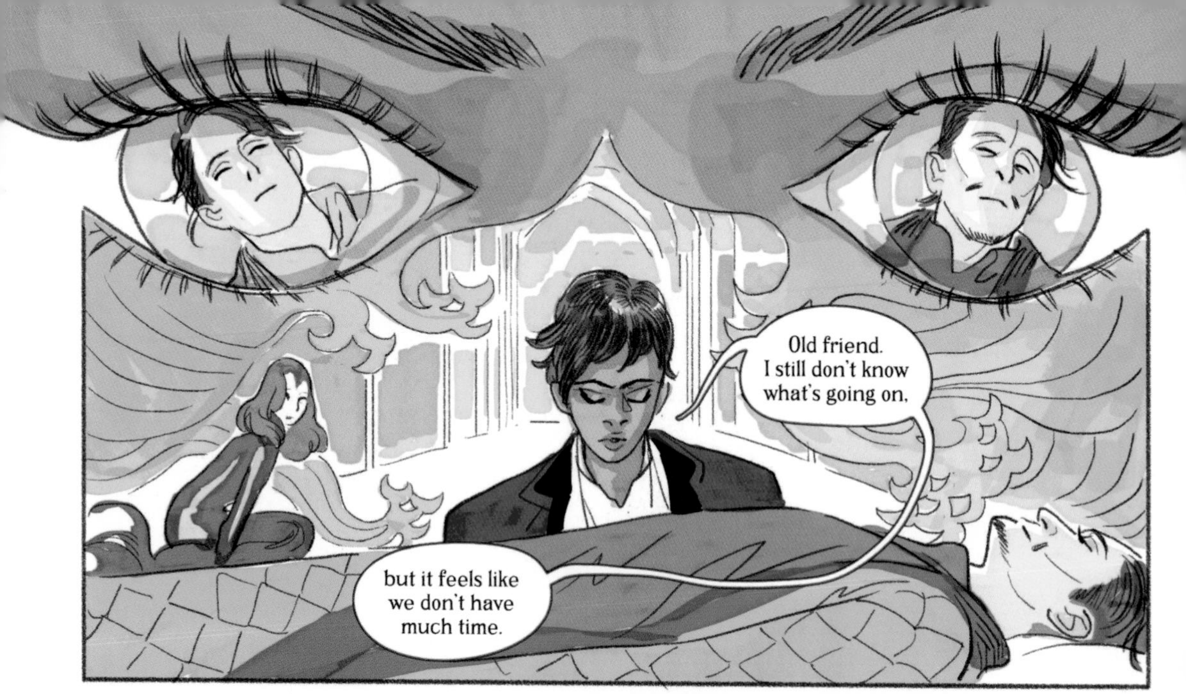
Old friend. I still don't know what's going on,
but it feels like we don't have much time.

Year 35 — Exodus

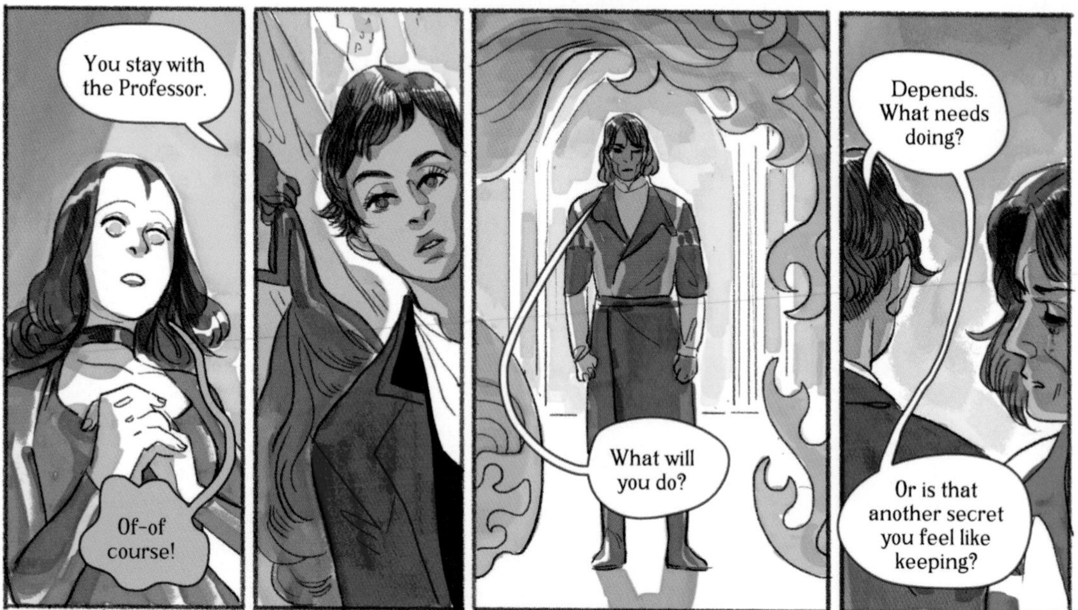
You stay with the Professor.
Of-of course!
What will you do?
Depends. What needs doing?
Or is that another secret you feel like keeping?

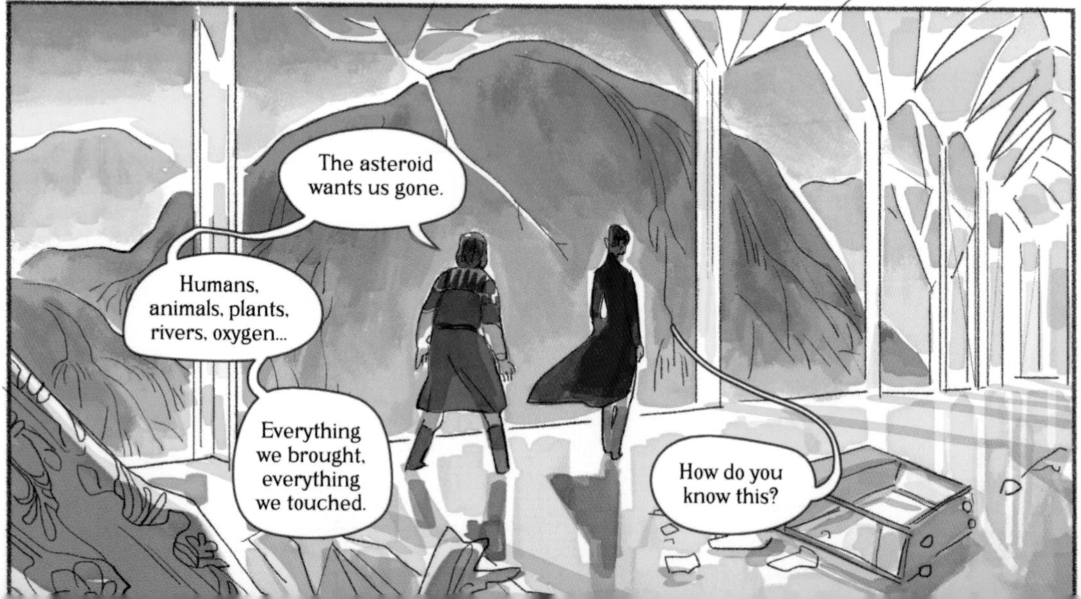
The asteroid wants us gone.
Humans, animals, plants, rivers, oxygen...
Everything we brought, everything we touched.
How do you know this?

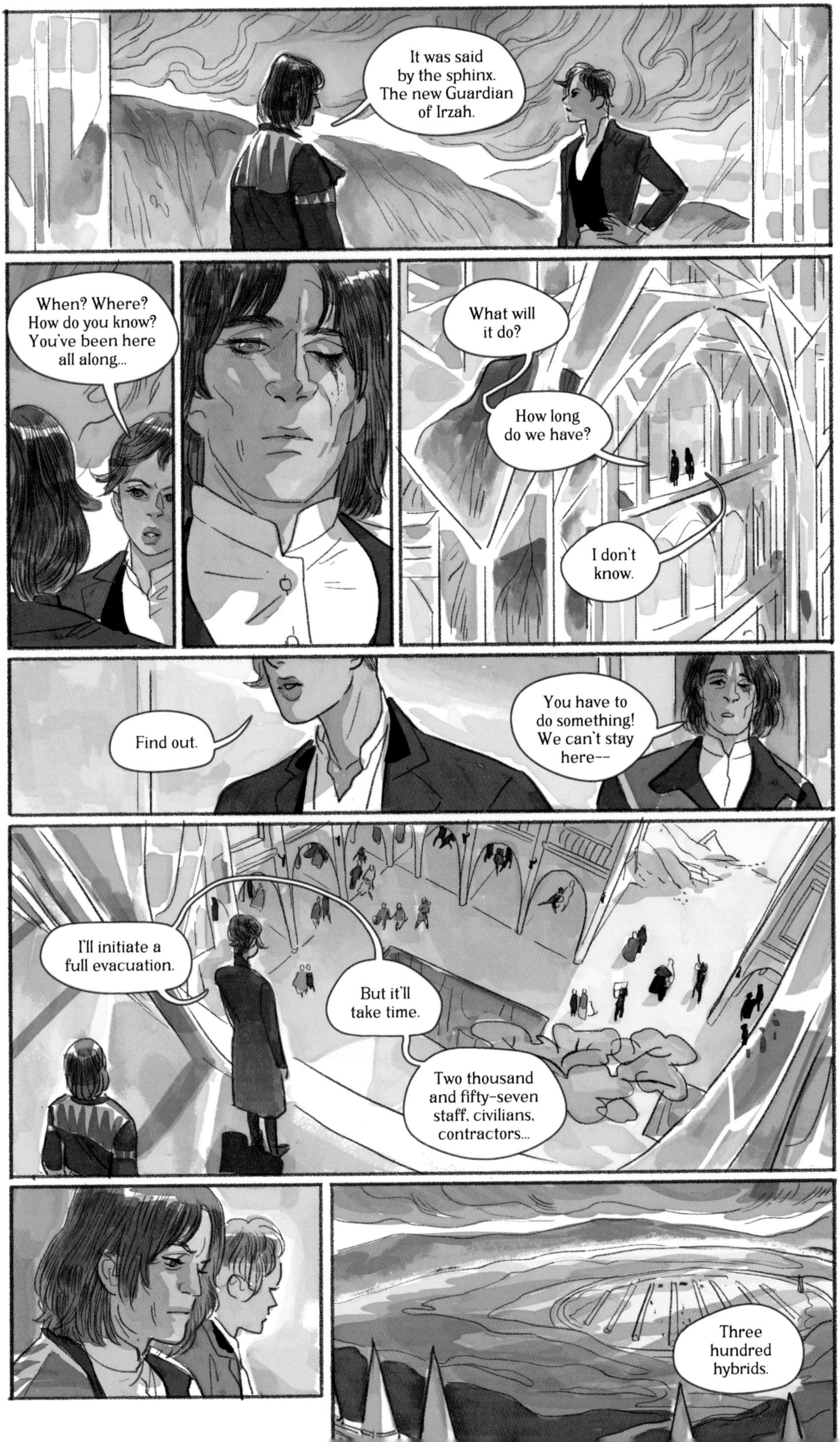
It was said by the sphinx. The new Guardian of Irzah.
When? Where? How do you know? You've been here all along...
What will it do?
How long do we have?
I don't know.
Find out.
You have to do something! We can't stay here--
I'll initiate a full evacuation.
But it'll take time.
Two thousand and fifty-seven staff, civilians, contractors...
Three hundred hybrids.

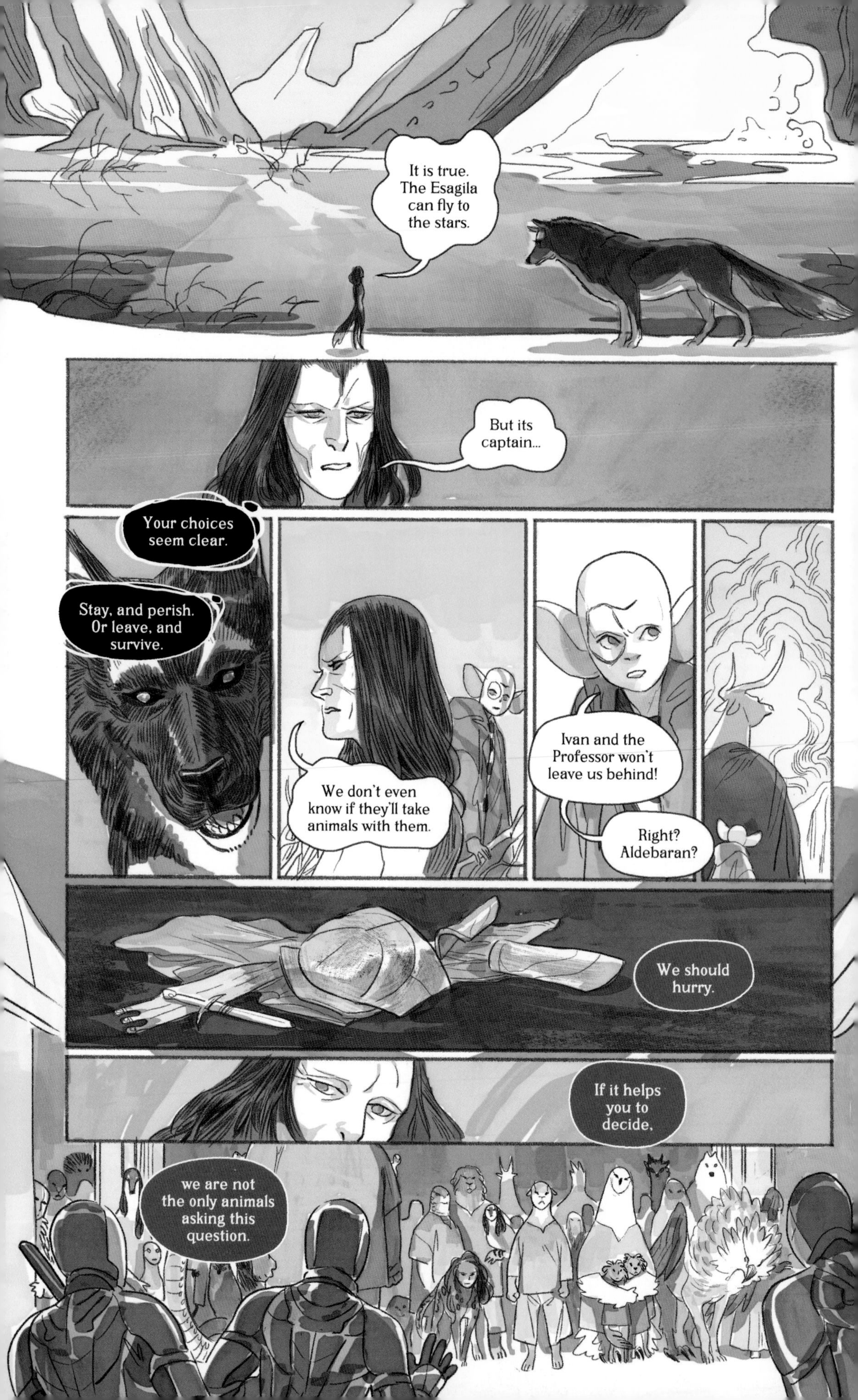
It is true. The Esagila can fly to the stars.
But its captain...
Your choices seem clear.
Stay, and perish. Or leave, and survive.
We don't even know if they'll take animals with them.
Ivan and the Professor won't leave us behind!
Right? Aldebaran?
We should hurry.
If it helps you to decide,
we are not the only animals asking this question.

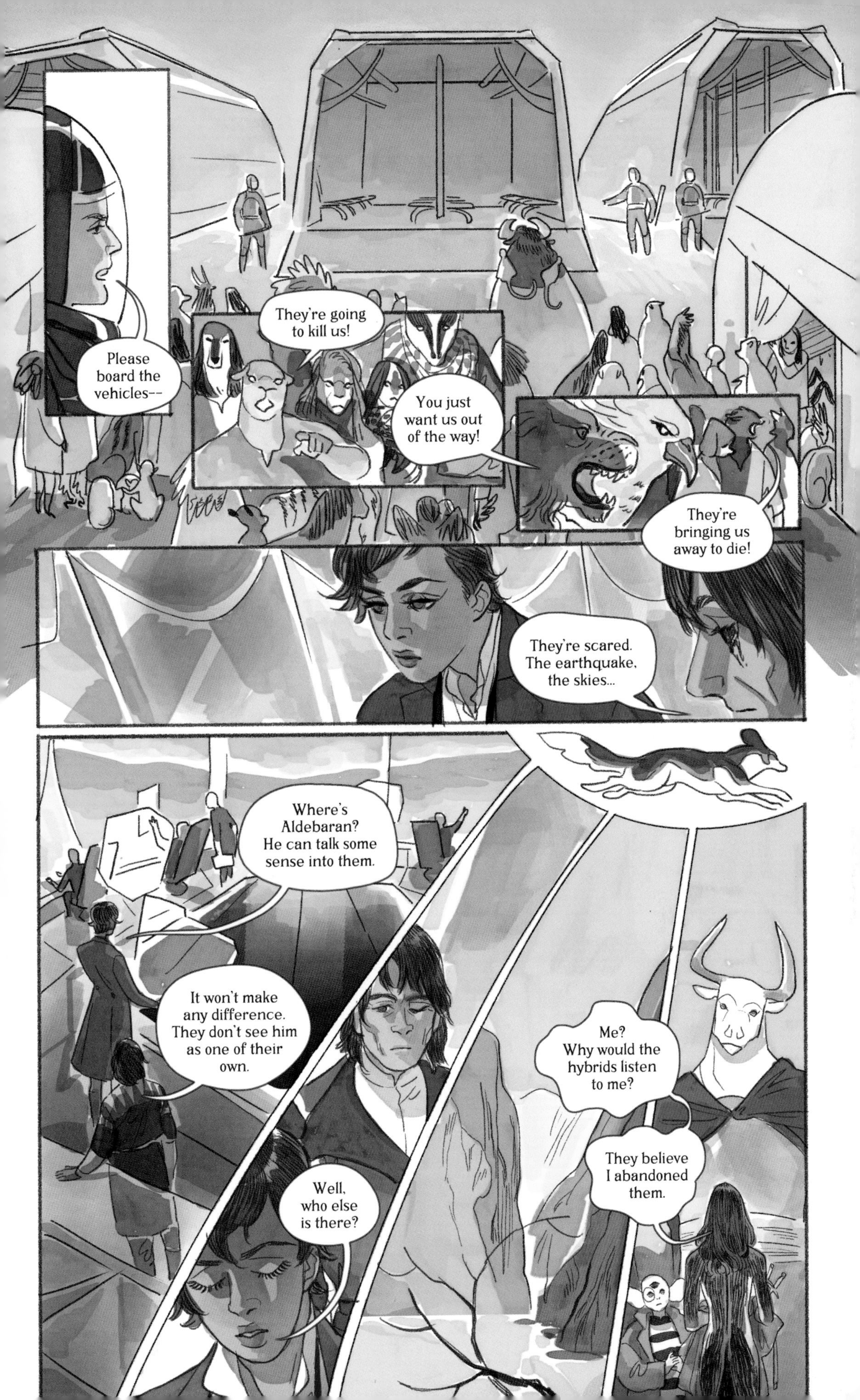
Please board the vehicles--
They're going to kill us!
You just want us out of the way!
They're bringing us away to die!
They're scared. The earthquake, the skies...
Where's Aldebaran? He can talk some sense into them.
It won't make any difference. They don't see him as one of their own.
Me? Why would the hybrids listen to me?
They believe I abandoned them.
Well, who else is there?

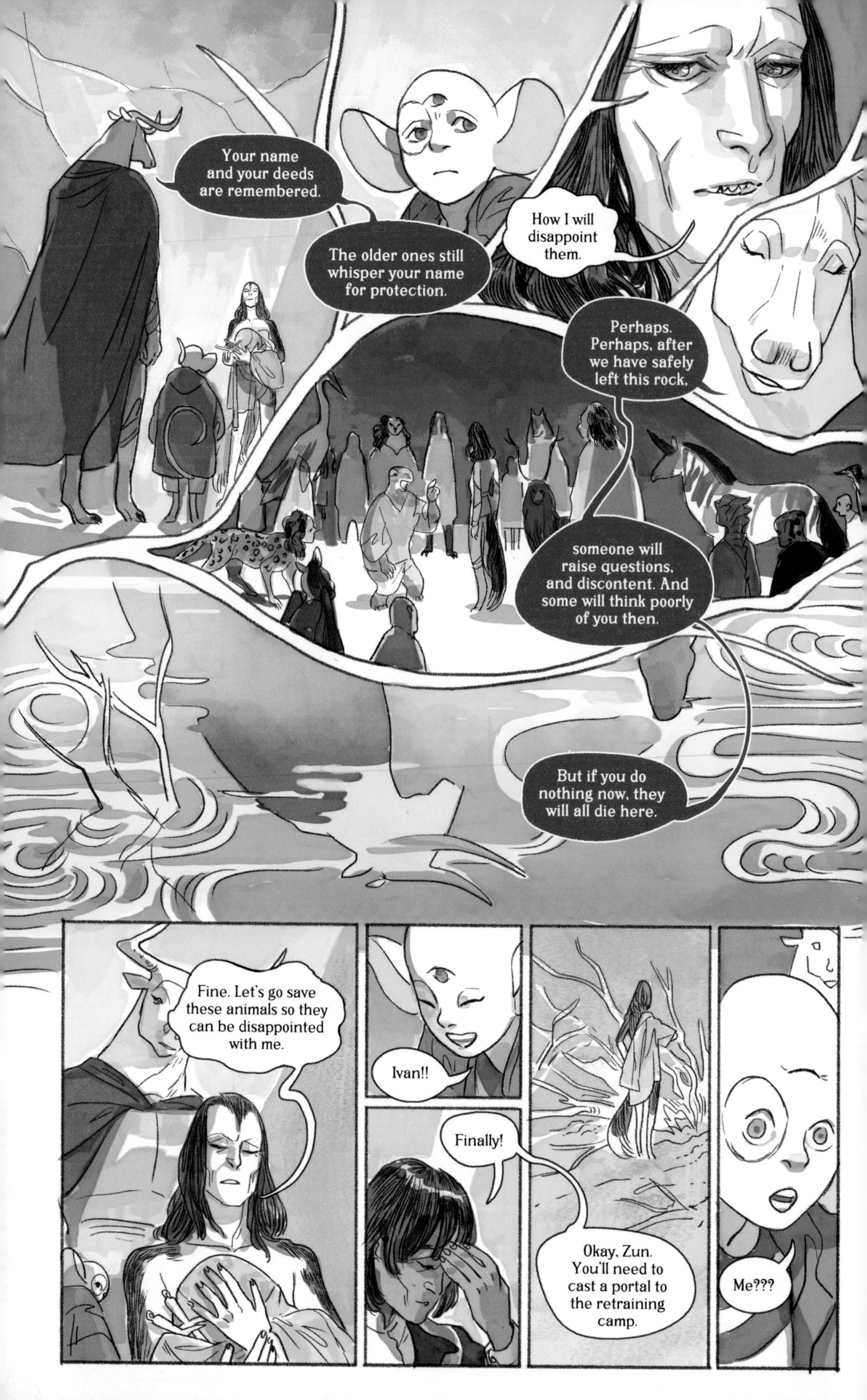
Your name and your deeds are remembered.
The older ones still whisper your name for protection.
How I will disappoint them.
Perhaps. Perhaps, after we have safely left this rock,
someone will raise questions, and discontent. And some will think poorly of you then.
But if you do nothing now, they will all die here.
Fine. Let's go save these animals so they can be disappointed with me.
Ivan!!
Finally!
Okay, Zun. You'll need to cast a portal to the retraining camp.
Me???

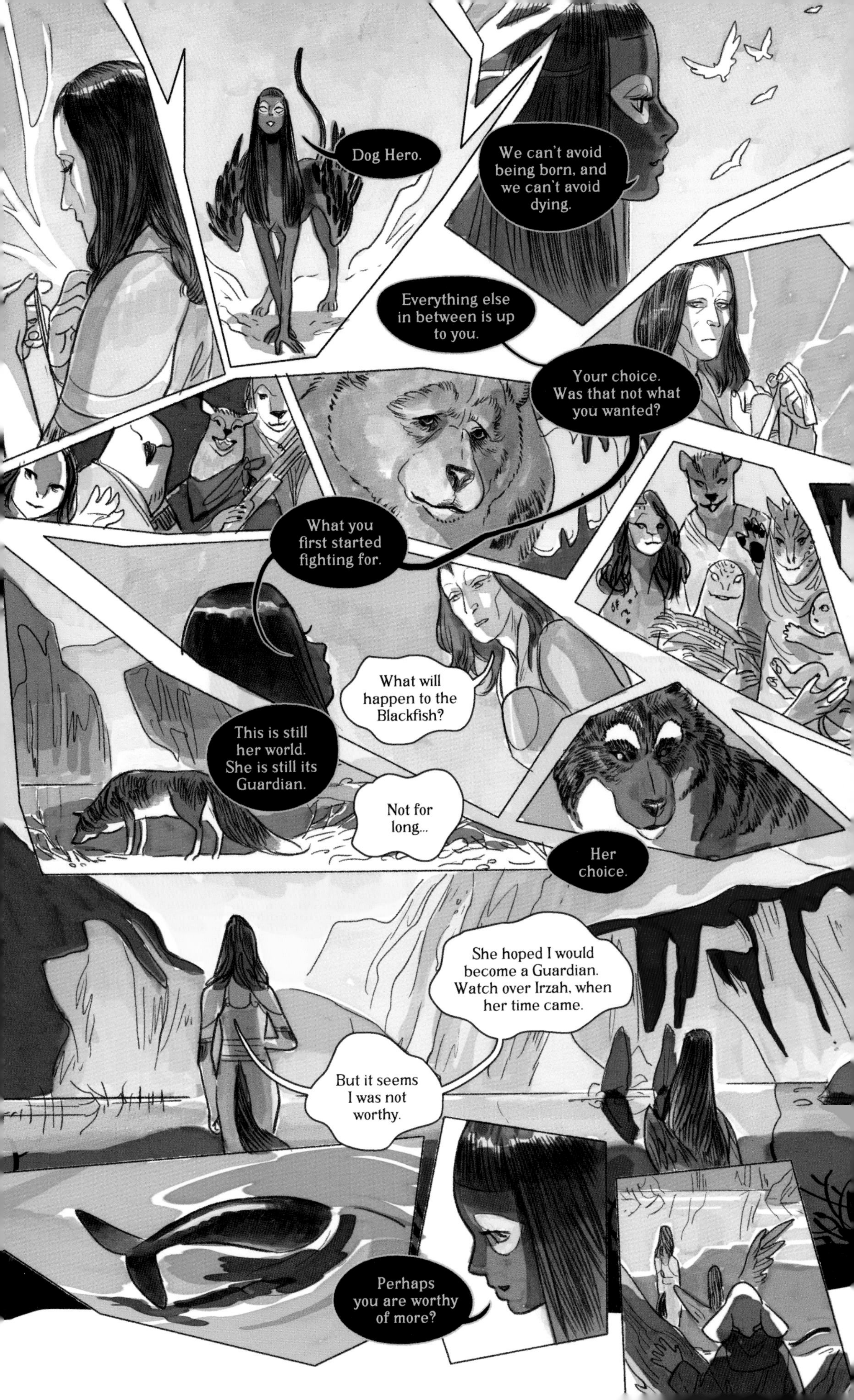
Dog Hero.
We can't avoid being born, and we can't avoid dying.
Everything else in between is up to you.
Your choice. Was that not what you wanted?
What you first started fighting for.
What will happen to the Blackfish?
This is still her world. She is still its Guardian.
Not for long...
Her choice.
She hoped I would become a Guardian. Watch over Irzah, when her time came.
But it seems I was not worthy.
Perhaps you are worthy of more?

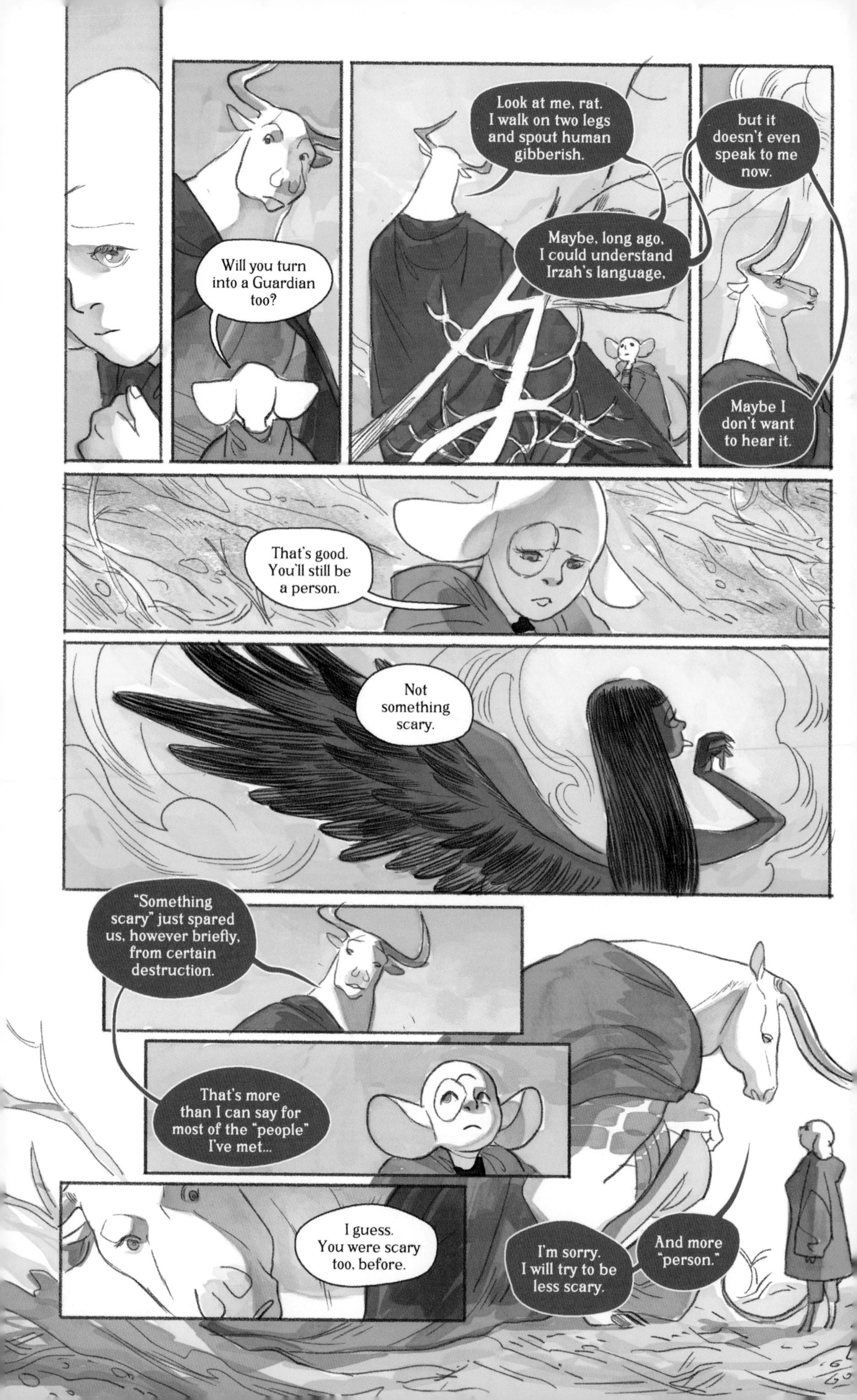
Will you turn into a Guardian too?
Look at me, rat. I walk on two legs and spout human gibberish.
Maybe, long ago, I could understand Irzah's language,
but it doesn't even speak to me now.
Maybe I don't want to hear it.
That's good. You'll still be a person.
Not something scary.
"Something scary" just spared us, however briefly, from certain destruction.
That's more than I can say for most of the "people" I've met...
I guess. You were scary too, before.
I'm sorry. I will try to be less scary.
And more "person."

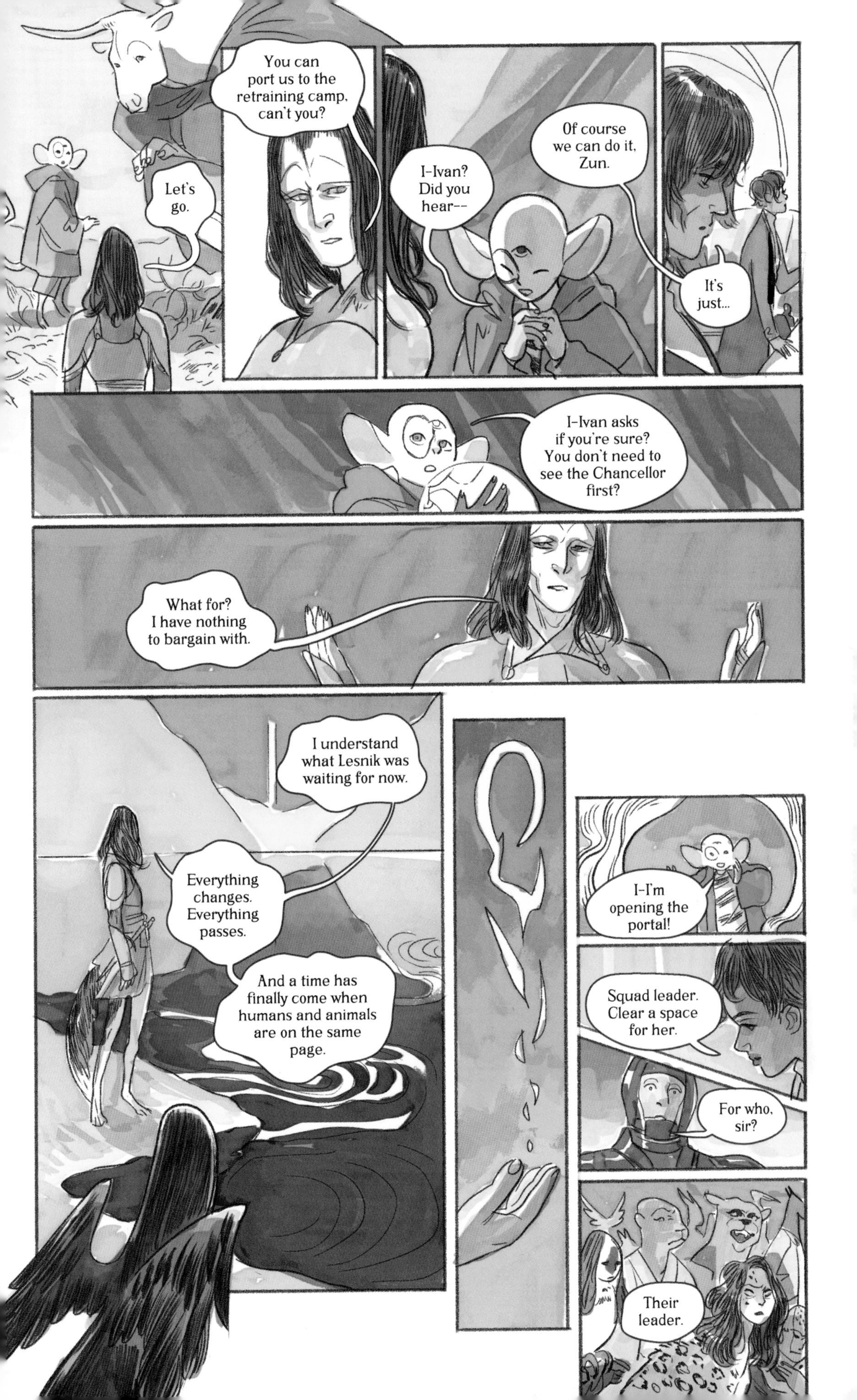
Let's go.
You can port us to the retraining camp, can't you?
I-Ivan? Did you hear--
Of course we can do it, Zun.
It's just...
I-Ivan asks if you're sure? You don't need to see the Chancellor first?
What for? I have nothing to bargain with.
I understand what Lesnik was waiting for now.
Everything changes. Everything passes.
And a time has finally come when humans and animals are on the same page.
I-I'm opening the portal!
Squad leader. Clear a space for her.
For who, sir?
Their leader.

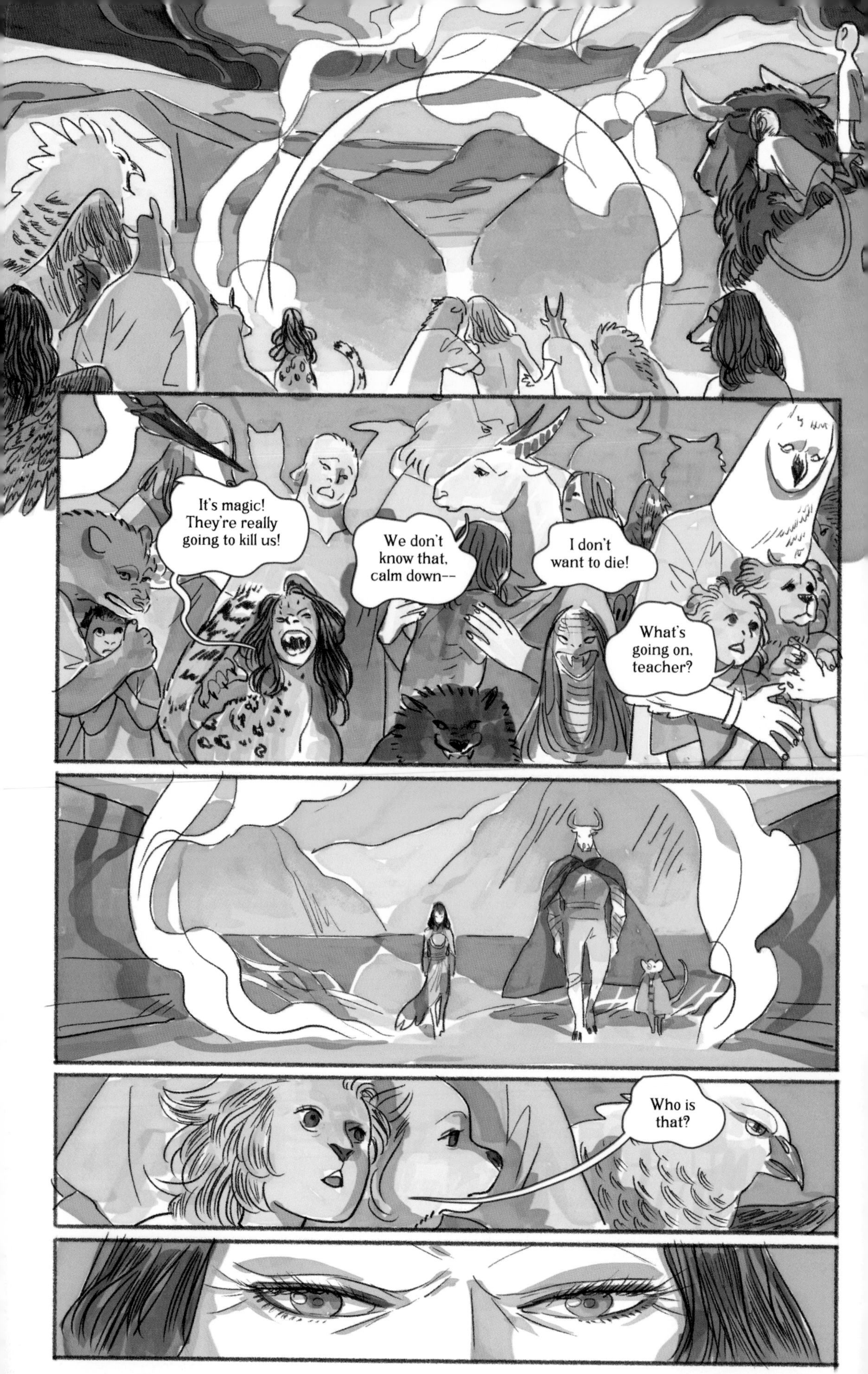
It's magic! They're really going to kill us!
We don't know that, calm down--
I don't want to die!
What's going on, teacher?
Who is that?

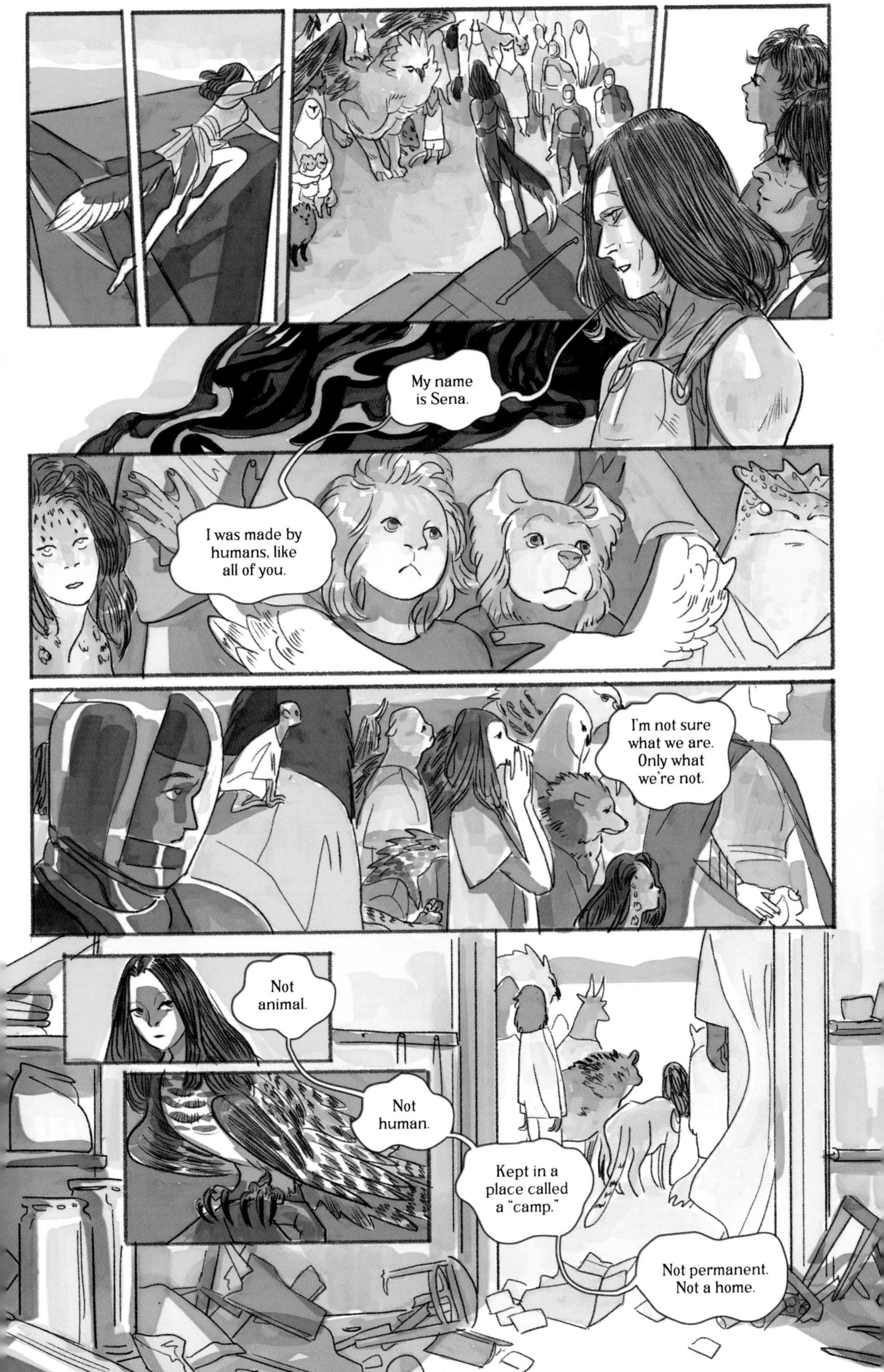
My name is Sena.
I was made by humans, like all of you.
I'm not sure what we are. Only what we're not.
Not animal.
Not human.
Kept in a place called a "camp."
Not permanent. Not a home.

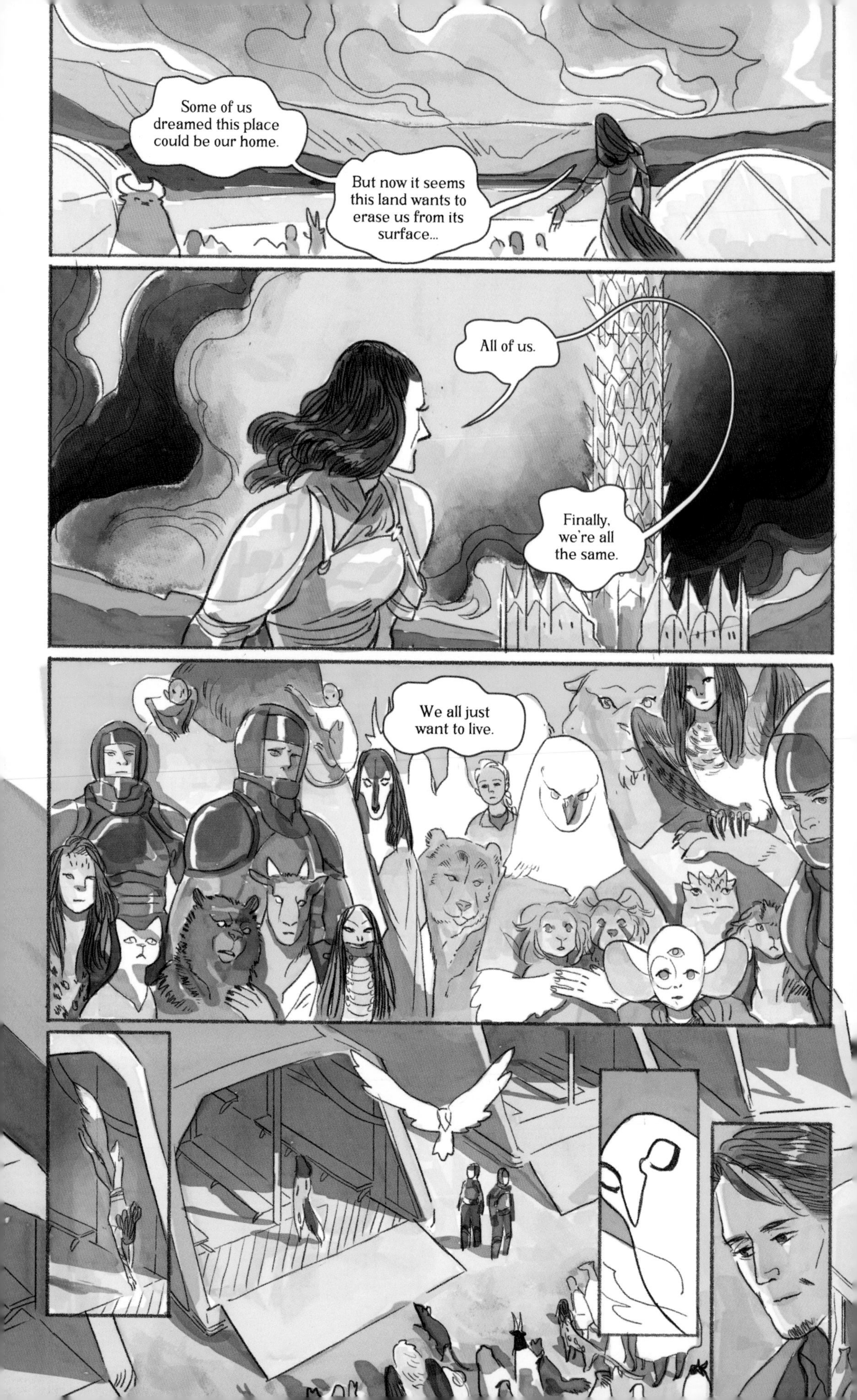
Some of us dreamed this place could be our home.
But now it seems this land wants to erase us from its surface...
All of us.
Finally, we're all the same.
We all just want to live.

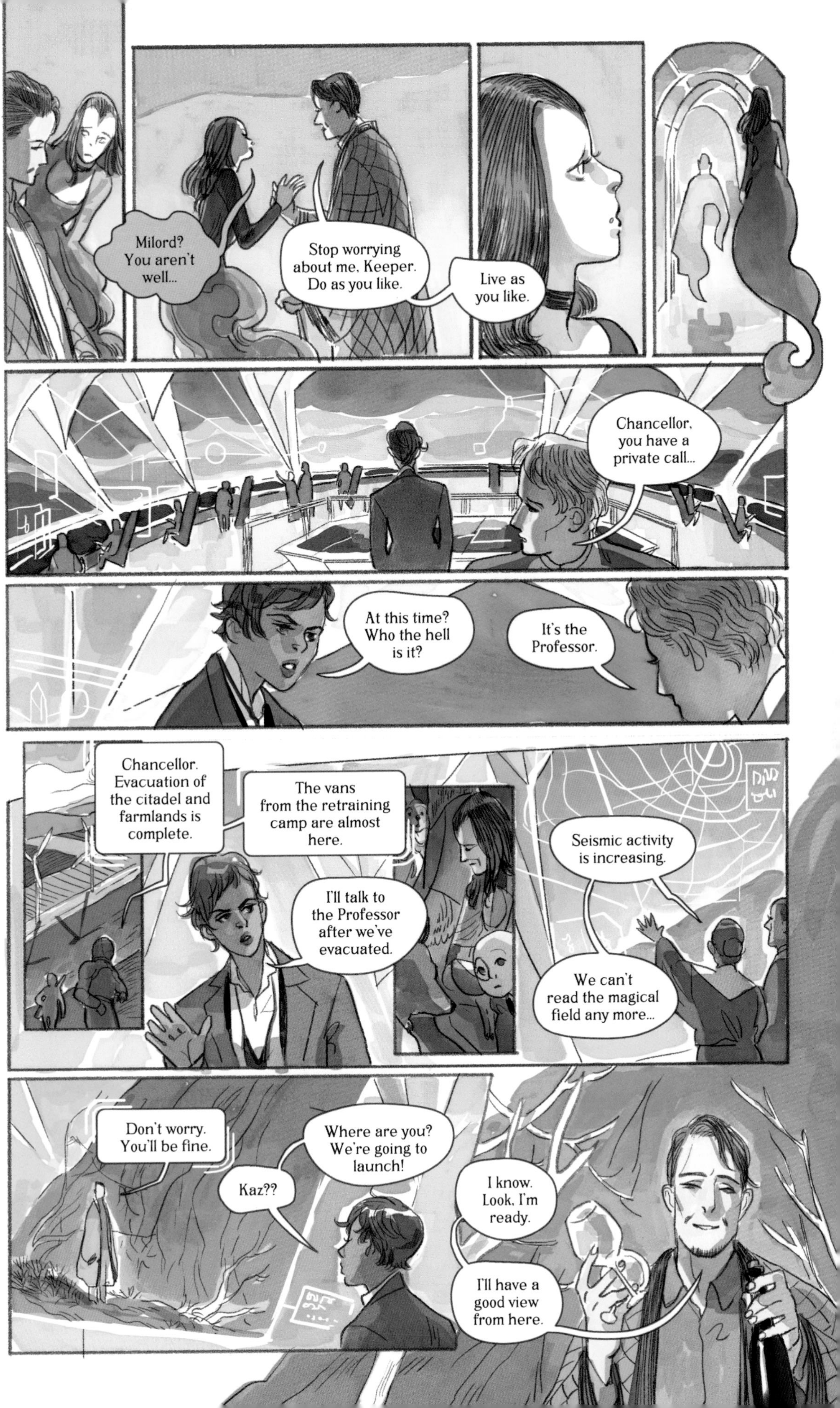
Milord? You aren't well...
Stop worrying about me, Keeper. Do as you like.
Live as you like.
Chancellor, you have a private call...
At this time? Who the hell is it?
It's the Professor.
Chancellor. Evacuation of the citadel and farmlands is complete.
The vans from the retraining camp are almost here.
I'll talk to the Professor after we've evacuated.
Seismic activity is increasing.
We can't read the magical field any more...
Don't worry. You'll be fine.
Kaz??
Where are you? We're going to launch!
I know. Look, I'm ready.
I'll have a good view from here.

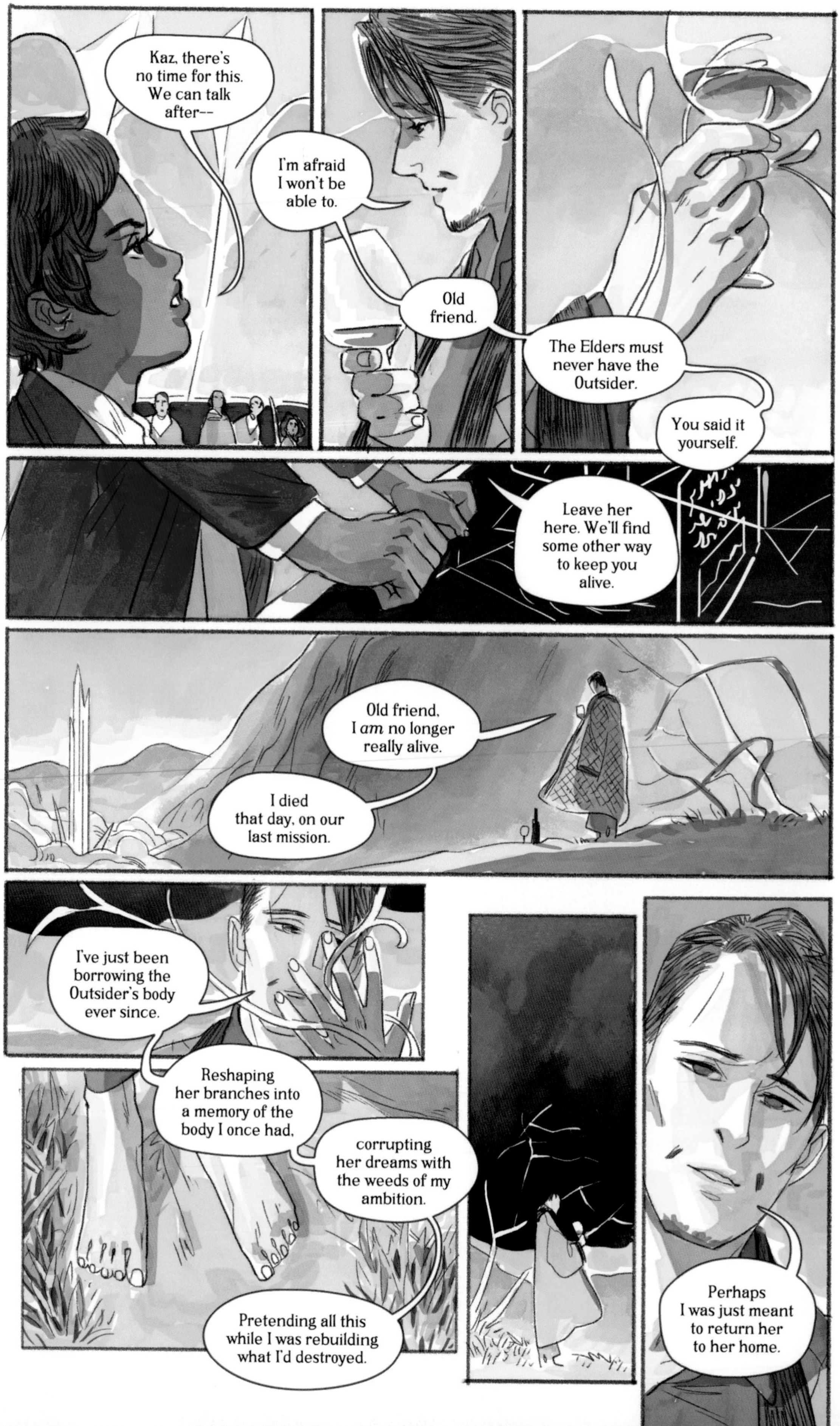
Kaz, there's no time for this. We can talk after--
I'm afraid I won't be able to.
Old friend.
The Elders must never have the Outsider.
You said it yourself.
Leave her here. We'll find some other way to keep you alive.
Old friend, I *am* no longer really alive.
I died that day, on our last mission.
I've just been borrowing the Outsider's body ever since.
Reshaping her branches into a memory of the body I once had,
corrupting her dreams with the weeds of my ambition.
Pretending all this while I was rebuilding what I'd destroyed.
Perhaps I was just meant to return her to her home.

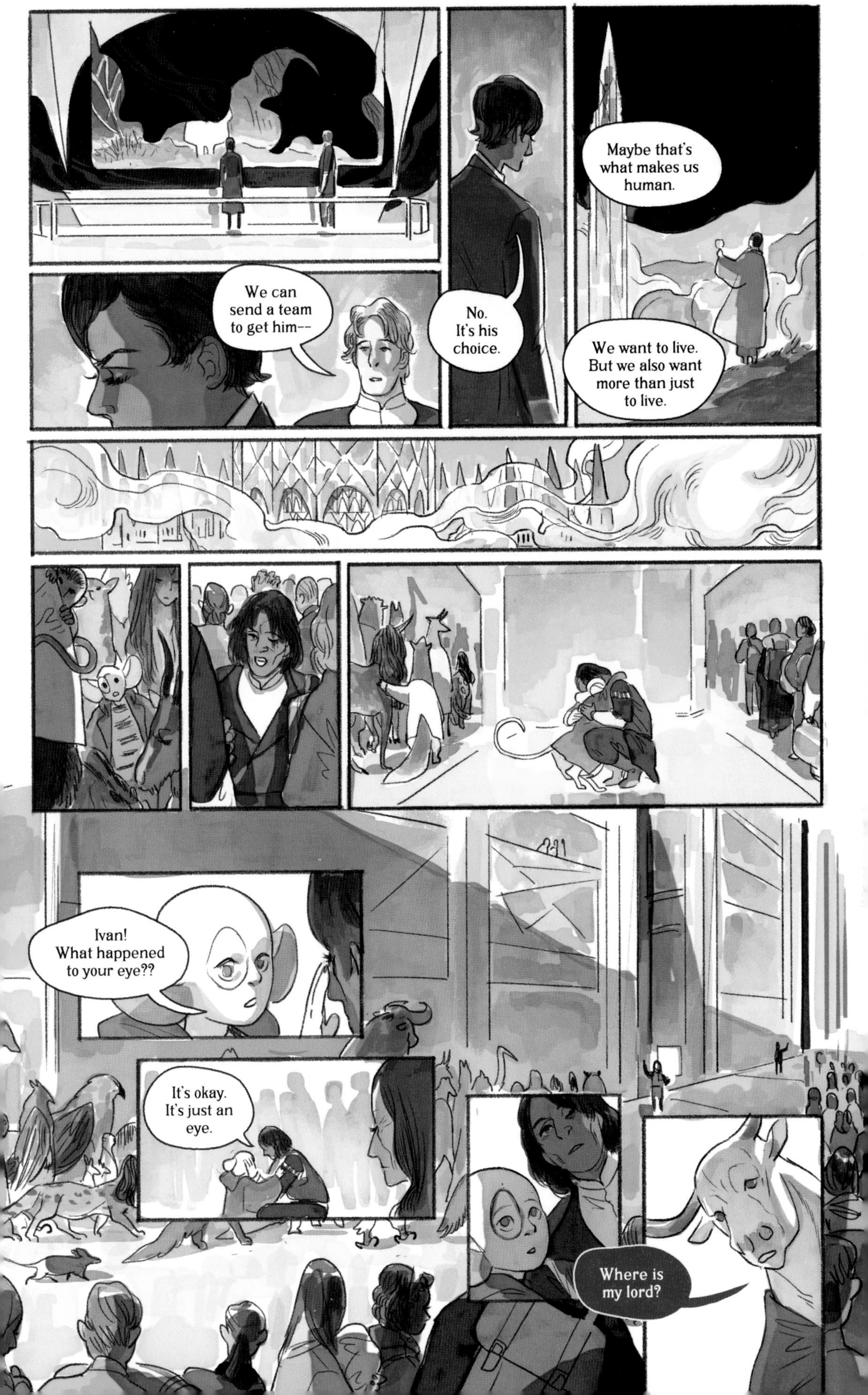

We can send a team to get him--
No. It's his choice.
Maybe that's what makes us human.
We want to live. But we also want more than just to live.
Ivan! What happened to your eye??
It's okay. It's just an eye.
Where is my lord?

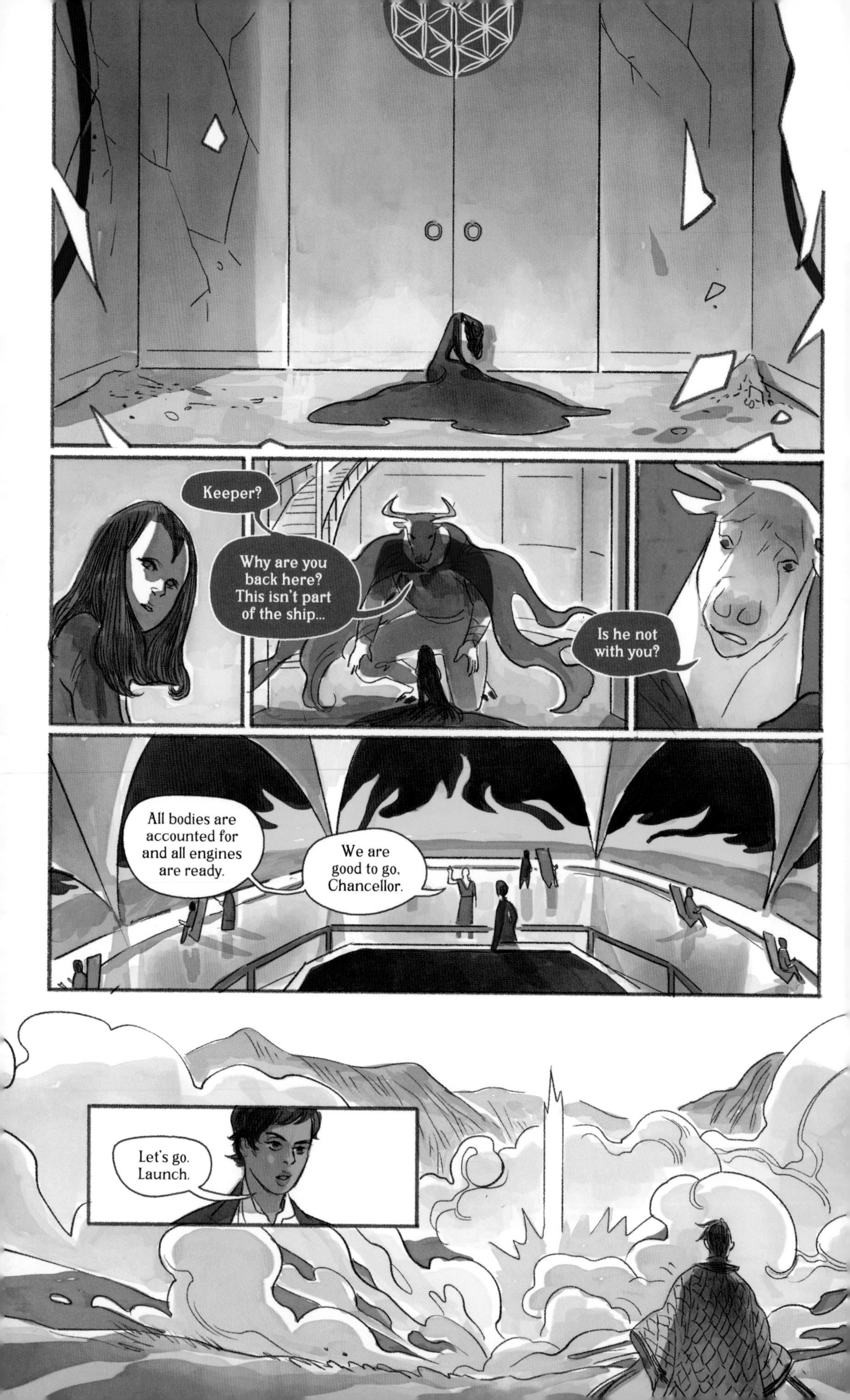
Keeper?
Why are you back here? This isn't part of the ship...
Is he not with you?
All bodies are accounted for and all engines are ready.
We are good to go, Chancellor.
Let's go. Launch.

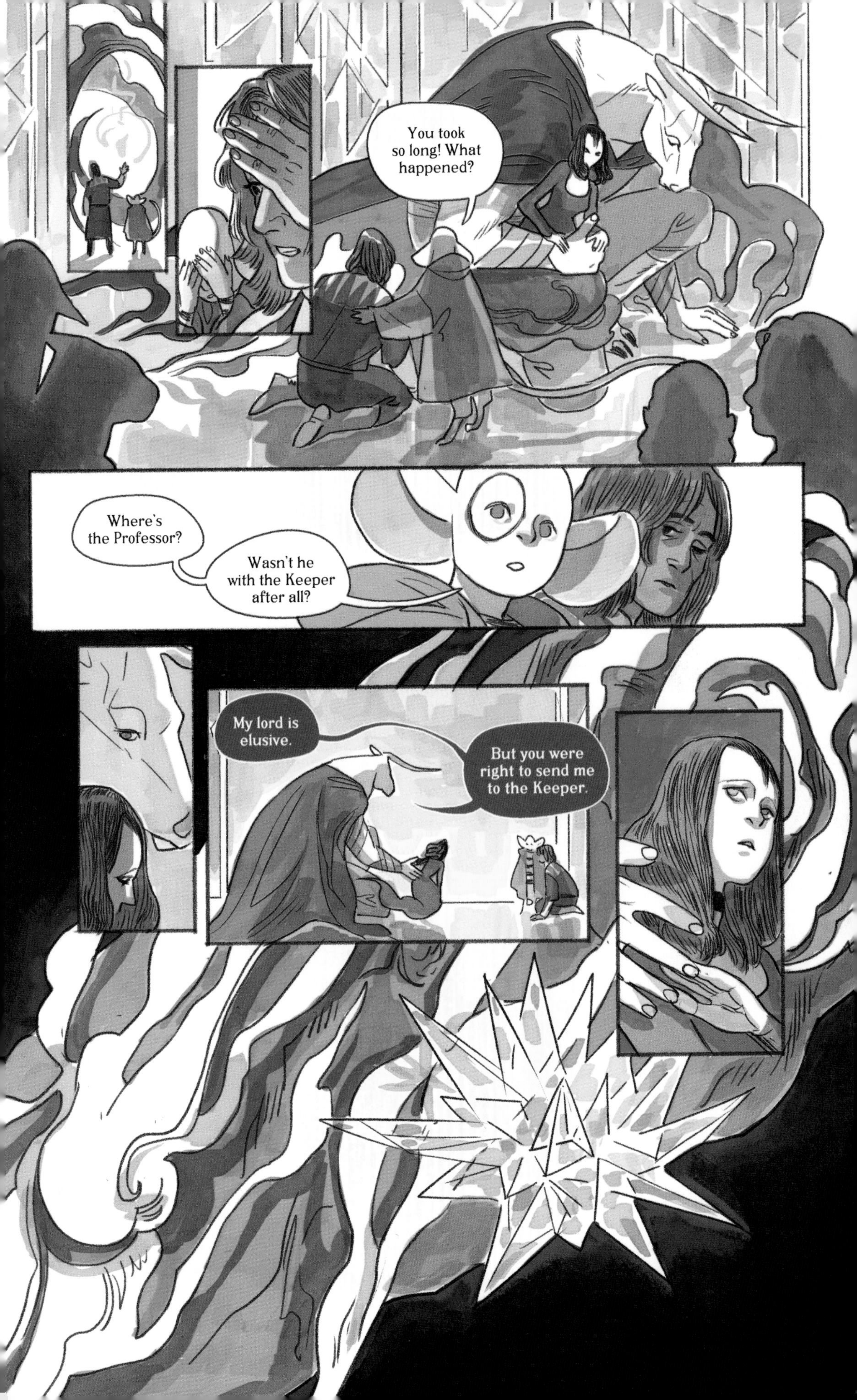

You took so long! What happened?
Where's the Professor?
Wasn't he with the Keeper after all?
My lord is elusive.
But you were right to send me to the Keeper.

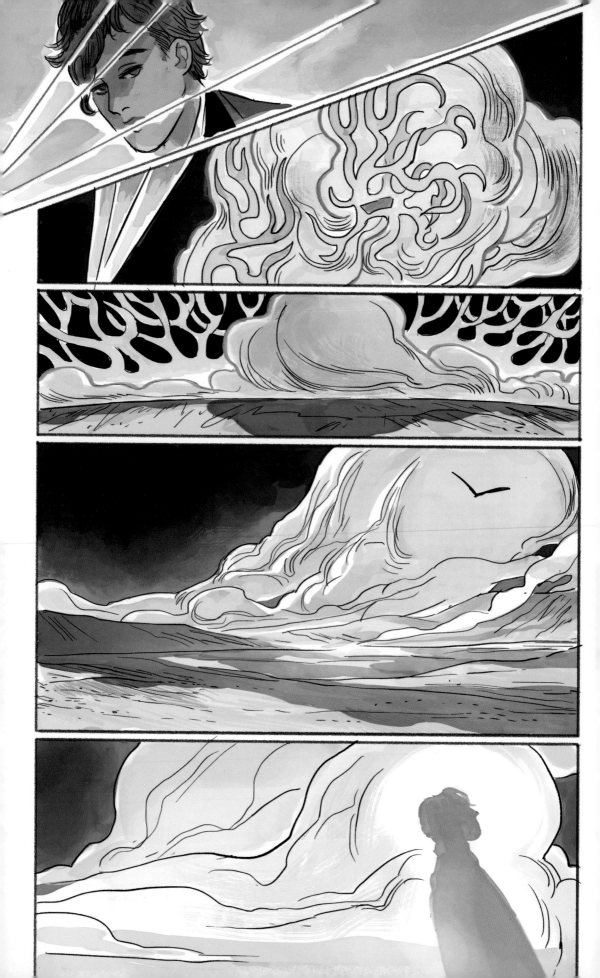

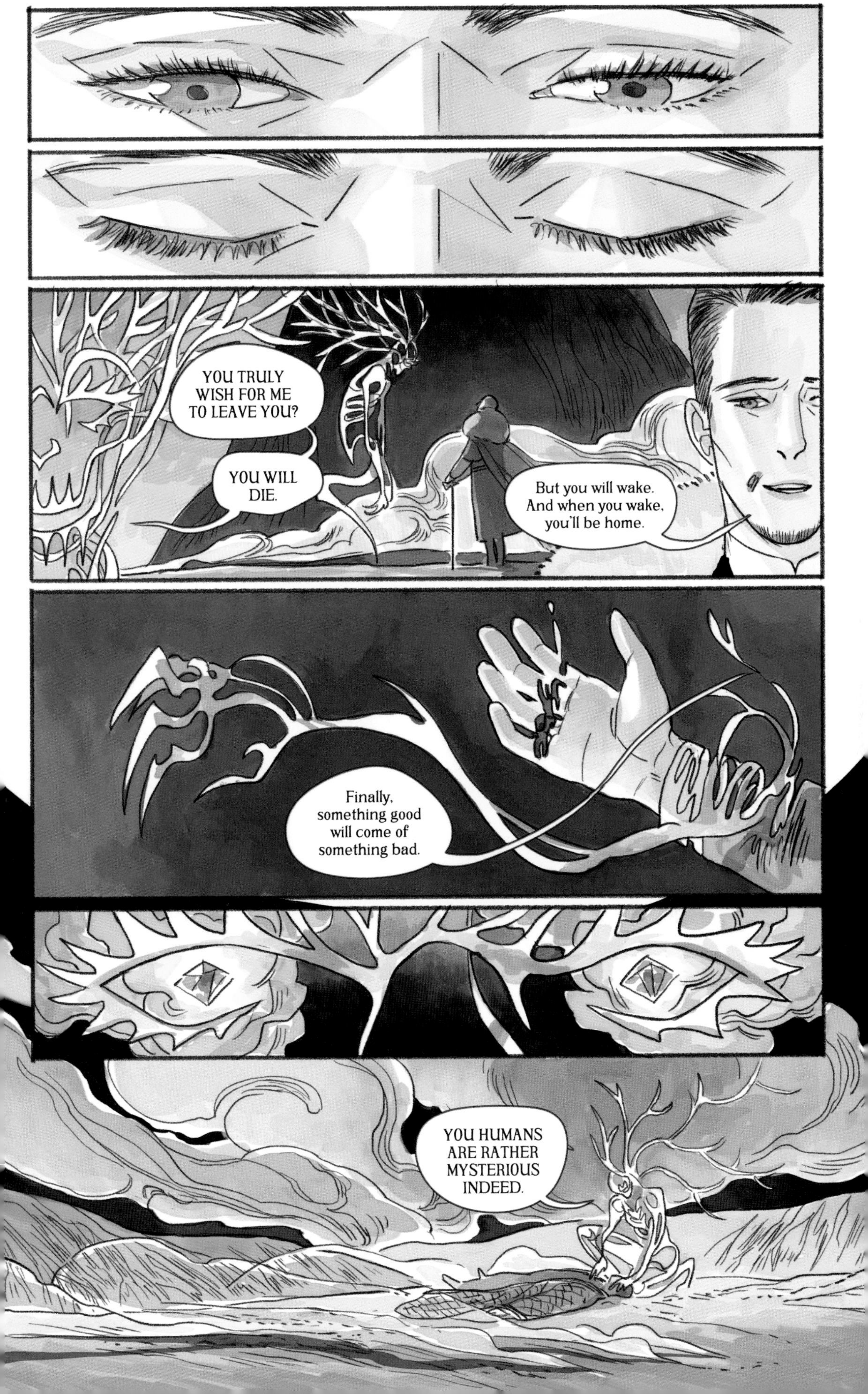
YOU TRULY WISH FOR ME TO LEAVE YOU?
YOU WILL DIE.
But you will wake. And when you wake, you'll be home.
Finally, something good will come of something bad.
YOU HUMANS ARE RATHER MYSTERIOUS INDEED.

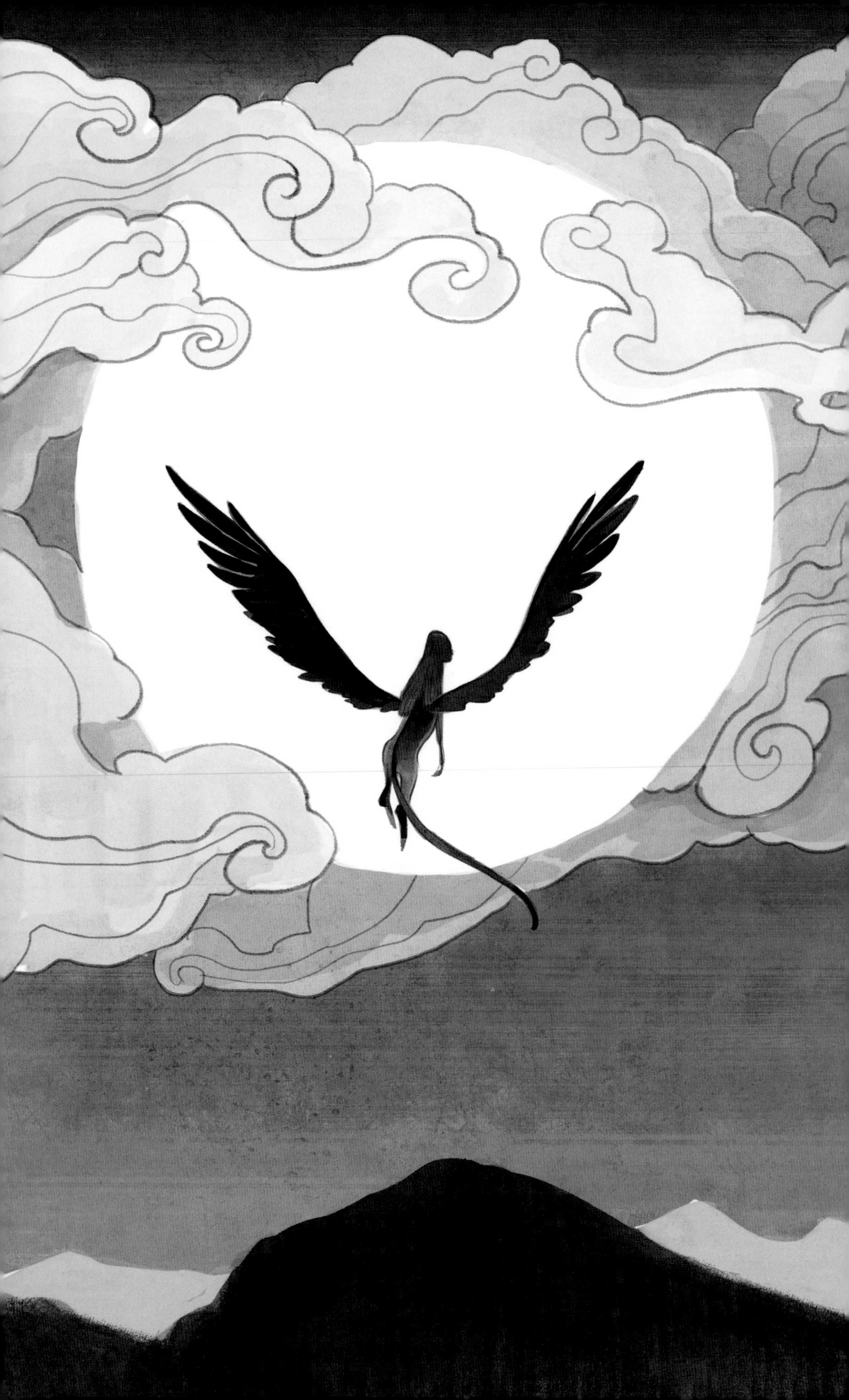

Mini Comics

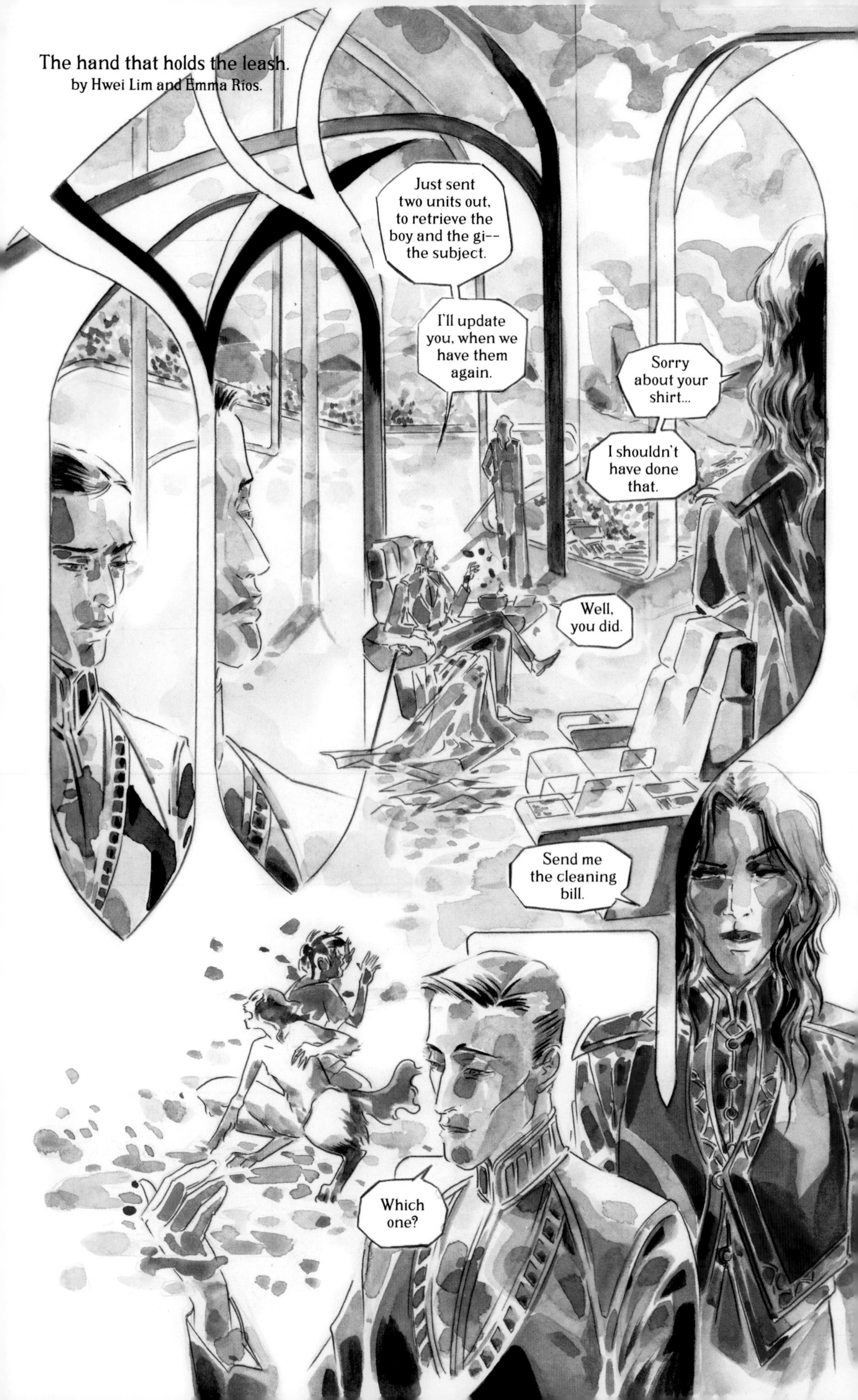
The hand that holds the leash.
by Hwei Lim and Emma Ríos.
Just sent two units out, to retrieve the boy and the gi-- the subject.
I'll update you, when we have them again.
Sorry about your shirt...
I shouldn't have done that.
Well, you did.
Send me the cleaning bill.
Which one?

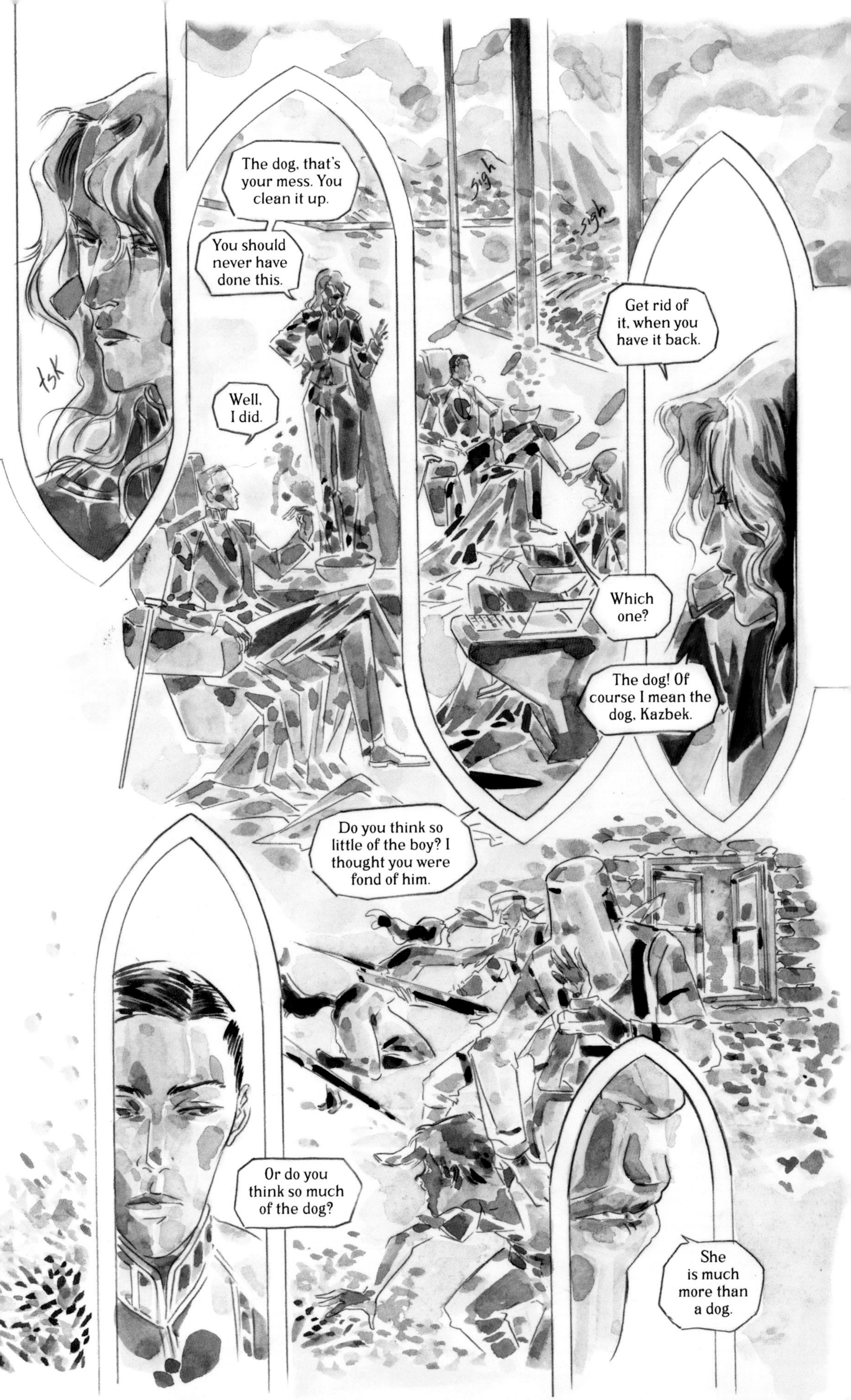
tsk
The dog, that's your mess. You clean it up.
You should never have done this.
Well, I did.
sigh
sigh
Get rid of it, when you have it back.
Which one?
The dog! Of course I mean the dog, Kazbek.
Do you think so little of the boy? I thought you were fond of him.
Or do you think so much of the dog?
She is much more than a dog.

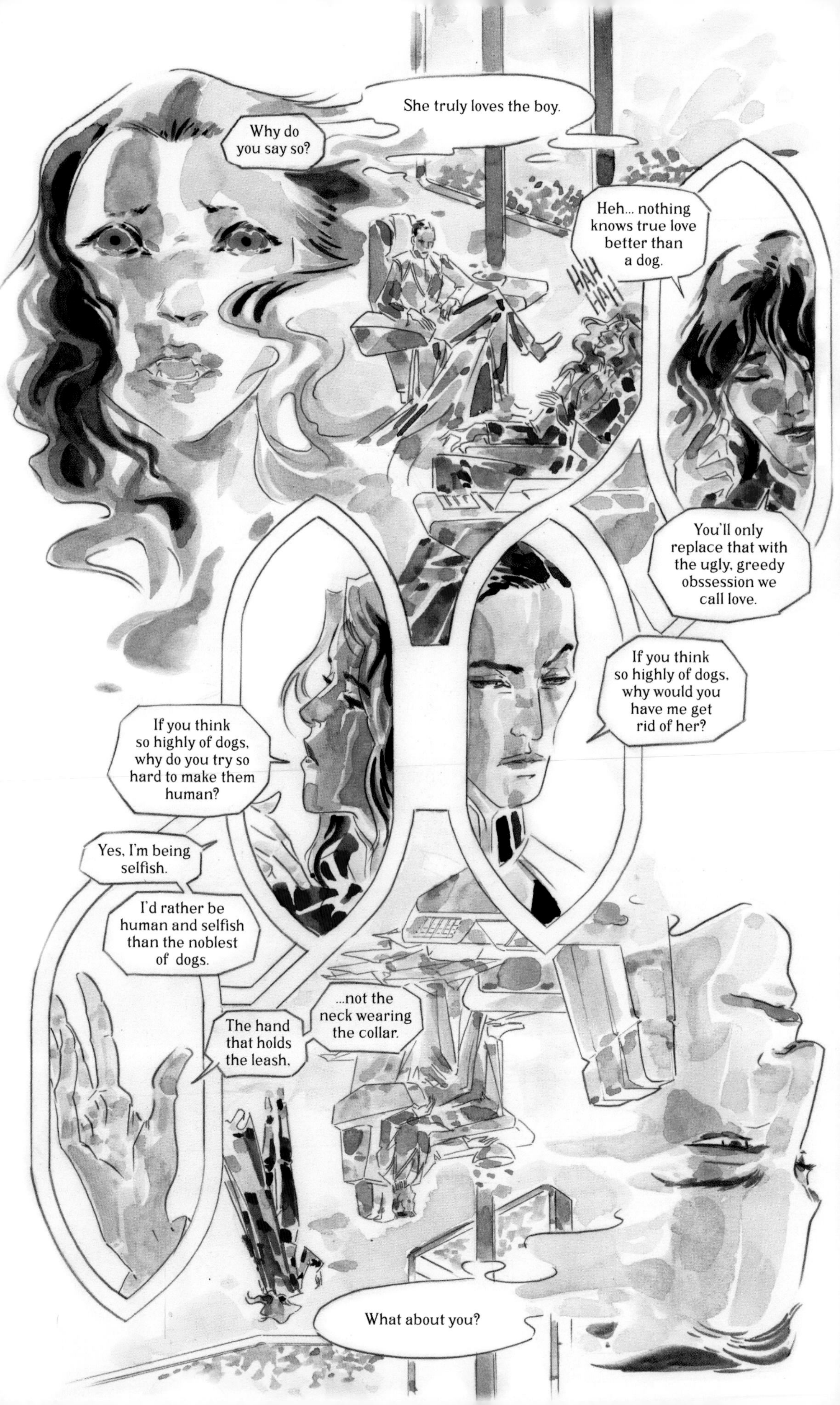
She truly loves the boy.
Why do you say so?
Heh... nothing knows true love better than a dog.
HAH HAH
You'll only replace that with the ugly, greedy obssession we call love.
If you think so highly of dogs, why would you have me get rid of her?
If you think so highly of dogs, why do you try so hard to make them human?
Yes, I'm being selfish.
I'd rather be human and selfish than the noblest of dogs.
The hand that holds the leash,
...not the neck wearing the collar.
What about you?

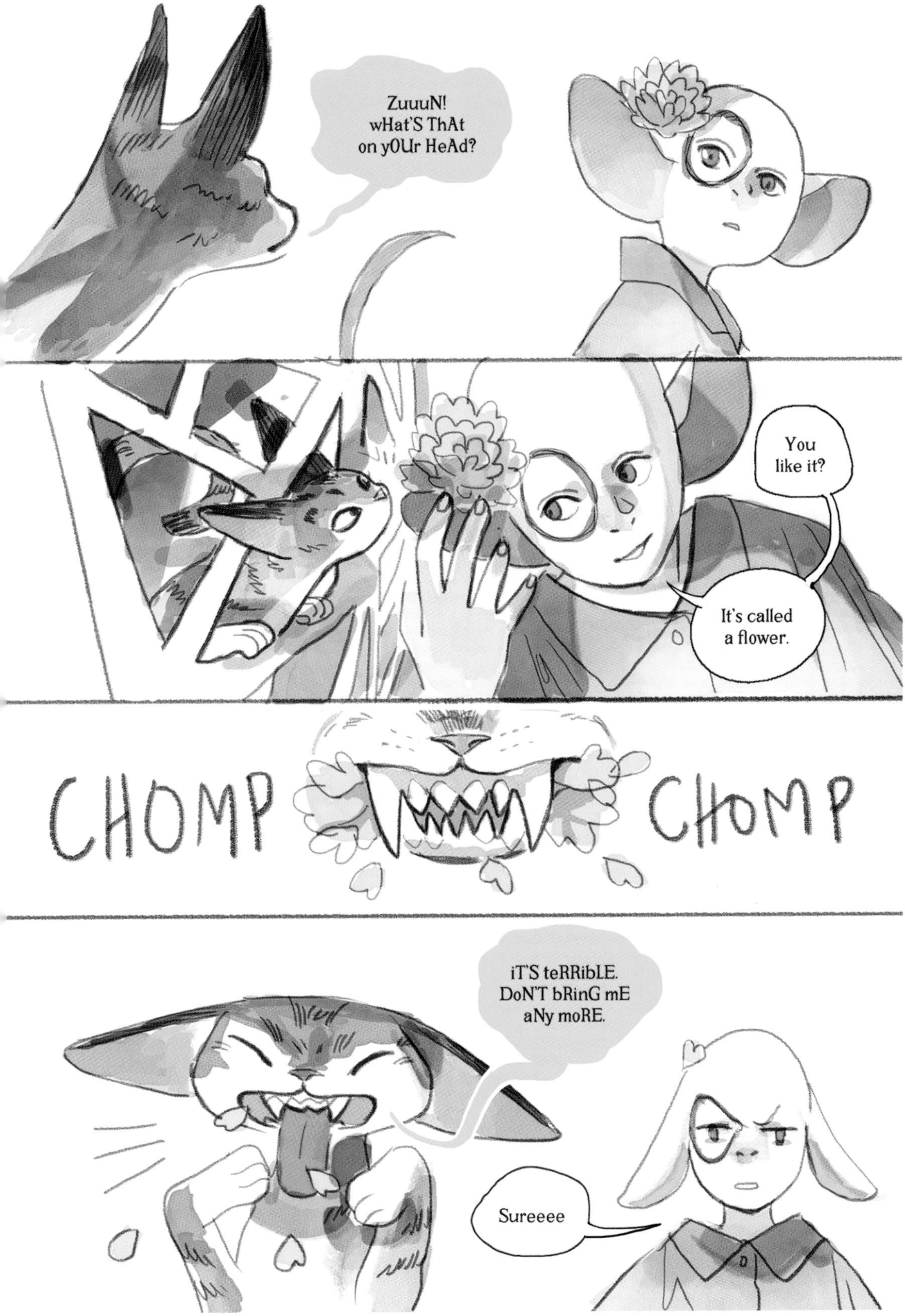
ZuuuN! wHat'S ThAt on yOUr HeAd?
You like it?
It's called a flower.
CHOMP
CHOMP
iT'S teRRibLE. DoN'T bRinG mE aNy moRE.
Sureeee

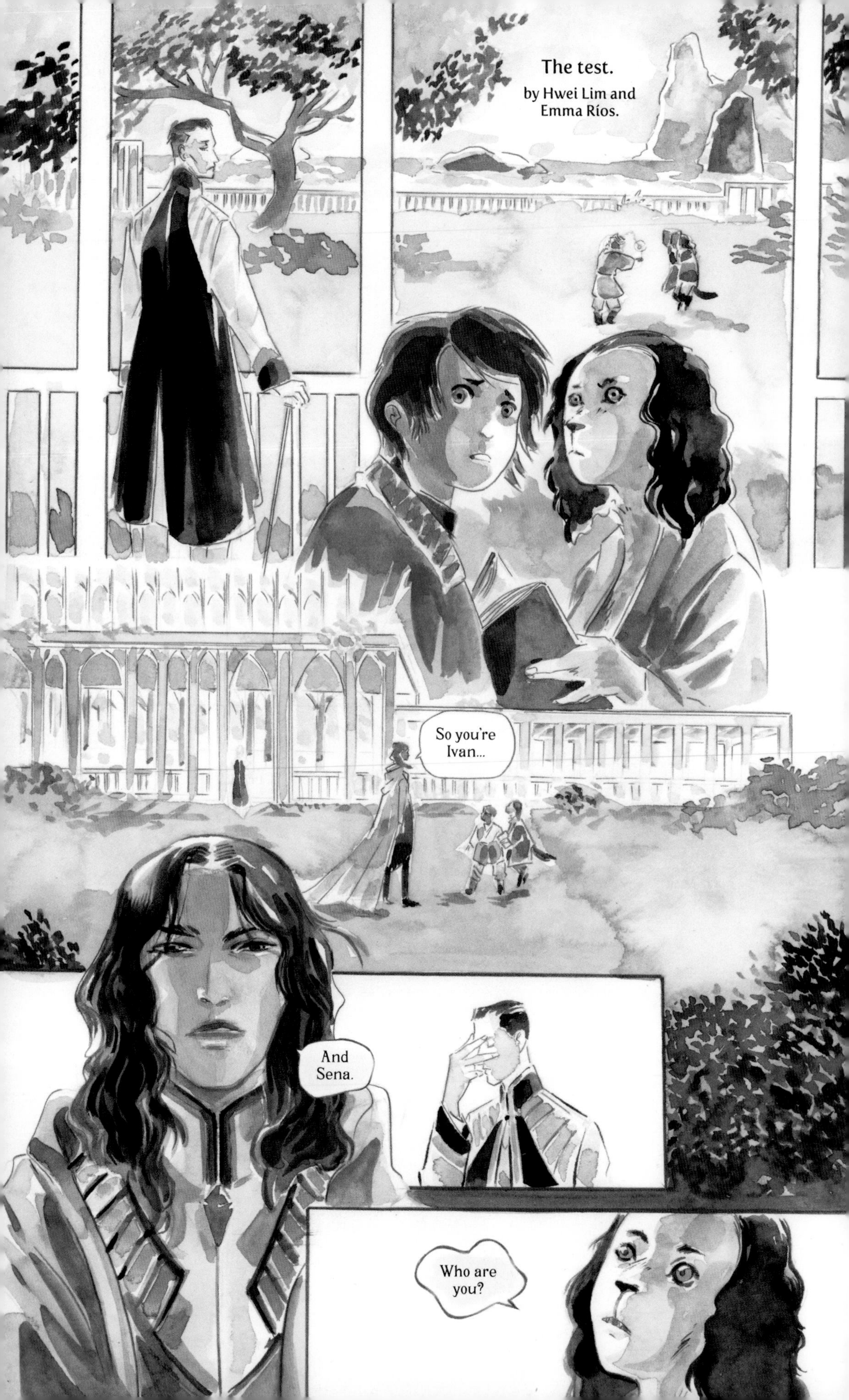
The test.
by Hwei Lim and
Emma Ríos.
So you're Ivan...
And Sena.
Who are you?

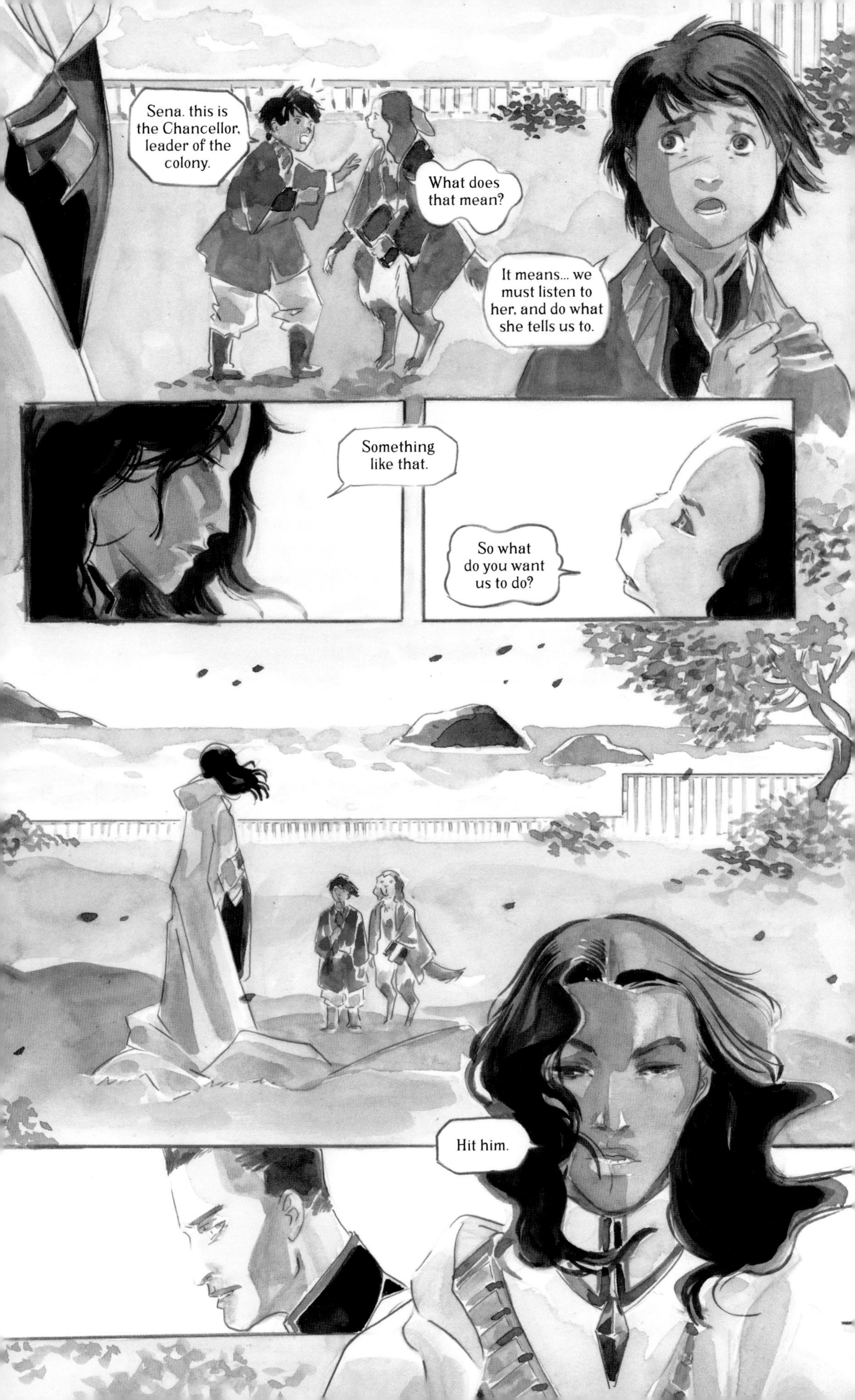
Sena. this is the Chancellor, leader of the colony.
What does that mean?
It means... we must listen to her, and do what she tells us to.
Something like that.
So what do you want us to do?
Hit him.

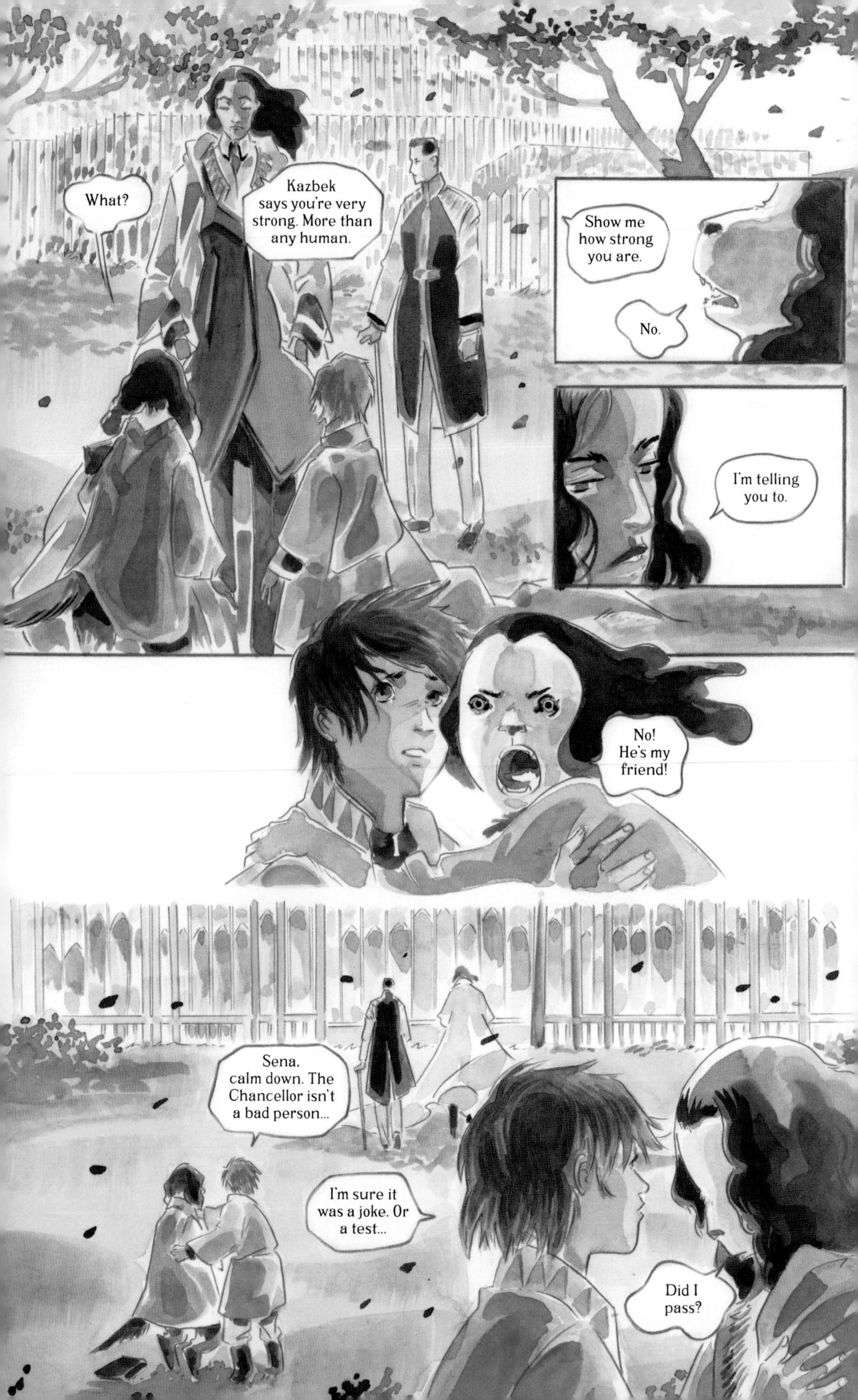
What?
Kazbek says you're very strong. More than any human.
Show me how strong you are.
No.
I'm telling you to.
No! He's my friend!
Sena, calm down. The Chancellor isn't a bad person...
I'm sure it was a joke. Or a test...
Did I pass?

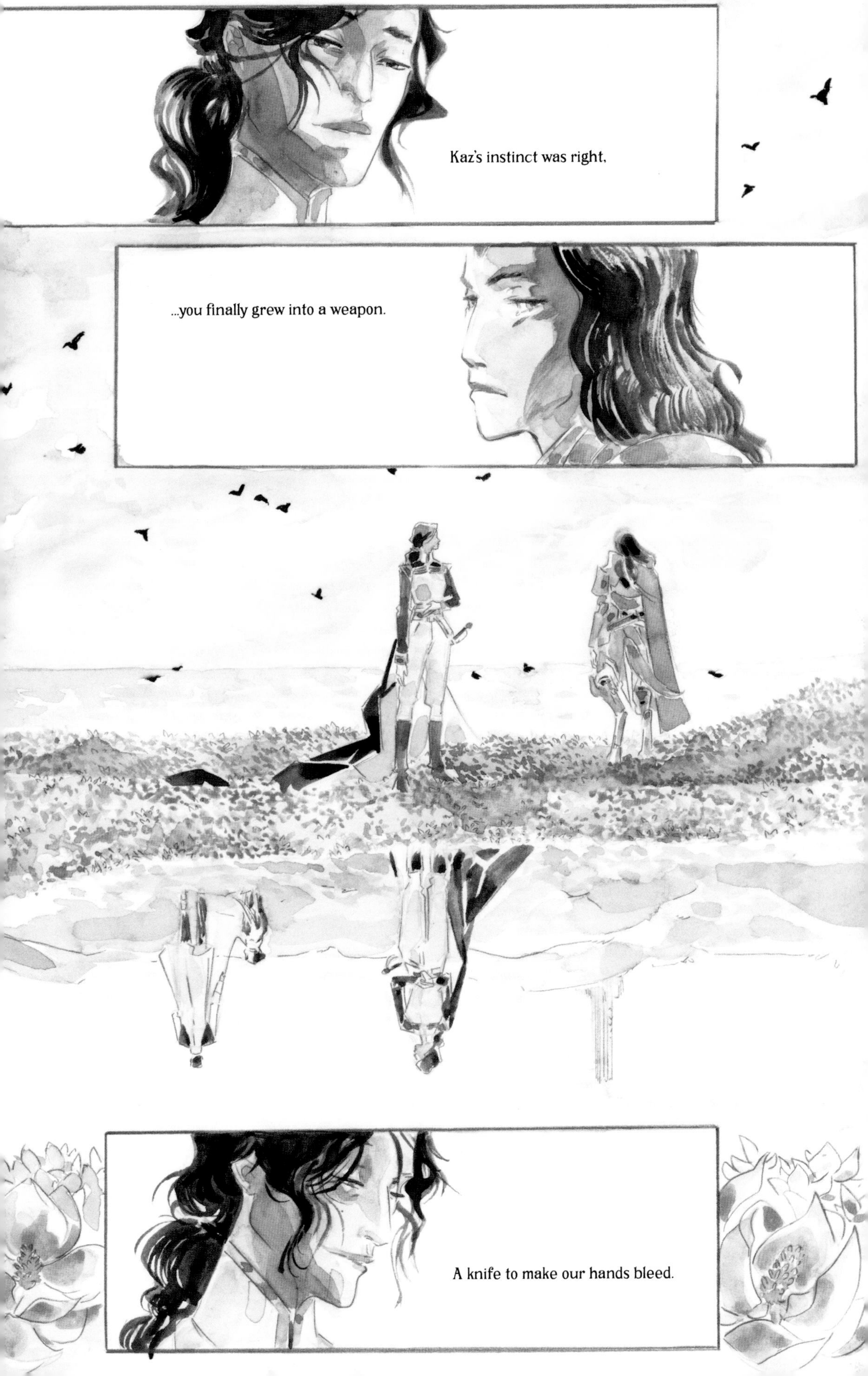
Kaz's instinct was right,
...you finally grew into a weapon.
A knife to make our hands bleed.

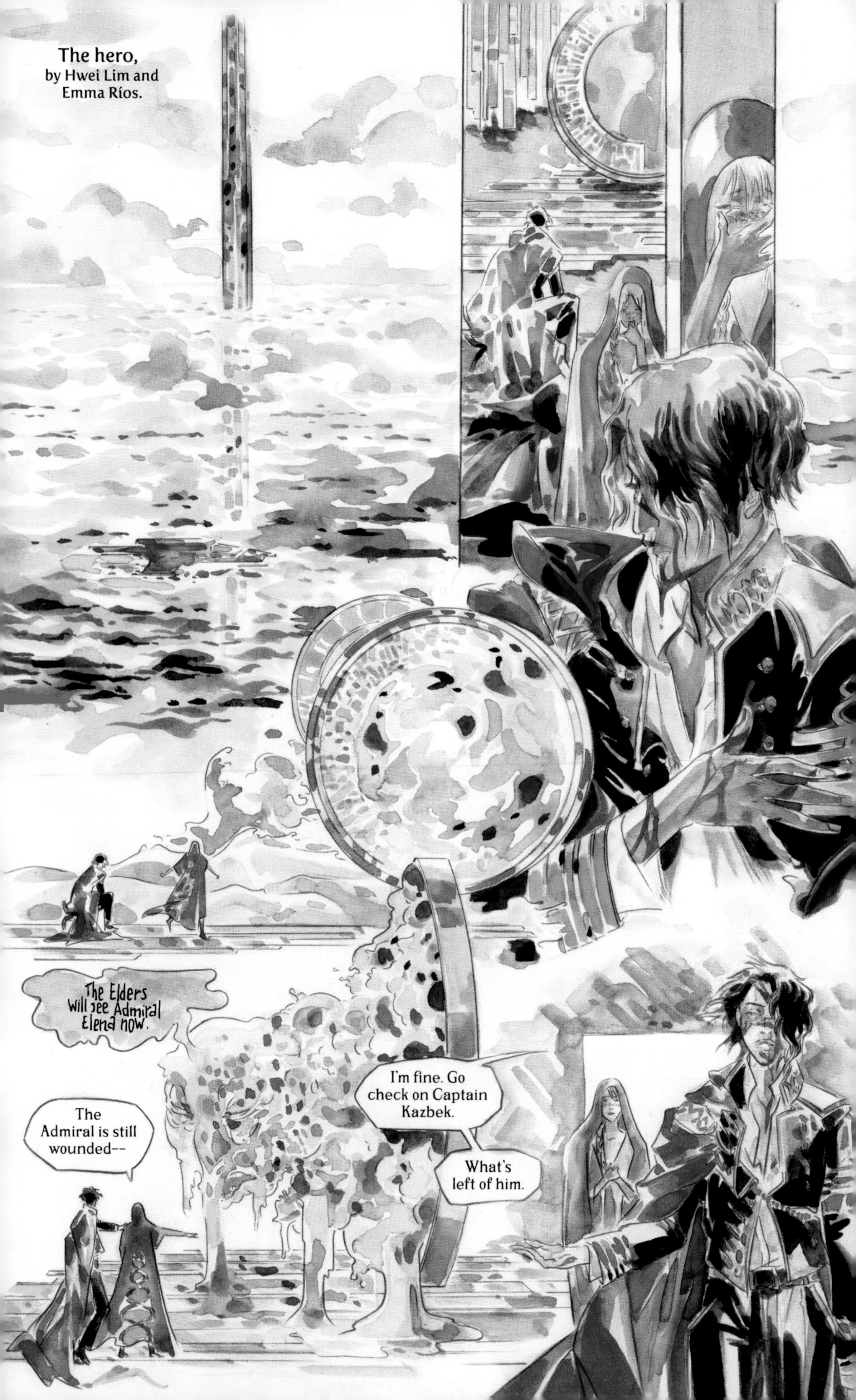
The hero,
by Hwei Lim and
Emma Ríos.
The Elders will see Admiral Elena now.
The Admiral is still wounded--
I'm fine. Go check on Captain Kazbek.
What's left of him.

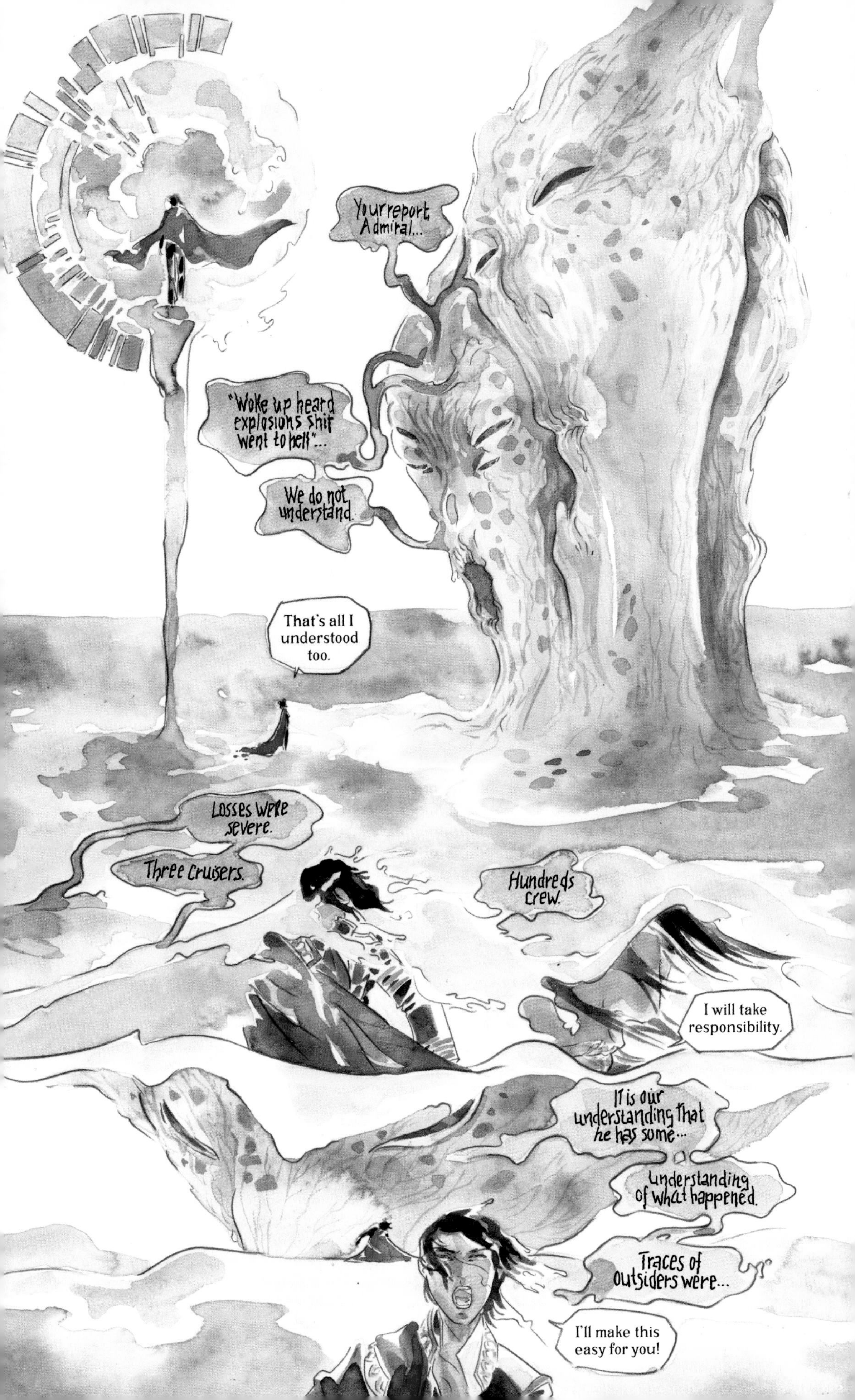
Your report, Admiral...
"Woke up heard explosions shit went to hell"...
We do not understand.
That's all I understood too.
Losses were severe.
Three cruisers.
Hundreds crew.
I will take responsibility.
It is our understanding that he has some...
understanding of what happened.
Traces of outsiders were...
I'll make this easy for you!

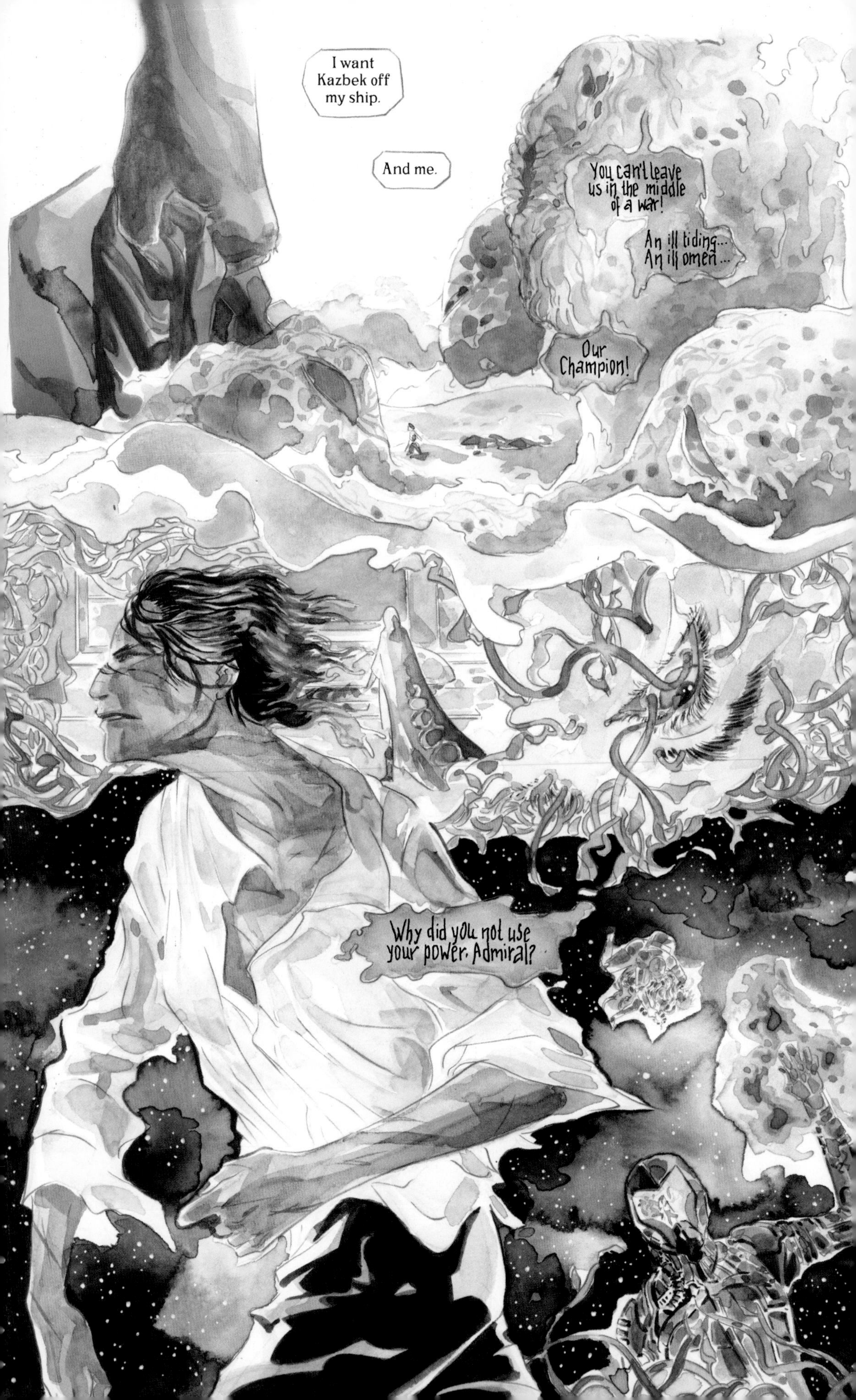
I want Kazbek off my ship.
And me.
You can't leave us in the middle of a war!
An ill tiding... An ill omen...
Our Champion!
Why did you not use your power, Admiral?

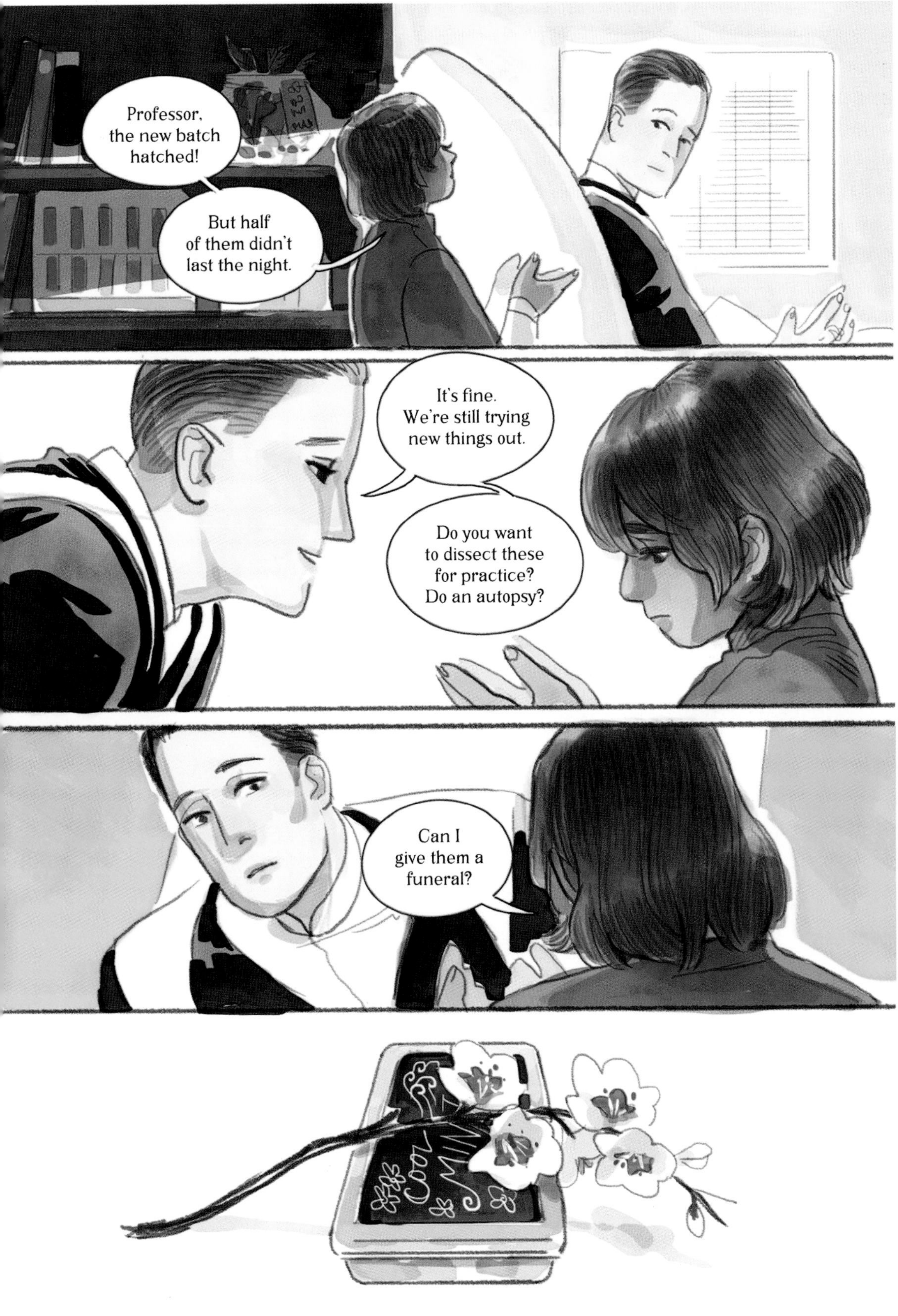
Professor, the new batch hatched!
But half of them didn't last the night.
It's fine. We're still trying new things out.
Do you want to dissect these for practice? Do an autopsy?
Can I give them a funeral?
Cool MINT

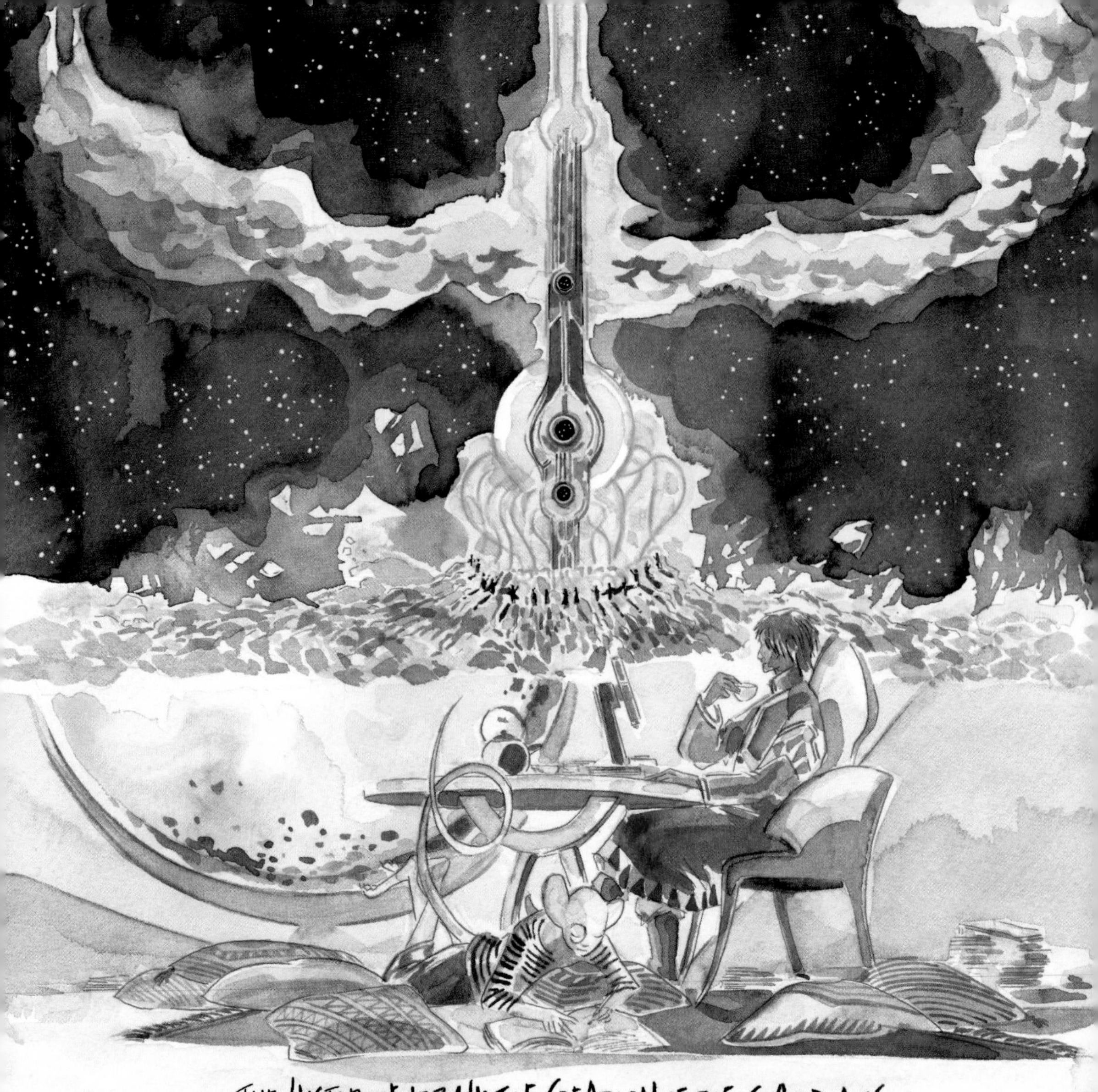

THE HISTORY OF IRZAH: THE CREATION OF THE GUARDIANS
(by Ivan and Zun)

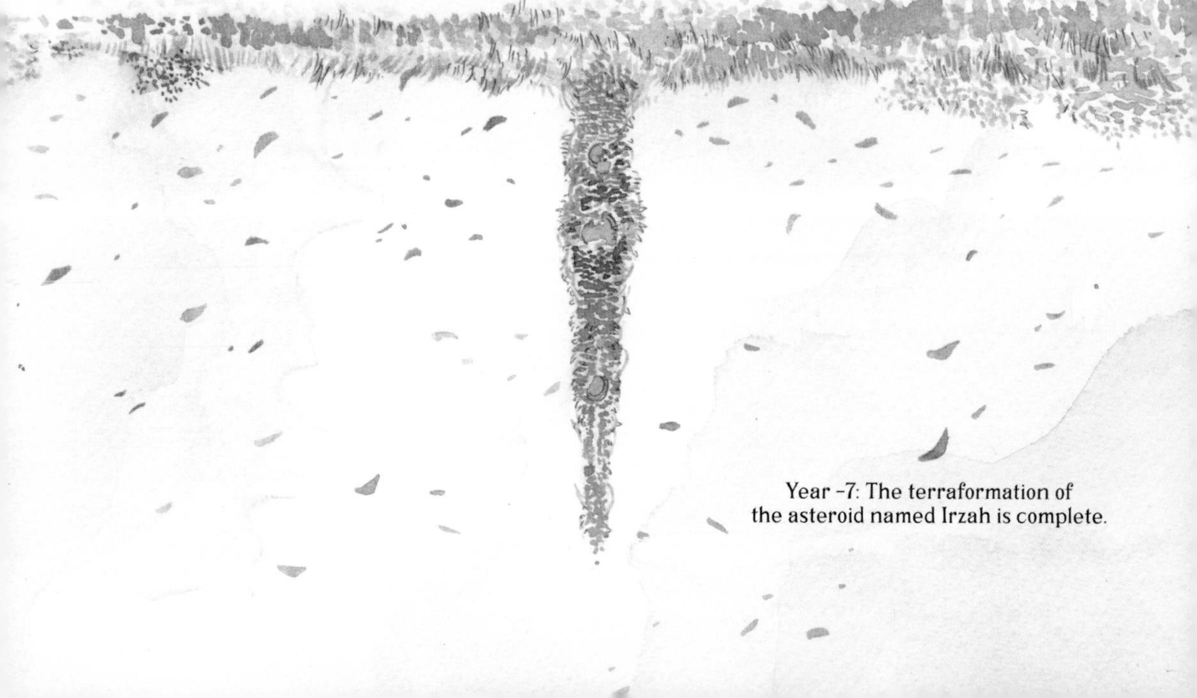
Year -7: The terraformation of the asteroid named Irzah is complete.

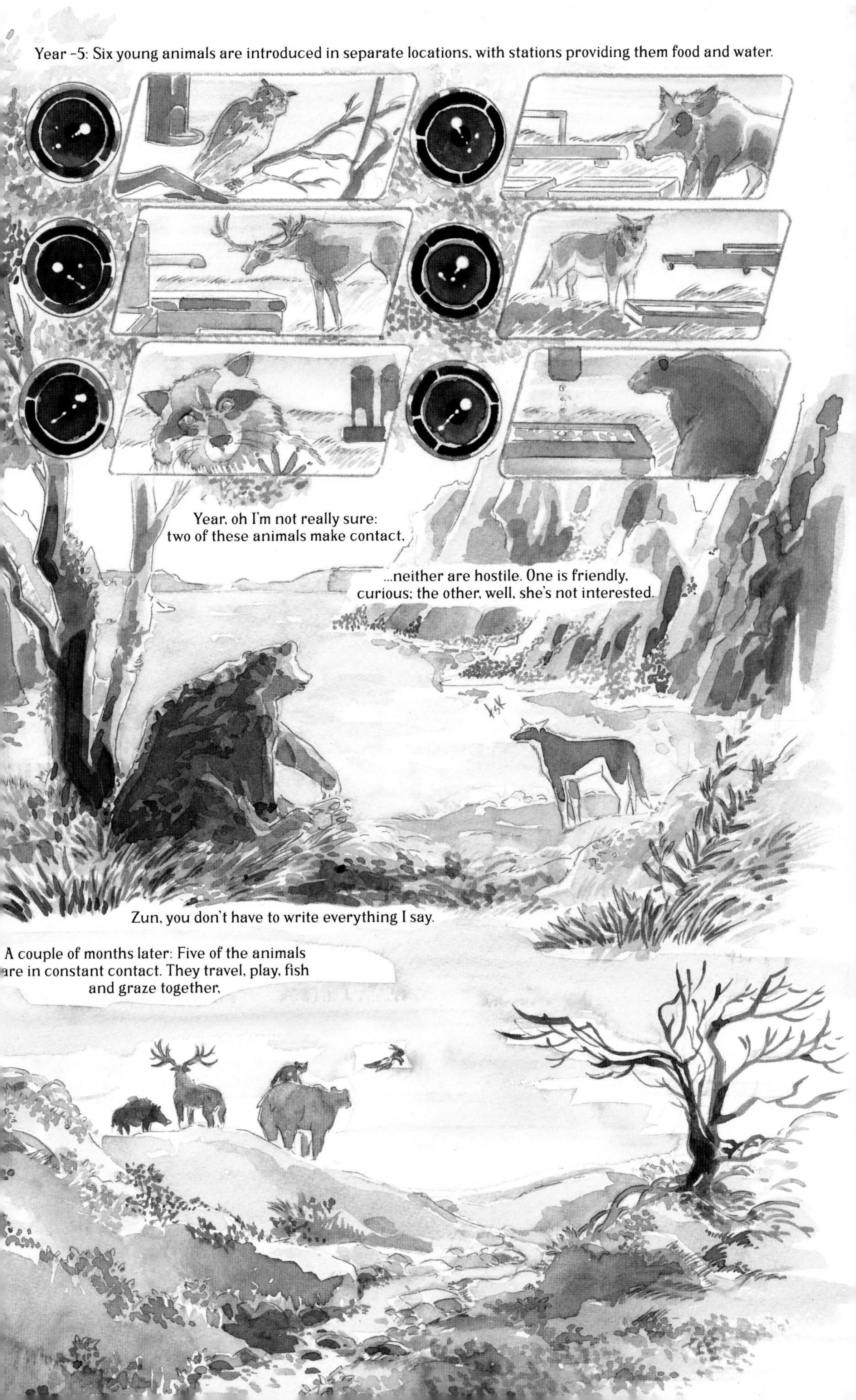
Year -5: Six young animals are introduced in separate locations, with stations providing them food and water.
Year, oh I'm not really sure: two of these animals make contact,
...neither are hostile. One is friendly, curious; the other, well, she's not interested.
tsk
Zun, you don't have to write everything I say.
A couple of months later: Five of the animals are in constant contact. They travel, play, fish and graze together,

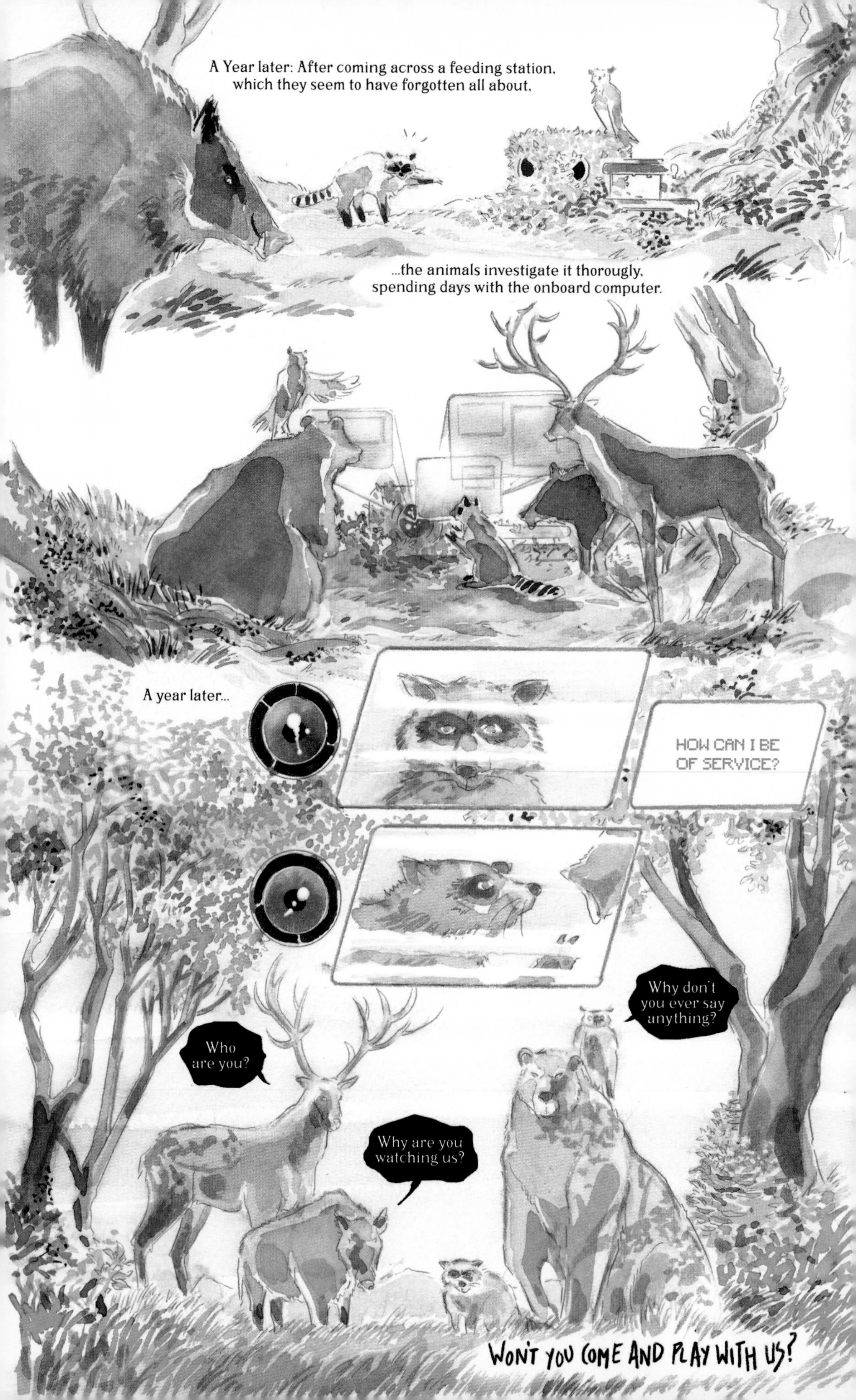
A Year later: After coming across a feeding station, which they seem to have forgotten all about,
...the animals investigate it thorougly, spending days with the onboard computer.
A year later...
HOW CAN I BE OF SERVICE?
Who are you?
Why are you watching us?
Why don't you ever say anything?
WON'T YOU COME AND PLAY WITH US?

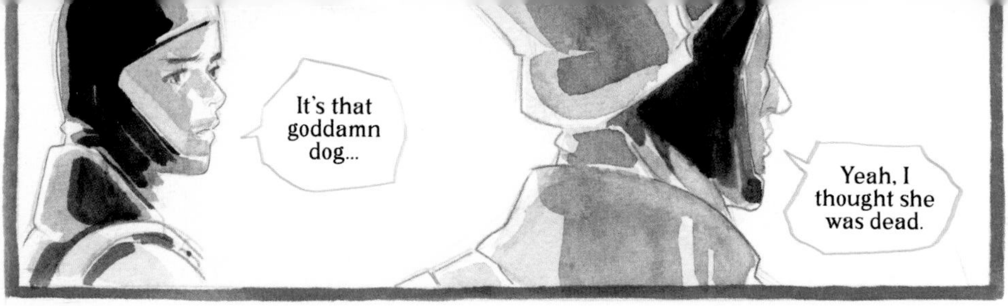
It's that goddamn dog...
Yeah, I thought she was dead.

Sirens chant, by Emma Ríos and Hwei Lim.

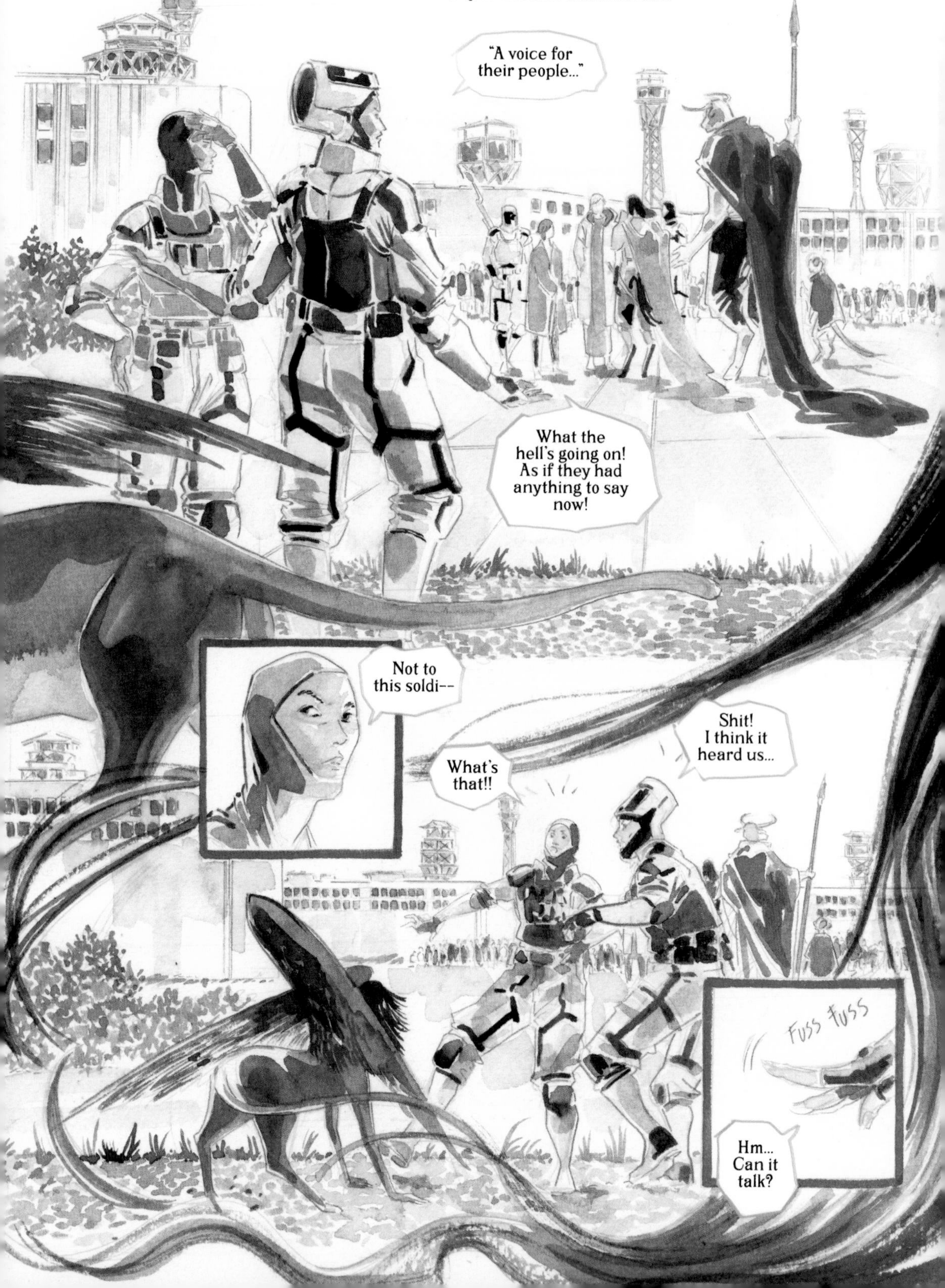
"A voice for their people..."
What the hell's going on! As if they had anything to say now!
Not to this soldi--
Shit! I think it heard us...
What's that!!
FUSS FUSS
Hm... Can it talk?

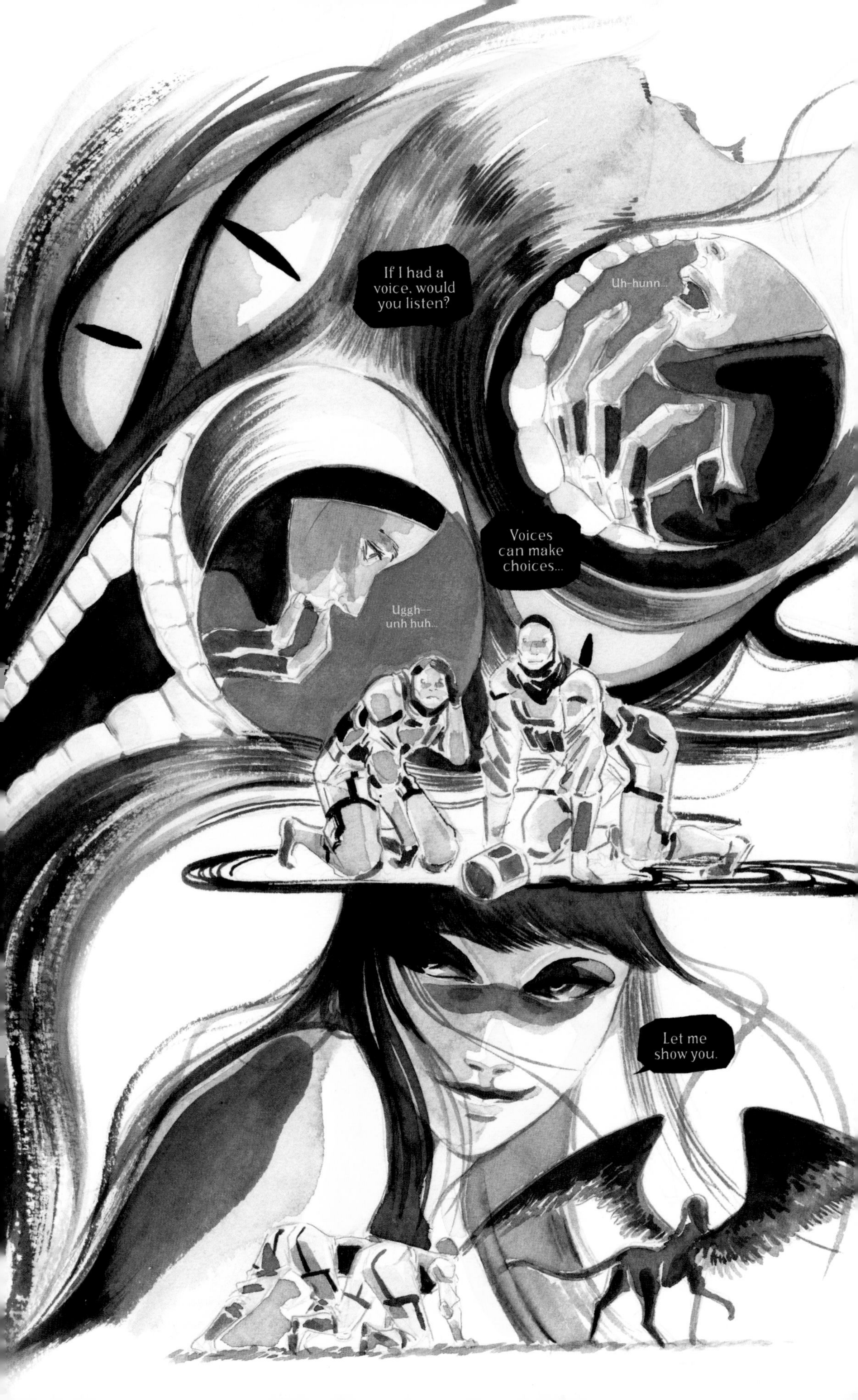
If I had a voice, would you listen?
Uh-hunn...
Voices can make choices...
Uggh-- unh huh...
Let me show you.

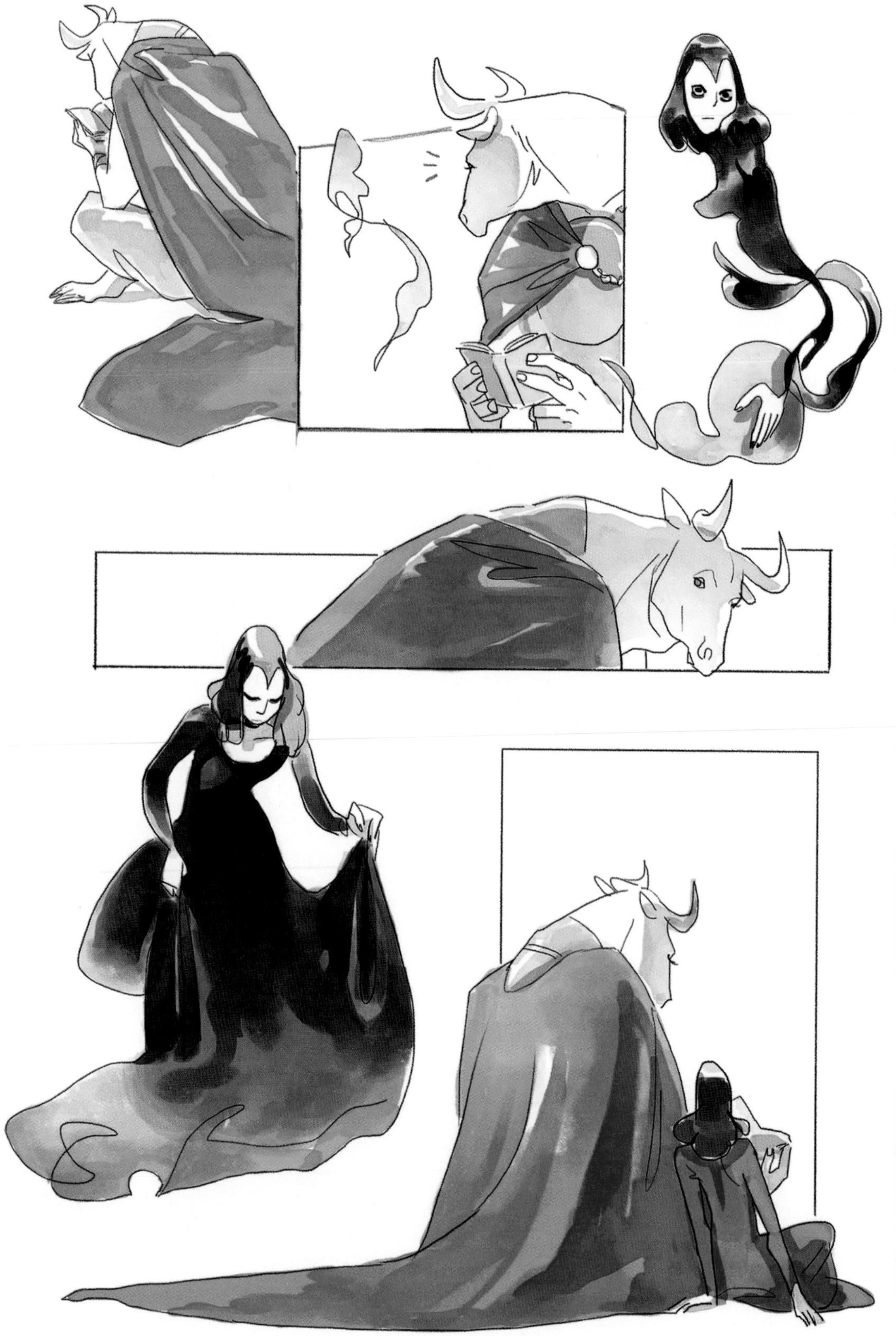

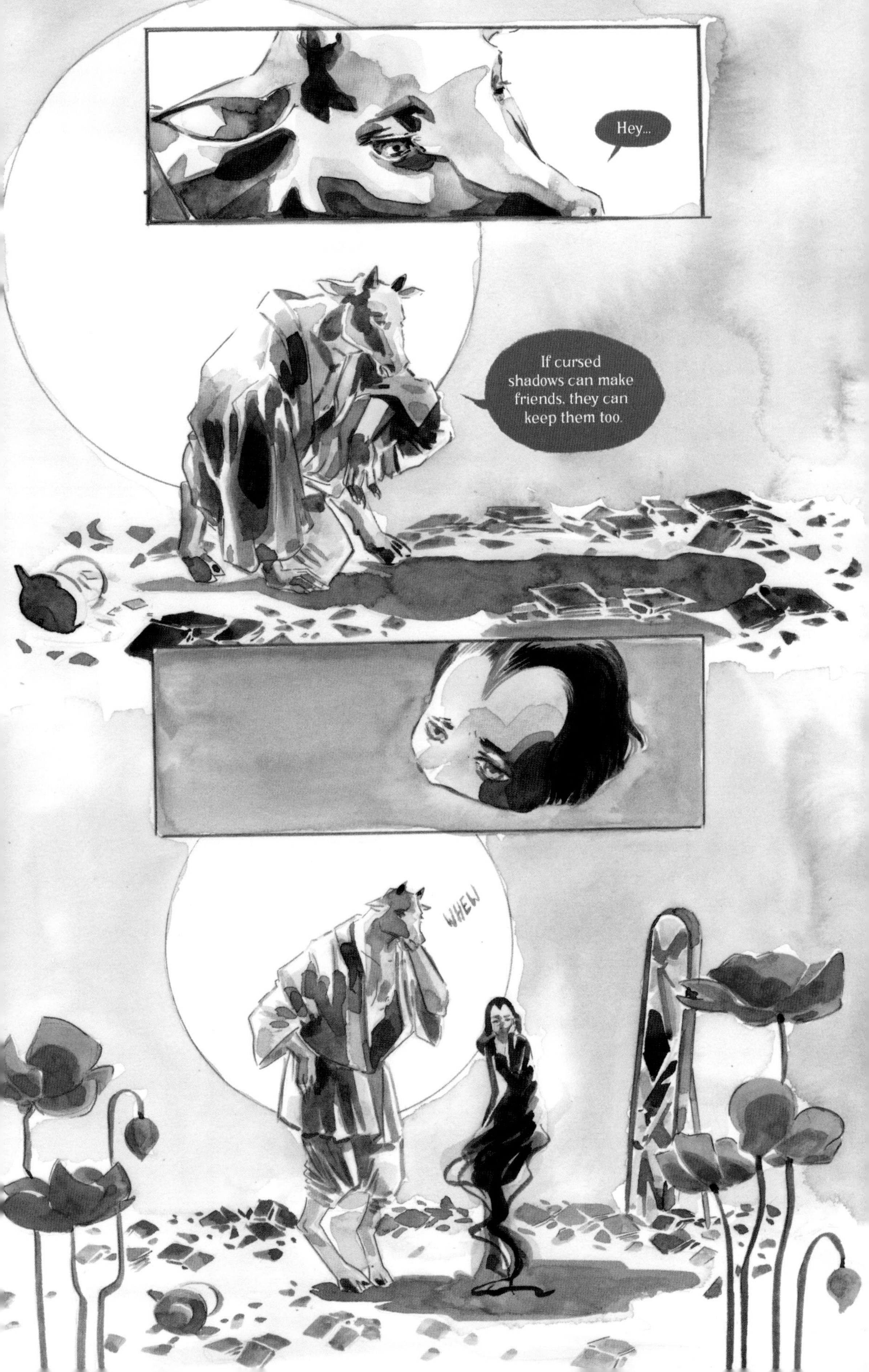
Hey...
If cursed shadows can make friends, they can keep them too.
WHEW

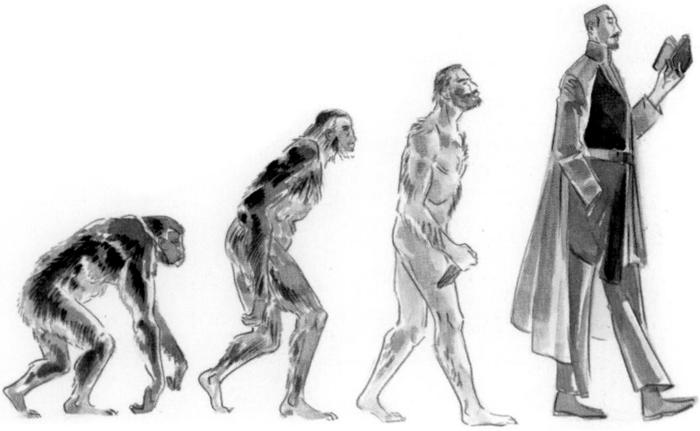

Animals
Sentient motile beings.

Humans (homo sapiens)
Rational beings evolved from a branch of great apes, characterized by an erect posture and bipedal locomotion. They are social creatures capable of creating and learning, and of developing complex language communication and art.

Evolved Animals
Rational beings characterized by an erect posture, depending on their branch. They are social creatures with strong instincts for survival, capable of creating and learning, and of developing complex language communication and art.

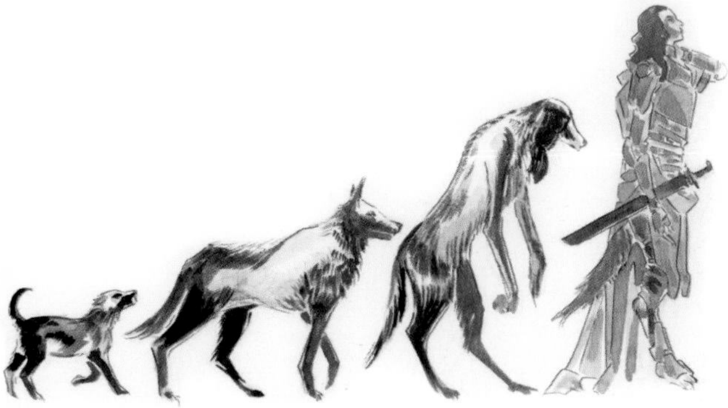

Minotaur
A mythological creature described as "part man and part bull" by the roman poet Ovidio (43BC-18AD) Born from a human woman and conceived as a symbol of protection and strength, the minotaur Aldebaran was a gift from the sentient Asteroid of Irzah to its new inhabitants.

Sphinx
A mythical and merciless creature - part human, part bird, and part lion - that symbolizes death, wisdom, and riddles.
The sphinx of the Irzah colony was apparently created by Kazbek in an attempt to decipher the asteroid's mysteries and show his own value.

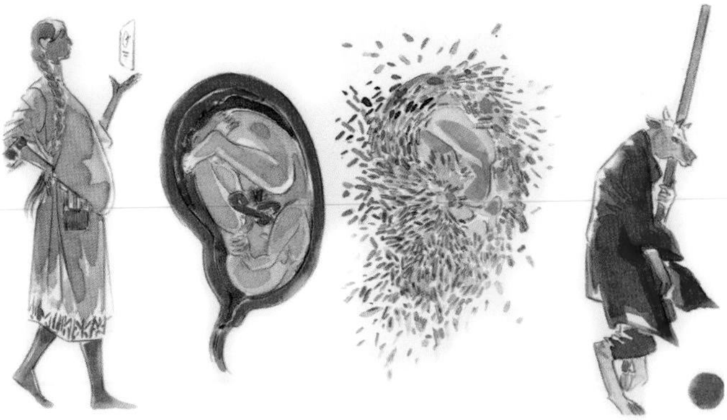

Curse
Ivan's curse, also known as Keeper or The Grudge, was a shadow of Sena casted by himself while he was adrift in sadness. An anathema turned into the sentient creature she is today by Kazbek, to help him deal with his sorrow.

The Guardians
The first animals taken to the Asteroid of Irzah, after being terraformed, to test the conditions of the environment. The grateful land made them not only survive, but evolve rational and clairvoyant.

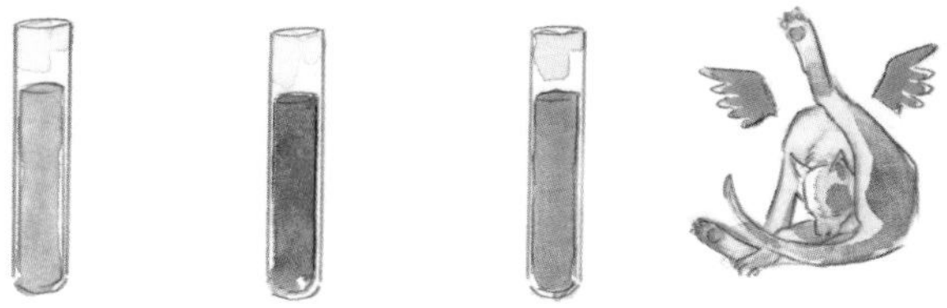

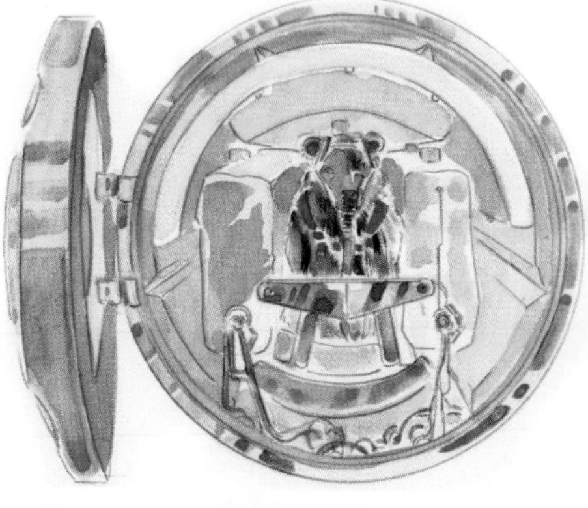

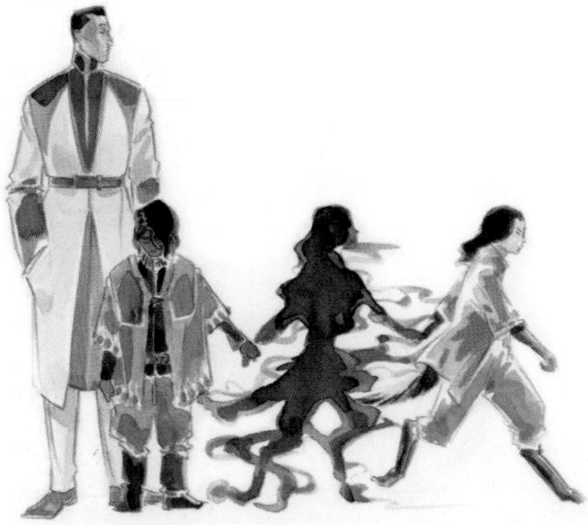

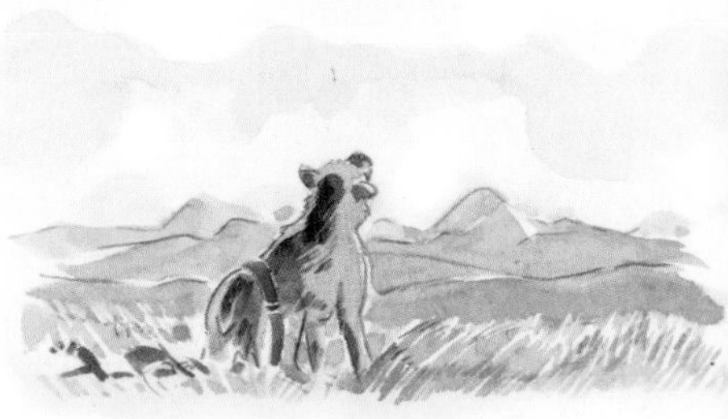

The Esagila

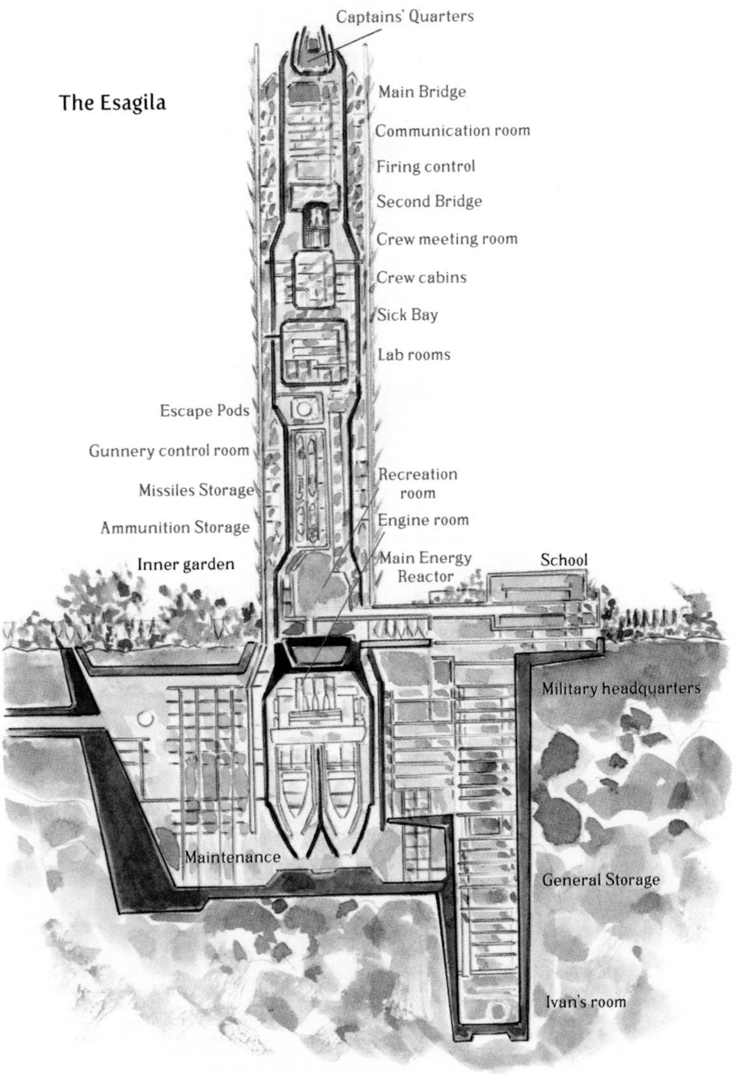
Captains' Quarters
Main Bridge
Communication room
Firing control
Second Bridge
Crew meeting room
Crew cabins
Sick Bay
Lab rooms
Escape Pods
Gunnery control room
Missiles Storage
Ammunition Storage
Recreation room
Engine room
Main Energy Reactor
Inner garden
School
Military headquarters
Maintenance
General Storage
Ivan's room

Irzah Colony

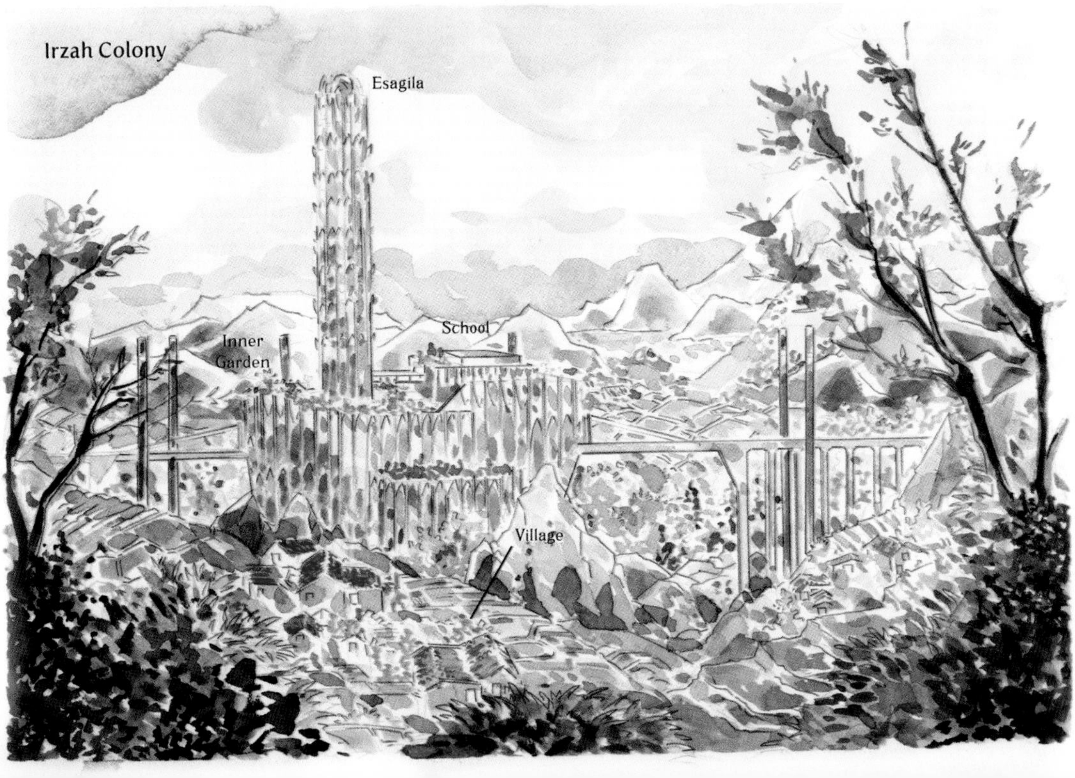
Esagila
Inner Garden
School
Village

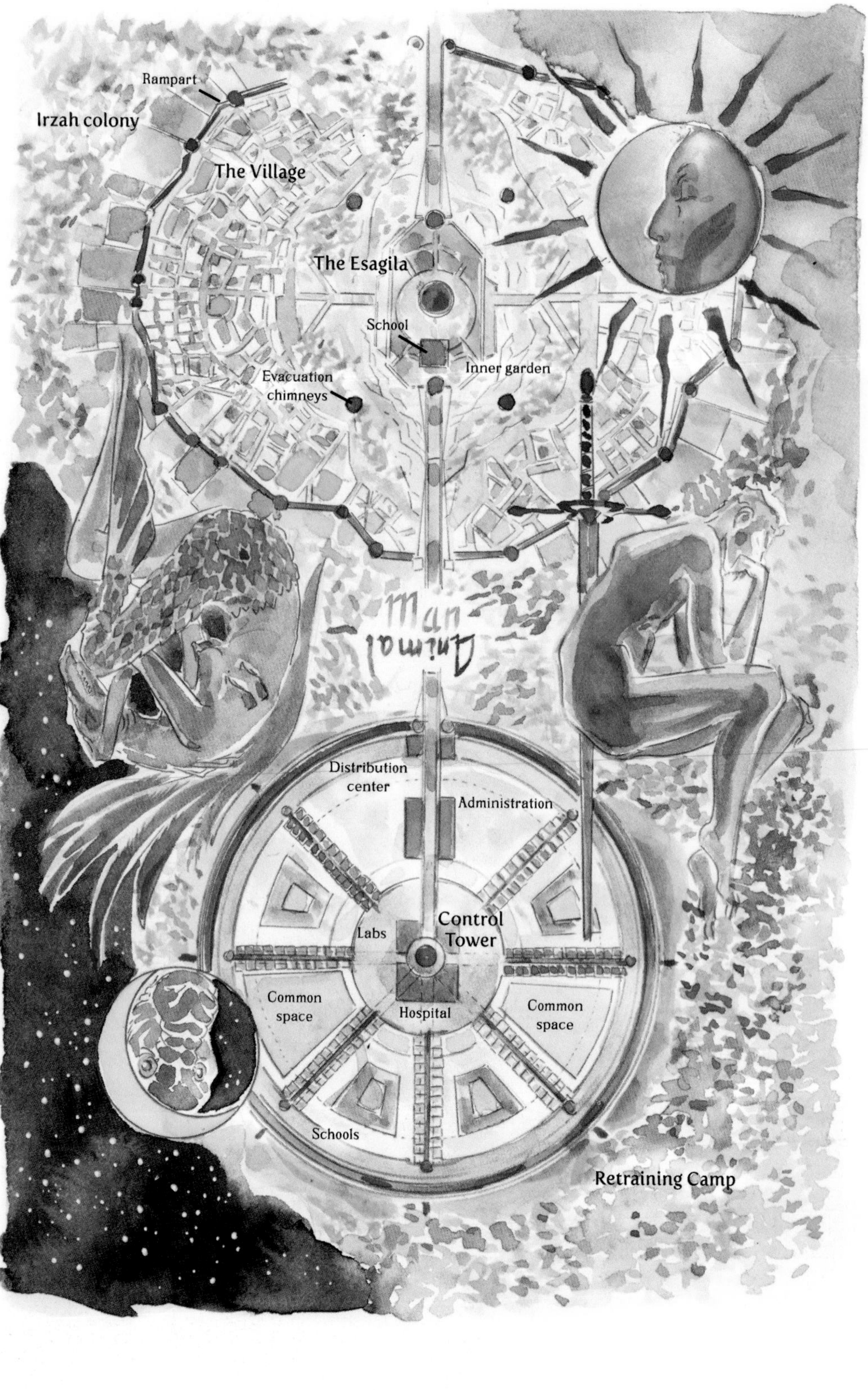
Rampart
Irzah colony
The Village
The Esagila
School
Inner garden
Evacuation chimneys
Animal
Man
Distribution center
Administration
Control Tower
Labs
Common space
Hospital
Common space
Schools
Retraining Camp

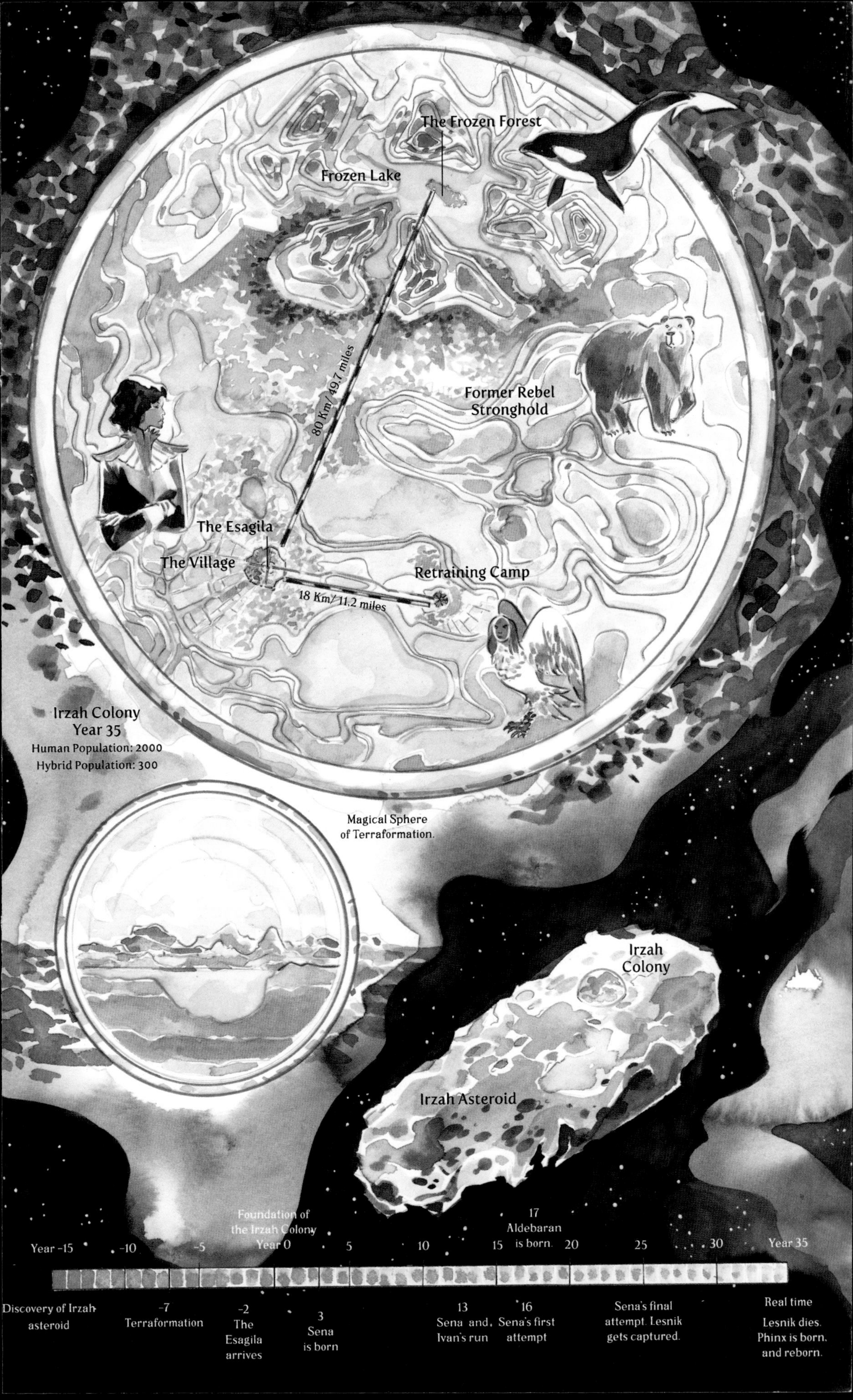

The Frozen Forest
Frozen Lake
80 Km/ 49,7 miles
Former Rebel Stronghold
The Esagila
The Village
Retraining Camp
18 Km/ 11,2 miles
Irzah Colony
Year 35
Human Population: 2000
Hybrid Population: 300
Magical Sphere of Terraformation.
Irzah Colony
Irzah Asteroid
Foundation of the Irzah Colony
17 Aldebaran is born.
Year -15
-10
-5
Year 0
5
10
15
20
25
30
Year 35
Discovery of Irzah asteroid
-7 Terraformation
-2 The Esagila arrives
3 Sena is born
13 Sena and Ivan's run
16 Sena's first attempt
Sena's final attempt. Lesnik gets captured.
Real time
Lesnik dies. Phinx is born, and reborn.

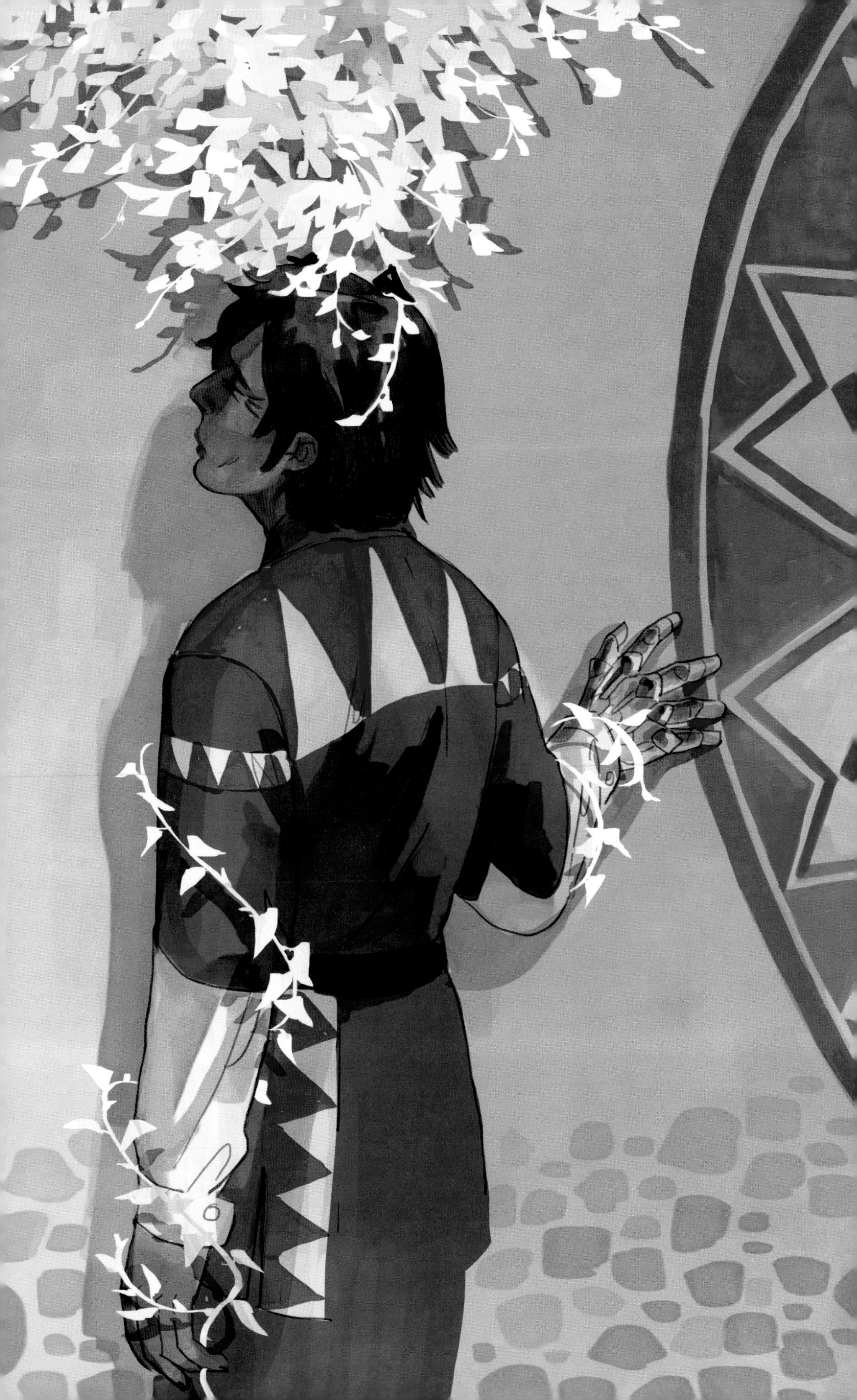

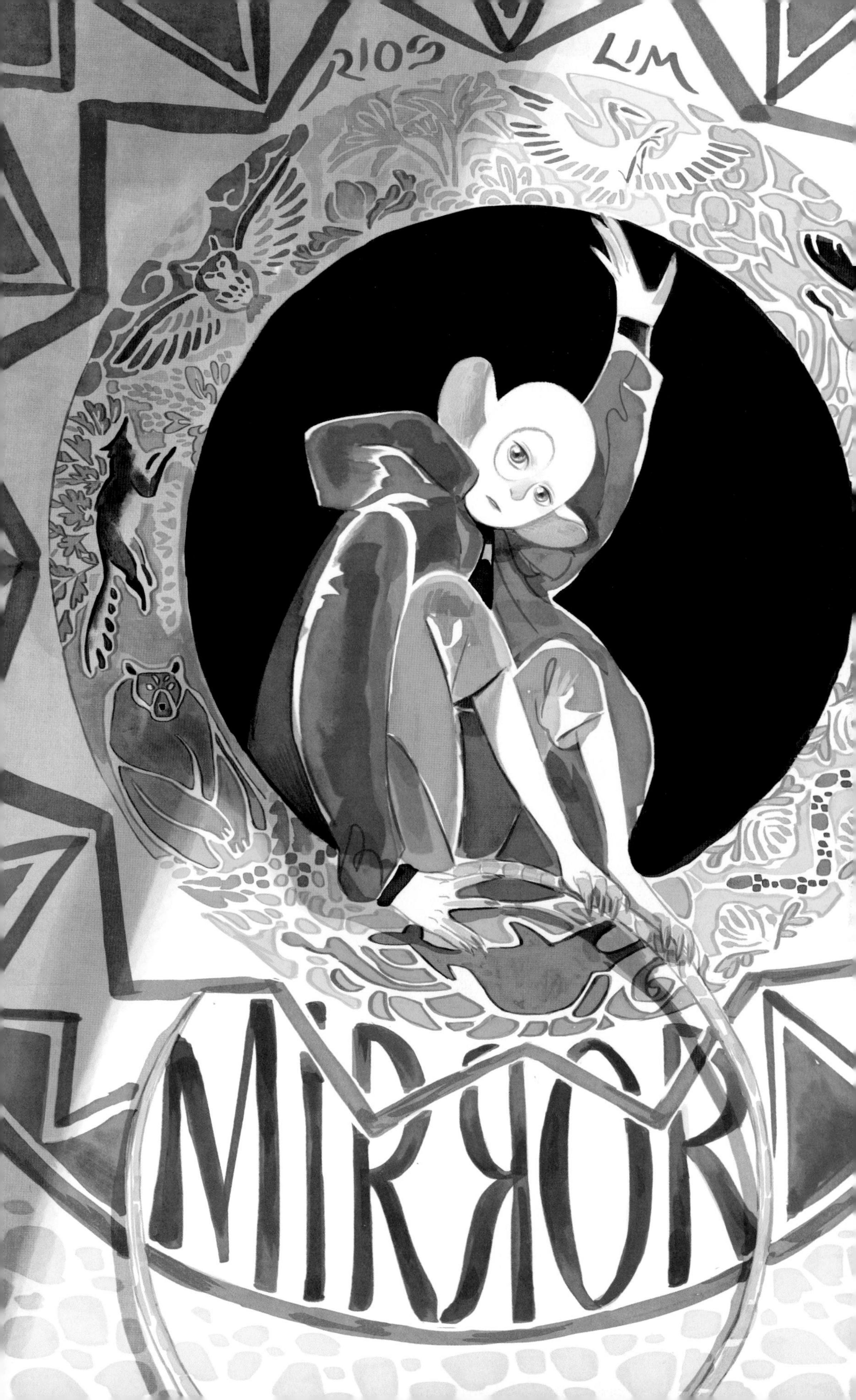
RIOS
LIM
MIRROR

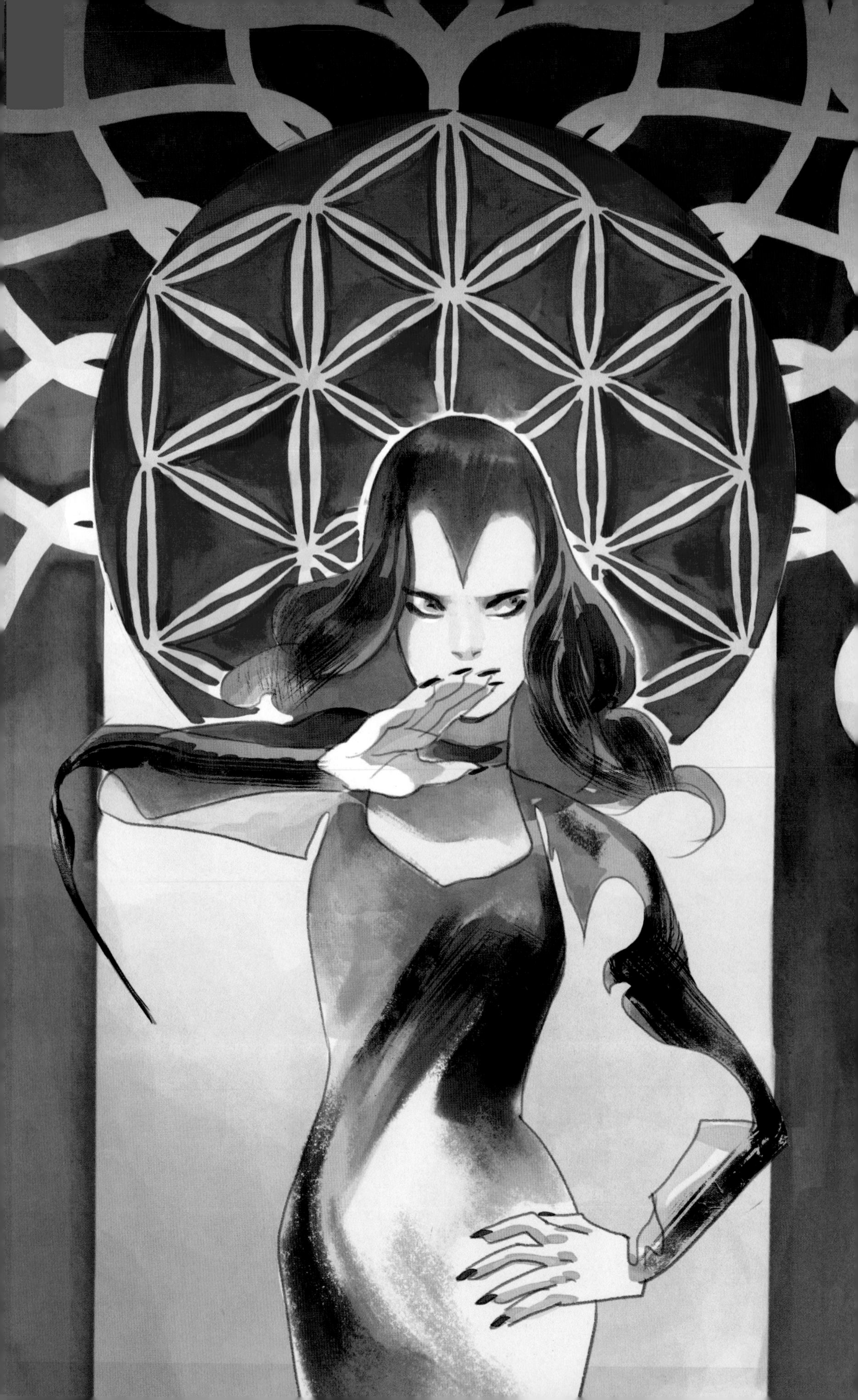

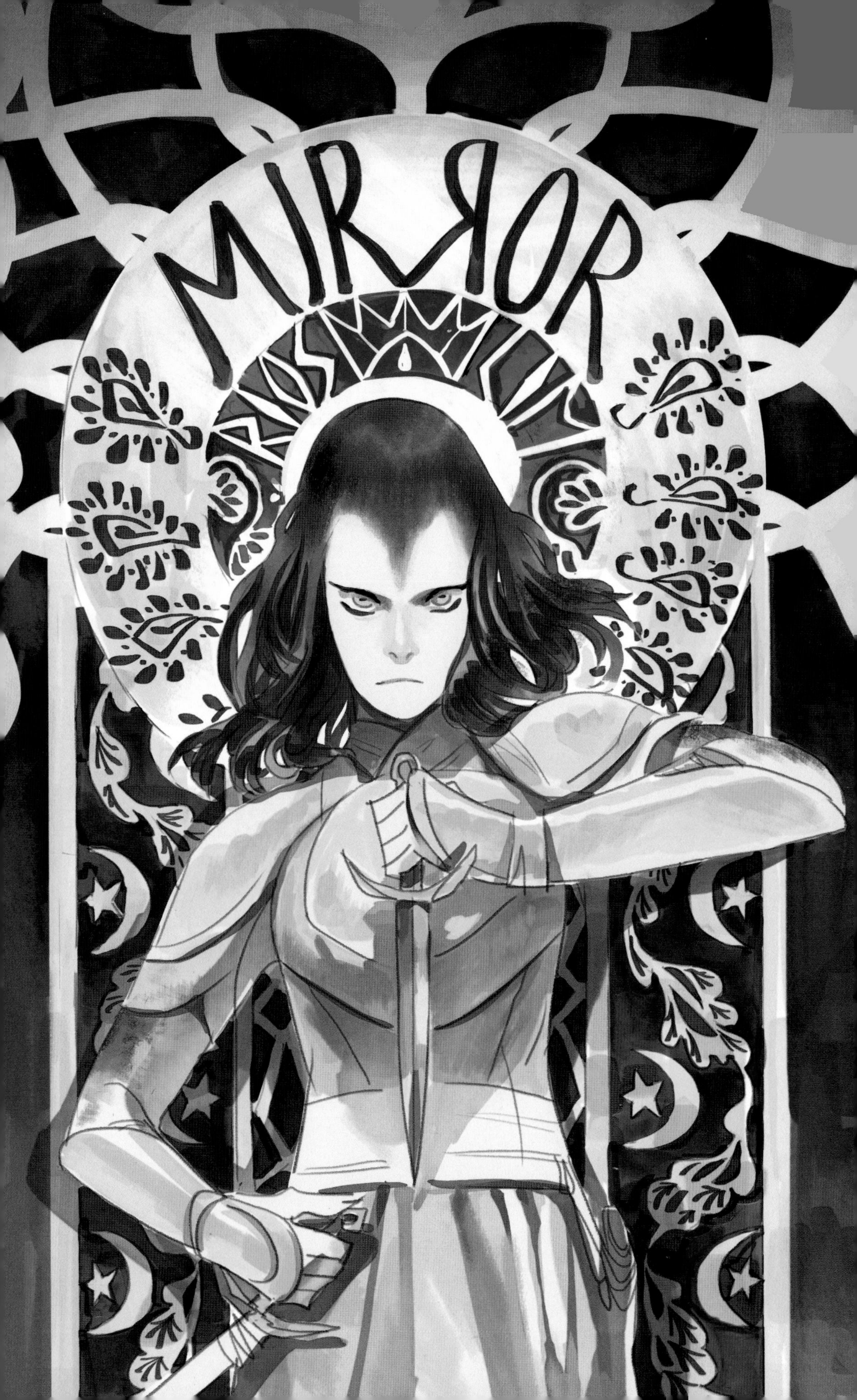
MIRROR

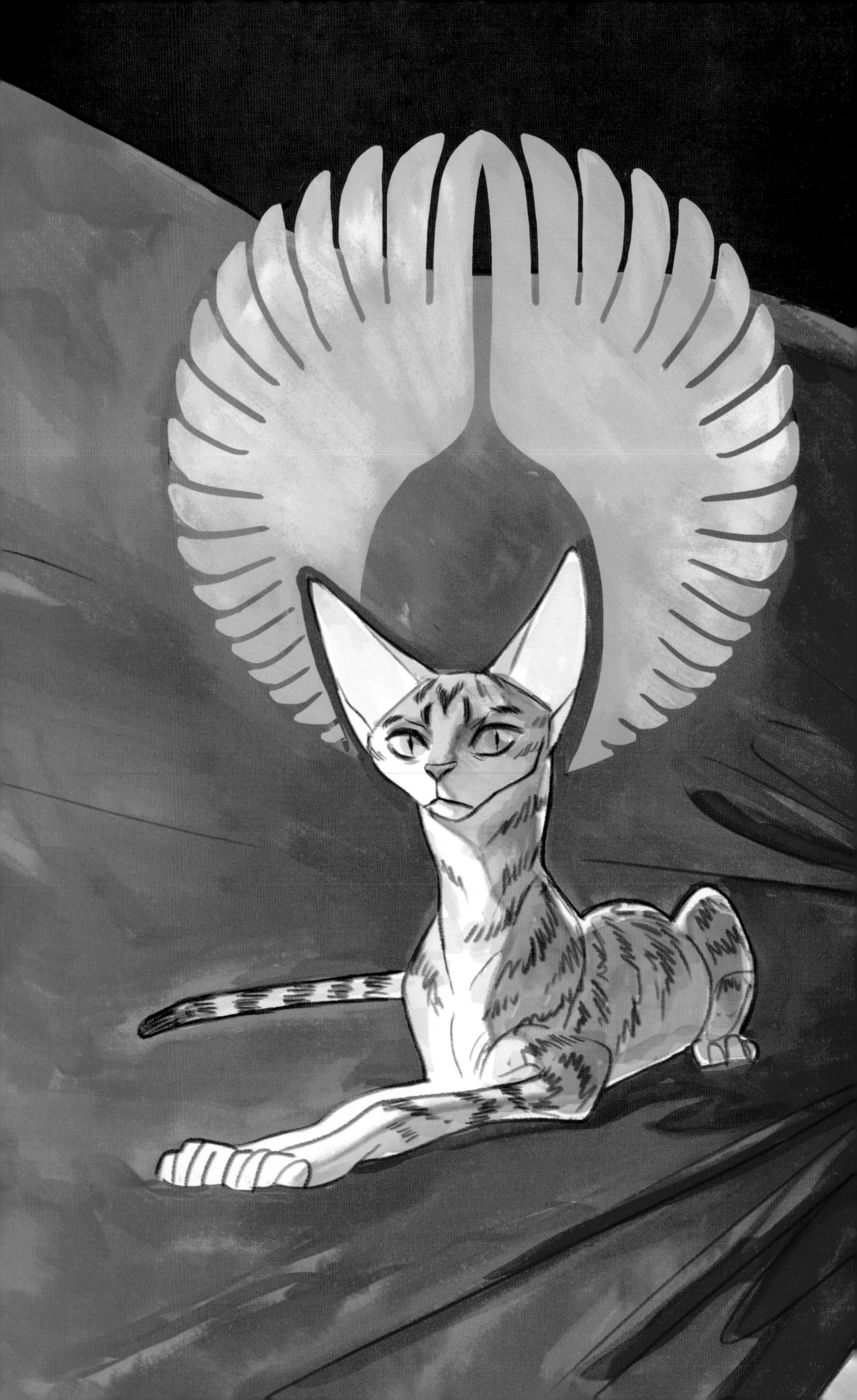

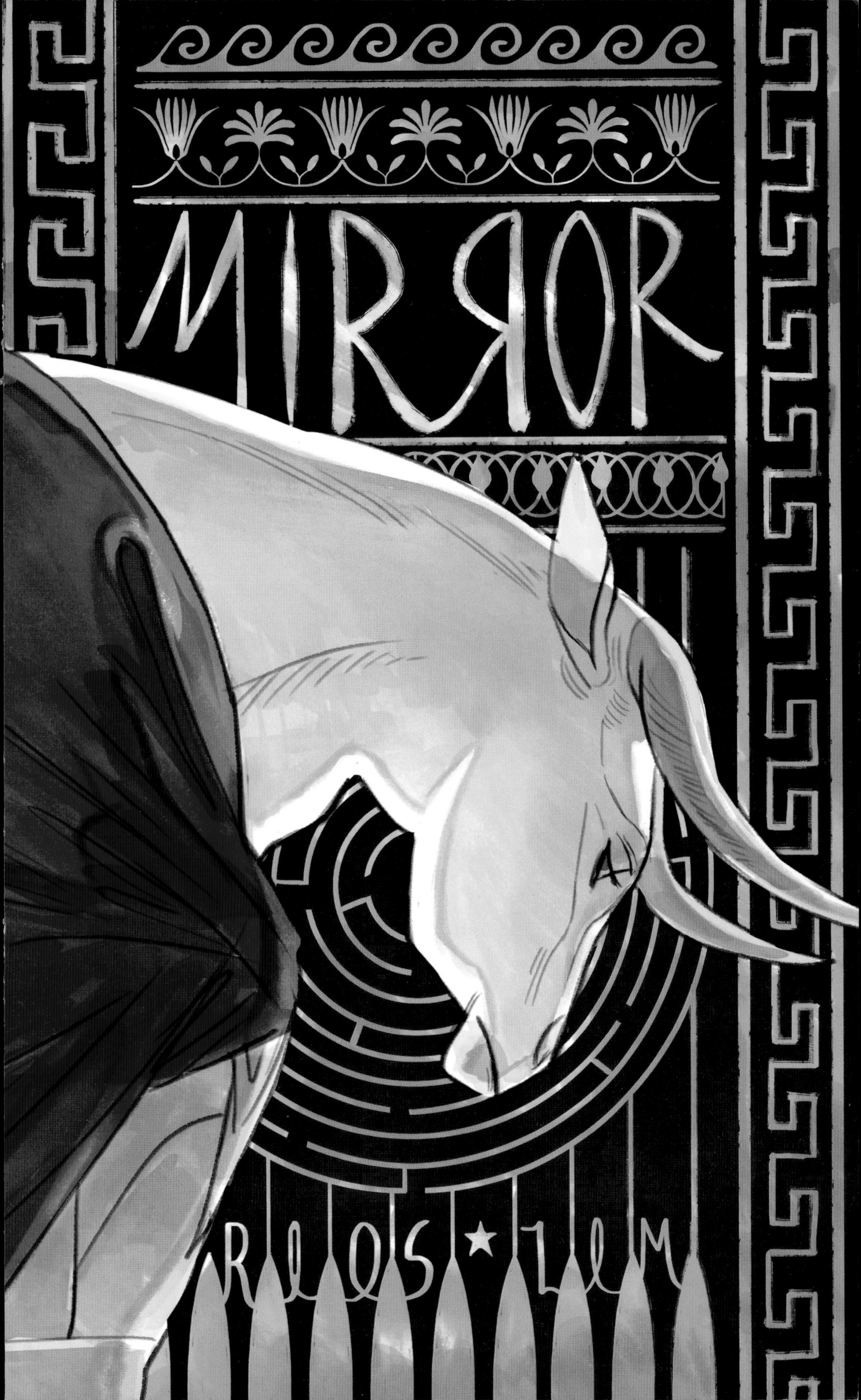
MIRROR
RIOS ★ LIM

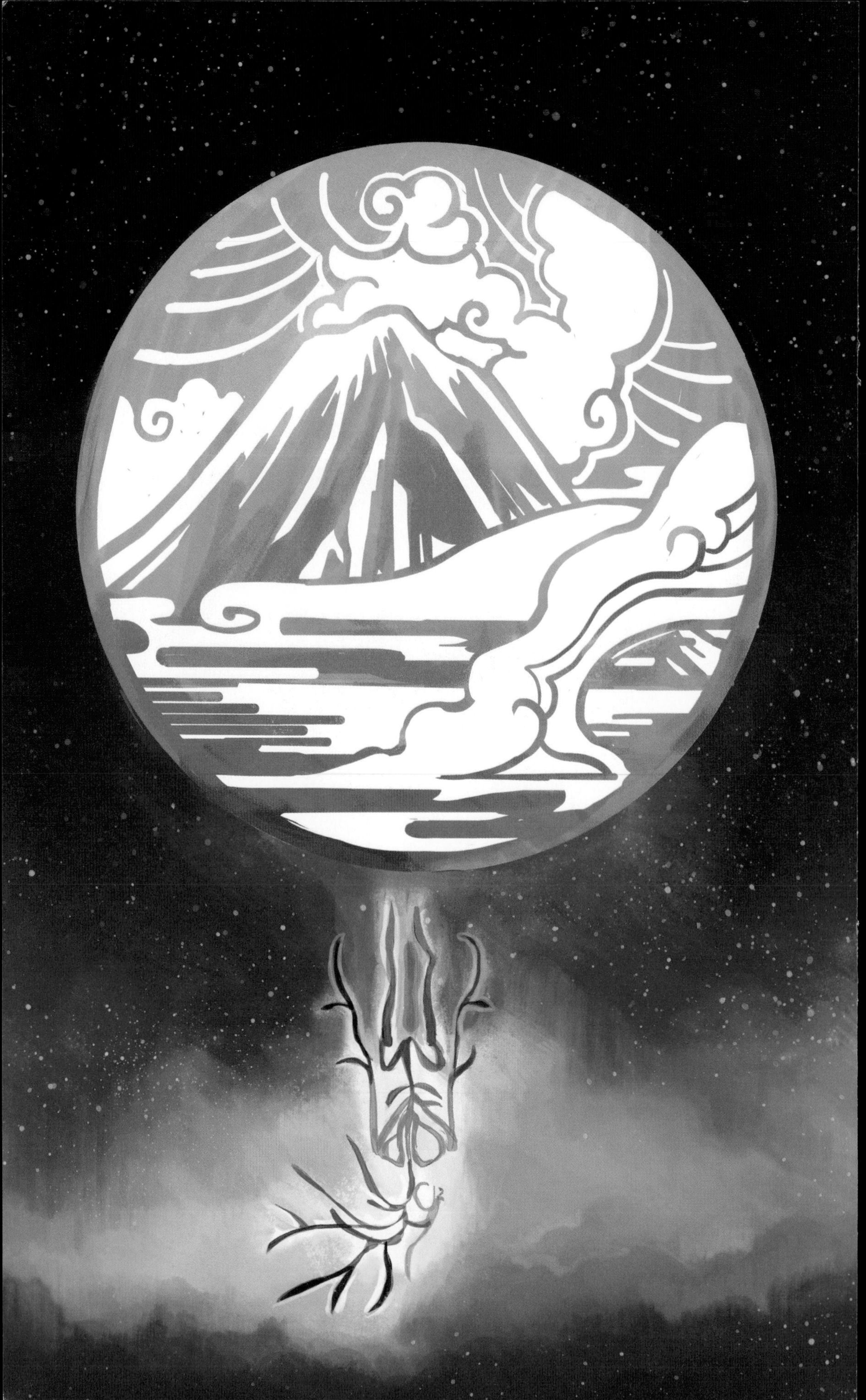

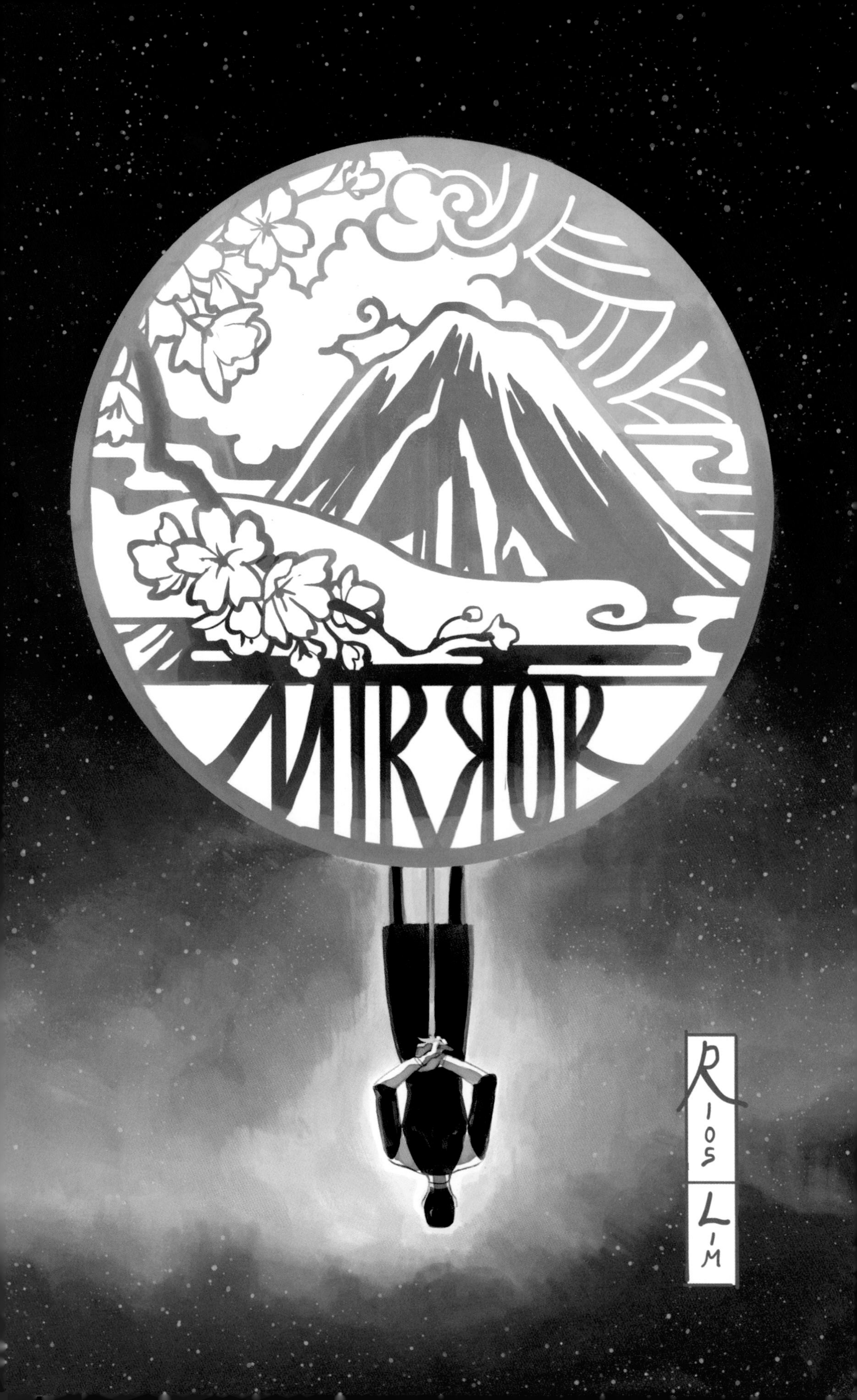
MIRROR
Rios
Lim

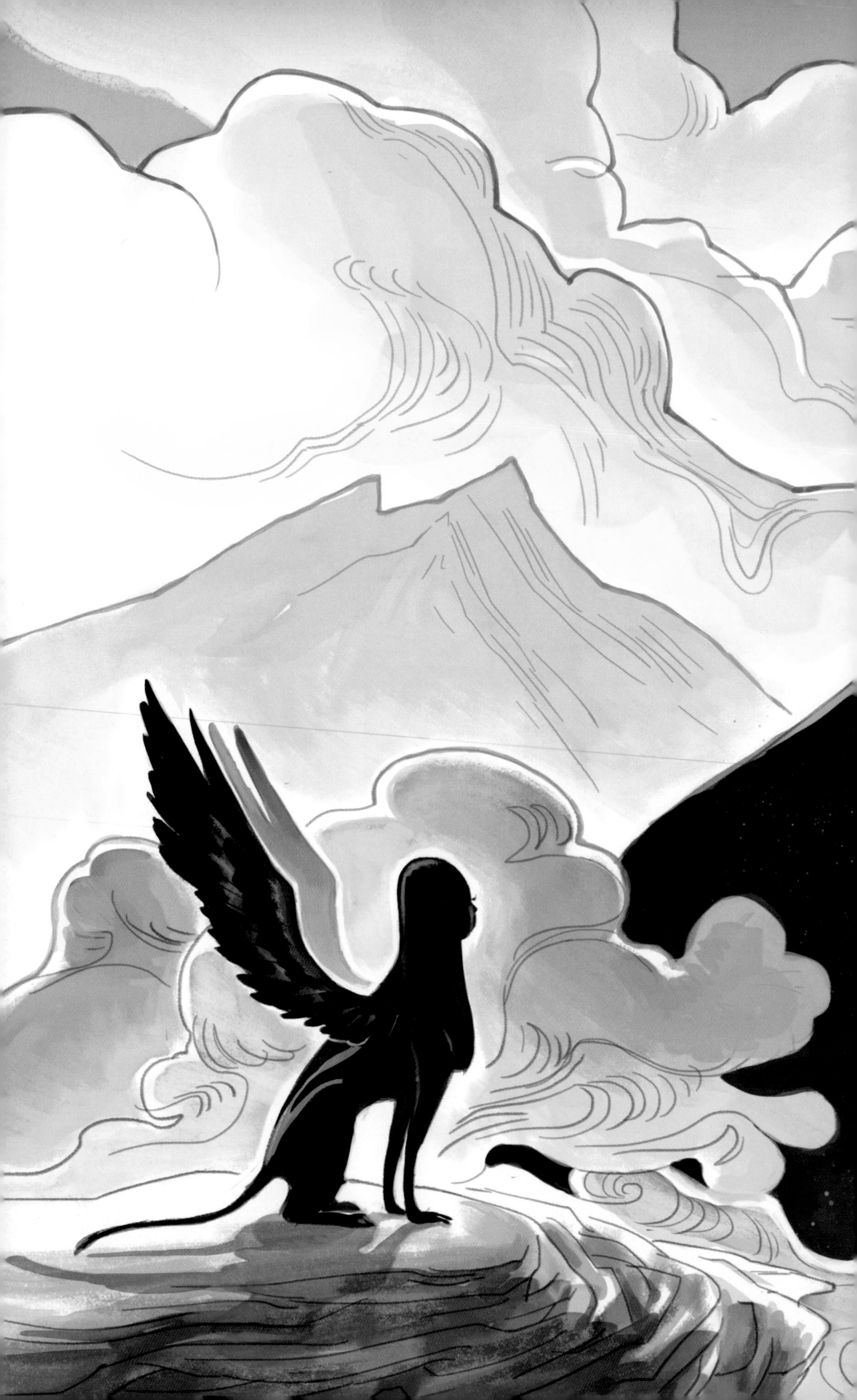

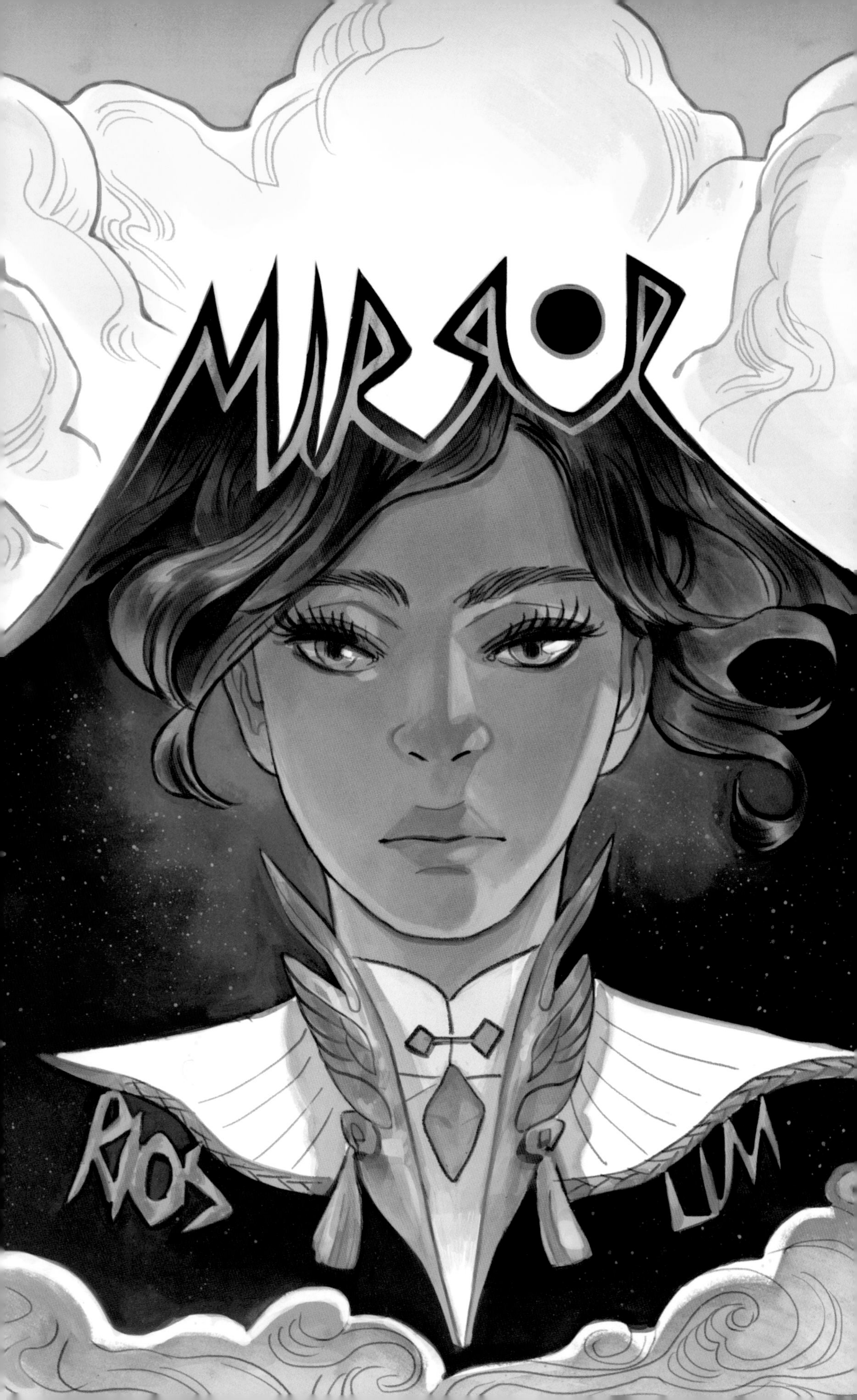
MIRROR
RIOS
LIM

MIRROR

Design

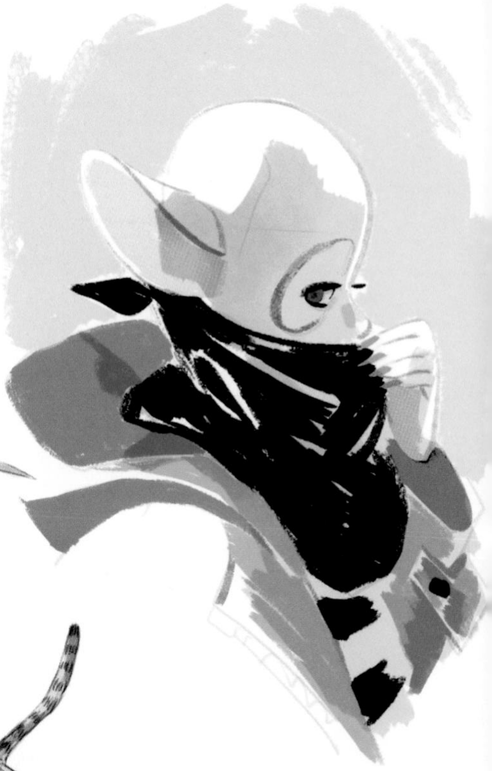

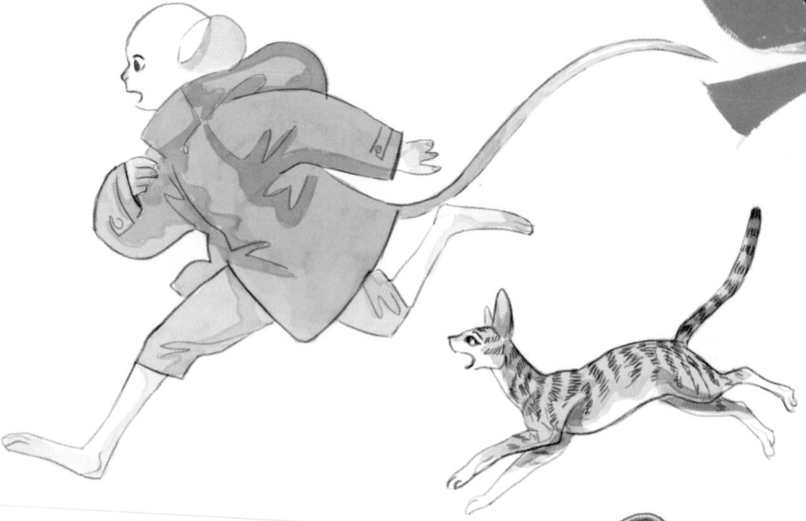

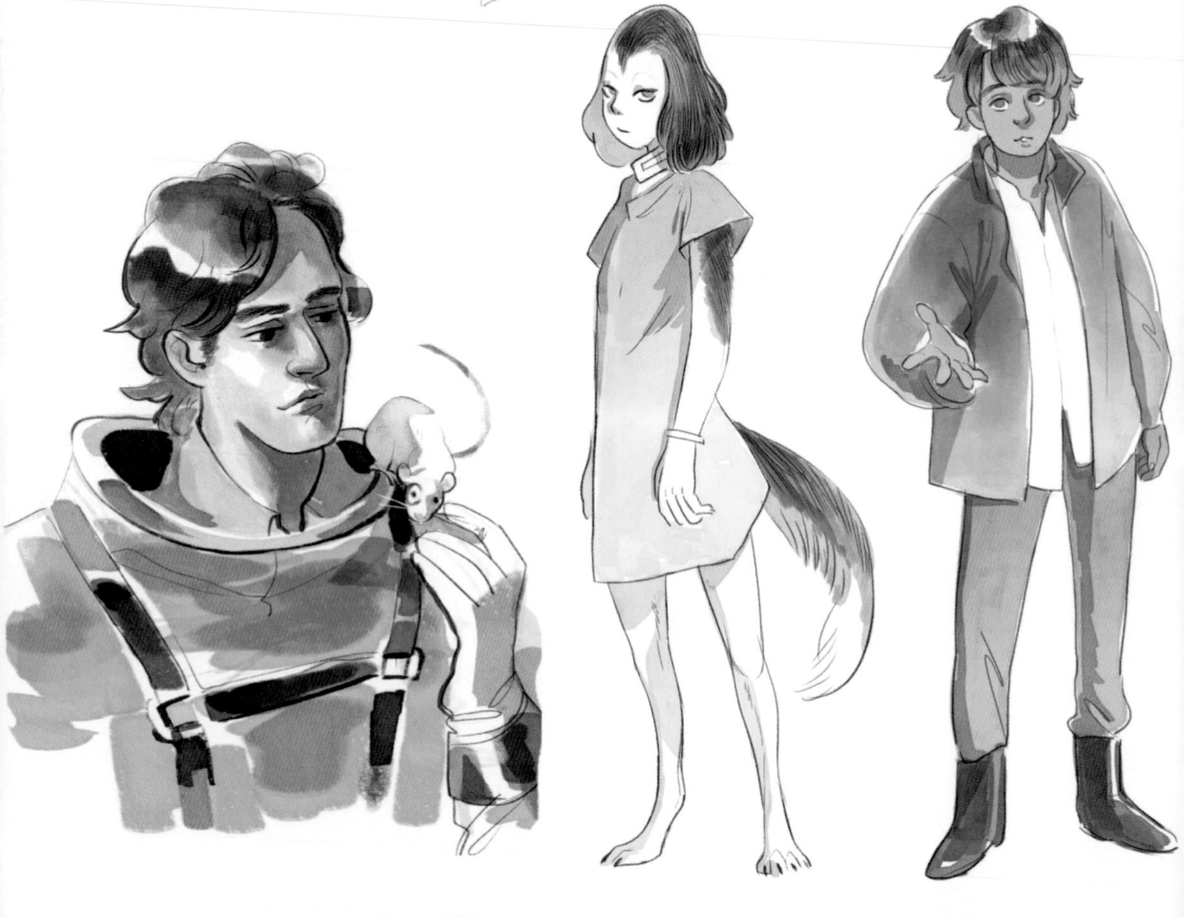

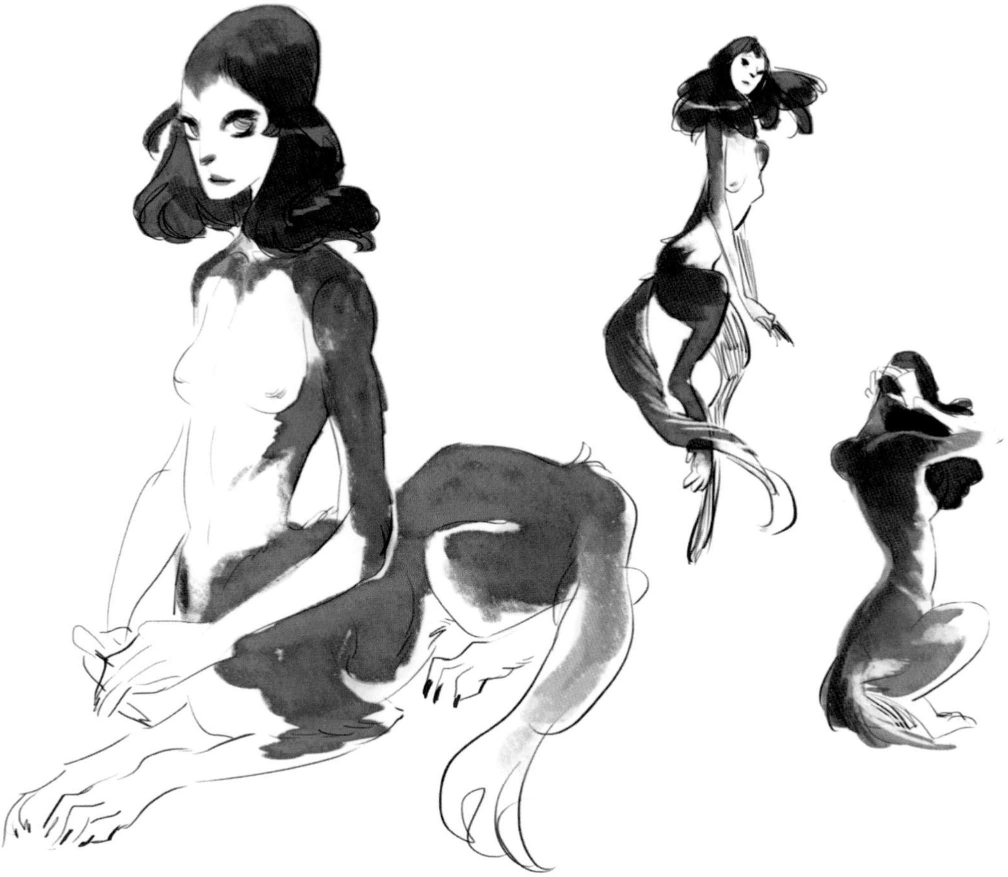

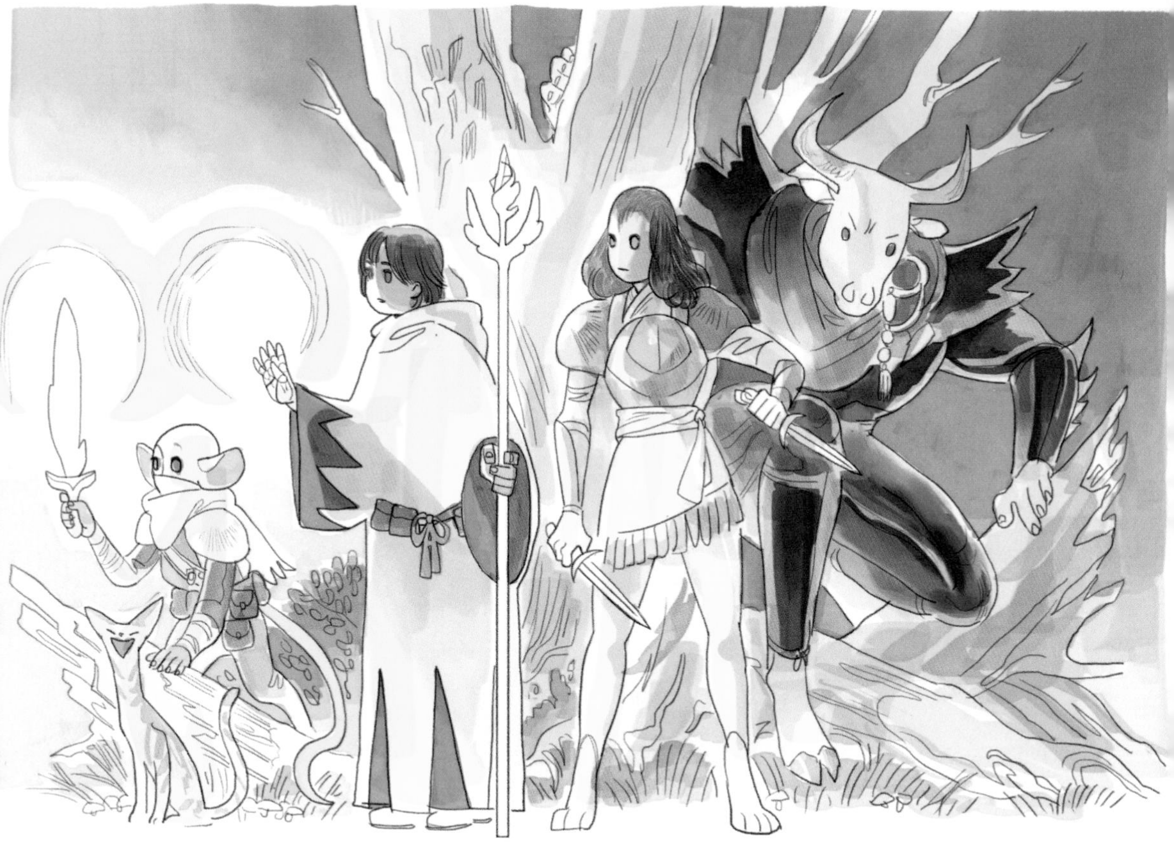

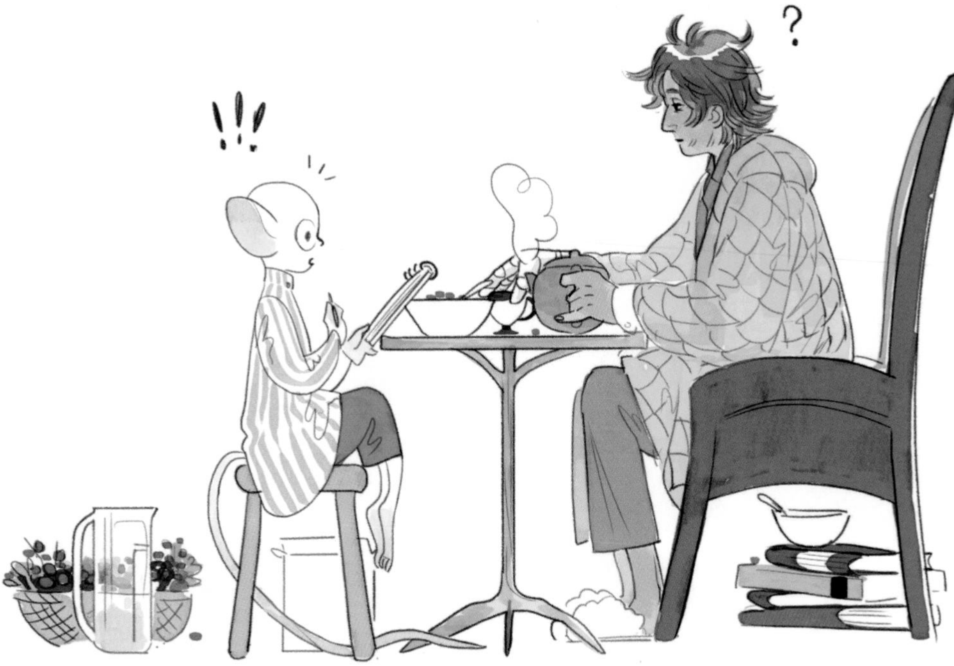

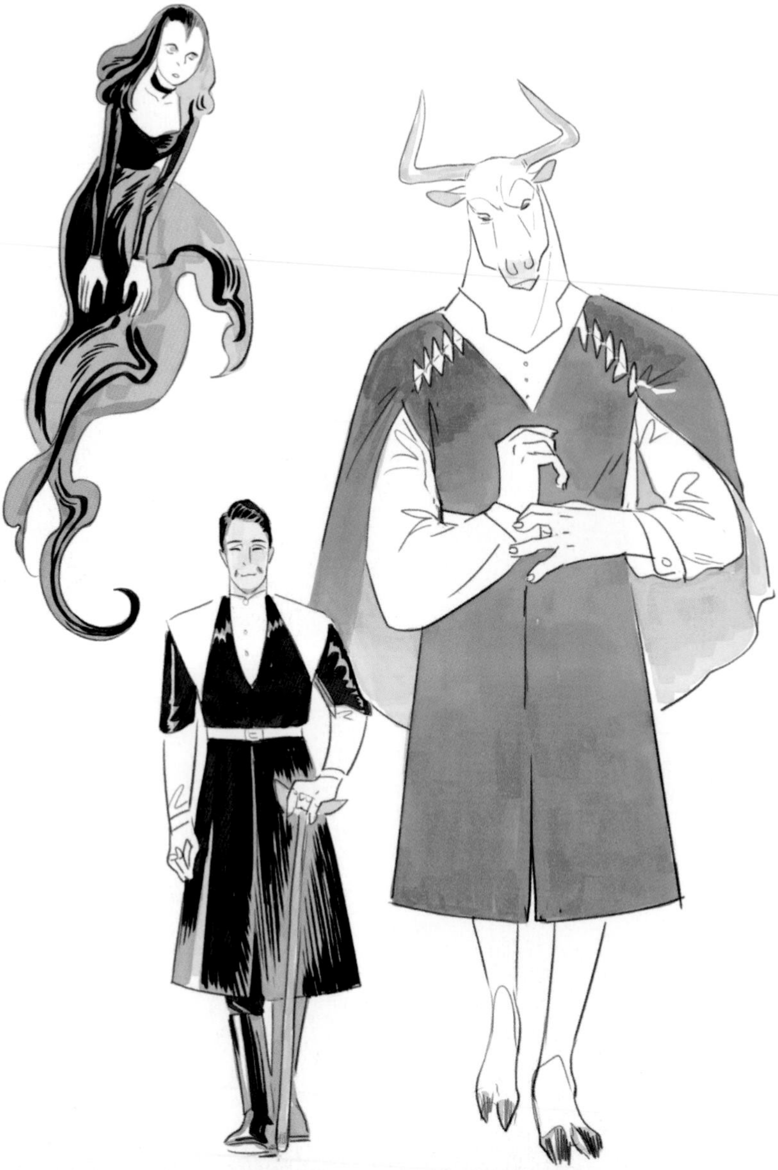

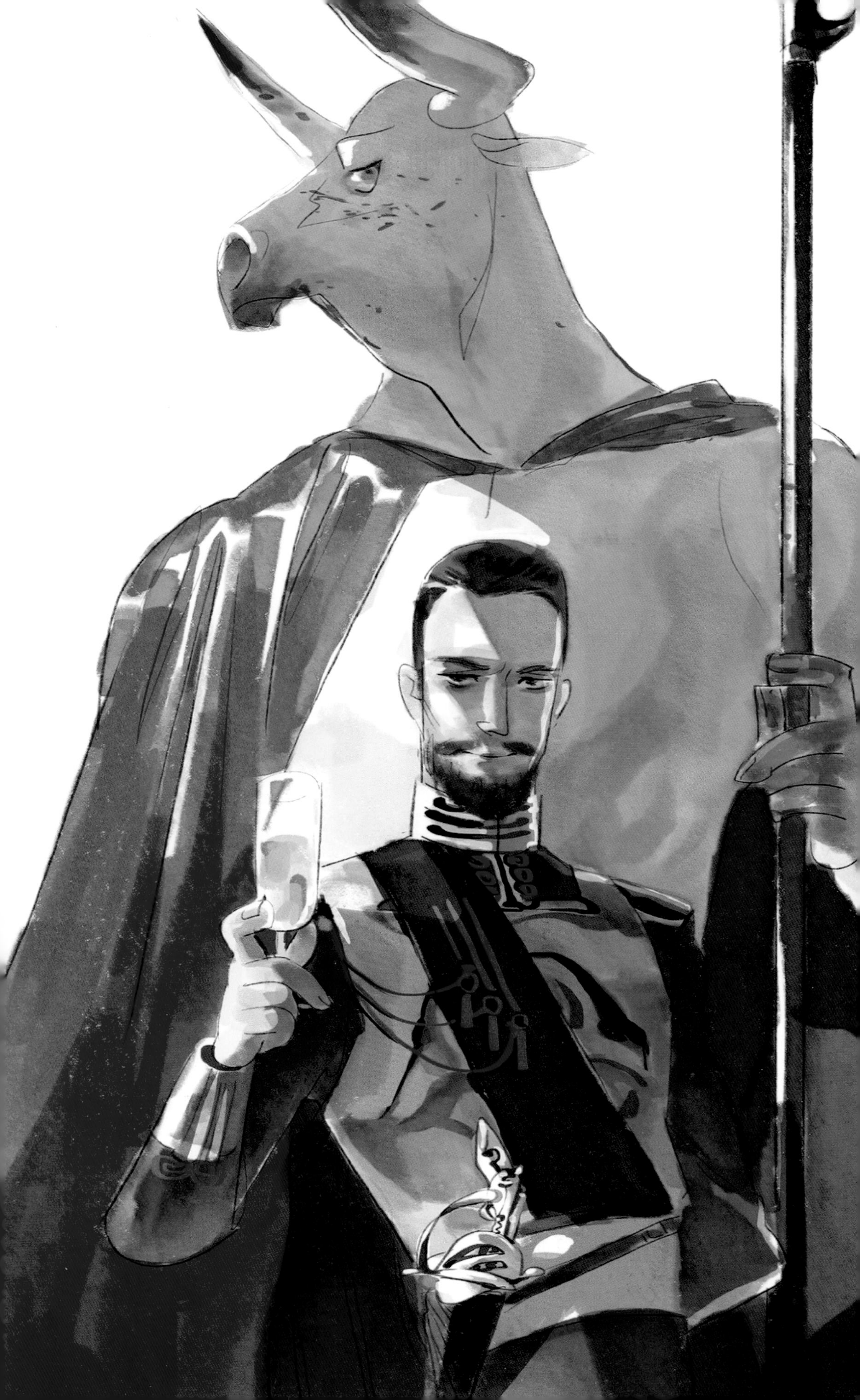

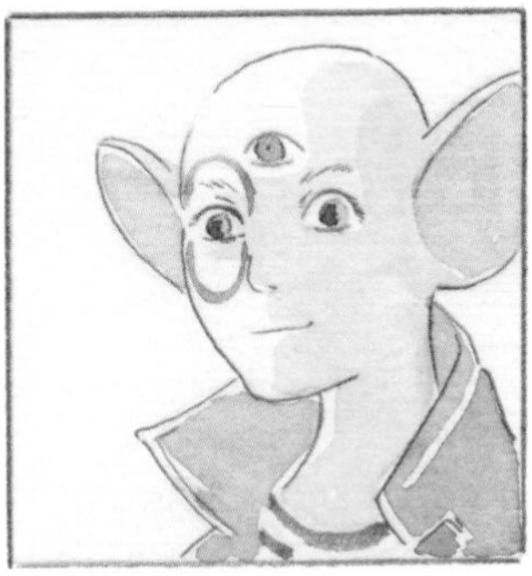

Zun was born a lab rat in the Esagila and transmuted into a hybrid by Ivan, her tutor and best friend, after showing evolved intelligence.

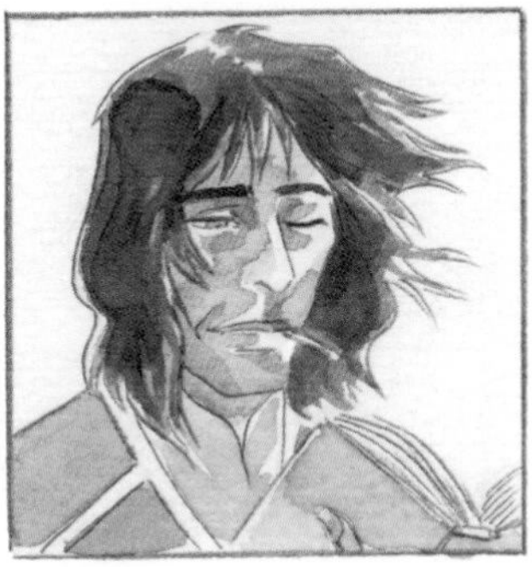

Ivan, born a gifted mage-scientist, was a talented child given to tutor under Professor Kazbek when he was only three. He was used as an incentive to make Sena accept evolution.

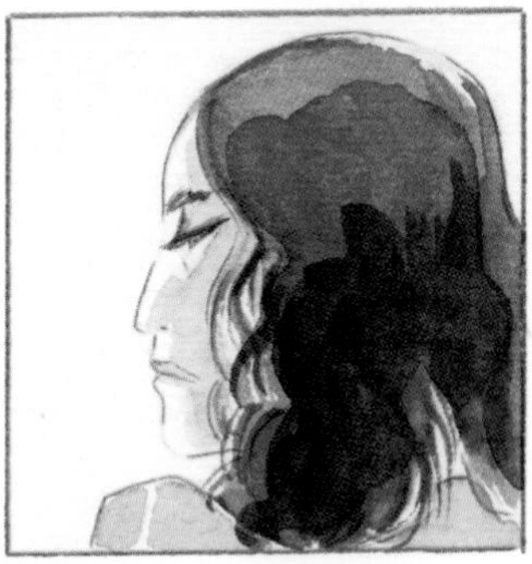

Sena is a dog evolved into a human, and the first man-made hybrid of Irzah. She grows up on the Esagila with Ivan and Kazbek, enduring a strict education that eventually makes a rebel of her.

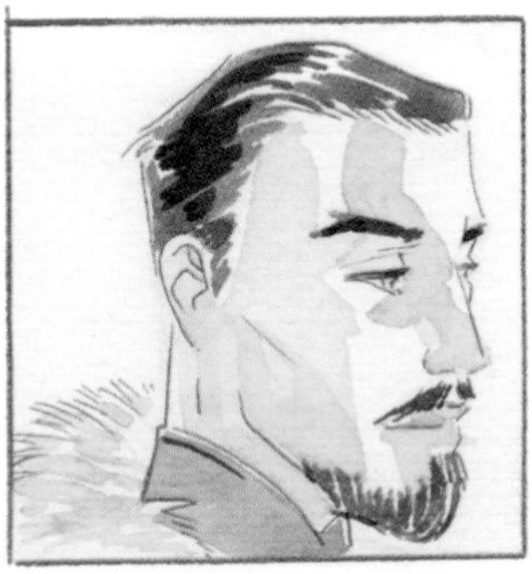

Kazbek Abkazhi is a mage-scientist of the Synchronia, where he used to serve under Elena's command. He hosts the Outsider within and is the master mind behind the Irzah colony.

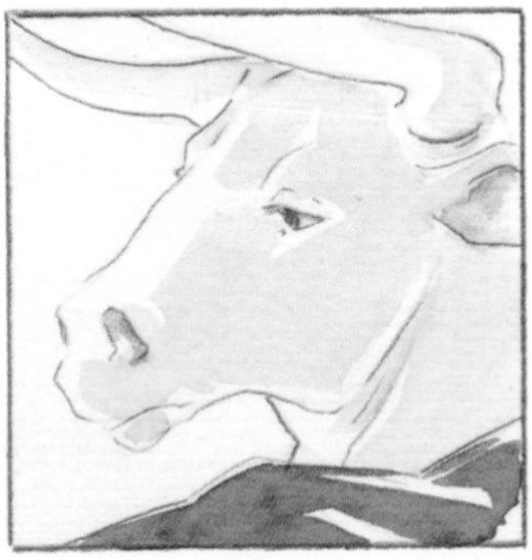

Aldebaran is a minotaur born from a human, Lia Zabat, after the Irzah Asteroid corrupted his gestation. He is devoted to Professor Kazbek, who considers him as a son.

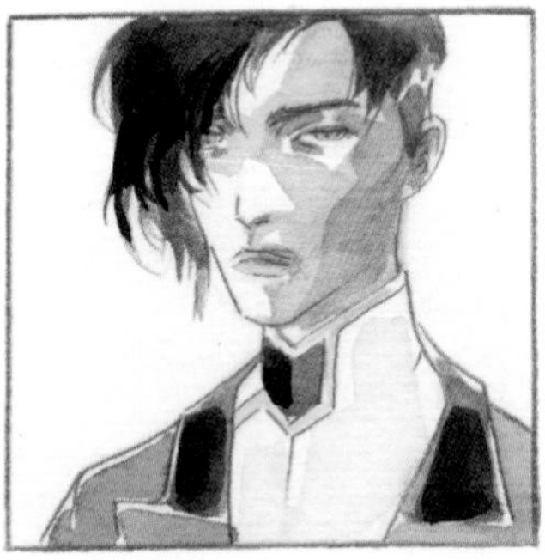

Elena Hagia is the chancellor of the Irzah colony. A former war hero fallen from grace after surviving the mission where Kazbek and the Outsider blend together.

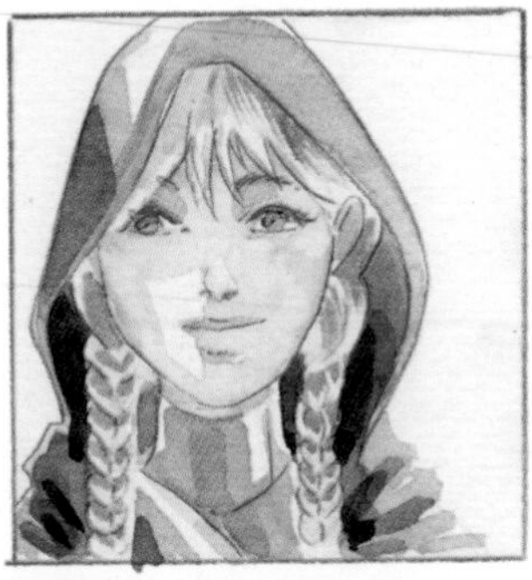

Lia Zabat was the captain of the star-ship Esagila when it used to be a field hospital belonging to Elena's fleet. Close friend of both Kazbek and Elena, she dies after giving birth to Aldebaran.

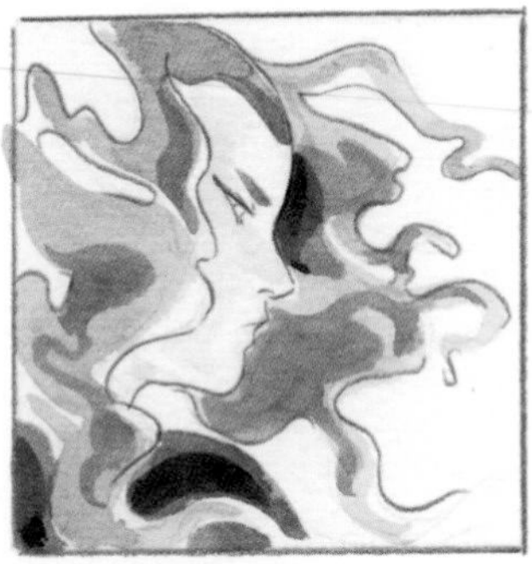

The Grudge is a curse Ivan casts upon himself as a kid, right after losing Sena. Finding out she's her shadow makes her lose any purpose of existence.

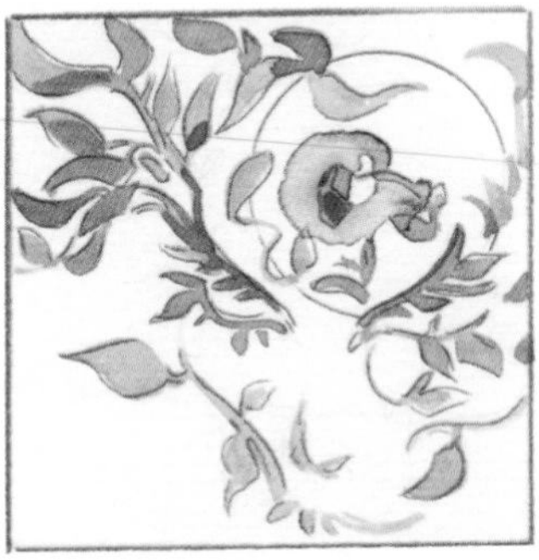

The Outsider had arisen out of three alien seeds found on the original planet of Irzah before being destroyed. She intertwined with Kazbek in order to save both their lives.

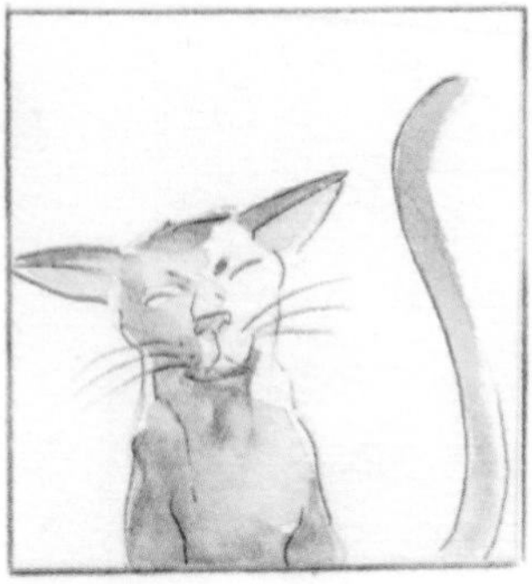

Phinx is Kazbek's creation, and the first experiment to succeed using DNA of a Guardian. Still an unnerving and selfish baby, she shows glimpses of incredible wits: a sphinx in the making.

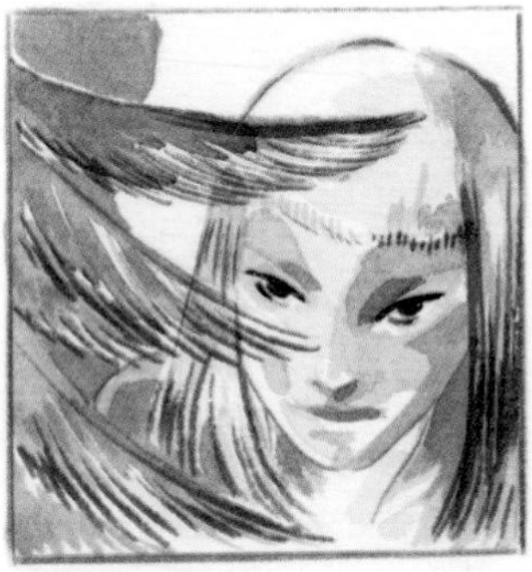

The Sphinx is the little cat touched by Irzah and transmuted into the true Guardian for the world to come.

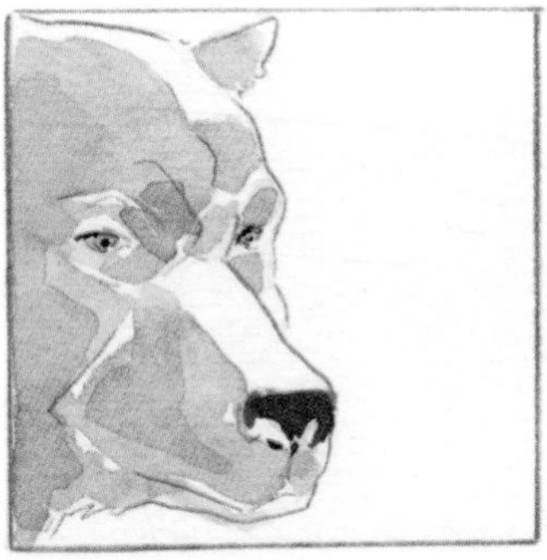

Lesnik the Guardian used to believe the man-made hybrids of Irzah were worthy of much more than what humans were giving to them.

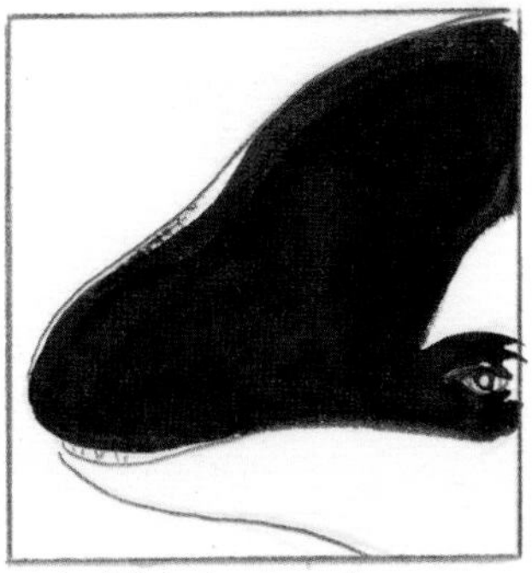

Blackfish the Guardian is the lone whale-wolf living in the lake of the Frozen Forest. After Lesnik is captured, she kidnaps Sena hoping to make a Guardian out of her.

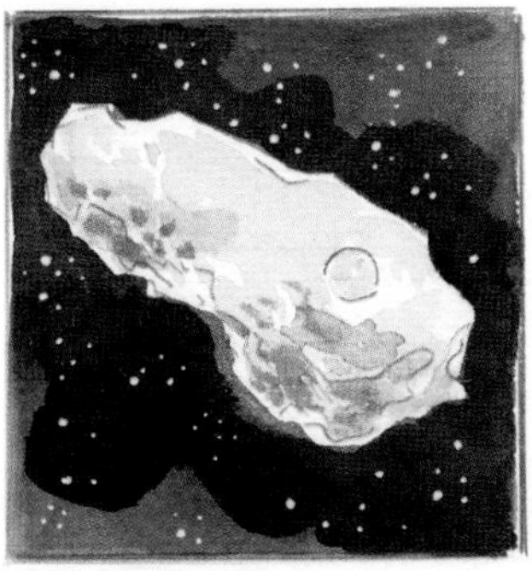

Irzah the Asteroid is debris from a mysterious planet destroyed by the humans of the Synchronia, and a sentient living rock eager to connect with the inhabitants on its surface.

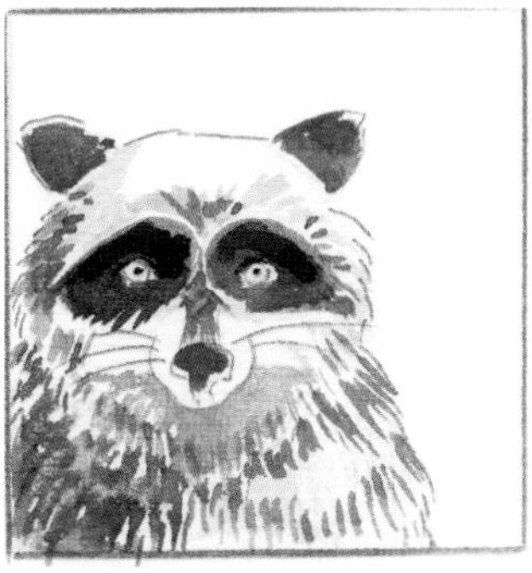

Linnae the Guardian was one of the first animals sent to Irzah that grew clairvoyant and able to communicate with the asteroid. She was also the first one to understand and manipulate a human device.

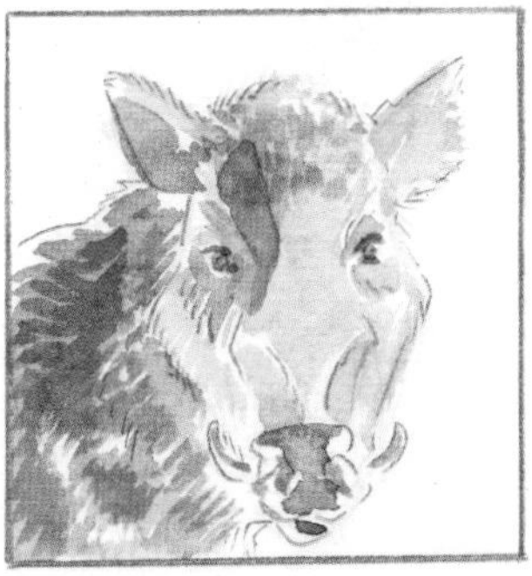

Locke the Guardian was one of the first animals sent to Irzah that grew clairvoyant and able to communicate with the asteroid.

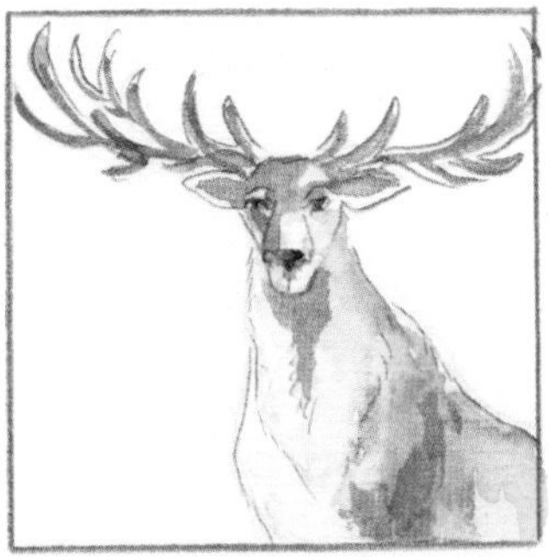

Cernuno the Guardian was one of the first animals sent to Irzah that grew clairvoyant and able to communicate with the asteroid.

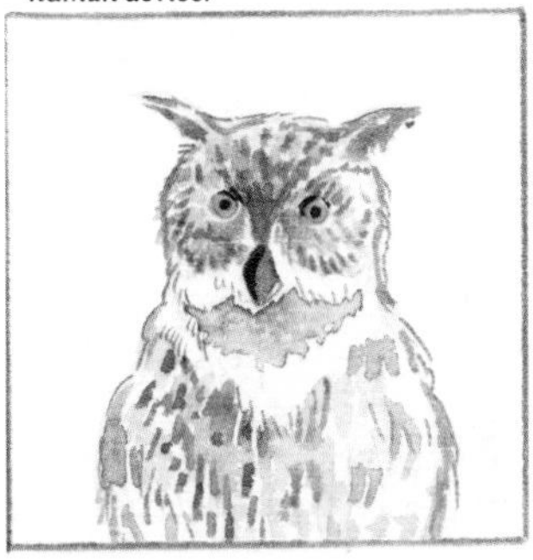

Bubo the Guardian was one of the first animals sent to Irzah that grew clairvoyant and able to communicate with the asteroid.

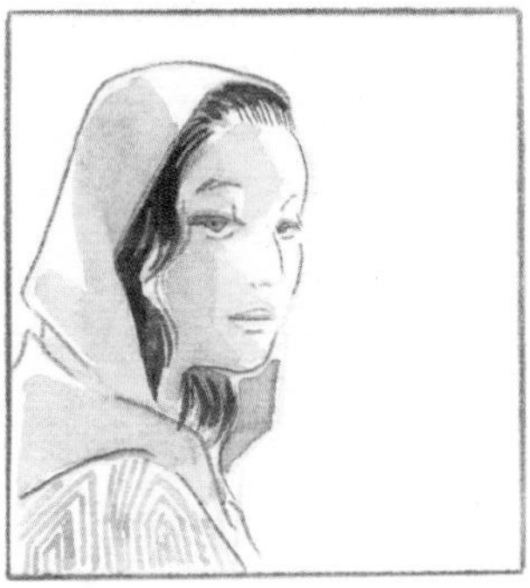

Dilara Hagia is Elena's older sister. An eccentric noble who had decided to keep her childhood appearance in order to make others feel uncomfortable.

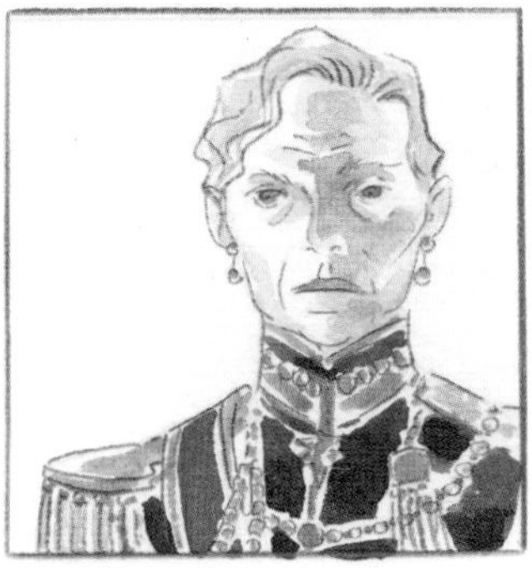

Stratigo Leto Hagia is the most valuable general of the Synchronia and the counselor of Planet Colossus. She's also Elena's mother.

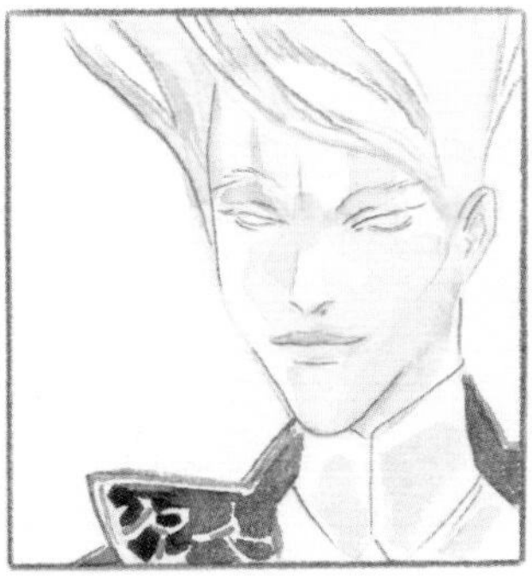

Enceladus is one of the three most powerful hermaphrodite Kybele representing the mages in the Council of the Synchronia. Ky was once Elena's instructor and former lover.

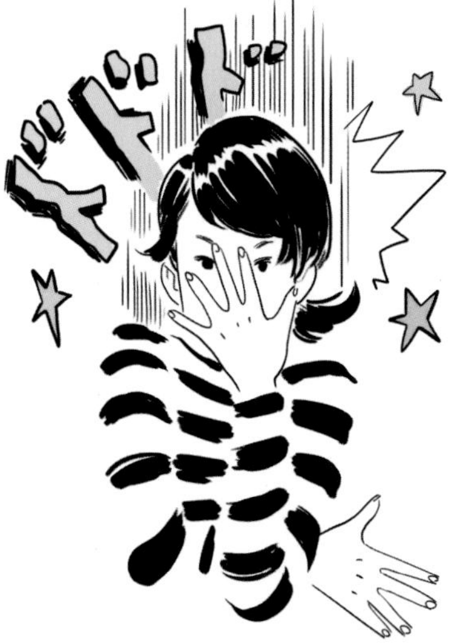

Hwei draws short stories about the rabbit Boris & child Lalage, a vague webcomic called *Hero*, illustrations for YA and children's books (*Spirit of the Sea*, *Dragonhearted*), and, most recently, an SF / fantasy story called *Mirror*, written by Big Boss Emma Rios...

Emma shifted her focus to a mix of both architecture and small press until working on comics full time. She's just published *I.D.* and currently co-edits *Island* with Brandon Graham, co-creates *Pretty Deadly* with Kelly Sue DeConnick and this book in your hands, *Mirror*, with Revolver Ocelot Hwei Lim.

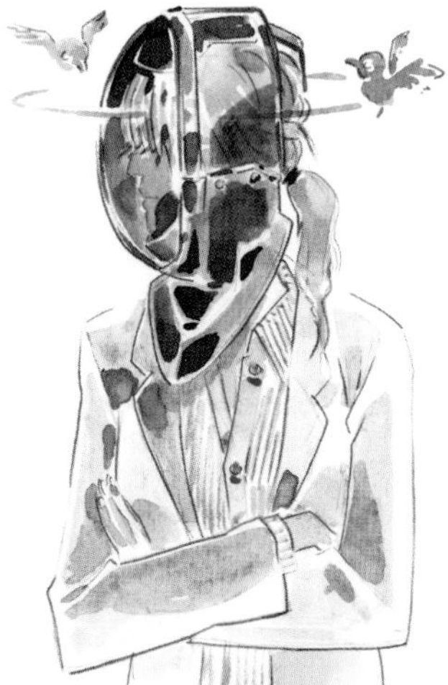

MIRROR: THE MOUNTAIN. First printing. September 2016. Published by Image Comics, Inc. Office of publication: 2001 Center Street, Sixth Floor, Berkeley, CA 94704. Copyright © 2016 Emma Ríos & Hwei Lim. All rights reserved. Contains material originally published in single magazine form as MIRROR #1-5. "Mirror," its logos, and the likenesses of all characters herein are trademarks of Emma Ríos & Hwei Lim, unless otherwise noted. "Image" and the Image Comics logos are registered trademarks of Image Comics, Inc. No part of this publication may be reproduced or transmitted, in any form or by any means (except for short excerpts for journalistic or review purposes), without the express written permission of Emma Ríos, Hwei Lim, or Image Comics, Inc. All names, characters, events, and locales in this publication are entirely fictional. Any resemblance to actual persons (living or dead), events, or places, without satiric intent, is coincidental. Printed in the USA. For information regarding the CPSIA on this printed material call: 203-595-3636 and provide reference #RICH-703343. For international rights, contact: foreignlicensing@imagecomics.com. ISBN 978-1-63215-834-5.

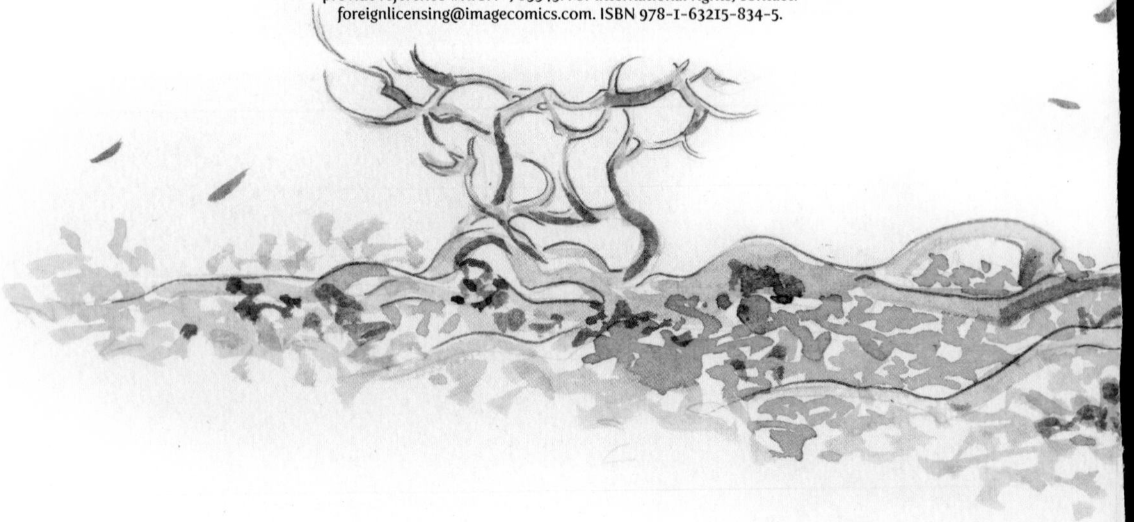